One dark night when the moon was green,
I came around the corner with my turd machine,
Shots were fired, screams were heard,
A lady got hit by my flying turd.

BROTHER

JACK STINGER

And The

HAUNTING OF WHITLOCK MANOR

PHILLIP WOLF

An Imprint of Wolf Entertainment Productions, Inc.
WolfEntertainment.NET

Library of Congress Control Number: 2022904789

First edition
1 2 3 4 5 6 7 8 9 10

ISBN: 978-0-578-39271-4 (paperback)
ISBN: 978-0-578-33686-2 (hardcover)
ISBN: 978-0-578-38438-2 (eBook)

Printed and bound in the United States of America.

For Destiny and Angelina

And thinking of Dad

PART ONE

Facing Fears

"Do the thing you fear most,
and the death of fear is certain."

—Mark Twain

CHAPTER ONE

The Ghost Riders

SUNDAY, MARCH 5, 1989. 9:30 AM

Jack Stinger would have slept past noon if it weren't for his friends ringing the doorbell. At the sound of the impatient *ding, dong, ding, dong,* he shot up in bed as if reacting to an acid reflux attack and ripped off his pj's. It was the fastest Jack had ever changed into his clothes. Any faster, and he'd probably discover a hidden talent as a quick-change artist.

"Who's at the door this early?" Jack heard his mother say from the kitchen. She was preparing breakfast while his father and brother still slept.

"I got it, Mom!" Jack said, speed-walking to the front door. He knew it was his friends because he rode bikes with them to the dirt trails every weekend. Today's forecast was partly cloudy, cool, and ten percent humidity—a near-perfect day to get out and ride.

He swung open the front door and found Stewart on the porch, sitting stationary on his blue Mongoose bicycle with mag wheels. Billy sat next to him on his black and yellow GT Pro.

Billy pointed to the corner of the porch. "You left your bike out last night."

Jack glanced at his bike leaning against the wall. He was

twelve when he got that silver Diamondback. He had wanted it for years; the chromed-out, freestyle, lightweight one with gel-filled rubber handle grips and foot pegs bolted to twenty-inch wheels. It was the holy grail of bicycles, but super expensive. Jack saved up money for years using the allowance he received from his mother for helping her clean houses as her second part-time job. And it was worth the wait.

"Wake your ass up!" Stewart said loud enough that Jack's mother overheard him.

"If that's Stewart," Jack's mother said, projecting her voice, "tell him I said to watch his mouth!"

Stewart leaned through the doorway over his handlebars. "Sorry, Mrs. Stinger!"

"Busted!" Billy cackled.

Stewart rolled back and punched him in the arm. "Shut up, you idiot."

Billy winced at the jab and rubbed his arm. "Asshole!"

Jack stepped out onto the porch and shut the door behind him. "Keep it down, guys."

"Well, if you hadn't overslept, none of this would've happened," Stewart said. "You ready to go?"

"Give me five minutes."

Stewart glanced at his watch. "Hurry up, the day's nearly half over," he laughed. "I bet there'll be a lot of riders there today—it's so nice out. Oh, and we need to hit up the old spook house later this afternoon."

Billy darted a gaze at Stewart. "Yeah, I don't feel like going there today."

"Come on, don't be a wuss." Stewart rolled his eyes, then regarded Jack with a faint smile. "Whaddaya say? You up for going there later?"

"Yeah, I guess so," Jack said, opening the door and stepping back inside. "Wait here." He shut the door on his friends.

Stewart spun his bike around on the porch and faced the front lawn. "You can't back out this time," he said, glaring at Billy. "It's Jack's turn to break in."

Billy felt he had no choice. "Sure, I'll ride the trails with you guys, but I'm not going inside that house if Jack finds a way in."

Stewart gave a sly grin.

Whitlock Manor was an old, abandoned three-story mansion located a couple of miles from their neighborhood. It stood alone at the cul-de-sac on Cemetery Hill. Jack, Stewart, and Billy had visited the place shortly before sunset once or twice a week ever since they first discovered it in the fifth grade. When rumors spread around school about the house being haunted, Jack decided to investigate it. He loved watching horror movies and reading scary books, and he also liked going to haunted houses every weekend in October. So of course this would be right up his alley!

In sixth grade, Jack formed the Ghost Riders bike club, creating it strictly for riding bikes with Stewart and Billy to Whitlock Manor. He wanted to keep the club between the three of them. If his other friends found out about it, Jack thought they might try to take advantage of the club and expand it with more members beyond his control. The smaller the better.

The mission of the Ghost Riders was to dare each other to enter the house alone. But no one had ever stayed around long enough to find a way inside; it was too creepy. Even Jack was afraid. Knowing there were no actors inside that would jump out and scare him made it feel different from the fake haunted houses he was used to walking through during Halloween.

This house was real, not just a maze of walls and panels with flame-retardant poly sheeting. Whether it was really haunted or not remained to be seen.

When Jack had first met his friends, he was just moving into the neighborhood and going into the fourth grade. Just days after moving into their new home, his parents dug a big enough hole to plant a weeping willow in their front yard. He spotted Stewart and Billy cruising through the neighborhood on their bikes as his parents were filling the hole with water. He invited them over to jump in the murky water hole while his parents took Polaroid photos of them seizing the moment, thus beginning their inseparable friendship.

Riding the bus to the arcade at the mall, drinking from the water hose, wading in creek beds, and smoking hollow twigs in the woods would go down as their fondest memories. They were responsible kids, rarely getting into trouble, returning home when the streetlamps turned on. Time flew by, and now they were sophomores in high school attending Remington High together.

———

Jack didn't want to keep Stewart and Billy waiting on the porch any longer than necessary. He brushed his teeth with one pass, then hurried into the kitchen and warmed a Pop-Tart in the toaster.

His mother was scrambling a bowl of eggs. "Let me guess. You're going to the trails with your friends."

Jack popped up the pastry prematurely from the toaster and headed for the front door. "How'd you know?" he said with half his breakfast in his mouth. "See you later!"

Back outside, his cheeks expanding like a chipmunk's, he

grabbed his bike. "Dammit, I forgot to bring water," he fretted as he took off down the sidewalk with his friends.

Several hours later, after a hot, fun-filled day at the trails, the Ghost Riders rode to their favorite burger joint, the Feed Bag, for a late lunch, then spent some time playing the *Kung-Fu Master* arcade game before finally heading to the old house on Cemetery Hill.

———

It was a thirty-minute bike ride to Whitlock Manor, and by the time they made it across town, it was 5:30 and the sun had stained a pinkish tint across the horizon. The Ghost Riders stopped at the top of the T-junction of Claybourn Street and Cemetery Hill for a quick break before proceeding. A couple of eerie, broken streetlamps leaned like lazy guards between them on either side of the street.

Sharing the same name as the graveyard half a mile behind the old house, Cemetery Hill was a secluded, quarter-mile street that led to Whitlock Manor. The city had recently planned to rezone the area to connect roads and develop a future apartment complex. The construction of a small business district was also in talks. But for some undisclosed reason, the city had delayed the project indefinitely.

"I think tonight's the night!" Jack said. "I can feel it!"

"I bet you can taste it, too—like my farts!" Stewart said.

"Since you mentioned it, it's *your* turn to enter. No excuses. I don't care if you have to knock a hole in the wall to get inside!"

Some things never changed between these boys—they were the type of friends that could embarrass your mother. Stewart was the tallest of the bunch and more apt to speak his mind.

His sarcastic personality was like his father's, which could get them both into trouble sooner than later. He was also a fan of Dungeons & Dragons, a game many parents hated for their kids to play. Until a few years ago, people thought it was a game of witchcraft, the work of the devil, and that the spells they learned in the game were real. Stewart played D&D with his other friends at least once a week. He enjoyed gathering around the table with them and creating adventures or developing quests with his imagination.

Billy was the skittish one amongst the Ghost Riders. In the beginning, he enjoyed visiting Whitlock Manor. But as rumors at school intensified about the old house, however, he became scared and lost interest.

"Sorry, guys, but I'm not going any further than the steps of the front porch this time," Billy said before they headed down Cemetery Hill. "Why did we even form this club? I *hate* that place!" He reached into his back pocket and pulled out a switchblade comb, pressing a button in the center of the handle. The comb flipped out like a real switchblade. The gimmick was a purchase he made from a pranks and gags catalog. Unfortunately, when it was shipped, it had a cracked handle. Rather than waiting another four to six weeks to receive a new one, he taped the handle and cut a slit down the seam so the spring-loaded comb could still function.

"You're going as far as we go, bro," Stewart told Billy. "You know we don't break tradition."

Billy ran the comb through his hair, folded it into the handle, and slid it in his back pocket. He had a habit of combing his hair when he was nervous. "You can't force me to do anything," he said. "I'll just go back home and—"

"Then you're out of the club!" Stewart snapped.

"Hey!" Jack intervened. "You can't cut members from the

14

club without a vote. So stop with the threats."

"Members stick together, man," Stewart reminded Jack.

Jack turned to Billy. "Are you really going to chicken out? I'd like for you to be here when we discover the truth about this house. You're part of this team."

Billy looked down at the ground for a moment, then said, "Look. I like being in this bike club with you guys, but what I don't like is when you try and force me to do something I don't want to do."

"Then you're not part of this team," Stewart said.

"Shut up, Stewart!" Jack warned.

"Fine, I'll come with y'all, but like I said, I don't want to go past the steps of the front porch," Billy insisted. "What do you say? Is it still cool that I hang with you guys?"

Jack glanced at Stewart, who shrugged in return. "Deal," Jack said back at Billy. "Now that we've wasted all this time, let's do this!"

The Ghost Riders set their bikes into motion down Cemetery Hill, their wheel hubs clicking in unison as they coasted between an infestation of potholes.

Coming up on the cul-de-sac, they eased their bikes to a stop and gazed up at the sinister-looking mansion surrounded by a conglomerate of trees. Vines snaked up the front of the house, completely covering the second-level bay windows, and weeds had grown over the winding pathway leading to the extended, wrap-around porch. The place looked as if it had been abandoned for centuries.

"Hey, the for-sale sign is gone," Stewart pointed.

Jack wiped his face with his shirt. "I never noticed it was missing before," he said. "I wonder if someone bought it!"

"I dunno," Stewart said.

Jack peeled his eyes from the upper window and over to Stewart.

"We've been coming here together for what, five years, right? It's time we debunk the rumors once and for all!"

Billy shook his head. "I'm staying right here," he griped.

"Not a chance, chunky," Stewart said. "Stop being a wimp and step out of your comfort zone!"

"Quit screwing around!" Jack snapped.

Stewart stared creepily into Billy's eyes. "Wuss," he said and got off his bike, the bicycle toppling to the ground as he stomped away.

Jack, shaking his head at Stewart's treatment of his bike, utilized the kickstand. He waited for Billy to set his bike down, and then they walked together to catch up with Stewart.

————

Ascending the front porch steps, Jack glanced behind him at Billy. Billy was sticking to his word and hung back at the bottom of the stairs.

The porch wrapped around the corners of the house and continued ten feet along both sides. A paint-chipped swing swayed from its rusted chains in the far corner, squeaking to a repetitious ghostly beat.

"That's not creepy at all," Stewart said, sarcasm dripping from his words.

Jack stepped to the swing and grabbed it to stop the irritating noise. "Oh, look." Stewart pointed at the lower corner of the window nearest to Jack. "The window is broken. Wasn't last time we were here."

Jack's curiosity antenna rose, and he stooped to investigate, tapping gently on the small hole at the impact point of the spider-crack. It looked like a BB or pellet from an air rifle had pierced the single-paned window.

"Hey, stop looking at the dumb crack and break the window!" Stewart intimidated Jack. "Then you can crawl through and finally get inside the house." He approached the front door and twisted the handle. "Damn, still locked. Yep, go for the window, dude!"

Jack pulled his hand away from the window, worried he might prick his finger on the glass. "No way! I'm not going to risk cutting my—"

A sudden gust of wind blew through the porch, and the swing behind Jack rammed against the side of the house. Jack's heart flew into his mouth, and he quickly jumped to his feet.

BANG! The swing hit against the house again.

Stewart flinched from the loud noise, his eyes swelling to the size of silver dollars. "Shh, listen, did you hear that?" he asked, taking a step back. "I heard someone talking."

Jack stood motionless, ears pricked. He could hear what sounded like the faint, garbled sound of someone's voice. A cold draft pecked at the back of his neck. "The window!" he suddenly remembered and stooped to the window again. "Listen."

But Stewart had already leaped back toward the stairs. "I think someone's living here. We should bounce before we get caught!"

Jack thought if Stewart had a tail, it would be curling between his legs right about now. Stewart, he thought, despite all that stuff he said to Billy, was apparently a coward.

When Billy saw Stewart at the top of the stairs, his eyes widened. He knew Stewart didn't back out of things so easily. So he turned and sprinted back down the pathway to his bike.

Jack remained on the porch, still trying to decipher the words as the voice spoke. He could hear it coming through the tiny hole in the broken window.

Five to enter, one to stay, the voice said.

Jack gasped at the words coming from the window and fell on his butt. He quickly got to his feet, shuffled around Stewart, and ran down the stairs.

Stewart did not hesitate and followed close behind him, toe to heel.

———

Billy mounted his bicycle, his foot slipping off one of the pedals as he tried to flee.

Jack and Stewart soon joined him, and the Ghost Riders fled as fast as they could back up Cemetery Hill until they knew they were at a safe distance from the house.

"I think we're in the clear," Jack heaved. He dismounted his bike and walked it the rest of the way up the incline to where the street intersected Claybourn.

Billy trailed behind, sweating profusely.

"Who said that back there?" Stewart asked, out of breath.

Jack shrugged. "I hope it wasn't someone who needed help. If we see on the news tomorrow about a body discovered inside that house, I'll feel guilty the rest of my life knowing we could've saved someone tonight."

"Wait—you guys heard someone in the house?" Billy said as he caught up to them. "Okay, that does it. I'm not riding this way ever again, let alone go back to that stupid house. Man, I knew this was a bad idea!"

Suddenly, a police cruiser's emergency lights flashed in front of them. The vehicle stopped, and the officer rolled down his window. He gestured for the teens to approach.

Jack felt his heart sink as he and his friends walked their bikes toward the cop.

Billy was so nervous, he reached into his back pocket for his switchblade comb. But the pocket was empty. *My comb! Where's my comb? Oh, no! It must've fallen out when I was running!*

"If it ain't Jack Stinger and his gang," the officer said, shifting the cruiser into park. As a black man in uniform, he looked cool with a high-top fade and his arm resting out the window.

Jack knew the officer. Mike Palinsky was his father's friend from when they were in the Army. After completing their first-term enlistment, they parted ways. Several years later, they ran into each other when Mike by coincidence moved to the same small town of Rusty, Texas, after being offered a job with the police department. Now he patrolled through Jack's neighborhood almost daily.

"What are you boys doing out this way? What kind of mischief are you up to?"

"Hey, Mike," Jack said, hanging his head low. "We're on our way home. We were just riding around."

"In case you didn't know, creeps roam around areas like this that are separated from neighborhoods. It's not safe around this place, guys. Being such a small town, you could easily get into some serious trouble."

"Yes, sir," the boys replied.

Billy thrust his hands in his pockets, feeling embarrassed. If only he had gone home when his friends set out to the creepy house after lunch, he would've never been in this predicament.

Mike turned his head to Jack. "Look, I'm not kidding. It's dangerous out this way. Get home before I notify your parents," he demanded sternly. "I don't want to be the one to take the call when you and your friends turn up missing."

"Yes, sir." Jack nodded. Sometimes he hated that Mike and his father were friends. The guy interfered too much with the family. *You're not my dad,* he wanted to say, but he kept his mouth shut.

Reaching into the breast pocket of his uniform, Mike pulled out a stack of football cards. "Here . . . these came in hot off the press this morning. They aren't current players, but they're some of the most memorable ones. I expect all of you to heed my words about playing around this area." He handed Jack and his friends each a Dallas Cowboys football trading card. It was something the police in this rural town practiced, targeting kids playing outside. Although the cards were not worth anything, the program was designed to make youths feel safe and keep them out of trouble.

Billy gasped like an excited little kid. "Thanks, Officer!" His eyes lit up when he looked at his card and then slapped it against his chest. "Roger Staubach! I'm going to keep this one sealed for sure! *This is cool!*"

"I got Danny White!" Stewart grinned.

"Stay out of trouble, and stay in school," Mike told them, then drove away, cutting off the emergency lights.

Stewart slid his card into his back pocket. "I wonder if he's going to check out the house."

"He's probably just turning around," Jack guessed. "I don't think he'll get out and walk around if that's what you mean."

He gave his card to Billy, who was already thrilled to receive his first "unofficial" football trading card. Jack saw Mike often, so getting another one for himself was easy. He wanted to make Billy happy, since he felt kind of sorry for him as an unwilling accomplice to an attempted break-in at Whitlock Manor.

Stewart hopped onto his bike with a concerned look on his face. "So, how does today affect the Ghost Riders? Since we can't come back here, is this the end of our bike club? The house is what started it all!"

"That's something to think about," Jack said, still wondering about the voice he heard. "Let's talk at school tomorrow."

CHAPTER TWO

Detour

MONDAY, MARCH 6. 6:30 AM
The alarm clock blared.

Jack usually hit the snooze button three times, once every five minutes, before crawling out of bed. This time, he anticipated getting up at the first sound of the alarm. He couldn't wait to visit Whitlock Manor by himself before school. Although it was tradition for the Ghost Riders to go together, and it was the purpose of the bike club, Jack didn't want to put up with the bickering between Billy and Stewart. What they didn't know would be his little secret. Besides, he was the president of the club, so he figured he could do whatever he pleased.

He reached for the alarm clock and pressed the OFF button. Then, experiencing another bad case of morning bed head, he rolled out of bed and proceeded down the hall to the kitchen.

Setting an empty bowl and a box of cereal on the table, he shuffled to the refrigerator like a zombie and retrieved a carton of milk. He skimmed over the information about this month's missing child printed on the back as he returned to the kitchen table.

Sliding into his chair, he overfilled his bowl with corn flakes. His mind was too busy thinking about who could have been whispering through the broken window at the old spook house.

Mike Palinsky's warning the previous night did not faze him, most likely because he knew his father was close friends with the guy. Which meant Mike was more prone to letting things slide. What was the worst he could do, slap Jack on the wrist?

Jack's mother rounded the corner into the kitchen wearing a fleece nightgown and fuzzy slippers. She was a bit shorter than him, and her shoulder-length blond hair was a morning disaster like his. She removed a carton of eggs from the fridge.

"Good morning," she said, noticing Jack eating rather quickly. "Do you have something going on this morning at school that you're late for?"

"Kinda," Jack said, wiping a bead of milk from his mouth and then stuffing his face with another heaping spoonful of cereal. "I'm meeting my friends a little early today. We're supposed to study for a science exam together."

Jack's mother was so gullible, Jack could easily lie about a teacher's in-service day and skip school without her fact-checking him against the school calendar. Since he wanted to stop at the abandoned house along the way, he wasn't in the mood to argue with her about its dangers. She was a charge nurse at the hospital, and she enjoyed exaggerating the same stories regarding how she saw hundreds of kids brought into the ER due to careless accidents.

"That's a good idea to meet up with your friends." Jack's mother smiled.

Jack tipped the bowl to his lips and slurped the sweetened milk, drinking as if he were dying of thirst. He stood from the table, placed his bowl and spoon in the sink, then started for his bedroom to finish getting ready. But his mother stopped him like she had eyes in the back of her head.

"Hey!" She pointed at the table. "Are you going to put that milk away?"

"Oops. I forgot," Jack said and grabbed the milk carton.

His mother slapped several strips of bacon onto a plate and covered them with a paper towel. Then she inserted the plate into the microwave and set the cook time. The microwave hummed to life. "I guess you're not hungry for bacon and eggs . . . or a waffle?"

"Nope," Jack said, opening the fridge and putting away the milk. He hurried out of the kitchen before his mother reminded him of something else to do.

As he traversed the dining room to the hallway, Jack's older brother, Victor, startled him around the corner with a swift punch to his upper arm. Jack, caught off-guard, winced at the pain. "What's your problem!" he said.

"You're in my way, dork," Victor growled. He was shirtless and still half asleep, his dark hair matted like a dirty cat's fur. He was a senior also attending Remington High, but unlike Jack, he was in no hurry to get ready for school this morning.

Jack rubbed at his arm. It had been a while since his brother punched him like that unexpectedly. Sometimes Victor would dead leg him instead. Victor's knee ramming against his thigh was always the worst. He'd take a punch over a dead leg any day!

Jack and Victor picked on each other daily, but not out of hate or jealousy. Their brotherly love also included vulgar one-liners and obscene gestures to one another.

"Crybaby," Victor muttered, ramming his shoulder into Jack's sore arm as he moved around him and headed to the kitchen.

Jack grunted, stomping down the hallway to the bathroom, where he combed his hair and brushed his teeth. As he tapped the toothbrush against the side of the sink, shaking the excess water from the bristles, he could smell the alluring aroma of cooked bacon creeping through the house. He heard his mother shout from the kitchen, "Charles, wake up! Breakfast is ready. I'm only telling you once!" But Jack knew she'd yell several more times before his father would finally hear her and climb out of bed.

Retreating to his bedroom, Jack stuffed his backpack with books, saving some room for a few other things (including his bulky VHS camcorder) to take with him on the detour to Whitlock Manor. He slung the backpack over his shoulder and headed into the kitchen, where he kissed his mother on the cheek. She had just sat down to eat, and his father was pulling a chair from the table to join her and Victor.

Jack noticed Victor was having a difficult time spreading a dollop of butter on his toast. He snickered when the knife tore a hole in the center of the bread.

"Shut up, mama's boy!" Victor roared at Jack. "Just for that, I'm not taking your skinny ass to school."

Jack raised a brow. "Serves you right, dummy. And I'm riding my bike today, thank you very much."

"Spoiled brat! At least I'll be able to listen to music without you holding your ears and telling me to turn the volume down like your mama does."

"The last time I checked, she's your mother, too."

Jack's mom, Lindsay, slapped a hand on the table, rattling the plates and interrupting Charles as he was slicing his fried eggs and mixing them with a pile of grits.

"Hey!" Charles barked.

Lindsay cut her eyes at him. Then she glanced back at Jack and Victor. "Stop fighting! You know I love you both equally and unconditionally."

Victor gave up on the toast and dropped it on his plate, scarfing down his scrambled eggs and bacon instead.

What a pig, Jack thought. He flipped Victor the middle finger, grinned at him like a psychotic clown, and bolted out the back door through the covered patio which led to the garage.

"You little tick turd!" Victor said with pieces of egg flying out of his mouth.

"Chew with your mouth closed!" Charles raised his voice.

Victor stood from the table and grabbed his dishes. "I forgot I'm supposed to pick up someone to take to school," he lied, still chewing his food, "so I need to leave soon." He dropped the dishes in the sink and wiped his hands on his shirt as he stomped back to his room.

———

Jack rode his bike down the sidewalk parallel with Main Street. Coming up an incline, he stood and pedaled faster, swaying the Diamondback side to side. Then, when the sidewalk leveled, he coasted to allow his burning legs a rest. He could hear his heart thumping in his ears.

Most of the cars driving past him were traveling well over the speed limit. However, Jack noticed one car in his peripheral vision pulling up beside him. He turned his head and saw Victor in his banana yellow 1974 Camaro. Jack could see his brother through the tinted windows jamming to rock music, apparently set to max volume because Jack could hear it from several feet away.

Victor glanced back at Jack and flipped him the bird, then floored it. The Camaro fishtailed down the road, the engine screaming like it was breaking the sound barrier.

Jack rolled his eyes, thinking it wouldn't be too long before his brother got another speeding ticket. He could picture his mother yelling at Victor now, grounding him from driving that car for several weeks. A smile stretched across his face. "Karma's a bitch!" he muttered.

Glancing at his Swatch and seeing he had an hour before school, he double-timed it and turned off Main Street, heading toward Cemetery Hill.

———

Squeezing the handbrakes, Jack skidded his bike to a stop. His eyes shifted from the two crooked streetlamps on either side of him to the old mansion at the end of the street.

After taking a short breather, Jack zoomed down Cemetery Hill's quarter mile of torn up road. Curving around the cul-de-sac, he stopped before the winding pathway leading to the ramshackle three-story house. He could hear the echoes from the swing bumping between the wall and corner post of the porch.

Leaves were blowing from the lot into the street, piling around Jack's bicycle tires and his feet. He glanced up at the dark cloud cover slowly rotating above Whitlock Manor. *Video!* he thought, and pulled the camcorder from his backpack. Powering it on, he popped the lens cap, framed the house in the viewfinder, and pressed the record button, panning the camera from left to right. Then he reset for another pass.

Movement from the lone third-floor window caught his eye. Jack tilted the camera up past the thick vines climbing the front of the house and focused on the third floor, the silent splatter of tiny raindrops accumulating on the camera lens.

A loud thunderclap startled him, breaking his concentration. Jack paused the recording and cursed up at the sky, pumping his fist in the air. Then he powered off the unit and reattached the lens cap, just in time before the downpour.

Stuffing the camcorder into his backpack, Jack extended the bike's kickstand and darted up the pathway to the house. He ascended the stairs of the front porch and sought shelter, figuring he'd wait out the storm before heading off to school. *So much for exploring the house!* Jack thought. But he knew being late for school was not an option. If his mother found out he was tardy, he'd be knee-deep in chores without an allowance. And she'd probably have him scrubbing toilets the next time she took him with her to clean houses.

The ceiling of the porch was beginning to leak, so Jack moved to a drier spot near the broken window. Moments later, he saw the sky had transitioned to dark green, and pea-sized hail was pelting the roof. With that noise mixing with the swing banging frantically against the house, it sounded like he was in the middle of a warzone.

Jack glanced at his Swatch. School was starting in forty-five minutes. "C'mon!" He raised a fist again, this time at the raging storm. He could see the trees beyond the porch bending like crippled fingers from the mighty gusts of wind.

Although he knew it would be risky for his camera, Jack figured he could use this downtime to film the storm. *At least I can get some good B-roll footage,* he thought.

After winding through a few minutes of tape filming the storm, Jack spun around and knelt at the broken window and zoomed in. He hoped to see something inside the house since he remembered seeing movement in the third-floor window. Maybe someone *was* living here. But with the autofocus overworking itself trying to display a clear image, Jack gave up and powered off the camcorder. Perhaps the window was too dirty for the lens to pick up anything inside the dark house, or Jack was just too close to the window. Packing away the video camera, Jack waited a while longer for the storm to finally calm. Then he hurried down the porch steps and sloshed through the muddy pathway to his bike, never glancing back at the towering mansion as he rode off to school.

CHAPTER THREE

The Plan

The bell rang for lunch, and students flooded the hallways of Remington High, scrambling to stash their books into lockers before piling into the cafeteria. The special for today was a square, overcooked slice of pizza the shade of a graphite pencil. But no matter what was on the menu, everything tasted the same.

Jack stood in his damp clothes, waiting in line to enter the kitchen. He felt water squishing between his toes from his wet socks as he glanced around the cafeteria, still embarrassed after having sat through the morning classes knowing he was the only one in school who had been drenched from the rain. Did no one else get wet from the storm? he wondered. At least the line was moving at a steady pace because the longer he stood around, the more people would see him shivering like a wet dog.

As he finally entered the kitchen, the aroma of bleach singed his nose hairs and made his eyes water. It was so strong he could taste the chemicals. Other students seemed irritated by the smell, too. It was like the janitorial crew was a little obsessive-compulsive about deep cleaning during a pandemic.

Jack peeled a clean tray from the top stack of trays, grabbed some plasticware, and thumbed a few napkins as thin as single-ply toilet paper. Next, he reached under the heat lamps for a slice of pizza, then moved down the line and grabbed a bowl of fries and a cup of fruit cocktail. He also snagged a pint-sized milk carton from a small cooler on the counter. Lastly, he eyed a slice of chocolate icebox pie for dessert before stepping to the cashier.

The smile stretching across Ms. Bagleweed's face could lighten up a funeral home as she counted the items on Jack's tray. Her long gray hair was bunched up in a hairnet. "Good afternoon, Jack," she said in a heavenly voice. She made annoying sucking sounds with her dentures.

Jack reached for a bottle of ketchup next to the register and doused his fries with it.

Ms. Bagleweed's jaw dropped, her fake teeth nearly slipping from her gaping mouth. She stared at the mound of ketchup that Jack used to blanket his fries with. "You like them fries soggy?"

"Yes, ma'am," Jack said proudly, his mouth watering.

"I'll have to charge extra for using that much ketchup next time," Ms. Bagleweed warned him.

Jack shrugged. She said this to him every time he came through the line. And he knew she'd repeat it tomorrow!

After paying her with a wet five-dollar bill, he pocketed his change, grabbed his tray, and proceeded to the table where he usually sat with his friends.

"Are there any fries under that mound of ketchup?" Stewart joked.

Billy was sitting next to Stewart with a disgusted look on his face.

Jack rolled his eyes as he took a seat facing them. He stabbed a plastic fork into a soggy fry and said, "Y'all don't know what you're missing!" He impaled a few more fries, stacking them on the prongs of his fork. Then he froze before taking a heaping bite.

Daisy Crawford was swaggering toward the table.

Jack's eyes found her petite wasp-waist, then scanned up to her small breasts, and finally to her dazzling blue eyes. Her long, smooth brunette hair bounced with each step. She never knew it (at least he didn't think she knew), but Jack had had a mad crush on her since the sixth grade. He just never had the courage to tell her.

"What's up, guys?" Daisy said, straddling a seat across from Jack, keeping an empty space between her and Billy. She flipped her hair back and dumped the contents of her sack lunch consisting of an apple, a peanut butter and jelly sandwich, a bag of chips, and a juice box onto the table. She usually brought her lunch to school because she couldn't stomach the cafeteria food.

"Trying to make it through this boring day so I can finish what I started," Jack said, stuffing the french fries he had stacked on his fork into his mouth. He wiped the ketchup dribbling down his chin with a napkin.

Daisy looked at him, intrigued by his comment, but disgusted by what he was eating. "What did you start?" she asked.

Jack glanced at Stewart and Billy, wondering if he should tell her about the old mansion on Cemetery Hill. Stewart and Billy didn't know he went there alone. If he said something, they would probably get on him about breaking their bike club rules.

Daisy leaned over the table toward Jack and grinned, her loose blouse drooping open at the collar. "What's wrong? Can't share your secret with me?" She and Jack had been friends since the third grade, and they were also neighbors living just four houses from each other. Other than his jaunts to the manor, there were no secrets kept between them.

Jack's eyes locked with hers, trying hard to keep from glancing down into her open shirt. He could feel his face getting warm. He opened his mouth to speak but delayed the thought of telling her about Whitlock Manor. He didn't think it was the right time yet. Instead, he tried solving the mystery as to why he was the only one in school drenching wet.

"Oh, it's nothing," he said. Then he included Stewart and Billy on the conversation and asked, "What did y'all think of that storm this morning?"

Stewart and Billy glanced at each other with confused looks on their faces.

Billy pushed his tray aside. "What storm? It never rained."

"Yes it did," Jack said, frowning. "Why do you think my clothes are still damp? Were you already at school when it started? I have video proof of the storm! Remind me to show you later."

Daisy swiped her apple from the table and chomped down on it. "Where were you that you got rained on?" she asked. "I walked the railroad tracks to school this morning and I didn't see a single dark cloud."

"Are you kidding? There was a downpour, and it even hailed at the old house on Cemetery Hill," Jack said.

Billy's eyes bulged. "You went back there?" he gasped. "Haven't you had enough of that place yet?"

"Dude! You can't do that!" Stewart glared at Jack.

"I know, I know," Jack said. "There's something about that place that made me feel like going back there alone this morning."

"Are you referring to Whitlock Manor?" Daisy asked, taking another bite of her apple. Now she was even more intrigued at what he had to say.

Jack flinched in his seat. "Yeah. Do you know something we don't?" he asked.

"My dad used to tell me stories about it a long time ago," Daisy said.

The noise in the cafeteria escalated, which usually meant only a few minutes remained until the end of lunch.

"What did he tell you?" Jack asked Daisy, curious if she knew any backstories about Whitlock Manor.

"He used to tell me the house has a secret room. An old homeless woman lived in that room until one day she died. My dad said someone working for the city was on the property mowing the weeds a few weeks later and smelled the decaying body. The police were called, and that's how the house was later condemned."

Jack rubbed his chin. Daisy's story didn't add up. "So, a dead body was found, and the house was condemned? If that's the case, then why aren't all of the windows boarded up? I've seen only a couple of windows covered."

"Well, that's what my dad told me," Daisy said with a shrug. "We talked about it just before he and my mom were divorced. Also, have you not been hearing the rumors going around school recently? A lot of people have been talking about that place."

"I know," Jack said. "And I want to be the first to debunk the rumors! Don't y'all want to know if that house is really haunted? Who's with me?"

"You can count me out!" Billy barked. "I don't ever want to go near that house again."

"I'm interested," Stewart said. "But I don't want to help with the research—too boring. And what about the club? Are we still a team?"

Jack's eyes cut over to Billy, then back at Stewart. "I don't know. One of us doesn't want to ride to the old house anymore."

"You two can keep the club going," Billy cut in. "But I'm out. Sorry, guys."

"Wait, what's going on? What club?" Daisy asked, confused.

"The Ghost Riders," Stewart said. "It's a bike club that Jack started just for riding to the creepy mansion on Cemetery Hill. It was pretty cool, until dillweed beside me here just dropped out!"

"I want in!" Daisy perked up. "Sounds like fun. How do I get in?"

"You're a girl," Stewart said.

Daisy pinched at her blouse and peered down inside at her chest. "Yep, as confirmed!"

The school bell rang, and Jack and his friends stood from the table and grabbed their trash.

"You're in!" Jack announced to Daisy.

"Oh wow, that's it?" Daisy asked, surprised.

"Hey!" Stewart frowned. "Adding members to the club requires a vote!"

Jack grinned at Stewart. "And so does getting rid of members, but you didn't seem to have a problem when Billy just quit the club. Besides, I'm president. I can overrule your objections."

"Then I'm out, too!" Stewart snapped. "No offense, bro. I'll still be your friend and all, but I think I'm done being a Ghost Rider. I can't stand scaredy-cats like Billy anyway."

"Shut your mouth!" Billy threatened.

"Make me, wuss!"

Billy gritted his teeth at Stewart and stomped off to class.

Surprised that he did not feel defeated by losing his two best friends as members of his bike club, Jack still wanted to confirm that Stewart was truly dropping out. "So, it's a no-go for returning to the house?"

"Negative," Stewart said. Then, as he parted from Jack and Daisy, he turned back and raised his voice over the crowd. "But let me know what you find out about that place!"

Jack nodded, respecting his decision. He turned to Daisy, grinning. "And then there were two. What do you say—wanna help me research Whitlock Manor? I mean, you're already a member of the club!"

Daisy's eyes lit up. "Come to think of it, I have a creative writing assignment that's due soon. This could make for a great story!"

"There you go!" Jack chuckled. "How about we meet up at the public library this afternoon? Do you have any plans after school?"

Daisy balled up her trash and tossed it into a nearby garbage can. "No plans. Four o'clock?"

"Works for me," Jack agreed with a smile.

"Good deal," Daisy said. "Catch you later!" She exited the cafeteria and disappeared into the crowd.

Researching Whitlock Manor with Daisy was a better idea than trying to break into the house by himself, Jack thought. He couldn't wait to see her again and hoped the next few hours of school would go by fast.

He stood outside the doors of the cafeteria, watching for a gap in the foot traffic. Then, when he saw the opportunity, he merged in with the flow.

CHAPTER FOUR

Grim Discovery

After locking his bike to the rack in front of the library, Jack found a seat on a park bench overlooking the well-manicured landscaped grounds. He took in the picturesque view. The weather was nice compared to what he experienced—apparently alone—at Whitlock Manor this morning. His clothes had dried finally but were wrinkled. Only his socks were still a little damp.

Jack's eye caught a black Cavalier Z24 pull up to the crosswalk. He watched as the passenger door sprang open, and Daisy stepped out of the vehicle.

Daisy grabbed her backpack and shut the car door, waving back at her mother. Then she cut across the grass and approached the park bench where Jack was sitting. "Sorry I'm late," she said with a cute smile, her teeth glistening white. "My mom had to work past her scheduled shift before she could pick me up."

"All good," Jack said, grabbing his backpack from between his feet.

The sweet almond smell of used books greeted them when they entered the library. Jack loved the scent of old paperbacks; it reminded him of when he visited his grandparents in Mississippi. He thought about the small town they lived in, where practically everyone knew each other. Stores, salons, and restaurants were all within walking distance from the house. He remembered Mr. Raven's Candy Depot and browsing the unique candy store stocked with nostalgic treats and toys. And reading books on the screened-in front porch of his grandparents' home while semis barreled down the road in front of the house. But the good ol' days were fading fast. Fashion trends were becoming harder to keep up with, business establishments were changing how they conducted business. The world was set at warp speed. Jack was old school; he hated change.

They walked past the central reception area in the library and headed for the nonfiction section where the microfilms were located. The machines used to be popular in gathering research back in the day. Still, the units in this library were gradually disappearing to make room for desktop computers soon to be installed. Jack remembered watching *Sounder* here on a film projector with his friends. He wondered if projectors were going the way of the dinosaurs.

"Grab a machine, and I'll catch up to you," Daisy said, taking a detour to the restroom.

Jack walked briskly toward a microfilm viewer that looked like a gigantic microscope. He set his backpack down in front of the machine and moseyed over to a row of alphabetized cabinets, then pulled open a drawer labeled CABINET 12: W - Z. Inside were several small rectangular boxes containing microfilm. Scanning his finger over the labels, he looked for the letters WHI for Whitlock. Once he found it, he removed the box and closed the cabinet drawer. Then, returning to his machine, he opened the box and pulled out the microfilm. The tightly rolled film contained microphotographs of newspaper clippings, book catalogs, and other documents.

Jack pulled the tray from underneath the projector lens and placed the spool of film on the spindle. Next, he secured the spindle onto the rollers and into the take-up reel. He manually wound it a few times, gently pressing the fast-forward button until it displayed the first image. When he pushed the tray back under the microscope, the image appeared magnified onto the large screen.

Daisy returned and sat next to him. She placed her backpack on the floor next to his and removed a pen and notebook from her bag. "What'd you find?"

"I just cued it up," Jack said, using a knob on the side of the projector to rotate the magnified image. He pressed and held the fast-forward button. "I didn't know if—" He released the button, staring at Daisy while she opened her notebook to a blank page. His eyes found the glossy, unblemished skin of her arm as she rummaged through her bag. Her delicate ears framed her dainty nose and puffy lips coated with a dark shade of red lipstick. It dawned on him that she was not wearing makeup when they first walked into the library together.

Daisy caught his stare, her rapture-blue eyes making his heart melt. "You okay?" she asked.

Jack blinked and returned to sifting through the film. "Yeah," he said, bashful. "I was just seeing what you were doing."

Daisy smirked and diverted her attention to the projector screen as images of old newspaper headlines passed underneath the lens. "Are you looking for Whitlock Manor?"

Jack's eyes moved with the images. "Yup, but I'm not sure where to start."

She followed along on the screen, tapping her pen on the cover of her notebook until something caught her eye. "Stop!

Rewind a few slides."

Pressing the button on the pullout tray, Jack rewound the film four frames.

"There!" Daisy leaned forward, pointing her pen at the screen. "Focus on that."

CONDEMNED HOUSE TO BE RESTORED
ON CEMETERY HILL

1897 - Things that go bump in the night are excuses for the energy that hangs on [ghosts] through means of communication via flashes of light, disturbing knocking, or furniture-dragging noises. When a human dies and passes on, is he stuck between our world and the afterlife? Perhaps the person stopped where he shouldn't have and lost his opportunity to move on, and the only thing keeping him from boarding the train to the afterlife was his attachment to a personal fortune, an object, his unfinished business, deep love for his spouse, etc.

William Whitlock, owner of Whitlock Manor located on Cemetery Hill in Rusty, Texas (inherited from his grandparents), has been experiencing unusual paranormal activity since residing in the house.

"I hear repeating noises the same time every day," Whitlock explains. "I hear glass breaking, but it's not like the sound of a drinking glass or a bowl shattering. It's more like a ceramic Christmas ornament dropping on the floor. I usually hear the sounds three times per day and at the same hours of 5:00 AM, 3:00 PM, and 8:00 PM. It happens in one of the guest bedrooms and in the great room near my great-grandmother's china cabinet."

Due to the disturbing sounds throughout the day, Whitlock restored sections of the house where the noises occurred. "I'm hoping this will resolve the situation. I plan to burn the china cabinet and move the chinaware into the kitchen," says Whitlock.

Jack scrolled to the next image on the screen. "Look at this one," he said and read the article aloud. *"Man found deceased in home. William Whitlock, resident of Whitlock Manor located on Cemetery Hill, was found dead in his home. He was fifty-two. Sources claim the cause of death was cardiac arrest. Medical examiner records indicate he had no prior health issues."*

"Interesting," Daisy said, jotting some notes.

"Yeah," Jack agreed. "I wonder if he ever had the chance to remodel the house before he died."

"Read on and find out," Daisy suggested, moving her hair that fell in her face and clasping it behind her ear.

Jack scrubbed through the film until something else grabbed his attention. "Check this out!" His eyes widened. "It's dated from two years ago."

"Read it," Daisy demanded.

"House scares away multiple owners," Jack read. "Whitlock Manor, notorious for its haunting structure and creepy history, has been occupied by many different families since 1899. Unfortunately, each family moved from the mansion due to disturbing sounds they claimed occurred about a month after settling in. As a result, the home remained vacant for approximately one year between each each homebuyer.

"City officials plan to vote to condemn the home and excavate the property to make ready for possible retail development. However, the current property owner (who remains anonymous) is pushing to keep the mansion standing due to its historical value."

"That's it?" Daisy asked, feeling as though the article did not provide much detail.

"I guess so," Jack said and pressed the fast-forward button. He searched for more articles. But when he found no more updates, he rewound the film and removed it from the machine.

Daisy closed her notebook and slid it into her backpack. "I don't know if this is going to be enough information to include in my writing assignment."

"I hope you can get *something* out of it," Jack said. He returned the microfilm to the cabinet, and when he came back, he noticed Daisy had her arms folded and was slouching a little in her chair, deep in thought. "What's on your mind?" Jack asked, sliding into the chair next to her.

"Paranormal investigations," Daisy said bluntly.

"Huh? What about them?"

"You tell me!"

"I don't know," Jack said, unsure of what Daisy was getting at. He tried guessing what was on her mind. "Um, you know I've always been interested in theories of the afterlife, so I guess you're saying you want to conduct a paranormal investigation on Whitlock Manor?"

"Bingo!" Daisy adjusted her posture. "Reading the articles sparked my interest in that house. I was thinking of other ways on how I could spice up this story for my writing class." She twirled the ends of her hair, a habit she had picked up recently whenever she brainstormed. "It might be too time consuming to find more public records on that house. Soooo . . . what if we checked out the house together in person? I mean, it makes perfect sense. You like to be scared. I like adventures. And I need a good story!"

Jack was intrigued by her idea. *Perhaps she's on to something,* he thought. "Can you keep this between you and me?" he asked.

Daisy raised an eyebrow. "Why?"

"If we do this, and someone from school finds out what we're doing, they might try and steal our idea. I want us to be the first to expose the truth about Whitlock Manor!"

Daisy tapped a finger on her cheek, thinking out loud. "It *would* be nice to debunk all the rumors," she said. Then she drew an imaginary X across her chest. "I cross my heart not to mention this to *anyone.*"

"Hope to die?" Jack added.

"And stick a needle in my eye!"

"Deal!" Jack said. "And since we're on the subject, remember at lunch I was holding back from telling you something?"

Daisy looked at him strangely. "Yeah?"

He paused, then continued. "Well, I heard a voice coming from the window on the front porch of that house last night."

"No way! What did it say—wait, is this a joke?"

"No joke," Jack said. "I think it was a woman's voice saying something about entering the house. But I can't remember what she, or it, said!"

"Maybe you'll hear it again," Daisy said. She grabbed her backpack. "Now you've *really* got me excited!"

Jack scooped up his backpack and got to his feet. "Are you free this weekend?"

"I think so. Why?"

"How about we make a trip to the old spook house on Saturday?"

Daisy's eyes widened. "Oh! Let me double-check my plans and

I'll let you know."

"Great! I'll call you later, and we can talk more," Jack said.

"Sounds good." Daisy smiled.

CHAPTER FIVE

A Surprise

Jack dug into his pocket for his house key and unlocked the front door. Being so late in the day, he wondered why his parents weren't home from work yet. His mother must be pulling a double shift. And he figured Victor had baseball practice after school. His father, a traveling sales consultant for an auto parts store, had an unpredictable schedule.

Jack walked into the kitchen, tossed his keys onto the table, and retrieved a box of gingersnaps and some milk.

Plopping onto the sofa in the den, he powered on the television and cycled through the channels with the remote. An episode of *Double Dare* slowly faded in on the screen. He propped his feet on the coffee table in front of him and dunked a gingersnap into the milk for a few seconds, getting it nice and soggy. Then he ate the cookie as he watched one of the game show contestants on TV reach into a gigantic nostril filled with green slime. The contestant grabbed a hidden envelope that contained a clue for the next obstacle in the game. The audience cheered, and Jack's hand dove in the box of gingersnaps, his eyes glued to the screen. As he repeated his routine of dunking the cookie into the milk and stirring it around, he thought he heard a noise coming from the dining room. He cocked his head to try and listen without having to mute the television.

His cookie, still submerged in milk, was swelling. Pieces of the gingersnap were flaking off and sinking to the bottom of the glass.

The noise Jack heard was constant, like the sound of a rodent trapped underneath the house. He set the box of cookies and his glass of milk on the coffee table and rose from the couch, heading into the dining room.

Sitting on the floor against the wall was a large open box, the flaps folded inward and secured with duct tape. Handwritten words in black lettering on the side of the box read: HIS NAME IS BEAR.

Jack stood over the box, peering down inside at a black Chow Chow pawing at the walls. The puppy's distressed face and tiny whimpering invited Jack to reach inside and scoop up the little fluffball.

"Whoa!" Jack smiled, cradling the puppy. "Where'd you come from?"

"I see you two have already met," Charles said, sneaking up behind Jack. He dropped a large bag of dog food on the floor next to the box.

Jack spun around. "Dad!" he said, his mouth gaping. "When did you get home? *Is this our dog?*"

"I helped work the counter today at the store instead of going out and chasing sales, and one of my co-workers brought her pups to work," Jack's father said. "I left early to bring this one home and went back out to get dog food. I figured it was time for a new pet. Your mother has been devastated since Guida died!"

It had been over a year since they lost their feisty overweight dachshund. She was a crazy dog but highly intelligent with so many human traits.

Jack's father scratched behind the puppy's ear. "Cute little fella, isn't he?" Still wearing his work attire smeared with black grease, he smelled like motor oil. "I was hoping to beat you home so I could see the look on your face when you saw him."

Jack rubbed his nose in the puppy's face. He loved the smell of puppy breath! "I can't believe you got us a new dog. Thanks, Dad!"

"Take him outside and see if he needs to pee," his father suggested. "He's been cooped up in that box for almost an hour." He peered down inside the box, looking for accidents. "I'm surprised he hasn't made a mess in there and rolled around in it."

Jack carried Bear to the backyard and set him in the grass. Bear sniffed around, hiked a leg and did his business, then trotted clumsily back to Jack.

"How are you already housebroken?" Jack muttered. He picked up the puppy and scratched under his chin. "Good boy!"

———

The sound of the garage door hummed. Jack's mother was home. Because she worked in a germ-infested atmosphere, she made it a rule not to allow physical contact until she showered. Instead, she greeted the family with a wave from the back door. Although she often came home stressed and tired, she still found the energy to prepare dinner, clean the house, mow the yard, pull weeds, and water the grass. The yard was her baby, and she pampered it like one.

Jack could not stop smiling when his mother walked into the house. He was curious to see how she'd react to the new addition to the family.

Charles folded the newspaper he was reading in his La-Z-Boy, slapped the paper on the marble-topped end table next to him, and stood to join Jack in welcoming Lindsay home.

Lindsay waved, then noticed Jack struggling to keep a straight face. She shuffled her eyes from him to Charles. "What's going on?"

Neither Jack nor his father said anything.

"What is it?" Lindsay insisted with a chip of irritation. She shifted a hand to her hip. "Did y'all break something?" The muffled sound of Bear whining and scratching inside the box in the dining room made her ears perk. "What was that?"

"I plead the fifth," Jack's father said.

Lindsay took a wide step around Jack and Charles and stormed into the dining room. She looked down inside the box.

Bear sat staring up at her with sorrowful, moist eyes.

"No more animals!" Lindsay shouted.

"C'mon, Mom!" Jack whined, scurrying to his mother.

"His name is Bear," Charles said.

"His name is NO!" Lindsay snapped. "Take the dog back to wherever you got him!"

"Why?" Jack asked, his heart sinking.

Lindsay glanced down at the puppy again. "For one thing, do you see how big his paws are? He'll be a *huge* dog, and we don't need another animal tearing up this house! Plus, you know I'll be the one feeding him and picking up all the craps in the yard!"

"But I'll help!" Jack insisted. "And I'll make sure Victor does, too."

"He's only a puppy. You know what puppies do? They chew on *everything*! We'll end up buying new shoes and furniture within a few months. I can't be dealing with all of that right now."

"But look at him, Mom! Look how cute and fluffy he is. I bet he'll make a good watchdog when he grows up."

Lindsay glanced down at Bear again, the puppy's unblinking eyes staring back at her. She picked up Bear and cradled him in her arms. Heaving a big sigh, she said, "Okay, he's adorable." She smiled, the puppy licking her face madly.

"*Yes!*" Jack cheered for the win.

———

Jack sat in the living room with his mother and father, playing with the puppy and discussing different names for him. Bear just wasn't a good fit for the dog. They needed something original.

Charles begged to differ.

Victor's car rumbled in the driveway, and Jack's parents looked at each other.

"Does Victor know about this dog?" Lindsay asked.

"Not yet," Jack's father replied.

Making his grand entrance through the back door, Victor tossed his baseball glove on the sofa and adjusted his ballcap. "What's the gathering for? Is this an intervention? *I swear I didn't do anything!*"

The puppy pranced clumsily toward Victor.

Victor did a double-take. "Wait, is that a dog?"

Jack rolled his eyes. "No, it's a furry frog!"

"Don't get smart with me, dillweed." Victor petted the puppy's tiny fuzzy head. "What did you name it? And are we keeping it?"

"He's a him, not an it," Jack corrected his brother.

Charles darted his eyes at Victor. "His name is Bear!"

"What? No! That's a stupid name," Victor argued. "We need to come up with something better if we're keeping this thing!"

"What do you suggest?" Lindsay asked.

Victor held his hand out for the puppy to sniff, buying him some time to think. He usually came up with the weirdest names for their pets. And the sad thing about it was that everyone agreed with his ideas!

Jack threw his hands in the air. "Well?"

"Bosco," Victor said with confidence.

"Yeah, I like that name better." Lindsay smiled.

"Y'all never like the things I suggest," Charles said, disgusted. Then, grabbing the TV remote wedged between his leg and the arm of the recliner, he took his frustration out on the device by pressing the buttons forcefully as he flipped through the channels.

Jack clasped his hands behind his back with a stumped posture, witnessing their father throw a childish tantrum. But this was nothing new, so he decided to grab his camcorder and capture footage of their new pet.

Beginning that night, boy and dog were inseparable.

CHAPTER SIX

Brotherly Love

SATURDAY, MARCH 11. 11:45 AM
Jack lay in bed, realizing he had not spoken to Stewart or Billy for nearly a week outside of school. Even though they were not part of his club anymore, they were still friends. He jumped out of bed to make some phone calls.

Jack picked up the handset of his Garfield telephone, its big cat eyes opening when the switch hook was released. He dialed Stewart's phone number first. When no one answered, he tried calling Billy. But all he got was a busy signal.

Jack pressed and held down the switch hook, and Garfield's eyes closed. They popped open again when he released the button. He dialed Daisy's phone number.

"Hello?" Daisy answered.

"Hey, it's Jack."

"Hey!" The tone in Daisy's voice was full of pep.

"Did you want to check out Whitlock Manor today?" Jack asked. "I meant to call and remind you about it earlier this week, but I got caught up in other things."

"I've been busy with schoolwork myself," Daisy said. "And my mom's been on this weird trip, making me do house chores and stuff. But I'm free this afternoon!"

"That sucks . . . about the chores, I mean."

"It's fine," Daisy giggled. "I'm used to doing them. So, when do you wanna go?"

Jack glanced at the clock radio on his nightstand. "Two o'clock?"

"Works for me!" Daisy chirped. "Meet at the lamp post at the end of our street?"

"Sure." Jack smiled.

"Okay, bye," Daisy said abruptly.

The phone clicked in Jack's ear. He hung up, grabbed his video game controller, and powered on the game console. As he waited for the game's title screen to appear, Victor barged into his room.

"Is that all you do is play video games?" Victor asked, glancing around Jack's bedroom at all the posters of video game titles taped to the walls.

Jack threw his hands in the air. "Don't you ever knock? And you play games, too. *Hypocrite!*"

"Not as much as you."

Jack fell silent. His brother was right. Then he griped, "What do you want?"

"I'm taking the motorcycle to the trails. I was gonna ask if you wanted to go, but it looks like you're too preoccupied with your TV."

"Of all days, you had to pick today?" Jack said. "I want to go, but I have plans with my friend. What about tomorrow? Will Mom and Dad be working?"

"Who knows," Victor said. "It's not my job to keep up with them."

Their mother discouraged them from sneaking the dirt bike out while she was sleeping before working the graveyard shift at the hospital. But Jack and Victor were clever boys and had a workaround. They would shift the motorcycle into neutral, walk it halfway up the alley, and crank the engine so she wouldn't hear it. Then they'd ride until the gas tank was nearly empty.

It was three months ago when their father had purchased the green Kawasaki 80. He thought it would give the boys something to do over the summer rather than stay cooped up in the house all day.

Victor took Jack for rides most weekends to the dirt trails where a new elementary school was breaking ground. The site had a huge mound that other kids on motorcycles gathered on the weekends to jump. What kept the kids out of trouble was there were no workers present on the jobsite over the weekends. The place was not fenced off, and it remained unsupervised.

Riders nicknamed the pile of dirt Mount Fear because it sloped at a ninety-degree angle five or six feet at the top. If you weren't a skilled rider, you were better off staying out of people's way.

Jack remembered Victor letting him ride the motorcycle by himself for the first time with hardly any coaching. "Give it some gas and switch to second gear when you get going," Victor said, barely giving Jack the basics. "Don't forget to use the clutch. Other than that, it's like riding a bike. Then, after you get the hang of it, take it up Mount Fear!"

Victor always made sarcastic remarks around Jack, and Jack didn't know if he was serious this time.

After adjusting the chinstrap to his helmet, Jack eased back on the throttle. The bike bucked a couple of times before he found his balance and finally sped away.

He practiced riding straightaways and switching to second

gear. Turning was easy—he got that down with no problem. But he was afraid to go any faster than second gear allowed without damaging the motor.

It was a solid five minutes before Jack returned to his brother with a big smile on his face. "That was fun!" he said over the bike's idling engine.

"You're not done yet!" Victor reminded Jack. "Take it up Mount Fear, and don't let off the throttle. You'll flip the motorcycle if you don't give it enough gas."

Jack wiped the sweat beads from his brow. He could feel the butterflies swarming in his stomach as he stared at Mount Fear like Evel Knievel concentrating on a world record jump.

Although he didn't want to ride up the steep hill, he did want to prove to Victor that he wasn't a wimp. So he lined up the motorcycle with the worn path leading to the mound, his heart racing in his chest.

Another dirt bike rider zoomed past him and took to the mound. The kid shot up like a rocket, getting some good hangtime before he made a perfect landing and sped down the other side of the hill to lap around and make the jump again.

Jack glanced over his shoulder at Victor, who watched him from a distance. "I have to do this," he muttered. It was either now or never. He slowly pulled back on the throttle and crept his way up the path. Then he threw it into second gear just before he started the climb.

Jack was near the top of the mound when the front wheel suddenly dug into the angled slope. The engine bogged down like it was about to stall, and Jack quickly twisted back on the throttle.

The motorcycle soared in the air!

Jack instinctively leaned forward in midair and brought the

front wheel down to make a clean landing, his feet slipping from the foot pegs when the bike touched down.

"You almost bit the dust!" Victor said when Jack returned. "But that was an awesome jump!"

Jack cut the engine and flipped down the kickstand. *That was so scary!* he said, removing his helmet.

"I know," Victor said. "I thought for sure the motorcycle was going to jerk back and land on top of you!" He grabbed hold of the handlebars. "C'mon, we need to get home before Mom wakes up. I'll drive."

———

Victor flicked the balled-up wrapper from a stick of chewing gum at Jack, the paper ricocheting off his head. "Grow up!" he said. "Your dumb game system will *never* compare to playing at the real arcade."

"Quit throwing your trash at me!" Jack yelled back. "Pick it up!"

Victor smacked his gum. "Make me," he chuckled.

"I don't make trash. I burn it!"

"Then burn the wrapper, butt-munch. And your joke is old. Come up with something better."

"Your face is old," Jack said, returning fire.

"C'mon, bro." Victor grinned, pointing at his own face. "You know you can't get enough of this face!"

"Whatever," Jack sneered.

"That's what I thought! Oh, and since you don't want to ride the motorcycle today, don't be ratting me out to Mom and Dad. You're dead if either one of them finds out!"

"Shut up," Jack muttered when his brother finally walked away. He lost interest in playing video games.

———

Jack stuffed his backpack with the items he wanted to take with him to Whitlock Manor. He packed his camcorder, a Polaroid instant camera, a few bottles of water, and enough snacks to share with Daisy. He gave Bosco a quick pat on the head before hurrying outside to the lamp post at the end of the street to meet up with Daisy.

Daisy showed up riding her pink Mongoose bicycle and wearing a fanny pack around her tight Daisy Dukes. Her smooth, long legs and curvaceous booty melted Jack's eyes!

One day I'll find the courage to express how I feel about her, Jack thought, hoping they could take their friendship further. He couldn't wait to tell her. But today was not the day to start getting mushy. They had an investigation to conduct.

"Ready to do this?" Jack cleared his throat.

"As ready as I'll ever be." Daisy smiled.

Jack set his Diamondback into motion. "Follow me!"

CHAPTER SEVEN

Trespassers

Cemetery Hill once had the sights and sounds of children jump roping and playing tag. It was difficult to imagine past homeowners who once resided on this creepy street going about their daily lives. But those days had long since been forgotten, eaten up by time itself. Cemetery Hill was battered, untouched by the city for years. There were few visitors, save for those who rolled into town who were lost, or an occasional group of hooligans who were curious about the old house.

Whitlock Manor reflected the memories of its birth and its history within the walls. The structure was rotted, roof shingles were stripped and nearly bare, and the upper balcony was missing part of a railing. The shutters were detached and dangled by threads from the windows.

Daisy set down her bike and gazed at the crippled mansion, sensing its negative energy yet oddly captivated by its sinister appearance. She loved old, abandoned sites, places that made her feel a sentimental attachment to them.

"I bet the city had a field day condemning this place," she said. "I see now what you meant the other day when you mentioned that not all the windows were boarded up. Did someone vandalize the house recently?"

Jack parked his bike next to Daisy's. "I don't know. And there had been a for-sale sign here for a long time. But when I was here last week with Stewart and Billy, it was removed. I think someone may have bought the house."

Daisy clasped her hands behind her back, eager to take a closer look around. "So, do we leave our bikes here?"

"Yeah, they should be fine," Jack assured her.

Daisy diverted her attention to a dark cloud emerging from behind the house. "Looks like rain soon, and we aren't prepared for it. Let's make this quick!"

"See, this is what I was talking about at school on Monday when you said it never rained that day!" Jack reminded Daisy. "I think the house releases supernatural forces that stir up the weather. Either that, or I don't think the house likes visitors."

"I never said I didn't believe you." Daisy wrinkled her brow. "I said I never saw it rain when you asked me. On the other hand, would the house really make it rain? Not sure how I feel about that. Anyway, let's get this over with before I change my mind."

"Wait!" Jack reached into the side pocket of his backpack and removed his Polaroid camera. "Let's get a picture first." He raised the flash compartment covering the lens and held up the camera facing him and Daisy with Whitlock Manor behind them. Then he pressed the shutter button.

Click . . . Churrr. The camera flashed and printed the film instantaneously.

Jack pulled the film from the picture exit slot and shook it to speed up the development process.

"I don't take good photos." Daisy grimaced as she looked at the picture.

"Not true," Jack assured her. He closed the flash compartment and stuffed the camera and photo in his backpack for safekeeping. "Let's go."

They ascended the winding path covered with crabgrass, dandelions, and other types of weeds leading to the house.

Halfway up, Daisy slipped but caught her footing and fretted over her clumsiness. And by the time they reached the rickety stairs of the front porch, she was out of breath with a mild case of vertigo. "Ugh! I keep feeling the illusion of the house leaning toward us!" she said. "I can picture monstrous skeletal arms bursting from the outside walls and grabbing us through the sun-bleached front door!"

"See, you'll have no problem with your creative writing project!" Jack said.

Out of nowhere, a crow suddenly swooped over their heads and perched atop the corner of the roof, cawing as it eyeballed the trespassers. The noise attracted dozens of other blackbirds, which circled above the house and then dispersed and either touched down on the edge of the roof or perched on tree branches surrounding the house. All the birds glared down at Jack and Daisy like they had no business being there, intimidating the teens with their annoying coos and clicks.

"Where did all these things come from?" Jack wondered.

"I have no idea, but they're creeping me out!"

The clouds, drained of color, parted above Whitlock Manor to welcome a streak of hot silver that split the heavens. A crackle of thunder shortly followed, scaring most of the blackbirds away.

"Get to the porch!" Jack insisted. "We're about to get soaked!"

No sooner had they taken shelter on the porch than the swing rammed against the side of the house.

"I kid you not," Jack said, stepping to the broken window near the swing, "I think this house hates me!" He bent to the cracked window.

"It doesn't hate you," Daisy said, and then, curious as to why he was leaning his ear close to the window, she asked, "What are you doing?"

"Listening."

"For what?"

"Voices, remember?" Jack replied, his ear covering the impact hole in the window. He suddenly remembered his camcorder and removed it from his backpack. "I want to get the sound on tape this time before I miss it again."

"Are you sure the voices weren't coming from your head?" Daisy snickered.

"I'm not crazy!" Jack said and hoisted the camera onto his shoulder.

"And you're positive no one lives here?" Daisy asked.

Jack sidestepped from the window to the front door and knocked. "Let's find out," he said, even though he knew no one was going to answer.

"Yikes!" Daisy moved behind him, not willing to be seen if someone should open the door.

"Hello?" Jack rapped on the door again. "Anyone home?"

"No one's answering," Daisy said after a brief pause. "Now what?"

Jack reached for the rusted doorknob and grasped it firmly. "We go inside."

"Shouldn't we see if there's a car parked around back or something first?" Daisy suggested, feeling a twist in her stomach.

Jack lowered the camera and spun around. "Are you wigging out already?" He remembered the last time she bailed on him, at the Funhouse of Doom several years ago. Daisy was so excited to enter while they stood in the long line waiting to get in. But when it was finally their turn to enter, the ticket taker held the door open for them and she was stricken with fear. She stood frozen with a blank stare.

"I'm not afraid." Daisy's voice pitched higher. "I just don't feel comfortable trespassing if someone is living here."

"If someone lives here, it's probably another homeless person, like in the story your dad told you. And I doubt a homeless person would harm us." He turned back to the door and twisted the knob. He and Stewart and Billy regularly checked the door each time they visited the house but found it always locked, so he didn't have any high hopes that it would open. But this time it was unlocked!

Although he maintained his composure, deep inside of him lingered the nightmarish feeling of terror waiting to be unleashed.

Jack pushed open the door, his ears resonating with the loud squeal of the rusted hinges. He leaned inside the doorway and peered through the darkness. A wave of uncertainty crashed over him as he cautiously stepped into the house and was greeted by a cold draft. His nose wrinkled at the rancid smell of rotting meat. "Eew! It stinks in here."

Daisy cupped her hand over her nose and mouth as she entered the
house behind Jack. "I don't think we should go any further than the front room today."

Jack glanced over his shoulder at her. "Still scared I see," he said, feeling an eerie stillness surrounding him.

CHAPTER EIGHT

Into the Darkness

The house welcomed Jack and Daisy into her dark, damp belly, challenging them to seek its treasures from the past. With its splendor stripped, the generations of its elegant features were replaced by thick cobwebs that laced the walls. The floors creaked with every cautious step. Dust particles trickled down from the rafters like ash during a volcanic eruption. The stench of mildew blanketed the air.

"Hey," Jack said to Daisy out the side of his mouth.

"What?" Daisy said in a nervous whisper.

"Can you grab a flashlight from my backpack? There's two, so you can use one if you want it. I didn't think the house would be *this* dark. Plus, I need more light for the camera."

Daisy rummaged through the bag and retrieved the two flashlights. She clicked them on and handed one to Jack. "I'm glad *you* came prepared. I forgot mine."

Jack grabbed the light from her and caught a whiff of the sweet aroma of her hair, still smelling fresh even after having ridden their bikes a couple of miles and breaking a sweat.

He scanned the area, the flashlight beam cutting through the stillness of the dark. He shined his light at the ceiling, where cobwebs drooped from an old chandelier like Spanish moss stretching from an old oak tree. "This place is creepy, but

I like it!"

"I don't like dark places," Daisy confessed. "I'd rather there be more natural light in here."

"I'm sure there would be if most of the windows weren't caked with years-old dirt," Jack said. "Let's check out the room where I heard the whispering through the window on the porch."

Daisy let out a sigh like a tire losing air pressure. "Can't we do that tomorrow, or maybe next week?"

"What's going on with you? I thought you were adventurous," Jack said.

"I am, but this just doesn't feel right! I mean, I love abandoned places, but this place . . . it has a weird vibe to it. I feel so claustrophobic right now."

Jack screamed in his head. He prepared to come here with Daisy, and now she wanted to back out. He didn't want to be rude or mean to her about it, so he tried to compromise with her and fumbled for the right words. "Why don't we just take a quick look around the room where the broken window is, and then we leave? If everything's good, we can explore the next area of the house next week."

Daisy gazed into Jack's eyes. "You promise we leave as soon as you look around the window?"

Jack made an X over his chest. "I promise."

"Stick a needle in your eye?"

"And stick a needle in my eye!" Jack smiled.

Daisy took in a long, deep breath and let it out slowly. "Okay," she agreed.

Finally pressing forward, Jack led the way into the next room. The house was a recipe for disaster; there was no telling what kind of trap lay ahead of them. "Watch out for loose boards!"

he warned. "Don't step on any rusted nails."

Waving his flashlight around the large open area, Jack discovered an oversized dirty rug in the center of the room. He hoisted up his video camera and zoomed in for a closeup in hopes to get a better look.

"That's odd. I wonder if that was left by the last occupant."

Daisy peered around him at the rug, unimpressed with it. "It's ugly."

Peeling his eye from the camera's viewfinder, Jack proceeded toward the rug. He stood over it, filming another clip. "Weird. What if it's worth something? And look at the faded patterns. It looks sort of like . . . a New Mexico design?"

"Who knows," Daisy said. "Can we move on?"

Jack lowered the camera and crept toward a cased opening leading into another huge area boasting a large brick fireplace. He could hear the muffled sounds of the porch swing outside banging against the wall in this room.

"Holy crap, this place is massive!" Jack's voice pinged in the room. He sniffed. "Do you smell that?"

"Yeah," Daisy said, pinching her shirt over her nose. "It smells like a rodent died in here!"

They waved their flashlights around the area, illuminating two windows covered with dust at the far end of the room.

"That's it!" Jack said with excitement. "The broken window! This has to be the room where the voice was coming from!" He frolicked across the room and knelt beside the spider-cracked window and swiped his hand on the thick grime, creating a clean streak that he could see through to the porch outside.

"Look how dark it got out there," Daisy said, peering over Jack's shoulder through the window. "That's some really bad weather rolling in!" Her eyes darted down at him kneeling at the floor. "You found your window, now can we—"

Something crashed in another room, and Jack jumped back from the window.

Daisy's reflexes were quick in catching her footing when Jack almost stumbled into her. She twisted around and shined her light behind her. *"What was that?"*

Jack stood motionless and listened for the sound again.

"Let's get out of here!" Daisy insisted.

"Hold on," Jack said. "What time is it?"

Daisy looked at her watch. "Three seventeen."

"Remember when we read the article at the library about Old Man Whitlock hearing strange noises in the house?" Jack recalled. "He said the sounds happened at different times each day. I think one of the times was around three o'clock!"

"That's right!" Daisy said. "The article stated the sounds happened in the two different rooms. The great room and one of the bedrooms."

"This must be the great room," Jack said. "But I don't think what we just heard came from in here. Do you?"

"I'm not sure," Daisy replied. "But do you remember the article also saying he moved his grandmother's chinaware to the kitchen? And Whitlock burned the cabinet that was in the great room." She jiggled her flashlight at the doorway where the crashing sound might have come from. "I think that room over there leads to the kitchen."

"Let's check it out!" Jack said.

"No way!" Daisy snapped. "You need to stick to your word about leaving after you looked at the window. You crossed your chest! Besides, my mom is probably wondering where I'm at right now, and I don't want to get chewed out when I get home. And with that storm brewing, she's probably flipping out already!"

"Just a peek, then we can go," Jack pleaded. "I promise!"

"You already made a promise, Jack!" Daisy whined. "Why can't we just go?"

"Because I want to see what that noise was. I wasn't expecting *that* to happen when I was looking at the window!"

Daisy threw her head back. "Ugh! I guess so but be quick!"

"Two seconds," Jack assured her.

Approaching the doorway at the opposite side of the room, Jack shined his flashlight in the newly discovered area. "She was right; this is the kitchen," he muttered. He hoisted his camcorder onto his shoulder and peered through the viewfinder. Although the picture was grainy due to the lack of light in the room, it looked like a tornado had struck this part of the house. The floor was caved in, and the walls looked like they weren't going to hold up much longer.

Jack panned the camera to the cupboards, warped and decayed with several missing doors. Tilting down, he took footage of the weeds growing through the cracks in the waterlogged floorboards.

"See anything?" Daisy whispered behind him. "Any idea what the noise was?"

Jack jumped; he'd thought she had stayed at the opposite end of the great room. "It looks like a swamp in here," he said. "I wonder if what we heard was the house shifting. This is definitely not safe to walk through."

"Then it's time to go," Daisy argued.

"Okay. Let's call it a day," Jack said, spinning around. He suddenly froze, shining his flashlight above Daisy's head. He forgot the camera was still rolling.

"What?" Daisy shined her light in Jack's face.

Jack was at a loss for words.

"You're scaring me, Jack! *What's wrong?*"

"Don't move," Jack whispered.

"Not funny!" Daisy said through gritted teeth.

Jack gazed at a figure with red glowing beady eyes, bobbing in midair indistinctly in steady successions behind Daisy. He closed his eyes for a second then opened them to be sure he wasn't seeing things. Unfortunately, the figure was still there.

"Jack," Daisy said in sheer terror, her heart squeezing painfully in her chest. The bulb in her flashlight flickered but did not burn out.

Jack's light dimmed, too, but the batteries held on for dear life. His camcorder, however, shut down.

He lowered the camera and leaped toward Daisy, brushing against her shoulder. "Run!" he shouted.

Daisy quickly turned but stood stunned at the red eyes bearing down on her. Her flashlight beam penetrated right through the figure's midsection. It looked like a wraith! "Jack! Wait!" she screamed.

Jack was already halfway across the great room when he noticed Daisy was not following him. He spun and shined his light toward her still standing near the kitchen doorway. "Daisy, c'mon!"

The wraith whipped around at Jack's voice, its demon eyes locking on him.

Daisy weaved her way past the apparition and sprinted across the room, hoping the ghost wasn't following her.

"Hurry, Daisy! Hurry!" Jack cried out. When she caught up with him, they both glanced back at the kitchen doorway.

The ghost was gone.

Huddling close, Jack and Daisy shuffled through the house back the way they came. Jack swung open the front door, but he quickly extended an arm out in front of Daisy, blocking her from running past him to the porch.

Mike Palinsky stood before them wearing a poncho with his hand on the hilt of his sheathed Glock 22, halting the teens from fleeing. "Whoa! What are you two doing here?"

"N-Nothing," Jack stuttered at the doorway, out of breath.

"The hell you're not! You're trespassing on private property."

"This place has been empty for years," Jack said, playing the dumb card.

Mike glared at him. "Someone owns this place, whether you know it or not, Jack." He took a couple of backward steps on the porch. "You two come on out of there."

"Where's all the no trespassing signs?" Jack asked, stepping onto the porch. Daisy was right up against him, trembling like a leaf.

The blood in Mike's face boiled at Jack's cocky attitude, but he stayed professional while in front of Daisy.

"We're sorry, Officer," Daisy pleaded with a dry mouth. Her stomach shifted uneasily, adding to the nervous twitching of her knees.

Mike acknowledged her apology and eased his hand off his weapon. "Listen, it's unsafe to be around here. That goes for your friends, too. I'll have to issue a citation and notify your folks if I catch you here again."

"You won't have to worry," Daisy said. "We *definitely* won't be coming back."

Mike noticed their backpacks and turned to Jack. "What's in your bags?" he asked, tilting his head at the camcorder Jack held at his side.

"*Were you filming in there?* I take it you didn't get a location agreement from the owner to take video of this place?"

Daisy opened her mouth to explain, but the buzzing from Mike's radio interrupted her.

"Central to 713," dispatch squawked over the channel.

"713, go ahead," Mike said over his shoulder radio.

"10-58. Traffic signals dark at West Main and Freeman."

"10-58. West Main and Freeman copy," he confirmed, then said to Jack and Daisy, "You two need a lift home? It doesn't look like this rain's going to let up anytime soon. I can return later to load up your bikes and drop them off to you at the end of my shift this evening."

Jack was stunned at Mike's offer to help. "Sure, but please don't tell my parents we were here. I know you and my dad are tight, but he'll *kill* me!"

Mike slapped a hand on Jack's shoulder. "This is between you and me, buddy—but only if you promise to stay away from here."

"I won't come back," Jack agreed.

CHAPTER NINE

Mike's Warning

After showering later that afternoon, Jack lay in bed with his hands behind his head and stared at the ceiling. Visions from the partial walkthrough at Whitlock Manor with Daisy repeated in his head. He couldn't unsee those disturbing glowing red eyes!

The storm had downgraded to a drizzle, and Mike hadn't returned with his bike yet—it had been a few hours. *Surely the traffic lights are working by now,* Jack thought.

Jack's mother appeared at his bedroom doorway. "Wash up. Time for dinner."

Bosco sideswiped Lindsay's leg and trotted into the room. "Dammit, Bosco!" she roared, then giggled at the puppy trying to jump up the side of Jack's bed. The height of the mattress rejected him, and he kept landing on his haunches.

When his mother left the room, Jack sat up and grabbed his backpack from the floor at the side of his bed. He hoisted Bosco onto the bed and emptied out his backpack. Removing his camcorder from the bag, he ejected the VHS cassette from the side compartment. Then he labeled the videotape with a black marker and set it on top of his dresser to review later. Although anxious to see if the ghost appeared on the video, he couldn't risk anyone walking into his room and seeing it as they stood over his shoulder. Especially Victor! Jack didn't have to worry about his father, who rarely came into his room.

Lindsay was setting the table when Jack entered the kitchen. Bosco trailed behind him until he pulled a chair at the table. "Smells good, whatcha making, Mom?"

"Fried salmon drizzled with pancake syrup, a side of mac and cheese, crisp yellow corn, and a garden salad," Lindsay replied. It was one of the family's favorite meals.

Victor plopped down in the chair across from Jack without warning. Lindsay was already by his side about to dump a heaping amount of lettuce and vegetable slices clasped in salad tongs into his bowl.

"Whoa!" Victor placed a hand over his bowl. "You can't pull a fast one on me this time, Mom! And you know I hate those nasty tomatoes, so get those away from my face!"

"You need to eat your vegetables," Lindsay insisted. "They're good for you!"

"Yeah, eat your veggies," Jack laughed.

"Stay out of this, punk!" Victor pointed at Jack.

Lindsay quickly took the opportunity when Victor was not looking, distracted from Jack's snickering at him, and dropped a pile of green lettuce with a couple of sliced tomatoes and cucumbers into his bowl.

Jack snorted.

"What's so funny?" Victor demanded. He looked down at his bowl and his eyes widened, stumped again by his mother's fast ninja-like movements. "Mom, are you trying to kill me? These things are *disgusting*!" He picked the tomatoes and cucumbers from his bowl and placed them on his napkin.

Lindsay giggled and scurried back to the stove to plate Jack's dinner.

When she returned with the fresh hot meal, Jack drizzled extra syrup over his salmon and added a touch of it to his mac and cheese. "Where's Dad?" he asked. "Is he not eating?"

Lindsay returned to the stove and slammed down the serving utensils. "Charles! Dinner's ready," she yelled. "It's getting cold!"

Jack heard the crumpling of newspaper and the recliner's footrest retracting. Moments later, his father entered the kitchen. "Yum! Fried salmon!"

Lindsay finally took her seat; like so many mothers, she was always the last one sitting down. She salted her food and reached to the center of the table for the syrup. "When's your science project due, Jack?" she asked.

Even though science was one of his worst subjects, Jack thought the assignment was kind of cool. The class was learning about force and momentum and the basic principles of Newton's Law of Motion. Additionally, students were to figure out how to protect an egg when dropped from the balcony over the cafeteria. "Two weeks," he said with his mouth full.

"Have you figured what you're going to use to protect the egg?" his mother followed up.

"Drinking straws or toothpicks—that's all we can use. But I'm not using toothpicks."

"I remember doing that stupid assignment a few years ago," Victor said. "My egg cracked."

"No wonder you're the way you are." Jack smirked, scooping a forkful of seashell-shaped macaroni and cheese. "Oh, wait—I forgot Mom and Dad told me you were hatched, so never mind."

"Eat shit, nerd!" Victor raised his voice.

"Watch your mouth!" Charles shouted over Victor. "Don't

be talking like that at the dinner table."

"Sorry, Dad," Victor apologized. "I'll remember to tell this nerd to eat shit after dinner then."

Charles cut his eyes at Victor.

"Ha!" Lindsay laughed, throwing her hand over her mouth to keep from spitting out her food. "Enough of the toilet humor!"

Victor moved a piece of pasta from his mac and cheese onto the edge of his plate. "Jack, you're such an idiot," he said and flicked the pasta at Jack. It missed hitting Jack and soared over his shoulder.

Bosco peeled out on the linoleum floor behind Jack and fetched the piece of cheesy pasta.

Retaliating, Jack tossed a crouton from his salad bowl and hit Victor between the eyes. "Bull's-eye!" Jack laughed.

"Oh, you're dead now, dude!" Victor snapped.

"STOP IT!" Charles roared. "If one of you throws something again, my belt's gonna have words with both of your rear ends!"

Bosco's ears perked at Charles shouting.

"Can we *never* have a decent meal without you two always picking at each other?" Charles continued, shaking his butter knife at Jack and Victor.

"Victor started it," Jack said.

"I don't care," his father snapped. "Y'all need to behave at the dinner table like civilized people."

"So it's okay not to be civilized anywhere else but at the dinner table?" Victor joked.

Jack burst out laughing.

Lindsay nearly choked on her food.

Charles gave Victor "the dad look" then said, "If I did what you two are doing when I was a kid, I'd be hung by my toes from the tree in the backyard!"

Jack didn't understand why his father was telling him and Victor this when he knew his father enjoyed embarrassing them in front of other people. In restaurants, for instance, if his food was not prepared correctly, or it came out cold, he'd make an epic stink about it for the thrill of causing a scene. Jack, Victor, and their mother would cringe as Charles spoke his mind to the waitress or manager.

Jack stabbed his fork at the last piece of lettuce in his bowl, ate it, then placed his silverware on the plate and gulped down the rest of his tea. It was the fastest he had ever eaten with the family, and he was surprised to be the first one done eating this time. He was used to being the last one finished.

"What's the rush?" Jack's father noticed him through the corner of his eye ready to excuse himself from the table.

Concerned about his bike, Jack needed to keep an eye out for Mike and couldn't let his family know about him and Daisy breaking into the house on Cemetery Hill. One slip of the tongue from Mike, and he'd be Bosco's next meal.

He stood from the table and took his dishes to the sink. "No rush," he lied to his dad. "I just want to try and beat a level on my video game."

"Don't you ever play enough of that crap?" Victor said.

"Shut your mouth," Jack retaliated, pushing in his chair at the table. Then he stormed off to his bedroom with Bosco at his heels.

———

Powering on the TV, Jack peeled back the curtains at his bedroom window and peeked outside, hoping Mike would be pulling up with his bike. Not seeing him, he stepped from the window and sat at the edge of his bed, thumbing through the channels with the remote. He remembered the VHS on the dresser while channel surfing and was tempted to review it, but he didn't want to scrub through all the footage yet, so he kept cycling through the stations on TV.

Flipping rapidly through the channels, Jack released his thumb from pressing the buttons on the remote and watched as his attention was drawn to a high-energy commercial advertising a new video game.

GalactiCats, Escape from Planet Warthole is the ultimate video game experience! Join Sergeant Smiley as he leads a team of space cat-ets on a wild journey to fend off the evil Toad Croak. Over forty hours of gameplay. Huge bosses and extraordinarily detailed visuals featuring a new technological supersonic graphics chip built right into the cartridge—you'll forget you're playing a game! Help the GalactiCats save the universe in this highly anticipated, ultra-addictive action-packed adventure and claw your way into becoming a new hero. GalactiCats, Escape from Planet Warthole blasts off to hit stores this summer!

"Whoa!" Jack's eyes enlarged. He didn't want the game; he *needed* it! If there was one addiction he admitted to, it was playing video games. He even considered addictive gameplay a form of therapy.

After watching the GalactiCats commercial, he suddenly had the itch to play a game. So he flipped the input device toggle switch on the back of the television to display the gaming console's startup screen. Then he grabbed a game and blew into the cartridge to remove dust particles on the chip—a quick fix for games that either froze on the TV or did not boot up correctly in the machine. The remedy was a hoax, but it was a habit since most other gamers did it.

After inserting the cartridge into the console, he waited for the copyright information and company logos to cycle through before the main title screen appeared. Finally, he pressed the start button on the controller. But his gameplay ended abruptly when he heard a car door shut outside. Jack leaped from his bed to the window and pulled back the curtain. Mike's police cruiser was parked in front of the house.

Jack dropped the controller on the floor as the first cutscene to the game's story began, then he darted to the front door before Mike could ring the doorbell. He opened the door just as Mike stepped onto the porch with his bike.

"As promised," Mike grinned, leaning Jack's bike against the wall.

"Thanks! Did those traffic lights start working again?"

"You're welcome. And yes, the power was restored."

"That's good," Jack said. "I bet you stay pretty busy."

"When it rains, it pours—no pun intended," Mike said. Then he pointed his thumb behind him at his cruiser. "I have your girlfriend's bike in the trunk."

"Daisy? Oh, she's not my girlfriend," Jack corrected him.

"Well, maybe you should think about asking her out one day," Mike suggested heartily.

"Like on a date?"

"You two would make a great couple." Mike smiled. "I grew up with a neighborhood friend that was a girl, too. Then I married her."

Jack didn't know if he believed him or not, or if he was just saying that to encourage him to go steady with Daisy. "Yeah, I don't think she's interested in me."

"Keep trying," Mike said. He glanced at his cruiser, then

back at Jack. "Would you mind if I give you the bike to take to her?"

"That's fine." Jack shrugged. "She only lives a few doors down anyway."

"Right on, buddy. I appreciate it."

They walked to the cruiser, and Mike popped the trunk. He removed Daisy's bike and set it down just as his radio squawked. He listened to dispatch while he closed the trunk. Since the call did not pertain to him, he proceeded to the driver's side then turned back to Jack. "Say, off the record, what intrigued you and your friend to snoop around inside the house this afternoon? You never explained since I got that call."

Jack knew Mike was going to try and pick at his brain, so he kept his answer brief. "We just thought it'd be cool to check out."

"Well, the house really does have an owner like I was telling you," Mike said. "The county has records of it. I'm not sure if it's going to be fixed up for use as a summer home or if the family will be moving in." He opened the door and slid behind the wheel. "As I warned you before, that place is private property. Trespassing can get you into trouble if the owner catches you."

Jack did not respond.

"I'm here to protect you along with everyone else in this city," Mike continued, shifting the vehicle into gear. "If it seems that I'm being too harsh about being around that old house, just know that I care about you, Jack. I don't want to see you or any of your friends getting hurt over there. In my opinion, that place should have been demolished years ago and not sold to another buyer. Breaking and entering is the charge if you or someone else other than the owner gets caught inside that place. Heed my words, Jack. *STAY AWAY FROM THAT HOUSE.*"

"I get it," Jack said, trying not to roll his eyes.

Mike shut his door, waved, then drove away.

"I guess no football card today," Jack muttered and grabbed Daisy's bike and walked it to her house.

CHAPTER TEN

A Well-Kept Secret

SUNDAY, MARCH 12. 11:00 AM

Stewart Johnson rode his bike to the Stoney Fields public park. A Little League baseball game was in progress as he rolled up to the concession stand and purchased two hot dogs and a large soda. After scarfing down the beef franks and chugging his ice-cold drink while watching a full inning, he set off behind the sports field and rode his bike down a winding dirt road secluded by trees to Eaglecrest Farm.

Sitting on his bike at the dead end where the gate entrance to the farm was located, Stewart waited for Rachael Eaglecrest to walk out of her house. She was the farmer's daughter, and Stewart had promised her that no one, including his friends, would know about their relationship. After four months and counting, it was the longest secret he had ever kept!

Stewart drummed his fingers on the handlebars to his own beat, recalling when he had met Rachael as he eyeballed the front porch of the farmhouse. He reminisced about the school field trip when he toured the campus of a community college. Rachael lived out of district and did not attend Remington High, but the class from her school merged with his group that day. After greeting each other during lunch break in the courtyard on campus, they were inseparable the rest of the day.

Stewart was attracted to her fiery red hair. She was big-boned, but that only made him more attracted to her. He liked thick girls. For Stewart, it was love at first sight!

Racheal warned Stewart about the situation with her family and how her father was so strict and overprotective of her, she had to keep any relationships discreet. Stewart didn't care; he had developed an infatuation with her.

At the end of the day, Rachael scribbled her address in Stewart's information packet. "I can't give you my phone number, but if you wait for me on Sunday mornings around eleven at the end of the dirt road outside the gate," she explained, "I'll come out and meet you. My father and brother attend stock shows in the mornings and are usually gone until dark."

Stewart remembered his heart thumping madly in his chest when he received Rachael's address that day. He had never picked up a chic so easily!

On the bus ride back to Remington High, he worried the entire way if meeting Rachael was just a prank, something she might've set up with her friends. It had happened to him several times before, getting stood up by girls, but this situation seemed different. Although negative thoughts wove in his mind about getting let down, his heart felt like it was in the right place. And after his first visit to Rachael's house proved true, that she did have feelings for him, they were officially in a boyfriend-girlfriend—albeit secret—relationship.

Stewart paused from tapping his fingers on his bike's handles when he finally noticed Rachael coming down the steps of the porch. She scurried up the gravel drive-up, stopped short, and waved at him from afar. It was the signal meaning the coast was clear.

Stewart rode up to the gate entrance and entered the combination to the padlock that Rachael had given to him the first day when he found her house. He rotated the dial three stops and popped the lock. Then he nudged open the rusty gate, squeezed his bike through, and pulled the gate closed behind him.

As always, he greeted Rachael at the ramshackle shed behind the farmhouse where they would be unseen. He leaned his bike against the outside wall and entered the shed, the smell of sun-soaked grass and aged timber lingering inside. Sunlight streamed from the cracks between the wall panels, illuminating the dust particles floating about like confetti. A variety of gas-powered tools and tractor parts hung along the back wall.

Stewart approached a sizeable wooden workbench in the center of the shed where Rachael leaned against it wearing a skimpy outfit. Her long red hair was positioned to one side and draped over the front of her shoulder, falling to the midsection of her curvy frame. Tiny freckles spread across her nose and cheeks like pointillism art. An addicting smile emerged between the gap in her lips when their eyes locked.

Stewart threw his arms around her, the intoxicating smell of her perfume tingling his senses with excitement. "Oh, God, how I've missed you," he whispered.

Rachael bit her lower lip. "You have *no* idea!"

Stewart slipped his hand around to the small of her back and pulled her close, embracing her with a hard kiss. Their moist lips fit perfectly through escalating breaths.

But Rachael peeled her lips away from his before things became more sensual. "We shouldn't be in here anymore," she said, taking Stewart's hands. "I think my brother's been keeping tabs on me lately, and it's kind of creepy."

Stewart could feel his face flush. "Sorry. I didn't mean to—"

Rachael pressed a finger to his lips. "It's okay," she said in a hushed voice. "I want to show you something." She led him outside to the barbed wire fence along the tree line behind the shed.

"What's over here?" Stewart asked.

"You'll see!" Rachael giggled. She pulled the two center barbed wires apart, making a gap for Stewart to slip between. "Quick, go through."

After transitioning through the fence, Rachael led Stewart deeper into the woods to a vast, desiccated area of fallen tree trunks. None of the trees seemed to have been chopped down on purpose. Instead, it looked like a storm had swept through the area and snapped them in half.

Sitting together on one of the fallen logs, Rachael took Stewart's hands and gazed deep into his eyes. "We've known each other for a few months now, right?" she said in a sweet voice.

Stewart nodded, anticipating what Rachael was about to confess to him.

"I know you've been itching for us to come out about our relationship. But I still think keeping it a secret is best for us right now."

Stewart regarded Rachael with a smile. He wanted to make out with her right then and there like they did in the shed. But being surrounded by decapitated trees did not fit the mood, and something seemed off about her; the way she had pulled away from him so abruptly in the shed was awkward.

Rachael leaned in and eased her head onto Stewart's chest, wrapping her arms around him. "I've never had feelings like this with anyone before. And you know my father is strict about who I hang around with, especially boys. I swear he'll kill me if he finds out we are more than just friends!" She cut her eyes up at him. "But this wasn't the reason why I brought you here."

Stewart ran his hand through her delicate hair, letting it fall in layers between his fingers. "I like you, Rachael," he admitted. "I just wish we could see each other more often and not on this same schedule once a week. I think your dad would like me—I'm a nice guy!"

Rachael pushed against Stewart's chest and sat up. "Are you kidding me! My father will *never* allow us to be together for as long as I'm living under his roof. He can't find out about us yet!"

"Whoa!" Stewart recoiled. "If you think it's *that* bad, then we need to figure out how to get you away from here!"

Rachael's posture slumped. "Not now," she disagreed. "Let's worry about that later."

"Then why did you bring me out here? You've never shown me this place before. It's kind of weird—all these dead trees and stuff."

"Over there," Rachael pointed behind them, "next to that big trunk. Do you see it?"

Stewart followed Rachael's finger to the area where she was pointing. "I see it. What's so special about it? The tree's dead, like all the others."

"No." Rachael frowned, standing up. "C'mon, I'll show you."

Stewart chased her to the log she had pointed to and walked around to the other side. Right away he spotted the tip of a metallic object protruding from the ground. He approached and crouched before the weird-looking device. "What is this?"

he asked, reaching down for the object.

"Don't touch it!" Rachael slapped his hand away. "It could be radioactive or something. What's up with guys always wanting to touch things anyway?"

"Well, what is it?"

"I have no idea," Rachael said.

"When did you discover it?" Stewart asked.

"I was herding one of the goats away from the fence last week when there was this loud crash. I looked in the direction of the sound, and I saw the tops of the trees snapping like they were twigs! I thought someone was coming through the woods with a bulldozer."

"Maybe it's the tip of a missile head!" Stewart joked.

Rachael frowned at him.

Stewart had another hunch. "Do you think this thing is what cut all these trees down?"

Rachael shrugged. "I don't know—I didn't see any smoke or fire. I don't even think my father or brother have been out this way to have seen this yet—I would've heard them talking about it."

"Maybe it's a piece that flew off a UFO!"

Rachael scoffed. "Don't be ridiculous. I don't believe in that stuff!"

"Or maybe it's the sphere from that movie *Phantasm*!" Stewart chuckled. His guesses were getting lame.

Rachael gave a fake smile. "I don't know what that is."

Stewart cocked his head down toward the metallic object, holding up a hand. "Listen! Do you hear that?"

Rachael furrowed her brow and stood motionless. "I've never heard that noise before. Is the sound coming from that thing?"

"I think so," Stewart said. "It sounds like an electrical transformer, or some kind of magnet giving off vibrations."

Rachael looked at him funny. "I don't know what you're talking about."

"My dad used to be a lineman," Stewart told her. "I bet he'd know what this thing is and why it's making a noise."

Rachael took a backward step. "I don't think that's a good idea for your dad to come out here."

"Oh no. It was just a comment," Stewart said, standing up. "I won't even mention this thing to him. Besides, he doesn't work in that field anymore since he was laid off last year. And you know what? This thing could be cancerous! Maybe we should—"

"Quiet!" Rachael interrupted and stooped down low. She waved at Stewart. "Get down!"

Stewart knelt back to the ground. "What happened?" he whispered.

"My dad and Reed just pulled up to the house! They shouldn't be back this early. I need to get inside before they see me!"

"Huh? How'd you see them from this far away?"

"I didn't," Rachael said. "I just heard my dad's truck tires in the gravel."

"Dang, girl." Stewart grinned. "You got some good hearing!" He snapped his head at Rachael and said in a deeper tone of voice, "You're kidding me, right?"

"I wish!" Rachael said. She leaned and pecked Stewart on the cheek then tiptoed through the crunchy leaves toward the fence line. "Get out of here!" she said in a loud whisper back at Stewart. "But wait until my dad and brother go inside the house." She ducked through the barbed wire fence, then hightailed it across the property to the back of the farmhouse.

Stewart dipped low and moved toward the fence, peering between the barbed wires. He couldn't see Rachael's father or her brother from the angle where he was positioned, but he could hear the squeaking of the entry gate closing. "Damn! I forgot I left the gate unlocked," he muttered. He listened for the pickup's doors to close, but instead heard the screen door at the front of the house bang shut. It wasn't Rachael, because she went inside through the back door.

That was his cue. Stewart parted the barbed wire and slipped through then bolted along the fence line to the shed where he had left his bike.

"Where's my bike?" he groaned upon approaching the shed. He noticed it wasn't where he had left it. He pressed his back against the outside wall of the outbuilding and sidestepped toward the front. Then, peeking around the corner inside, he caught a glimpse of someone's back to him standing at the workbench.

That's got to be Reed, Stewart thought, knowing Rachael's father was probably much older than the person he was looking at.

Reed was shirtless and barefoot with mud smeared on his feet and his cuffed, battered jeans. His buffed frame closely resembled a plastic, bowlegged superhero figurine with a bulky upper torso and a thin waist. As he shifted to a profiled position, Stewart saw his square-jawed face was streaked with grease. He was hard at work behind the bench working on something.

My bike! Stewart screamed in his head when he spotted one of his bike's blue mag wheels disassembled on the table. Clenching his teeth, he jerked his head back from the doorway and whispered angrily, "That skunk head's taking apart my bike!"

Retreating to the fence line, Stewart reentered the woods. He followed the fence to the front of the property, then squeezed out onto the dirt road where he had traveled on his bike to get here.

It was going to be a long walk home.

CHAPTER ELEVEN

Awkward Situations

MONDAY, MARCH 13. 8:45 AM
      Jack sat at his desk in science class, his textbook open to the chapter his teacher, Mr. Jenkins, was lecturing.

Mr. Jenkins taught freshman and sophomore science at Remington High. A middle-aged man, he was short and stout with a thick handlebar mustache and thinning salt-and-pepper hair. His daily attire was bland and boring and mostly out of style. The heavy scent from his cologne lingered in the classroom every morning.

This morning he lectured to his sophomore class on the theory of perception. Most of his students were half asleep. "People believe heavier objects fall and sink faster than lighter objects," he said in a raspy voice. "Sometimes these ideas are wrong and continue to exist even in the face of inconsistent evidence."

Jack, aimlessly doodling in his notebook, was part of the group of kids who weren't paying attention. He hated this class as his first period. His brain wasn't awake enough to experiment and make observations.

Sitting next to Jack in her boyfriend's green and gold varsity letterman jacket was Susie Harwood. She was biting on a chipped nail, rolling her eyes at the boring instruction.

Patrick Ryan (aka Nerdy Patrick) sat across from Susie with his glasses pushed firmly against his face with no room to breathe. Obviously, this was his favorite subject, his attention glued to the chalkboard at what Mr. Jenkins was writing.

Next to Patrick sat Devin Morton, or Masquerade Morton as people called him because the bridge of his large nose arched like an ugly carnival mask. But no one dared call him Masquerade Morton to his face, let alone within hearing distance. He was a heavy metal enthusiast and Remington High's most feared bully. The kid wore the same wrinkled Pantera T-shirt to school nearly every day, reeking of body odor. His long hair always looked greasy, and his breath smelled horrible due to his toxic halitosis condition.

Devin slouched in his chair with his legs sprawled out, chewing on his pencil eraser and spitting the pieces onto the floor. Patrick turned and gave him a disgusted look, rolling his magnified eyes behind his thick lenses.

Devin leaned toward Patrick with a death stare. "What are you looking at, Nerdy Patrick?" He grinned, pieces of eraser wedged between his teeth.

Mr. Jenkins turned from the blackboard. "You got something to say, Mr. Morton?"

Devin sat up, his backbone pressing firmly against the back of his chair. "I'm cool, Mr. Jenkins!"

Mr. Jenkins scowled at him. "What I'd give to have five minutes with that belligerent kid," he muttered quietly to himself like a ventriloquist. He stared at Devin until Devin's eyes glanced away, then continued with his lecture.

Mr. Jenkins spoke in a slow, monotoned voice. Halfway through his instruction, he scanned the room for a student to participate in an example. He eyeballed Jack. "Mr. Stinger!" he projected his voice.

Jack's fist slipped from underneath his chin, where he was keeping his head afloat, and he sat up, suddenly alert.

"Tell me which is heavier, a pound of lead or a pound of feathers?" Mr. Jenkins smiled.

"A pound of lead," Jack responded with confidence.

Mr. Jenkins was a statue, pausing to see if Jack would change his answer.

Jack looked at Mr. Jenkins like a cow staring at an oncoming train.

Other students were restless in their seats, wanting to give the correct answer.

"Why do you think a pound of lead is heavier?" Mr. Jenkins asked, ignoring those who raised their hands.

Jack cleared his throat. He hated being put on the spot. "Um, because it has more weight than a feather?"

The class giggled, and more arms shot up. "I want Jack to explain," Mr. Jenkins said, glancing around the room at all the kids itching to blurt out the answer.

Then, back on Jack, Mr. Jenkins said, "Listen to the question again and give it a little more thought. Which is heavier, a pound of lead or a pound of *feathers*?"

Jack felt a lump in his throat. "The feathers?" he said, thinking Mr. Jenkins had emphasized the word as a clue.

The class burst out laughing.

"Quiet down!" Mr. Jenkins raised his voice. "Let him answer."

"What an idiot!" Devin sneered, watching Mr. Jenkins to see if he was going to call him out again for yelling across the room.

Jack knew Mr. Jenkins would not let up until he gave the correct answer, because he was persistent in calling out individuals to wake up their brains.

"I'll ask one more time—which is heavier, a *pound* of lead or a *pound* of feathers?" Mr. Jenkins asked.

Jack ignored the whispering around him. Then the answer finally hit him. He leaned forward and bounced his forehead on his desk. His face red, he looked up at Mr. Jenkins and said, "They both weigh the same!"

The class cheered.

"Very good!" Mr. Jenkins smiled. "It's okay that he answered incorrectly," he addressed the class. "This is an example of how people can perceive heavy objects. When I said *lead* first, the brain tricks you into thinking it's heavier than a feather without first analyzing the question." He grabbed a piece of chalk from the corner of his desk and pecked at the board.

As he scribbled, Devin reached and slapped Patrick on his arm. "Hey! I bet you didn't know that answer either, nerd boy!" he chuckled. "One thing about you smart kids is y'all don't have any common sense."

Patrick kept his attention on Mr. Jenkins writing on the chalkboard, trying to tune out the bully next to him.

Devin held his hand out toward Patrick and made a disgusting sound with his throat. "Check this out, Nerdy Patrick!"

Patrick turned his head toward Devin, looking down at his hand.

Devin spat a loogie in the palm of his hand, then slurped it back into his mouth and swallowed like he was eating an oyster.

Patrick and the students sitting around Devin cringed.

"You're sick!" Patrick said, looking away.

Even Susie heard Devin sucking his spit back into his mouth from a few seats away. *"Disgusting pig!* Leave Patrick alone, you bully! What did he ever do to you?"

Jack twisted in his chair to see what all the fuss was about with Devin. He watched as the kid continued picking on Patrick. "Did he make Patrick do his homework for him again but Patrick gave him the wrong answers or something?" he said to Susie.

"I don't know, but that idiot needs to let up on that poor kid," Susie responded. Then she said loud enough for Devin to hear her, "I can't believe *MASQUERADE MORTON* is still allowed in school!"

"Who said that?" Devin perked up. "Say it again, and I'll beat your ass!"

Mr. Jenkins peered over his shoulder with a slacked jaw a second too late. The bell rang, ending first period. He set the chalk down and yelled over the noisy students packing their belongings and shuffling in groups out of the room, "There will be a quiz tomorrow! Study your notes and read chapters sixteen and seventeen in your textbook. And don't forget your hypothesis on force and momentum, as well as the egg drop project, are due at the end of next week before spring break!"

———

Jack entered the combination to his locker and tossed his science book inside, then pulled out a Turbo Pascal workbook for his next class. The assignment he was working on was an intro to animation project. Because of his interest in level grinding, he had an excellent idea for programming a sample role-playing game. It was something too advanced for his class, but he loved the tedious task of programming and hoped he'd get extra points for creating something none of his peers could do.

He shut his locker, and Stewart suddenly appeared in his way.

"What's up?" Stewart said.

"Hey! Where have you been?" Jack replied, surprised. "I've been trying to reach you and Billy for days! Are y'all mad because you quit the bike club? What's going on?"

"Nah, I just thought I'd take it easy for a while before spring break starts next week," Stewart lied. "You know how crazy it usually gets."

Jack rocked back on his heels looking askance at his friend. "Uh, we usually go to the rec center and ride bikes during spring break. How is that crazy?"

"Oh, yeah," Stewart scratched the side of his head, "about my bike. I wrecked it the other day."

"What? How!"

"You know that ramp Billy's brother built at the trails?"

"Yeah?" Jack said.

"I jumped it and my back tire popped when I landed and the rim bent!"

"No way!" Jack said, shocked. "What'd you do, land on a huge rock or something? And are you okay? You don't look injured."

"I'm fine," Stewart said. "Just pissed that I don't have a bike to ride now. Oh, hey—what else did you find out about the old spook house?"

Jack glanced at his Swatch. "I'll tell you about it during lunch. We better get to class. You know how Principal Jerkoff—I mean Jerry—likes to give tardies now to those still in the halls when the bell rings!"

"Yeah, I know." Stewart smiled. "Okay, catch you later, Jack!"

"See ya," Jack said, and fumbled through the crowd to class, wondering if something else was the matter with Stewart than what he was telling him. His excuse was far-fetched. He and Stewart were tight and didn't hide things from each other. Jack wished lunch period would come sooner so he could find out what was wrong.

CHAPTER TWELVE

Jack's Terrible Mistake

Jack got pizza for lunch again, with a side of fries doused in ketchup. Last week, Ms. Bagleweed chewed him out for hogging the condiments. Standing in line waiting to check out with her again today, he anticipated another lecture. *"I'll have to charge you extra next time for using that much ketchup,"* he recalled Ms. Bagleweed telling him last week. And, as predicted, she told him the same thing again when it was his turn to pay. *Is she suffering from dementia?* he thought, grabbing his tray and exiting the kitchen.

Jack sat at his usual table, but this time he was alone. Stewart and Billy were always sitting there before him. He was hoping he'd have a chance to talk to Stewart more about his bike and what was eating at him.

Sitting near Jack several seats down from him was Denise Bevins—Devin Morton's girlfriend. She was eating alone, too. Her dark aesthetic seemed a bit much, consisting of thick black lipstick, heavy foundation lighter than her skin, thick mascara, short, jet-black hair, black fingernails, and a vast collection of onyx rings.

Jack watched her as she opened a pint of milk and placed it on the table in front of her. Then she unrolled her thin napkin, smoothed it out, and set the plasticware spaced evenly on top.

She picked up her square slice of pizza with her pinky fingers tucked underneath keeping it level, then took a large bite and stared off into space as she chewed. Before swallowing, she took another bite, her cheeks expanding like balloons.

Obsessive compulsive much? Jack thought, knowing that sounded rude even in his head.

A food tray slapped down on Jack's table, the ear-piercing whack silencing the cafeteria for a split second.

Daisy took a seat in front of him.

"Hey!" Jack said, his voice drowned out by the noise escalating in the cafeteria.

Daisy's face was pale with dark, heavy bags under her eyes. She glared at Jack maliciously. She could've cut a sheet of paper with those sharp eyes.

"Um, you okay?" Jack frowned.

Daisy pursed her lips as she started taking items from her tray and placing them on the table. "For starters, I forgot my lunch and had to buy *this* nasty stuff. Ugh! And I haven't been able to sleep because of the nightmares I've been having since we broke into that stupid house."

"The food's not *that* bad," Jack teased.

Daisy grimaced, holding up a greasy fry between two fingers, then releasing it. "Gross!"

"You don't know what you're missing." Jack grinned, trying to cheer her up, but it wasn't working. "Hey, have you noticed anything strange about Stewart? And have you seen Billy recently? I mean, you obviously know he hasn't been here eating with us at the table for a while."

"I haven't seen either one of them outside the cafeteria," Daisy replied, still sulking over the cafeteria food. "Why?"

"Stewart showed up at my locker this morning, and he didn't

seem like himself—said he wrecked his bike and was relaxing before spring break starts. *Who relaxes before spring break?* Something just seemed . . . off about him. And as for Billy, he hasn't responded to me in over a week."

"Maybe Billy's sick," Daisy suggested. "Stewart's always been kind of weird in my opinion."

"Well, Stewart said he'd talk to me more at lunch today, but obviously, he's not here. Something's up."

Daisy shrugged in response.

Jack stared down at his fries and half-eaten pizza, his appetite gone. He pushed his tray aside and folded his arms over the table, watching Daisy pick at her food. "Sooo . . . when do you want to go back to the house?"

Daisy slapped her hands on the table, causing Jack to flinch and attracting Denise's attention down the table. *"You're kidding me, right?"*

Denise glanced at Jack and Daisy, eavesdropping on their conversation.

"I'm not joking," Jack said. "I still wanna check out the kitchen and see what's upstairs. There's three floors, you know."

"You're crazy!" Daisy responded. "Didn't you say the kitchen was a disaster? And the thing with the red eyes—was that even real?"

"It sure looked real to me," Jack said. "I think we can get around in the kitchen; we would just need to take it slow. What about paranormal investigations? I thought you were interested in finding out if that place was haunted."

"Are you saying that ghost thing we saw wasn't enough proof for you? As far as the investigation, we don't even have the right equipment to do something like that anyway. Plus, you know I get scared easily. I want to help you, I really do. But the house is so rickety, I think it's too risky to explore any further."

Jack slumped at the table. "So, Mike pumped you full of fear."

"What? Oh, the cop. No! Come on, you saw how flimsy the floor was in that house."

"You know, I've read about spirits getting trapped between reality and the afterlife as lost souls," Jack said, motioning with his hands. "Maybe that thing we saw has unfinished business it needs to carry out before it can move on. I do agree it was kinda unsafe in there, but I think we should still find out the truth. What if it wasn't a ghost at all and someone has rigged that house to scare people? I mean, I've seen some nifty life-like things in fake haunted houses. This could be someone's idea of a joke and it'd be cool if we could catch them in the act!"

"Oh, so now you're Fred and I'm Daphne?" Daisy finally cracked a smile. "What would we do, try and hold a conversation with that red-eyed thing?"

Denise continued staring at them with unblinking eyes.

"Maybe we should go there at night next time and see if anything else appears," Jack said.

Daisy leaned from the table. *"Absolutely not!"*

"Well, I still want to know who or what was whispering at me through that broken window," Jack said. "What if it's a person somewhere in the house who's been missing for years? We could be town heroes if we find them! There must be a logical explanation to what I heard. And no, it was not all in my head!"

Jack caught Daisy shifting her eyes in the direction where Denise was sitting. He turned and spotted Denise staring back at him. "Can I help you?"

Denise placed a quick hand over her chest. "Excuse me?" Her jaw dropped.

Jack cleared his throat and spoke with more emphasis. *"What are you looking at?"*

Daisy waved her hand in Jack's face, warning him to cease communicating with the weirdo.

"Well, that was rude!" Denise gasped. "Keep your stupid comments to yourself. By the way, I know that house you're talking about. Better stay away like your girlfriend says."

Jack looked at Denise sideways. "And just what do you know about that place?"

Denise shook her head. "The less you know, the better."

"Hey! You brought this up!" Jack said, irritated that she would not give any details. Perhaps she knew nothing about the house and was just bluffing. After all, she was Devin's girl-friend—she could be messing with him. *"Tell me what you know, freak!"*

"How dare you!" Denise said, her eyes widening.

Daisy slapped a hand over her face. "Jack, stop! You're gonna get yourself in trouble."

"You better watch your back, *jerk*," Denise threatened Jack.

"I'm not scared of you *or* your dumb boyfriend," Jack snapped.

Denise stood and stomped out of the cafeteria.

"You left your food tray!" Jack called after her. Then he said under his breath, "And take that attitude with you!"

Daisy's eyes leveled with Jack's. "Seriously? She's a rat, and she'll go tattle to her boyfriend about you!"

"Let her. I don't care," Jack said. "Her boyfriend's in my science class, and he's a real douchebag."

"Wow!" Daisy's eyes widened. "You're really gonna start

something, aren't you? I've never seen you like this!"

"Listen, I've been pushed around a lot, but I don't let it happen anymore," Jack said. "And you know what? I bet Denise knows *nothing* about Whitlock Manor. I think she was just interested in what we were talking about. I wouldn't be surprised if she goes to check out that place with Devin and they trash it."

The bell rang, ending the lunch period.

"Let's talk later," Daisy said. "And watch your back!"

Jack followed Daisy out of the cafeteria. "I'll call you," he said, his pinky finger to his lips and thumb to his ear like he was holding a telephone. Then he merged into the crowd and headed to his locker.

———

Jack pulled out the textbook he needed for his next class. He slammed the locker door and gave the combination dial a quick spin. And that's when he spotted Denise walking toward him. *Here we go,* he thought, and sighed.

Everyone around him seemed to be moving in slow motion when he saw Devin suddenly emerge from behind Denise. Kyle Jenkins, whom Jack recalled seeing hanging around Devin sometimes, flanked him on his right.

Jack knew if he tried to bolt, it would only make matters worse. It wouldn't stop Devin from catching him. He'd get him in science class. Jack had nowhere to hide.

"I told you to watch your back," Denise reiterated as she, Devin, and Kyle stopped in front of Jack.

Devin leaned his crooked nose close to Jack's face. "Whatever words you're having with my girl stops now!" he threatened.

Jack couldn't hold his breath forever and caught a whiff of Devin's halitosis.

Kyle cracked his knuckles. "Rip 'im apart, Devin!"

Denise stood with her arms folded and a grin that stretched from ear to ear.

An audience was already forming around them. It would only be a matter of time before teachers noticed what was going on and would step in to break up the confrontation.

"I know you," Devin said. "You're in my science class. I saw that you grew a microscopic brain today," he chuckled, "and finally figured out that lead weighed the same as feathers."

Denise wrinkled her nose and Kyle darted his eyes at Devin in confusion.

"Answer this riddle for me, hot shot," Devin continued. "I have two fists. My left one delivers fifty pounds of force, and my right one delivers fifty pounds of force. Which one would you rather have bust your face in?"

Jack stuck out his chest. "Your girlfriend started it, so back off!"

"He's lying!" Denise snapped. "Kick this scrawny kid's ass!"

"Fight!" someone erupted within the crowd, summoning more bystanders.

Devin clenched a fist and held it inches from Jack's face. "You don't have the privilege to talk to my girl. Do I make myself clear?"

Jack could feel the blood pumping through his veins. He wasn't going to let this loser talk down to him, even if he was outnumbered.

Kyle stepped forth. "Hey numbskull, are you *that* stupid? I'd answer him if I were you!"

Jack cut his eyes at Kyle. "I plead the fifth."

"What?" Devin wrinkled his brow.

"Just as I thought," Jack said. "You're not so bright yourself."

"Ooooh! That's grounds for death, Devin!" Kyle snickered. "Don't let him off the hook that easy, man."

"No one's ever stood up to him like this," a voice said from the crowd. Then another person shouted, creating a chant that the crowd started repeating, "Masquerade Morton's gonna get shortened! Masquerade Morton's gonna get shortened!"

Devin gritted his teeth, then relaxed. "I'll cut you a deal. If you kneel before me, kiss my shoes, and beg for forgiveness, I'll let you go with a warning today."

Denise glanced at Kyle with a gaping jaw. "Oh, this I'd love to see!"

Jack knew Devin's intention was to embarrass him in front of the crowd and make him feel weak. But he refused to submit.

"Well?" Devin stepped back.

Jack thought of all the times Devin had bullied other kids in school, and how they always succumbed to his intimidations and threats. What if he did something about it on behalf of all those who never had the courage to stand up for themselves against this bully? What if retaliating against this sore loser instilled a fearlessness in those who underestimated their own power? What if—

Jack caught Devin off guard and threw a mean punch, popping him between the eyes. He heard the crack and felt the bridge of Devin's nose dislocate.

The crowd immediately stopped chanting and the hallway fell silent for a moment, everyone in shock.

Devin stumbled backward, cupping his hands over his face

as dark red blood seeped between his fingers and trickled down his forearms. And as the pain surged, Devin's tears flowed, and he gagged from clots of blood draining down his throat.

Kyle, like the coward he was, quickly slipped into the crowd and disappeared.

Denise dashed over to Devin and tried comforting him as the crowd burst into cheers and laughter. Some students gave high fives, while others celebrated the significant milestone of a defeated bully. The good guy stood his ground for once.

Devin pushed Denise away from him. "Get away from me!" he cried and spat a clot of blood on the floor. Backing against the wall, he scowled at Jack. "You're dead meat! You hear me? DEAD MEAT!"

Denise burst into tears and took off down the hall before the faculty showed up.

Jack, still trying to process what had happened, looked at his hand. His knuckles were red as beets. He couldn't believe he threw his first-ever punch at a bully!

Someone broke from the crowd and ran up to Jack. "You gotta get outta here before the teachers catch you!"

Jack looked up. It was Tommy Crenshaw, Billy's older brother. He was a junior.

Jack hesitated, trying to figure out why Tommy was helping him.

"Come on!" Tommy insisted.

"Why are you helping me?" Jack finally asked, following Tommy down the hall.

"My little brother looks up to you," Tommy said. "You guys are good friends."

"Where's Billy?" Jack asked, feeling like he was in a dream from punching Devin's lights out.

"We've been having issues with our mom lately," Tommy said. "Billy's taking some time alone right now. But he'll be in touch with you soon."

They stood in front of a classroom doorway. The room emitted the smell of sawdust. "This is my woodshop class. If you get questioned by the faculty later, let me know. I'll vouch for you, bro. Now get out of here!"

Jack turned and walked to a stairwell around the corner. His next class was located on the second floor, and according to his Swatch, he was already tardy.

CHAPTER THIRTEEN

A Night of Anguish

TUESDAY, MARCH 14. 12:00 AM
Sarah Crenshaw lay on the sofa, passed out next to her Chihuahua and two cats. Her arm was stretched over the edge of the cushions, wrist limp with her thumb and forefinger balancing a half-empty beer bottle over the pet-stained carpet.

Tonight was the second anniversary of her husband's death, and she had started on the bottles early yesterday afternoon.

The screen from the television flickered, illuminating the darkened room. The station was initiating its nightly broadcast sign-off with an image of the American flag and the playing of the National Anthem. After the music died away, color bars filled the screen, followed by static and white noise.

A creak from upstairs splintered the air, and Sarah gagged and sat up, the beer bottle slipping from her fingers. Her sudden movement frightened the animals, and they scattered the living room like frantic mice.

"That you, Billy?" Sarah slurred, rubbing her bloodshot eyes. She glanced over her shoulder at the stairs. "Or is that you, Tommy?"

No response.

"Y'all better not be up this late—you have school!" She picked up the bottle and placed it on the coffee table with the other empty longnecks. Then she staggard toward the staircase and grabbed the handrail.

Tommy stood at the top of the stairs. "Mom, you're drunk!" he growled. "You're the one who needs to go to bed!"

Sarah struggled to keep her balance, her heart pumping in a rapid, unstable rhythm.

"Drinking's not going to solve your problems!" Tommy reminded her.

Sarah cringed and looked up at Tommy, speechless, her eyes swelling with tears. Her legs weakened, and she collapsed and passed out again at the foot of the steps.

———

Sarah woke up hours later on the floor before the staircase, her head pounding. She grabbed the handrail to help herself up and hobbled to the living room. She started on clearing the beer bottles from the coffee table before Tommy and Billy stumbled upon the mess. But she still wasn't finished when Tommy rushed downstairs and whisked past her on his way to the kitchen.

Sarah glanced at Tommy with her arms full of bottles, wondering why he didn't acknowledge her. *He always says hi to me in the mornings,* she thought. She set the bottles down back on the coffee table and followed her son into the kitchen. Grabbing a bottled water from the fridge, she asked, "Is your brother awake?"

Tommy inserted two slices of bread into the toaster without responding to her.

Sarah pulled a chair from the table. "Well?" she said, taking a few swallows of cold water.

"I didn't check on him," Tommy answered with a defensive attitude.

"Why not?"

The toaster pinged, and Tommy grabbed his breakfast and stepped to the table, jerking the chair out. "I'm not his father," he said. "Billy's a big boy; he can take care of himself. Why do you always rely on me and make him my responsibility? *You're his mother*. Oh wait, that's right, you're always drunk. And you never come out and watch me race my

bike at the events anymore. What gives, Mom?"

Sarah wiped the tears gliding down her face.

"I'm serious, Mom," Tommy continued. "Dad's gone, and there's nothing we can do to bring him back. I'm not trying to be mean, but that's life, and we all need to move on. I think you need to get some help, like looking into counseling or going to church . . . just do *SOMETHING!*" He rose from the table, kicking his chair back and sending it screeching across the floor.

Sarah looked at her son in silence.

"I'll be in my room finishing breakfast," Tommy said. "And yes, I'll make sure Billy's getting ready for school."

Sarah wiped away more tears, feeling disappointed in herself and ashamed that she was not providing for her children as she used to. She found herself depressed more often when she was laid off from her job shortly after losing her husband to a car accident. Her peppy attitude and charisma were no longer her distinguishing traits.

The queasiness in her stomach intensified, and she could feel what was inside barreling up her esophagus. She leaped from her chair at the table and hunched over the kitchen sink . . . and puked.

———

Tommy didn't have the patience to knock before entering, so he burst into Billy's room. "Hey, get your butt out of bed!"

The room was messy, clothes strewn about the floor and hanging off the edge of the bed. The sheets were bunched up at the foot of the mattress, but there was no sign of Billy.

Tommy checked the bathroom. Billy wasn't there, either. He dashed downstairs, irritated that he had to waste his time in finding his brother when he should be getting ready for school.

He checked the garage and noticed Billy's bike was gone. "Huh. Guess he already left for school," he muttered, and returned inside the house to finish getting ready.

———

Sarah spent the morning cleaning the kitchen and vacuuming the house while Tommy and Billy were at school. Although she felt like crap most of the day, she figured she owed this to her children because of her carelessness and bitter attitude around them for so long. She'd get on her kids for not picking up after themselves, but who would get on her for not leading by example?

Opening the refrigerator, Sarah stared at the alcohol taking up an entire shelf plus the lower panel in the door. It was going to take a great deal of mental strength to pour out every ounce of liquid from each can and bottle. Knowing quitting cold turkey would be risky, she breathed deeply, reached inside the fridge, and got to work.

By the afternoon, Sarah had filled two garbage bags full of empty cans and bottles. She set them on the floor in the garage and would let Tommy take them to the recycling facility and split the cash he'd receive with Billy. If she kept the cash herself, she knew she would blow the money on more alcohol.

With twenty minutes to spare before the kids came home from school, Sarah escaped to the bathroom and peeled off her clothes, slipping into a warm bubble bath. She dozed off in the tub, allowing the soothing suds to take away the stress from the day.

———

Sarah's eyes popped open when she heard the front door close and footsteps pounding up the stairs. She hurried out of the tub, because she wanted to see the looks on Tommy's and Billy's faces when they noticed the house was cleaned. She especially wanted to see their reaction when she told them the good news about her quitting drinking!

She quickly dried off, slipped into sweatpants and a T-shirt, and walked briskly into the kitchen.

Tommy was preparing a grilled cheese sandwich when she snuck up behind him and put her arms around him. "I'm sorry," she whispered, her chin resting on his shoulder.

"I doubt it," Tommy said harshly, spreading mayonnaise on the two slices of bread. Mayo instead of butter on a grilled cheese sandwich layered on for a smoother spread and did not burn easily on its way to golden-brown. "You'll just be sorry again next week," he added. "And then the week after that. I know your pattern, Mom."

Sarah controlled her irritation at Tommy's remark. Instead of bad-mouthing him, she pecked him on the cheek and shifted over to the refrigerator. She opened the door, gesturing inside the fridge like a model on a TV game show introducing the grand prize. "See? I threw it all out." She smiled. "I'm starting over . . . *today*!"

Tommy slapped a slice of bread, mayo side down, into the preheated pan on the stove. He let it sizzle for a few seconds, then layered two pieces of cheese and topped them with the other slice of bread, mayo side up. "Good for you. So, how long before you restock?"

Sarah frowned and closed the refrigerator door, then slid into her chair at the table. "I'm trying to do better, Tommy," she said. "And you being sarcastic doesn't help."

Tommy flipped over the grilled cheese and browned the other side, smoke rising from the pan when it hit the heat. "We've gone through this before, Mom. It's the same routine every day."

"But this time I really want to do this!" Sarah insisted.

Tommy took a seat at the table across from her. "I actually made this for *you*," he said, pushing his plate toward her.

Sarah didn't know what to say. Her kids *never* cooked for her.

"If you say you're gonna get help this time," Tommy said, "I want communication, dedication, and honesty playing a huge part. No more bullshit—jeez, I sound like Dad!"

Sarah reached across the table and placed her hand over Tommy's. "I *promise* to try my hardest."

Tommy pulled his hand away. "Did you know the word *try* means no?"

"Since when?" Sarah cocked her head. "Let me rephrase. I promise I'll work hard at staying focused. Listen, the death of your father has taken an extreme toll on me. I'm sorry I never got the help I needed before it became this bad. I want to see you and Billy happy again. I know you're both frustrated with me. So, I want us to be a family again."

Tommy sighed. "I guess all I can do is wait to see what happens."

Sarah smiled and pushed the plate back to Tommy. "You know good and damn well you didn't make this sandwich for me. Eat it before it gets cold!"

"I guess I thought I'd try and be nice," Tommy chuckled.

"I thought you said try means no?" Sarah smirked.

Tommy shook his head and took a bite of the grilled cheese.

"By the way, where's your brother?" Sarah asked. "Did he have something going on after school that I don't know about?"

Tommy shook his head. "Not that I know of. He's probably playing with his friends somewhere. He didn't come home with me today."

Sarah stole a quick bite from his sandwich and stood from the table. "Welp, I suppose we'll just have to give him the good news later."

———

Sarah sat on the sofa stroking the fur of one of the cats in her lap. She had the table already set for dinner, waiting for the pizza she had phoned in to be delivered.

She flipped the channels with the remote to a rerun of *I Dream of Jeannie*. She giggled at a scene with Jeannie feeding Jhinn Jhinn on the kitchen table. Then Sarah suddenly realized she hadn't fed her own pets their dinner! Since she was too comfortable to get up, she yelled from the couch, "Hey, boys, come down here for a minute!"

Tommy was the only one who came down the stairs. "What's up?" he said when he entered the living room.

"Can you feed the animals for me?" Sarah grinned.

"Really? You called me down for *that*?" Tommy said. "What happened to your legs?"

"Cocoa's on me," Sarah laughed, scratching behind the cat's ear. "I called for Billy, too. Where is he?"

"He's not here," Tommy replied, heading into the kitchen.

"Have you heard from him *at all*?" Sarah projected her voice.

"Nope," Tommy said, peeking around the corner from the kitchen. Then he returned to the counter and spooned a can of dog food and then cat food into separate bowls. Both cats and dog came running into the kitchen, the cats rubbing against his legs and the Chihuahua spinning in circles behind him.

"What about his friends?" Sarah asked. "Do they know where he is—he better not have ridden his bike to that creepy house I've been hearing him talk about lately!"

Tommy set the dog bowl on the floor and placed the cat bowls on the counter. "I can call his friend Jack and see if he knows where he might be."

"Yes, please do!" Sarah said. "I'm getting worried."

"I'm on it," Tommy said, grabbing the telephone.

———

Sarah was on the verge of an anxiety attack when she sat at the table with Tommy eating pizza. "This is so unlike of Billy not to check in all day!" she said, her hands shaking. She was getting scared, but the side effects from quitting cold turkey were also starting to kick in. She wanted a drink so bad right now!

"I'm worried, too," Tommy said. "He's been pretty upset with you like I have. But something feels kinda off."

"Like what?" Sarah asked.

"I don't know. My gut tells me he might have tried running away again."

"I hope not," Sarah said, slapping her slice of pizza down on her plate. She had lost her appetite.

———

"It's after nine o'clock!" Sarah cried. "Where's Billy? Oh, God I hope he hasn't been struck by a car or something! I know he rides his bike in that damn street!"

Tommy paced the living room, checking the time on his watch. "He's usually in the shower by now and getting ready for bed. I can ride my bike around and look for him. Or would you rather we call the police?"

"Yes!" Sarah perked up from the sofa. "That's something we should've done a long time ago!" She reached for the cordless telephone on the end table and dialed 911, her hands shaking and her legs in an anxious bounce.

"Nine-one-one, what's your emergency?" the operator answered after the first ring.

Sarah suddenly burst into tears. "My son is missing!"

———

Sarah wiped the tears from her eyes while Tommy stood at the window in the living room, watching for the police to show up.

When the sound of two car doors shut outside, Sarah's face tightened with fear. She didn't know if she could handle talking to the police without bawling.

"They're here," Tommy confirmed, and moved to the front door to await the knock.

CHAPTER FOURTEEN

Daisy's Haunt

Daisy sat leaning against the headboard of her bed, re-reading the paragraph she had written thus far for a creative writing assignment. She tapped her finger on her composition notebook to the beat of an '80s mixtape playing through the boombox in the corner of the room. Her eyes caught a glimpse of the time on the clock next to her. "Ugh! It's already ten o'clock?"

It was rare for her to suffer from writer's block. She always found it easy to crank out stories and essays. But this assignment had her frustrated.

Annoyed by the assignment, Daisy threw her notebook across the room like a Frisbee, the pages snapping in the air. She stormed out of her bedroom and into the bathroom off the hallway. She slipped on a headband to keep her hair pulled back and splashed water on her face.

She patted her face with a hand towel and looked at her reflection in the mirror, the bags under her eyes dark and puffy. If she hadn't procrastinated and put off doing her homework, she could've squeezed in some rest. Time management had always been her weakness when it came to homework.

Removing the headband, Daisy fixed her hair into a ponytail then turned to exit the bathroom. Her mother startled her in the doorway, making Daisy flinch. "You scared the bejesus outta me!"

"Are you still doing homework?" her mother asked.

"I barely even started," Daisy grumbled.

"It's not healthy for you to be staying up late every night," her mother argued. "Take a break. I made some cherry turnovers, so come get one."

"Okay," Daisy said, switching off the bathroom light and following her mother into the kitchen.

The pastries had already been plated when Daisy sat with her mother at the small round table. "Ooooh. This looks good!"

"I've been wanting to make these for a while," her mother said, cherry pie filling oozing when she cut into the dessert. "I've been having to stay late at the salon lately."

"Should you even be eating this since your health scare?" Daisy asked, recalling when her mom coughed up blood one day. She had been a heavy smoker since Daisy was an infant.

"I don't think eating this will affect my lungs, baby girl," her mother said, grabbing an ashtray from the center of the table. She struck a match and lit a cigarette, taking a few quick puffs as she shook the match, extinguishing the flame. She blew a stream of smoke out the side of her mouth and asked, "How's Jack been lately?"

"He's fine," Daisy said, trying to avoid the secondhand smoke by taking shallow breaths.

Her mother took a long drag and tapped the curling ember into the ashtray. "Have you two been getting intimate with each other?" she asked bluntly, smoke spewing from her mouth and nostrils like a chimney.

Daisy's mouth gaped. "Really, Mom? That's gross!"

"You seem to hang out with him more than you do with any of your other friends," her mother said, balancing her cigarette out the side of her mouth. "I thought maybe you two had some sort of spark." She leaned back against her chair and exhaled another thick stream of smoke into the air.

"We're not a *thing*," Daisy made herself clear and pushed her chair from the table. She grabbed her saucer and rinsed it off in the sink. "I need to finish my homework, then I'll try and get some sleep. G'night, Mom." As she headed to her room, she heard her mom strike another match.

———

Daisy sat on her bed, picking up where she left off with her creative writing assignment. She read the paragraph multiple times as she thought about how she could begin the next sentence.

BRAIN AND DYNAMITE

The brain is a ticking time bomb. Like the traveling spark from a dynamite's fuse, the mind spreads information throughout the body. Upon combustion, a plethora of knowledge stimulates the cells as a climactic finale of fireworks.

Daisy wished she would have drawn a different topic the day she got the assignment for writing a simile. Her creative writing instructor called it the fruit basket assignment. Each student drew two labels with a different topic on each one and had to compare the two. Comparing the brain to a stick of dynamite was dumb but obviously a challenge. She hated it.

The cassette tape in the boombox reached its end, and the bedroom fell silent. In addition to the crickets chirping outside her window, Daisy could hear the inner workings of her ears.

The tension inside her was building. She slapped the heel of her hand down on the mattress. Then she threw her pencil across the room, where it bounced off the wall and rolled next to the closet door, coming to a rest against the baseboard. "I can't do this," she cried, warm tears flowing down her cheeks.

She felt like giving up and taking a zero for the paper, or at least a fifty since she already had a paragraph written to show she at least put some effort into her writing.

"This is so stupid!" Daisy muttered and slid out of bed to retrieve her pencil.

Picking up the pencil from off the floor, she paused to the faint sound of tapping. "Mom?" Her voice cracked. "Is that you?"

She waited a few seconds for a response before opening her bedroom door and peeking into the darkened hallway. *"Mom!"* Daisy said louder, then reached and flipped on the hall light.

The hallway was empty.

As Daisy switched off the light, she caught a glimpse of a pair of red eyes staring back at her at the end of the hall. Seconds later, the red dots faded like two LED lights with low voltage drops.

Flipping the light on again, Daisy saw the hallway was still empty. "I must be losing my mind!" she said, closing her door and returning to her bed. She slipped underneath the sheets and clenched them to her chin with white-knuckled fists, watching the undercut of the door for moving shadows from the hall light she had left on.

Daisy woke in the middle of the night and shot up in bed to a scratching sound in her room. *Stay calm; it's only your imagination,* she told herself, maintaining a watchful eye on the bedroom door. But the sound was not coming from the bedroom door. It sounded like it was inside the closet!

She thought about playing the mixtape to help ease her busy mind. When she visited the therapist to cope with her parents' divorce several years ago, one of the doctor's suggestions was to dance to music to clear her mind. However, she couldn't find the courage to reach for the boombox, flip the cassette tape over, and play the other tracks.

The noises in the closet were getting louder, like fingernails tapping on the door from the inside. Then, the sounds became a repetitive beat of tapping and scratching like Morse code. Tap, scratch, tap, tap, scratch, tap, tap, scratch, tap, scratch, tap, scratch, tap.

When the sounds stopped, Daisy eased herself out of bed and stood with a hawk's eye on the closet door. She planned to make a mad dash to the living room and sleep on the sofa the rest of the night. She wouldn't be able to sleep another minute in her room even if the disturbing knocking ceased forever.

Diverting her attention to the base of the closet door, Daisy noticed a thin layer of smoke seeping from underneath. *Fire!* She reached to feel the door for heat but retracted her hand—not because the door was hot, which it wasn't, but because the smoke was thickening and becoming darker. It billowed up from the undercut and accumulated in a circular pattern around her ankles. Then it rose to her waist in a corkscrew pattern and shifted in front of her as one big mass.

Standing frozen, Daisy could see within the smoke a dark shadow bobbing steadily in place. *The thing at Whitlock Manor!*

A chill trickled down her spine, tingling the back of her neck. She continued to stand frozen, like the entity had paralyzed her.

Daisy tried forcing a scream, but whatever was floating around inside the odorless smoke seemed to have a hold of her larynx, too. She shut her eyes, hoping she was only hallucinating, and that the smoke and dark figure would go away when she opened them again. Unfortunately, wishing it away was not an option. A fierce pair of red eyes pulsated within the smoke like something from a carnival sideshow.

Daisy couldn't breathe. Her throat felt as if it were being squeezed, choked by the demon before her.

Then the figure shapeshifted, molding into a cloak with a hood like what Daisy had seen at the old house on Cemetery Hill. Within the dark void of the hood came a low-pitched voice. "Return," it seethed. Then the smoke-shape dispersed and seeped back under the closet door like it was sucked up in a vacuum.

Daisy could finally breathe again. She hunched with her hands over her throat in a coughing fit. With a hand over her mouth, she ran into the bathroom, dropped to her knees, flipped up the toilet lid, and vomited the cherry turnover.

Catching her breath as she hunched over the commode, Daisy debated whether to wake up her mother or call the cops. But who would believe her? She knew her mother would blame it on her lack of sleep. And the police would probably just jot down a report and file it away forever.

Daisy got up and rinsed her mouth and washed her face. She dared not go back into her room again tonight. Her legs trembled as she staggered down the hall to the living room and plopped down on the sofa, the pale moonlight spilling through the curtained windows. Her head was spinning with so many thoughts going ninety to nothing.

The door to the primary bedroom creaked open, and Daisy's eyes darted toward the silhouette of her mother standing at the doorway. Her eyes hadn't fully adjusted to the room yet.

"Why is the light on in the hallway?" her mother asked in a groggy voice and stepped into the living room.

"Mom?" Daisy cocked her head and drew her knees to her chest. "You okay?"

"Return," her mother hissed from afar, and the silhouette blended into the shadows of the room.

CHAPTER FIFTEEN

Details on the Tracks

WEDNESDAY, MARCH 15. 6:05 AM

Jack woke from a troubled sleep. Bosco stood from the foot of the bed and plopped down beside him, resting his head on his chest.

"Hey, buddy," Jack said, rubbing the puppy's floppy ear between his thumb and two fingers. "You hungry?"

Bosco perked up, cocking his head. Then he touched his wet, twitchy nose to Jack's face.

"Pffffft!" Jack blew raspberries. He hopped out of bed, scooped up the dog and tucked him under his arm like a football, then headed for the back door.

While Bosco did his business in the backyard, Jack sat at the cast iron table in the corner of the covered patio where his father usually smoked. He could smell the stale odor from the cigarette filters piled in the ashtray on the table. He glanced around the enclosure at the work he and his father and Victor had accomplished. Although it was a couple of years ago, he remembered like it was yesterday when they started the project. It was a grueling two weeks of sawing, hammering, and climbing amidst a heat index over 100 degrees every day. But it was one big project he was proud to have completed with his family.

Bosco trotted from the yard to the patio and sat close to Jack's feet.

"You're done already?" Jack petted the puppy's head. He returned inside the house and dumped a scoop of dry dog food into Bosco's bowl.

"Don't you want to *enjoy* your food?" Jack said when Bosco scarfed down the food like he hadn't eaten in weeks. Then he filled another bowl full with fresh water from the kitchen sink.

The telephone rang, and Jack jolted, water sloshing out of the bowl as he set it down next to Bosco. *Why does the phone sound louder in the mornings when it rings?* he thought, annoyed that he had a mess to clean up now. He stepped toward the phone hanging on the wall near the fridge and picked up the receiver, wondering who was calling so early. "Hello?"

"Hey, it's Daisy."

"Hey!" Jack said, surprised. "What's up?"

"Are you riding your bike to school today?"

"Yeah. Why?"

"Can you walk with me instead?" Daisy requested. Her voice sounded different to Jack.

Jack leaned against the refrigerator, winding the phone cord around two fingers. "Sure," he said. Daisy had never asked him to walk with her to school. "You all right?"

"Yeah," Daisy replied. "I need to talk to you about something, and it can't wait. Can you be ready by seven?"

Jack's mother stepped into the kitchen. She had only been home from work for a couple of hours and was about to make breakfast. "Who are you talking to?" she mouthed at Jack.

Jack cupped his hand over the phone, pulling the handset away from his mouth. "Daisy," he whispered, then returned the phone to his ear and said, "I can be ready by seven."

"Good." Daisy sounded relieved. "I'll meet you outside your house. Let's take the railroad tracks."

"Sounds good," Jack agreed, and hung up the phone.

"What was that all about?" Jack's mother asked, greasing a frying pan.

"I'm walking to school with Daisy."

"Oh?"

"I'm not sure, but I don't think she's been getting along with her mom lately."

His mother turned the stove to medium heat and set the pan on the burner. "Don't be walking on those railroad tracks," she warned him.

Jack didn't want to hear it from her this early and knew she'd argue with him until he left for school. "We're not taking the tracks," he lied before she could begin with one of her long-winded lectures, then hurried out of the kitchen.

———

Jack saw Daisy waiting for him at the edge of the lawn when he walked outside. He met up with her, and she threw her arms around him.

Jack leaned back and raised Daisy's chin with the tips of his fingers. He gazed into her teary eyes, her face as pale as a sheet. "What's wrong?"

Daisy sighed. "I'll explain on the way." She wiped the tears from her face with the heel of her hand.

They walked between houses, crossed over an alleyway, and proceeded onto the next neighborhood street. The railroad tracks were located on the other side of the chain-link fence beyond the last house at the end of the road.

"So, what is it?" Jack asked.

Daisy glanced up at him. "Can you have an open mind?"

"Daisy, you know me!" Jack said. "I promise it'll stay between us."

Daisy sighed nervously, then said, "You know that thing we saw inside Whitlock Manor?"

"The ghost, or whatever it was with the red eyes?" Jack said. "Yeah."

"What about it?"

Daisy hesitated, then said, "I think it latched itself to me before we escaped the house!"

Jack felt a chill course through his body. "Huh? Whaddaya mean?"

"I've been experiencing strange things ever since that night I got home," Daisy explained.

"What kind of strange things?" Jack asked.

"Cold drafts nipping at my neck and creepy noises in my bedroom . . . you know, like when a house settles. But it kept getting worse. And last night, I was attacked!"

"No way!" Jack gasped. "Are you sure it wasn't a dream?"

Daisy cut her eyes at him. "I told you to keep an open mind," she reminded him. "It was as real as I'm talking to you right now."

"Well, how were you attacked?" Jack asked. "And how did it follow you home? I didn't see anything odd about you, other than being scared out of your wits when Mike drove us home. Are you like possessed or something?"

Daisy rolled her eyes. "Let's get over the fence to the tracks, and I'll tell you the rest."

They finally reached the intersection at the end of the street and could see the railroad tracks through the chain-link fence from across the way.

Crossing the intersection, they approached the fence line and removed their backpacks. Jack tossed them over the fence and climbed up first.

When she saw Jack make it to the other side, Daisy began her climb. Her shoe slipped from one of the zig-zagged diamond shapes in the fence near the top. "Jack, help!"

Climbing back up the fence, Jack met Daisy at the top and helped her over.

"Thanks!" Daisy breathed when her feet touched the ground. Burrs clung to her shoelaces and socks.

"Sure," Jack said, and grabbed their packs. He handed Daisy's to her, then proceeded up the hill and through a thick rock bedding before stepping foot on the railroad ties.

"I couldn't finish my homework assignment last night so I was up late," Daisy continued to explain. "My body went numb while this . . . *thing* stared deep into my soul. It even spoke to me!"

"What!" Jack's eyes widened. *"What did it say?"*

"It was *so* disturbing, even though it was just one word—*return*. It said '*Return*.'" She looked at Jack, anticipating what he would say.

"That's it?" Jack asked. "What do you think it was trying to tell you?"

Daisy squinted at the sun peeking over the horizon. "I don't know. Maybe it wants me to return to the house? Now I *never* want to go back there after what happened to me last night!"

Jack stayed silent for a moment, thinking. Then he looked over at Daisy. "There's something strange going on at that house," he said. "We *have* to figure it out. I wonder if what visited you was also the same thing that spoke to me on the porch."

"I'm afraid, Jack," Daisy confessed. "I don't want that thing appearing in my house again!"

Jack took Daisy's hand. "I understand if you don't want to go back to that house."

Daisy looked Jack in the eyes and smiled as they continued their stroll amidst the orange glow of the morning sun.

CHAPTER SIXTEEN

An Unwelcome Visitor

FRIDAY, MARCH 17. 4:45 PM
Spring break had begun, and the first thing Jack did when he got home from school was play a video game. The telephone rang.

Jack paused the game and picked up his Garfield telephone, the cartoon cat's eyes popping open. "Hello?"

"Okay," Daisy responded in a soft voice.

"Okay, what?" Jack said.

"I'll do it." Daisy raised her voice a notch.

"Huh? You'll do what?"

There was a brief pause.

"I'll go back to the house with you," Daisy finally said.

"*Really?*" Jack was taken aback. "What changed your mind? I mean, I don't want you thinking I'm forcing you to go back there or anything."

"You're not," Daisy said sharply. "I had another haunting last night, but it was just the creepy noises this time. I haven't slept in my own bedroom in days! I figured if I go back to the house, we might can stop this thing from paying me visits."

"Are you sure you want to go back?"

Daisy sighed. "As much as I don't want to . . . yes. Like you said before, we gotta figure out what's going on at that house."

"Well, we have the whole week ahead of us," Jack said. "When do you want to go?"

"What about tomorrow afternoon?" Daisy suggested.

"You're that desperate, eh?"

"Yeah."

"Okay . . . let's do it!"

"Two o'clock?" Daisy proposed.

"Sure," Jack agreed. "Meet at the streetlight?"

"Yep. See you tomorrow," Daisy said, and hung up.

———

SATURDAY, MARCH 18. 11:15 AM

Sitting on the floor in his room, Jack was stuffing his backpack with video gear, a couple of flashlights, and some extra batteries when he saw Victor appear at the doorway. He wore a sleeveless T-shirt and shorts, and tube socks that were pulled up over his calves. Jack thought he could pass as a dancer from one of those aerobics championship competitions—minus the head and ankle bands.

Victor scanned the video game posters taped to the walls in Jack's room. "I see you added more stupid posters," he said, then glanced down at Jack. "Where do you think you're going? Finally running away?"

Jack eyeballed his brother. "Mind your own business."

Bosco walked from behind Victor, squeezed between his legs, and plopped down in front of Jack.

"Hey, I got an idea," Victor said. "Why don't you do something constructive other than play video games all day?"

"Does it look like I'm playing video games?" Jack said. "Besides, what are *you* doing? And when was the last time you took a shower? You smell like a bean burrito. Get out of my room!"

Victor raised his arm and blew at his armpit hairs. "I haven't showered since you were born, which was about two days ago. Besides, I'm about to work on my car. I came in here to ask if you wanted to help, but it looks like you're too preoccupied tinkering with your baby toys."

"You're always working on your car," Jack said. "It breaks down like every week. When will you ever stop adding crap to it? And you know I'm not a mechanic—I have a life." He zipped up his backpack.

"One day, my car will be passed down to you, and I'll be getting my dream car," Victor said. "You better start learning auto parts, bro."

"What dream car, a Pinto?" Jack laughed. "No thanks on the hand-me-down."

"No, stupid! A Pontiac Trans Am with a firebird hood graphic like in *Smokey and the Bandit*."

"Better get a job like Mom says," Jack mumbled. "That dumb newspaper delivery gig you have won't even pay a single bill. And I know you throw half the bundles down gutters—scammer!"

"Suit yourself, butthole," Victor said, walking away.

Jack gave Victor the finger, then grabbed a blank VHS tape from his dresser, remembering he still hadn't reviewed the footage he captured the first time with Daisy at Whitlock Manor. He unzipped his backpack and stuffed the tape in the bag along with a roll of gaffer tape (a great invention because it didn't leave a sticky residue) for securing his flashlight to the camera.

Watching Jack's every move, Bosco suddenly perked his ears, his attention diverting to the window. He whimpered and wagged his tail.

"What is it, boy?" Jack scratched behind Bosco's ears. "You don't want me to leave or something?"

A car door shut outside.

Bosco woofed and trotted to the window.

"Oh, that's what you were whining about," Jack said, meeting Bosco at the window and peeling back the curtain.

A candy apple red 1966 Mustang convertible was parked in front of the house.

Jack saw two people sitting in the front seats, and one person was in the back. *Who was it that got out?* he wondered. He figured the person was probably walking to the front porch right now, about to ring the doorbell. He dashed out of his bedroom and through the living room (passing his father in his recliner reading *The Dallas Times Herald*) to the front door and looked through the peephole.

"Oh no!" Jack muttered under his breath when he noticed the bruised face. "It's Devin Morton!" Then stepped away from the door and ran back into the living room, announcing in a hushed voice, "Don't open the door!"

Jack's father looked up from reading the newspaper, his spectacles settled at the tip of his nose like a librarian. "Huh?"

Victor reentered the house through the back door, wiping his greasy hands on a shop towel. "What's wrong with you?" he asked Jack.

"Someone from school is here," Jack replied in a faint voice. "I never told you, but I was in a fight with this dude the other day, and I think he's come over here to kick my ass!"

"Really?" Victor cracked a smile. "Now *this* I gotta see!"

"*No!* Don't answer the—"

Rap! Rap! Rap! The blows to the front door were powerful, like pounding echoes in an empty warehouse.

Bosco yapped like a Yorkie and ran to the front door.

"Who's at the door?" Jack's mother stepped out of her bedroom with an empty laundry basket.

Jack placed a finger to his lips. "Shhh!"

Lowering the footrest to the recliner, Charles stood and slapped the newspaper down on the seat cushion.

"Dad, don't open the door!" Jack said nervously.

"I'm only looking through the peephole," his father said.

Rap! Rap! Rap!

"Jesus!" Charles grumbled before he could see who was at the door. He checked to be sure the deadbolt was in the locked position then looked through the peephole. Seconds later, he turned to Jack. "Who the hell is this kid?" he said as he stepped away from the door. "He has a sword! *Why does he have a sword?*"

"Are you serious?" Jack gasped.

Lindsay approached the family gathered in front of the door. "Who
is it?"

Charles peered through the peephole again and studied the hooligan standing at his doorstep. "That's a damn samurai sword!"

"Let me see," Jack said, his father stepping aside. He peeked through the peephole and saw Devin in a striking stance, blade raised with his feet shoulder-width apart and his body turned slightly at a forty-five-degree angle. He was wearing bleach-splattered jeans and a solid black T-shirt. His greasy hair was in a ponytail. His face was as pale as the skin of spoiled milk, except for the prominent bruises around his malevolent eyes.

"What did you do to this deadbeat?" Jack's father whispered.

"Call the police!" Lindsay demanded.

"No!" Jack said.

"This punk could bust down the door and massacre all of us!" Jack's father whispered loudly. "I'll call Mike Palinsky. He'll know what to do. In the meantime, everyone keep away from this door." He turned to Victor and ordered him to lock the back door.

Jack slapped a hand to his forehead. If the cops showed up, Devin would know he called them, and he'd taunt Jack the rest of his days at school.

Victor ran to the back door and locked it, then darted back to the front door and looked through the peephole.

"Get away from the door!" Lindsay said. She looked terrified. "Didn't you hear your father?"

"Calm down!" Victor retorted, glancing back at her. "I'm just looking." He peered through the peephole again. "Dang, Jack. You did one hell of a job to his nose! How in the hell did you—hey, he's walking back to the car. What a coward. Aaaaand . . . they're gone."

"Mike's en route," Charles finally returned. "Thankfully he's on duty today."

"Too late," Victor said. "He's gone."

"I'm sure we'll be able to file a report," Charles said. Then he asked Jack, "Do you know where that kid lives?"

Jack's face was grave and filled with worry. "No."

"Then how did he know where you live?" Victor asked.

"I've seen him a few times in our neighborhood when I was riding bikes with my friends. He probably saw me going into our house one day when I didn't notice."

"When did you get into a fight with him?" Lindsay asked. "And why hasn't the school called me about it?"

"There were no teachers around when it happened," Jack said.

"At least not that I saw. The hallway was packed with kids. It happened so fast, too."

"His face looked pretty bad," Charles said. "You popped him pretty good—no wonder he's out for retaliation!"

Victor slapped Jack on the back. "Good job, little bro. I'm proud of you for finally standing up for yourself."

"That's not something to brag about," Lindsay said. She glared at Jack in disappointment. "You could've gotten yourself seriously injured. I don't want you outside for a while until we know for sure it's safe. I'll be calling the school to inform them what happened here today."

"Do you really have to go to that extreme?" Jack asked.

Victor slipped away from the escalating argument, something he didn't want to get caught in between.

"It's the right thing to do," Jack's mother said. "Besides, if we—"

Ding-dong!

"And that would be Mike," Charles said, looking through the peephole to confirm. He unlocked the deadbolt and swung open the door. "Greetings! Come in."

"Hi, Mike," Lindsay greeted Mike with a smile. "Thanks for stopping by."

"It's my pleasure." Mike nodded, pulling the shades off his face and hanging them over his breast pocket. "Good thing I was nearby when you called. Looks like I missed all the action?"

"Unfortunately," Charles said. "He left about five minutes ago. You
may have passed them on the way—red convertible Mustang."

"Didn't see one," Mike said, pulling a notepad and pen from a pocket of his uniform. He licked his finger and flipped to a blank page and said to Jack, "I'm guessing the incident was geared toward you from what your dad told me over the phone."

"Yeah," Jack said, looking at the floor.

"Tell me what happened."

———

By the time Jack had explained everything, from when he upset Denise at lunch, to the moment he punched Devin's lights out, Mike had written two pages of notes. He circled a few items of importance needing follow-up and said, "You mentioned your friends Stewart and Billy weren't at the table with you during lunch on Monday, but you had seen Stewart in the halls. Do you believe Billy would have had any prior altercations with Devin?"

"No, as far as I know," Jack replied.

"Do you have any idea where Billy is?"

"His brother called me on Tuesday after school and told me he and Billy were having issues with their mom. He wanted to know if Billy was over here, but he wasn't."

"The reason I ask is because Billy's mother filed a missing persons report a few nights ago," Mike said.

Jack's eyes widened. "What! Tommy never mentioned that when I talked to him!"

Charles and Lindsay glanced at each other in shock.

"Well, you may notice more frequent patrolling around the vicinity of your neighborhood for the next few weeks," Mike said. "On a side note, please contact me if you have any leads as to Billy's whereabouts."

"I will!" Jack said.

Mike flipped to another blank page in his notepad. "Sorry to have veered off subject . . . Did you happen to get a plate number on the Mustang?"

"No," Charles answered. "We didn't want to open the door. It's quite a distance from here to the street to have read the plate through the peephole or a window."

"Well, you did the right thing by not opening the door," Mike commended Charles. "I'll visit the school and get some additional information on Devin."

"It's spring break," Jack reminded Mike. "No one will be there."

"Someone will be there," Mike said. "But if they aren't, I can get ahold of the superintendent."

Jack felt his stomach drop. "Won't Devin come back over here knowing we called the police on him?"

"Your safety is my priority," Mike said. "Right now I'm just after information. This will be handled appropriately." He turned to Charles. "Do you want to press charges? Disturbing the peace would be the offense in this case."

"You bet your ass I want to file charges!" Charles raised his voice. "The kid wielded a sword on my front porch! To me, that's clearly a sign of attempted murder."

"Dad!" Jack protested. This was getting out of control.

"Can you provide evidence proving he intended to kill you? Did he make any threatening phone calls before he showed up, or make any verbal threats toward you while at the door?"

"He just about knocked the door down by pounding on it so hard! Does that count? Oh, and make sure you note his family as accomplices. The person driving the Mustang was older, so it may have been his dad."

Mike jotted in the notepad. "I can mail you the documents, and you'll have to appear in court to answer to the charges."

"That's fine," Charles said. "I'll show this punk who he's dealing with!"

Mike smirked and stashed the notepad and pen in his pocket. "You're a hoot, Charles. I've always admired your sense of humor and persistence."

"You know me as well as I know you. Just livin' the dream, man."

"I feel you on that one," Mike chuckled. Before he let himself out, he faced Jack once more. "You haven't been snooping around that old house, have you?"

"No, sir," Jack said.

"Good," Mike said, opening the front door and stepping out onto the porch and slipping on his sunglasses. "Let me know if Devin bothers you again, whether here or at school. Then you can get him on harassment charges. If I'm unavailable, call the station."

Charles gave a thumbs-up and closed and locked the door. He glared at Jack. "What house was he talking about that you were snooping around in?"

Jack gulped, then lied, "I'm researching Whitlock Manor on Cemetery Hill for school, and Mike happened to drive by while I was there with my friends."

"Don't be hanging around that creepy old place," his father said. "I've driven past that house a few times, and it *does* look dangerous. See if you can find other ways to research the place without having to go over there, like at the library or city hall. And that's my two cents." He pulled a pack of cigarettes from his pocket and headed toward the back door to the patio.

Jack's mother sighed. "He needs to stop that damn smoking!" Then she looked Jack in the eye. "Listen, I want you to be safe. Keep an eye out for that kid when you're out there riding your bike."

"I know, Mom," Jack said, rolling his eyes, then remembered he was to meet up with Daisy to visit Whitlock Manor. He stomped back to his bedroom and made the call to her, letting her know he couldn't risk going out there today.

CHAPTER SEVENTEEN

A Sneak Peek

Victor stood from leaning over the engine of his car, set his tools aside, and closed the hood. Back inside the house, he stepped to the kitchen sink and scrubbed the grease off his hands and forearms with a bar of Lava soap. Then he headed to his bedroom to grab his wallet but stopped outside Jack's bedroom when he noticed the door ajar. As nosy as he was with Jack, he peeked inside the room. No sign of his brother, so he entered and snooped around.

The first thing he did was check Jack's backpack on the floor. He unzipped it and peered inside. "Hmph, I wonder what he's filming this time." Uninterested, he zipped up the bag and scanned the room.

The VHS tape on Jack's dresser labeled "Whitlock Manor" caught his eye. He glanced over his shoulder to be sure he wasn't being watched, then grabbed the tape and whisked to his bedroom next door.

Victor fed the VHS into his TV VCR and sat at the foot of his bed to see what was on the tape. The video played automatically, and a static blue overlay appeared on the TV, followed by a few seconds of black. Finally, a shaky image of a room in Whitlock Manor appeared. "This is dumb," Victor said.

A moment before he pressed the stop button on the remote,

something caught Victor's attention. The camera moved past Daisy and revealed a battered kitchen behind her. Victor could hear whispers from the audio, but he couldn't decipher the words. He leaned close to the television screen. "What is this crap?"

The video glitched and cut to black. A moment later, a closeup of Daisy's face came into focus. She looked frightened, staring into the camera. "What?" Daisy asked in a hushed voice, her flashlight flickering.

Another glitch.

"Oh my God." Victor rolled his eyes. "This is so awful!"

He reached to eject the VHS but suddenly paused when he noticed a pair of red eyes over Daisy's shoulder. "What the hell was that!" Victor pressed the rewind button on the remote then played the scene again. As soon as the red eyes appeared, he paused the tape and studied the image. "What the—"

"Hey!" Jack busted into the room, startling Victor. "Are you watching my tape?"

"Dude! Don't be sneaking up on me like that!" Victor yelled. "What is this crap? Are you summoning demons on this video or something?"

Jack swiped the remote from him and pressed the eject button. The VCR regurgitated the tape. "Stop going through my stuff! I don't do that to you. That's an invasion of privacy!"

Victor wiggled his fingers at him like a magician does before a trick. "Ooooh! What other fake stuff did you film? I bet you have footage of you and Daisy making out, don't you? Pervert!"

"What? No! And that video isn't fake." Jack pulled the tape from the VCR and dropped the remote in Victor's lap, then stomped out of the room.

Victor followed him. "Stop pouting and tell me what I was watching on that tape, fool."

Jack slammed his bedroom door in Victor's face. "Go away!"

"Hey!" Victor banged on the door. "What was I watching? You better answer me, tick turd!"

Lindsay barreled down the hall. "What's with all the yelling?"

Victor spun around to her with a sly grin. "Jack's filming pornography."

"No I'm not!" Jack shouted behind the closed door.

"Y'all are crazy," Lindsay said, walking away.

Victor placed his lips against the doorjamb. "Tell me what's on that tape. What I saw wasn't normal. You can't make stuff look that real—you're not that good of a filmmaker yet, dork."

Jack creaked open the door. "I can't trust that you'll keep your mouth shut if I told you."

"Try me," Victor said.

"Daisy and I went to that old house on Cemetery Hill," Jack said rapidly, the words rolling off his tongue. "There, you happy? Now go away!"

Victor pushed against the door when Jack tried closing it in his face again. "Why did you film that place?" he asked.

"Why do you care?"

"Curious minds want to know," Victor replied. "And maybe it'll make a good headline for the *National Enquirer* when I pitch them your story. They're always looking for quirky ideas."

"I don't think so," Jack said.

"Tell me, you butt munch!"

Jack threw his hands in the air. "Ugh! We're trying to debunk the rumors going around at school. People are saying the house is haunted."

"So I've heard," Victor said. "I wouldn't be surprised if a homeless person lives there. But what were the red eyes I saw on the tape? That's mainly what I was concerned about. Everything else I saw was just garbage."

"Gee, thanks. You're a real critic now, aren't you?"

"Don't be stupid. What was it?" Victor demanded.

Jack paused. "A ghost or something," he finally said. "And we're going back there soon to check out the rest of the house."

"That explains why you were going through your backpack this morning," Victor said.

"Yeah, well, don't tell Mom or Dad about it—especially Mom! She'll freak out and ground me for life."

"I told you, I won't say anything," Victor assured him. "I'm not a snitch like you."

"Whatever."

"Maybe you should make a movie about that place. You know, document your experiences instead of just filming random stuff. Hell, I might even watch it if it's good."

"There's a lot involved in making a movie," Jack explained. "More than you think. But right now, I'm just capturing stuff to use as evidence."

"Oookay," Victor said and returned to his room. He grabbed his wallet, and on his way back, he stopped at Jack's doorway again. "I'm taking Dad's Good Times Van to the auto parts store. I need something for my car. Wanna go?"

"Can you stop at the gas station to get slushies?" Jack asked. "They just got the *Street Fighter* arcade game I want to play. We won't have to go out to the mall anymore to play it!"

"Oh yeah, I forgot they were getting that game," Victor chirped.

"Tell you what, since you let me in on your secret video, I'll buy your drink and lend a quarter for the game—your first round of me kicking your ass is on me."

CHAPTER EIGHTEEN

The Dig

Stewart knew it was risky to return to Eaglecrest Farm knowing Rachael's father and brother were there, but he had to be sure Rachael was okay. He felt she was in danger and knew her family was not treating her right. If they were hurting her, he'd take the matter into his own hands, but he also knew that calling the authorities would be safer. Again, a risk that he was willing to take.

Rummaging through his father's toolbox in the garage, he searched for something to use to dig up the metallic object. "I gotta see what that thing was," he muttered, disorganizing the toolbox. "Screw the shovel, I don't wanna carry that thing way out there."

Stewart slid closed the drawers and checked around the gardening tools hanging on the opposite wall of the garage. Like the shovel, most of the equipment was too big to carry when he walked back to Eaglecrest Farm. "There's gotta be something!" he snarled. Then his eye caught a hand trowel propped against the wall between bags of fertilizer and potting soil. "Perfect!" He grabbed the trowel and slipped it in his back pocket. He pulled his shirttail over it, keeping it hidden when he returned inside the house.

The house was a pigsty, reeking of mildew. Bills were scattered around the dining room table, clothes were strewn about the floor in the living area, the sofa had stuffing seeping out of the cushions, the windows were filthy, and the list could go on and on.

Stewart's father slapped a stack of past due bills on the table to add to the current pile and ran his hand through his mullet.

"You look stressed," Stewart said. He noticed his dad wearing the same button-up sleeveless denim shirt from two days ago.

"That's an understatement," Stewart's father replied. "Not sure how we're going to make ends meet this month."

"Sorry, Pops," Stewart said, grabbing a handful of ice cubes from the freezer and dumping them into a thermos.

"What do you have going on today?" Stewart's father asked.

Stewart topped off the thermos with cold water. "Just hanging out with my friends—not sure what they want to do yet, though," he lied. He hated this place. The less he had to hang around here, the better. His mother brought home most of the income, even though she worked a dead-end job. It was a miracle they were still living in the house due to their delinquent payments.

"That's cool," Stewart's father said. He opened the top envelope from the stack of bills. The look on his face went from mellow to disheartened in a split second.

"Where's Mom?" Stewart asked, tightening the thermos lid.

"She's in the bedroom getting ready to go grocery shopping, with what little money we have anyway. Why, you wanna go?"

"Nah. Tell her we need more milk, and I'm out of popcorn." Stewart headed for the front door shouting, "I'll catch you later!"

———

Stewart stood at the end of the dirt trail where he usually waited on his bike for Rachael to exit the farmhouse. This time he was hoping to see her father and brother leaving the premises. But the truck was still parked in the gravel driveway. "Not good," he said. Then again, it was Saturday. Sundays were when Rachael's father and brother spent the day at the stock shows.

Since the coast looked clear, Stewart started toward the barbed wire fence and slipped between the center wires. He made his way into the woods and through the thick brush behind the house, keeping an eye on the shed for Reed. If Stewart was spotted trespassing, he knew he'd probably be shot dead.

Approaching where he had sat with Rachael around the group of dead trees, Stewart stopped, frowning. The area had been cleaned. The fallen trees were removed, and their stumps preserved with a polyurethane wood sealant. The ground was blanketed with leaves. *Her dad and brother must've found out about this place!* Stewart thought. He headed to where the metallic object was buried, hoping it hadn't already been dug up. But with all the leaves, he couldn't tell where the object was located. "Dammit, where are you!" he said, kicking the leaves around. Then he remembered the thing emitted a low-frequency noise, so he paused to listen.

There were no sounds.

Leaning against a tree stump, disappointed that he couldn't find the object, Stewart took a drink from his thermos. Instead of scavenging around for the location of the metallic sphere, he planned how he could get Rachael to come out of the farmhouse without himself getting caught. *I swear, if I find out her dad laid a hand on her, I'll burn the place down!* he thought, and tightened the cap on his thermos. Then he stood and walked to the fence line and slipped between the barbed wires.

Stewart glanced up at the upper windows of the two-story farmhouse from afar, thinking one of the windows was to Rachael's bedroom. He glanced around for anyone to make sure no one was watching him, then dashed to the back porch. His plan was to peek through the screen door—if the front door was open—in hopes he'd catch Rachael lounging or moving about inside the house.

Glancing behind him once more as he ascended the porch steps, Stewart approached the screen door and froze.

Reed stood inside the dark house, blending in behind the screen, glaring at Stewart like a psycho. He pushed open the door with such force that it knocked Stewart off his feet, the trowel in his back pocket skidding across the porch and tumbling down the steps.

Stewart crawled backward on his hands and feet as Reed stood towering over him. Unless it was the angle that Reed stood, Stewart noticed the guy's frame was bulkier than the last time he saw him in the shed. He looked like an imbalanced cartoon character with his bulk tapering down to his absurdly thin ankles. His forearms were the size of spaghetti squash!

Reed stooped and picked Stewart up by his shirt collar, hauling him to his feet like he was a life-size nutcracker figurine. "I can't wait 'til the old man sees what I caught!" he said, excitement written on his face.

Stewart swallowed, his throat bone-dry.

"Nighty night," Reed said, and threw an uppercut so fast, Stewart had no time to blink.

CHAPTER NINETEEN

The Getaway

Mike Palinsky stared humbly at the stacks of unorganized and overdue paperwork on his desk. He needed a better system.

Behind his cubicle, criminals were being escorted to and from booking stations. It was noisy, and the place smelled of body odor.

Rick Silvestrie and Joe Milberry approached Mike's desk. Joe's glistening bald head was so clean, you could eat off his scalp. "What's up, Mike?" Joe said. "We're getting lunch with the sarge at noon. You coming?"

Mike looked up at Rick and Joe from his computer monitor. "Go ahead without me," he declined. "I'm following up with something for a friend. I'll catch you guys next time."

"Suit yourself," Rick said. He slapped Joe's arm with the back of his hand. "C'mon, let's see if the sarge is ready."

Mike performed a search in the database for Devin Morton's criminal history, waiting for the info to appear on the screen as the computer took its slow time compiling the file.

When the results finally appeared, Mike skimmed through the details. Devin's record was clean. "Must be a first-timer," he said. "Just another teenager looking for attention." He peeled a sticky note with Devin's address written on it that was stuck to the bottom of the computer monitor and stuffed it in his pocket. Then he shut down the computer and marched outside to his cruiser.

———

Pulling up to Devin's house, Mike realized it was only three blocks from where Jack lived. He slid from the driver's seat and proceeded up the walkway to the house and rapped on the door. "Rusty Police Department!" he announced. "Please open the door."

No one answered.

Mike knocked and announced his business again.

No answer.

He stepped from the porch and was walking back to the cruiser when he picked up on a noise coming from the back of the house. It sounded like a garage door rolling up or down. He quickly advanced to his vehicle and drove around back.

As Mike drove up the alleyway, a blue and white Bronco II pulled out of the driveway of Devin's house. Mike stopped briefly and noticed a red convertible Mustang inside the garage as the rollup door was coming down. After making a note of the license plate before the garage door sealed shut, he caught up with the Bronco II.

Following the vehicle down the residential street, Mike saw the right taillight was out. "Excellent, now I have a reason to stop them," he said, then picked up his radio to announce his intention to dispatch. "713 to Central."

"Go ahead, 713," dispatch replied.

Mike read the Bronco's license plate aloud, so dispatch had it if things went astray when he made the stop. But it wasn't safe to pull them over yet. Too many cars were parked along the street. "Jeez, don't people use driveways and garages anymore?"

He continued following the Bronco until the street became less crowded, then flipped on the overheads and tapped on the air horn to get the driver's attention.

The Bronco pulled over at the end of the street.

Mike flipped on the front-facing floodlights, the swiveling spotlight, and the high beams. He always played it safe no matter what time of day. The bright lights provided some concealment from the occupant in the vehicle who might try to see when he was approaching. "713, we landed in the residential area of Bellview and Hargrove Court," he announced into the radio on his shoulder.

"713, Bellview and Hargrove Court, copy," dispatch confirmed.

Mike stepped out of the cruiser and closed his door softly. Why give the occupant a hint that he was walking up to them? He approached the Bronco carefully, his attention torn between the unknown occupant and a car he heard driving up from behind. He hoped the passing driver would slow down and give him some space. After the car passed, Mike touched the Bronco's taillight, leaving his thumbprint in the event he should become incapacitated during the stop. He glanced in the back and side windows of the Bronco for anyone in the rear seats but found no other passengers.

He saw the driver had already rolled down the window upon his approach and hoped both of the driver's hands were on the steering wheel. "Good evening, my name is Officer Palinsky—"

"Is there a problem?" the unattractive woman interrupted, looking irritated that she had been pulled over.

Mike remained calm, even though he knew the woman was

going to be uncooperative. He dealt with people like her all the time. "My name is Officer Palinsky, badge number 1329. The reason I stopped you is because your right brake light is out. May I see your driver's license and proof of insurance? And is anyone else in the vehicle with you?"

The woman was hesitant to answer. "No. It's just me. I didn't know my brake light was out." She handed him her driver's license.

"Insurance?" Mike asked.

"It's in my bag in the back," the woman replied nervously.

"It needs to be on you, or in your glove box or somewhere accessible from where you're sitting," Mike told her.

The woman frowned. "Well, that's just stupid! I have insurance; it'll only take a second to get it."

"No need," Mike said. He read the woman's name on her license. "Suzanne Morton, are you related to Devin Morton?" he asked.

"I'm his sister," the driver responded. "What does he have to do with this?"

"Is this driver's license up to date? I see the address is different from where you pulled out in front of me in the alley."

"I don't live here," Suzanne said. "I was just visiting. The address on my license is correct." She gripped the steering wheel tighter.

Mike's eyes caught the slight movement in her hands then noticed the large rock on her finger. *She's married,* he thought. *Why does she not have her married name printed on her license? He* glanced at the license again to double-check he had read it correctly. *Yep, last name Morton—this is his mother!*

"Can you not tell me why my brother is in trouble?" Suzanne asked again. "I should have a right to know!"

"He's been involved in an incident," Mike said. "I'm collecting facts for the case."

"So, why are you questioning *me*? Why even mention him if you're stopping *me* for a light that's burned out?" Suzanne looked at him sideways. "Wait, how do I know you're really an officer of the law and not some random guy about to rob me or something?"

"I introduced myself and gave you my badge number. Again, I'm Officer Mike Palinsky, badge number 1329."

"That tells me nothing!" Suzzanne argued.

"713, are you 10-4 on your stop?" dispatch squawked over Mike's radio.

"10-4," Mike replied. He glanced back at Suzanne. "Please stay in your vehicle. I'll return in a moment." He took Suzanne's license back to the cruiser to run the information through the system, glancing back at the Bronco every few steps.

Sliding into the seat with his door slightly ajar, Mike stuck one leg out as he typed the information into the computer. The results displayed faster here than on his computer at the station. Reading the information on the screen, Mike learned the Bronco had been identified as a getaway vehicle in a series of fraudulent check writing schemes. "Bingo!" he said and looked up, thinking he saw movement in the back seat of the Bronco. As a result, he updated his status to an escalating situation. "713 to Central. 3939—requesting backup."

"713 copy. Backup en route," dispatch confirmed.

Moments later, the passenger front door of the Bronco flew open, and Mike watched as a male with long hair hopped out of the vehicle and fled the scene on foot. He matched the description that Jack had given him.

"That's twice she's lied to me!" Mike said, grabbing the transceiver radio and flinging open his door.

He jumped out of the cruiser and drew his weapon, shielding himself behind the door. "Central, I have gunpoint!" he said through his shoulder radio. Then he spoke through the transceiver, his voice projecting through the speaker mounted behind the front grille of the cruiser. "Driver, please shut off your vehicle and place the keys on your dash."

Suzanne stuck her head out the window. "What? *Why!*"

"Shut off the engine, place your keys on the dash, and step out of the vehicle," Mike repeated through the speaker, anticipating backup to arrive at any moment.

People in the neighborhood were starting to come out of their houses to witness the commotion.

Suzanne stepped on the gas, peeling away. The vehicle drifted into the intersecting street and nearly clipped the stop sign at the corner lot.

"Son of a bitch!" Mike raged. He secured his weapon and slid back into the cruiser, taking off with his sirens blaring.

"713 to Central. 6182—in pursuit of suspect heading east on Melbourne. A second suspect has fled on foot and was last seen crossing Bellview heading north through a residential area."

"Vehicle heading east on Melbourne, copy. What's the description of the suspect on foot?"

Mike suspected it was Devin who had fled the scene and replied with Jack's description that he had previously given to him. "Caucasian male. Long blond hair. Roughly one hundred twenty pounds. Jeans. Black T-
shirt."

"Copy that. Units en route to patrol the area for suspect on foot."

Heading into rush hour traffic, Mike spotted the Bronco about six car lengths ahead of him. Another cruiser suddenly swerved in front of him and took the lead.

Mike accelerated and approached the onramp to I-35. The freeway was backed up, and he saw the Bronco finally pulling over up ahead and ending the chase peacefully.

———

Devin stopped to catch his breath. When he fled from the Bronco, he ran three blocks, zigzagged between several houses, and ended up in Jack's neighborhood. He thought his mother telling the officer she was his sister was golden. But he knew if she had given him her real ID the first time, with the actual address printed on it, the cop would have found out the truth.

Coming up on Jack's house, Devin hocked a loogie in his front yard, then cut through the side of the house and advanced two blocks over to the street where Denise lived. He had a last-minute idea to hide out at her place in case the police happened to prowl through the area looking for him.

Devin knocked on Denise's door.

"What are you doing here?" Denise whispered when she cracked open the door.

"Why are you whispering?" Devin asked. "Is everyone sleeping or something? Can I come in?"

"Are you crazy!" Denise said.

"The cops are looking for me. I need a place to hide until it's safe to go back home."

"Let me guess, that Jack kid called the cops."

"Yeah, and he's made a *huge* mistake!" Devin said.

Denise yelled back into the house, "Mom, I'll be outside

hanging with my friends for a bit. She stepped onto the porch and pulled the door shut behind her. "You can't stay here."

"I need a place to hide," Devin pleaded. "My parents have been doing some illegal stuff that could cost them years in prison. If the cops catch either one of them, especially my mom since they're hot on her trail right now, they'll probably issue a search warrant to gain access to my house!"

"What!" Denise slapped a hand to her face. "What about hiding at the place where you meet up with your friends at that sewer sometimes?"

Devin rubbed at his chin. "You know, that's really not a bad idea." He grinned. "And it can buy me some time while I figure things out."

"I'll go with you!" Denise smiled, her black lipstick smeared over her yellow-stained teeth. "I can sneak my mom's keys to her car, and we can take the back roads to the park."

"What if she catches you taking her keys?" Devin asked. "I'm already wanted. If you get caught driving your mom's car, and I'm with you, I'll be shit out of luck with a criminal record slapped to my name!"

"Don't worry," Denise said. "I do it all the time and I haven't been caught yet."

"Well, with the luck I'm having today," Devin said, frowning, "you might've just jinxed yourself."

———

Devin sat with nervous tics in the passenger seat of Denise's mother's Tempo. He leaned his seat back so no one could see him. He'd never been in the car with Denise driving before, so he had to trust they would arrive at Porter Park in one piece.

"Oh, look!" Denise pointed as she pulled into a parking

space. "Ducks! I should've brought some bread."

Devin returned his seat to its upright position. "Those things need to stay away from me," he said, stepping out of the car. "I hate ducks!"

Denise glared at Devin over the hood of the car. "I didn't know you had a fear of ducks."

"Yeah, and it's really a thing," Devin said. "It's called anatidaephobia. If there's one strange word I can pronounce correctly, it's that one."

"I've never heard of that," Denise said.

Devin kept his distance from the ducks waddling toward him. "Well, now you know."

————

An oily film topped the murky embankment water.

"That's gross." Denise wrinkled her nose.

"It's where the sewer empties, what do you expect?" Devin said. He pointed at the large pipe extending over the water. "That's where we need to go."

"I'm not wading through all this nasty stuff to get over there!" Denise cringed.

"Do you know a better place I can hide?" Devin asked.

"If you say your parents are in trouble, it will only be a matter of time before the entire city starts looking for you!" Denise said. "And don't forget about school—they have tabs on you, too. So what's the point in hiding?"

"Don't you be a snitch!" Devin seethed. "If you don't want to help me figure out how—"

Devin paused.

Denise darted a gaze at him. "What? Figure out how to what?"

Devin looked around his surroundings. "Listen! Do you hear that?" he whispered.

Denise scanned the trees along the perimeter of the embankment. "Hear what?"

"Exactly . . . nothing!" Devin said. "No birds and no wind."

Behind them, across the grassy knoll, a small dog barked. Devin caught a glimpse of a Pomeranian trying to slip from its leash on the sidewalk. The elderly lady walking the dog stooped to pick up her feisty little furry friend and continued down the sidewalk, giving Devin and Denise a vile stare along the way.

"What are you looking at!" Devin shook his fist at the old woman. "Shut your dog up!"

The old lady looked away and picked up her pace.

Denise grabbed Devin's arm. "Hey! She didn't do anything to you!"

Rage swelled in Devin's vibrant eyes. He seized Denise's throat with one hand and squeezed. "Don't you *ever* grab me like that again!" he snapped, losing all self-control.

Denise flailed her arms, her face turning bright red. She kicked Devin at the knees, and he finally released his grip. Backing away, she held her hands to her throat. "What the hell is wrong with you!" she gasped between coughs.

Devin curled his fingers to fists, his knuckles turning white. "Serves you right!"

Denise looked at him, appalled, her mouth agape. Her eyes twitched over his shoulder at the water behind him, and she took another step back.

Devin uncurled his fists and took a breath. "C'mon, Denise, I didn't mean to hurt you," he said, extending an arm toward her. "There's been lots of bullshit happening in my life lately, and I'm just sick of it all."

"It's not that." Denise shook her head. She pointed behind Devin. "Something is moving under the water."

Devin squinted at Denise. Hearing a splash behind him, he turned around and watched for movement in the water. "Probably just fish," he said, shrugging his shoulders.

"I don't think fish can live in water that looks like that," Denise said matter-of-factly.

Devin crept to the edge of the water, craning his neck at something forming out in the center of the water and moving toward him.

"What *is* that?" Denise wondered, stepping to the edge of the water and standing next to Devin. "It looks . . . toxic."

"It looks like tar," Devin said. He spotted a branch on the ground nearby and grabbed it, then extended it over the water.

"Don't get too close," Denise warned him.

"It's fine," Devin said, angling the stick over the substance gliding toward him and Denise.

"It's got a mind of its own," Denise said.

An air bubble formed in the black mass, and the substance stopped inches before their feet at the edge of the water.

Devin poked at the bubble with the stick. "It's ballooning." He jabbed at it repeatedly until the stick pierced through and a thick, slimy substance seeped out like chocolate syrup.

Denise moved away from the edge of the water. "Eww!"

Devin studied the glob of film for a moment. "Something's moving underneath," he noticed. "Do you see it?"

The hole he punctured with the stick dilated, and the tar-like substance expanded across the water. He pulled the stick away from the mass and looked at the black, gooey stuff at the tip. The substance was slithering down to his hand in a candy cane pattern.

"Drop the stick!" Denise barked. But it was too late. The goop latched onto Devin's hand and hardened in an instant.

Devin's hand froze underneath the hardened slime. He tried shaking it off, but the substance cracked, and he yelped as a string of dark tendons leaped from the goo and stretched over to Denise next to him, latching onto her arm.

"Get it off me!" Denise screamed. "It hurts! Get it off!" She grabbed the substance and tried pulling it off, but it maintained a tight grip around her arm.

"Tug of war," Devin spoke quickly. "Let's pull on three. One . . . two . . . *three!*"

As they tugged on the substance, two more strings suddenly lashed from the tar that floated over the water in the embankment. Like eyeless eels, the strands wrapped around Devin's and Denise's necks and reeled them, pulling them toward the organic mass. Their screams pierced the air as they were dragged into the water and the thick film closed over them.

As though satisfied after a quick snack, the mass glided back to the center of the water, Devin's and Denise's bodies never resurfacing.

CHAPTER TWENTY

Tommy Takes a Ride

Tommy knew his mother was tempted to start drinking again. Trying to quit cold turkey was unpleasant, as opposed to gradually tapering off an alcohol addiction. Thankfully, he was there to prevent her from drowning her sorrows again. With the police confirming Billy was "officially" missing, his mother's withdrawal symptoms were becoming more noticeable.

The phone rang off the wall every day, and Tommy's mother would answer it in a self-loathing tone, hoping good news would eventually come through about Billy's whereabouts. But it was primarily friends and family checking on her and Tommy. For years, they had never heard from many of these relatives. And the ones who did call them, they had not heard from in ages. Never once did these same people ever check up on Tommy's mother when *she* needed help.

Tommy prepared a fruit salad for his mother and took it to her bedroom. The flickering of the television screen illuminated her pale face when he entered her room. She was losing weight like she had come down with a virus. "I made you this," he said, setting the salad bowl and glass of water at the side of the bed.

His mother looked up at him, not speaking. She looked so

drained of energy, the frown on her face had stuck.

"You need to eat, Mom," Tommy said. "You'll get sick if you don't. You know this because that's what you always told me." Since it looked like she had no intention of picking up the salad bowl, Tommy grabbed it and placed it in her lap. He scooped some cottage cheese and held it
to her lips. "Eat, Mom."

Frustrated that his mother would not open her mouth, Tommy tossed the spoon in the bowl like a dart. "I'm going outside to get some fresh air," he sighed. "You should try and eat while I'm gone. This isn't like you, Mom."

His mother cut her eyes at him. "Can you call the detective and see if there are any updates on your brother?" she asked, her speech slurred. "His card is on the refrigerator."

"I'll give him a shout when I get back," Tommy said.

His mother nodded and sank her head into the pillow.

———

Tommy rode his bike through the neighborhood, crossing a major thoroughfare and into an empty parking lot. He and Billy used to hang out here when the lot was a convenience store before it burned to the ground. Then it became a popular meetup for some thrashers until the city ran them off. Tommy was hoping to find a clue that might lead him to his brother's whereabouts.

Nothing out of the ordinary stood out at him, so he bunny hopped the curb and crossed the street to another neighborhood, a shortcut he and Billy took to the place behind the fire station. He curved around the bend and approached the intersection of Claybourn and Whittle Way. Crossing over, Tommy followed the sidewalk parallel to Claybourn and rode over the railroad tracks. Then he turned into the entrance to the fire station and circled behind the building through the parking lot.

Crossing the parking lot, Tommy jumped the curb and pedaled as fast as he could in the grass, hoping no one would see him passing alongside a daycare center. He was surprised a fence hadn't been built yet to keep people from trespassing where he was headed. He coasted down a short hill and squeezed the handbrakes as he approached the entrance to the sewer system.

Tommy rested his front tire on the coping of the cement and glanced down into the gully. It looked like a tiny version of the spillway drain hole at Hoover Dam. *Let's call this The Bowl*, he remembered telling Billy when they first stumbled upon this place years ago. *Because it looks like a giant cereal bowl!* It was referenced by other kids as a half-pipe, and Tommy and Billy used to come here and watch skateboarders perform professional tricks like nose and backside pivot stalls, frontside sweepers, and rock to fakies. But it was Tommy who usually stole the show and performed advanced BMX maneuvers with some massive hang time and always stuck the landing. The challenge was the water below that flowed between the sewer pipes on either side at the bottom. If he didn't hop over the puddle on his way up the high-sided curved wall on the other side, his wheels would become slick, and he'd risk wiping out. Thankfully, it never happened.

Tommy could hear the sewer water trickling below from the larger tunnel on his left, the entry to the sewer line which measured about seven feet in diameter. The smaller tunnel on the opposite end was about five feet in diameter and passed underneath the railroad, emptying into a small levee on the other side.

Thinking he'd have a little fun before heading into the larger tunnel, Tommy dropped in the hole, bunny hopped over the trickling water below, and rode up the other side. He banked in the air and grabbed the seat of his bike with one hand while turning the handlebars ninety degrees and whipping the tail end around. Then his wheels touched down and came to a skidding stop, his feet planting on either side of the trickling water.

Tommy stared into the entry of the sewer. He could feel the humidity like warm breath blast him in the face.

Easing his bike into the pipe, the musty smell nearly gagging him, Tommy could hear cars passing above on Claybourn. He shouted for Billy at the first curve where the natural light ended. From this point forward, he'd be traveling in the dark. But this wouldn't be the first time he rode his bike about a mile through the tunnel until it emptied
into the storm sewer outlet at Porter Park.

"Billy!" his voice reverberated. "You in here?" He listened for a response, but all he heard was the constant traffic above.

Tommy debated if he should risk riding all the way through. It had been years since he'd ridden down here with Billy. What if another pipe had been added further into the system and branched off to somewhere else? "Screw it!" he decided, and rode into the darkness.

———

The smell of hydrogen sulfide and ammonia intensified the further Tommy progressed. The light beaming through gutters he passed from sections of neighborhoods helped him to see once his eyes finally adjusted to the dark. He followed the trickling water down the center of the pipe and shouted for Billy at random along the way.

Thinking he heard someone talking, Tommy stopped and listened. Voices of kids reverberated through the tunnel. *That could be Billy,* he thought and continued riding through the sewer.

Having ridden for a while now, he knew that any moment he'd see natural light bouncing off the walls at the final curve, like tubing in an enclosed waterslide.

The voices of kids grew louder. But when Tommy splashed through a large puddle of water as he rounded the final curve and squeezed the handbrakes, the voices suddenly stopped.

Tommy could see the end of the tunnel and three kids crowding the rim of the pipe. "The Jenkins brothers," he muttered. "Dammit! I hate these idiots."

Andy, the youngest brother, tossed a rock out into the murky water below while his oldest brother, Kyle, sat next to him exhaling smoke out his nostrils. The cigarette was pinched between his fingers, his hand limped over a knee. Standing next to Andy and Kyle was Stephen, the red-headed middle brother with a serious case of acne.

Tommy watched as Andy spun around and spotted him sitting on his bike.

"Um, guys?" Andy said.

Kyle and Stephen turned their heads.

Tommy recognized Kyle as the coward who had tagged along with Devin the day Jack had punched him in the face at school. He remembered seeing him blend in with the crowd when Devin ran to the restroom with a bloody nose.

Stephen stood and pulled the handle of a switchblade from his pocket. He approached Tommy, tossing the object back and forth between his hands. "Well, well," he said, grinning. "Looky what we have here! Where'd you come from?" He glanced back at his brothers and chuckled. Then he spun back around to Tommy and pressed a button on the handle. A comb flipped out instead of a blade, and Stephen ran it through his hair.

Tommy recognized the switchblade comb when he saw the black electrical tape wrapped around the handle. "Where'd you get that?" he asked.

"This?" Stephen held up the comb to show Tommy.

"That's my brother's!" Tommy grew angry. "He has tape around it just like that one. *Where did you find it?*"

Stephen folded the comb back into the handle and slid it in his pocket. "Finders keepers." He smirked.

Kyle flicked his cigarette over Andy's head, where it landed in the water outside the pipe. He stepped around Stephen and stood in front of him. "This is our territory. State your business or prepare to get the living shit kicked outta ya!"

"You guys live down here?" Tommy joked. "I didn't know you owned this place." He stretched his arm over his handle bars and opened his hand. "The comb . . . it belongs to my brother. Hand it over!"

Kyle glanced back at Stephen, then took a step closer to Tommy. "And what if he doesn't—cry to your mommy?"

Although it was three against one, Tommy stood his ground, determined to get Billy's comb. *They must know where Billy is if they have his comb,* he thought.

"Well?" Kyle said, sticking out his chest.

Tommy got off his bike and engaged the front brake. He tilted the bike forward on its front wheel and kicked the rear tire, the frame tail-whipping 180 degrees. The peg on the back wheel struck Kyle's thigh.

Kyle fell against the sewer wall, howling in pain as he held his leg.

Defending his brother, Stephen leaped and grabbed the wheel of Tommy's bike before Tommy could reset and do the same thing to him. Then he counteracted and pushed Tommy with his other hand.

Tommy stumbled backward and fell on his butt in the water running through the center of the pipe.

Before Tommy could get to his feet, Stephen hopped on Tommy's bike and rode toward Andy at the rim of the pipe. "Hold on to the bike while I finish off this punk," he said to Andy, then returned to help Kyle.

Andy's face lit up. But instead of holding the bike like he was told, he set the front wheel at the edge of the pipe. "Hey, guys!" he shouted back into the sewer. "Check this out!" He pushed the bike out of the sewer, and it splashed into the discharge below.

Not paying attention to their little brother, Stephen and Kyle ganged up on Tommy and grabbed him by the collar.

"You're mine now!" Kyle snarled in Tommy's face.

"Get your filthy hands off me!" Tommy pushed Kyle into the side wall. Then he spun to Stephen and shouted, "Give me the comb!"

"Over my dead body!" Stephen barked, and suckerpunched Tommy.

Tommy doubled over, gasping for breath, his hands holding his abdomen.

Kyle pushed himself up from the curved wall and limped toward Tommy. He grabbed and yanked his arm. "Get his other arm!" he commanded Stephen. "Drag 'im to the water!"

Andy was jumping around like a spaz, excited that he had tossed a bicycle into the nasty water, when Kyle shoved him out of the way. "Hey!" Andy yelled.

Kyle and Stephen stood holding Tommy at the rim of the pipe.

"On three," Kyle said. He started the countdown. "One . . . two . . . *three*!"

Andy caught on to what they were about to do and joined from behind and pushed as his brothers tossed Tommy out of the sewer, sending him splashing into the nasty water two feet below.

Tommy stood in the water, flinging globs of muck from his face as Stephen and Andy howled with laughter.

Kyle pulled a cigarette and a lighter from his pocket. "Let's get out of here," he said, lighting his cigarette.

The Jenkins brothers climbed out of the sewer and onto the mushy perimeter of the embankment, then proceeded up the incline to their bikes.

Tommy spotted his bike's handlebars poking up from the surface and grabbed the handles. He pulled the bike dripping with mud and some kind of tar-like substance out of the water and carried it over his head to the sewer pipe. He figured it would be safer to ride back through the sewer rather than risk running into the Jenkins brothers again if he took his bike up the embankment and rode through Porter Park.

Climbing into the sewer, Tommy mounted his bike, cleaned the handlebars and frame with his bare hands—flinging the gooey substance against the sewer walls—and rode back the way he came. He shot out of the reinforced concrete piping fifteen minutes later, ascended the wall of the Bowl, and hightailed it home before daylight's end.

PART TWO

Escaping Fears

"He never walked away from a problem,
but occasionally liked to bury it
and dig it up later."

—James Herbert, *The Fog*

CHAPTER TWENTY-ONE

The Return

SUNDAY, MARCH 19. 11:15 AM

Jack grabbed his backpack and made his way to the garage, treading softly past his father sawing logs in the recliner.

He entered the garage and found his mother filling the gas tank in the lawnmower. Nothing could stop her from doing her weekend yard work. She'd kick over dead before she would let someone else break a sweat over the yard. "Where are you going?" she asked, topping off the tank.

"Going to feed the ducks with Daisy at Porter Park," he lied, knowing his mother was easily fooled.

"Oh, that sounds fun," his mother said. "Why the backpack?"

"I figured I'd bring my camera and get some B-roll. I can probably use the footage for something later."

"Well, don't be throwing rocks at them turtle heads while you're out there!" his mother warned him. "You know what happened last time when you were at that park with Victor, and y'all got caught shooting those things with the pellet gun."

"I know. Victor's gun was confiscated, and you paid a hefty fine to get it back from the police station. You don't have to keep bringing this up every time I go to the park. And I'm not taking a gun!"

Jack's mother wiped her hands with an oil-stained shop rag. "I'm just making sure you know to be careful. Don't be out too late. And come straight home if you see that Devin kid. You shouldn't even be outside further than the front yard with that idiot running around."

"I won't be out late," Jack promised, wheeling his bike out of the garage and onto the driveway.

Victor was leaning halfway over the engine bay of his Camaro with a leg kicked up like he was searching for a nut or bolt he had dropped.

"What's wrong with your car now?" Jack asked.

Victor pushed himself from the car and stood with his arms and face streaked with grease. Sweat dribbled down the sides of his face. "Don't worry about it. You wouldn't understand."

"Whatever." Jack rode his bike into the alley. He pedaled to the end of the alley then turned onto the sidewalk and followed it around then back up his street to Daisy's house. He parked his bike in the front yard and proceeded up the walkway to the front porch and rang the doorbell.

Daisy opened the door, shielding herself behind it.

"Ready to go?" Jack asked, wondering why she was hiding behind the door.

Daisy glanced behind her, then back at Jack. "I don't want my mom knowing I'm leaving the house," she said. "Hold on."

Jack flinched when Daisy shut the door on him. He retreated to his bike and sat on it, fiddling with the textured, gel handlebar grips as he waited for Daisy.

Moments later, Daisy appeared from the side of the house on her bike and pulled up next to Jack.

"I see you came prepared." Jack smiled, noticing Daisy had

ditched the fanny pack this time and wore a backpack.

Daisy shrugged. "Easier to carry things in," she said. "I packed a few survival items, too. Let's get this ghost hunt over with!"

Jack chuckled, then spun his bike around and popped a wheelie into the street.

"Show-off," Daisy said, and caught up to him.

———

Jack and Daisy stood on the porch at Whitlock Manor.

"This is new." Jack pointed at a latch and padlock secured to the door. The broken window and all the lower windows around the house were boarded. "When did this happen?"

"Now what?" Daisy asked.

Jack rubbed his chin. "How much do you want to bet Mike was the one responsible for this?"

"The cop?"

"Yeah."

Daisy walked around the porch, searching for another way inside the house.

Like clockwork, crows perched in trees and lined the edge of the roof. Dark clouds rolled in directly above the house. The porch swing swayed, the rusty chains singing a squeaky tune.

"I guess we could go around back and see if there's another way in," Jack suggested.

"I was wondering the same thing," Daisy said. "Get out of my head before I start charging you rent!"

"Wait a minute," Jack said, kneeling at the boarded window close to the swing and placing his hand on it.

"What is it?" Daisy asked.

"Shhh!" Jack placed his ear to the plywood. "I can feel a vibration in the board." He moved his hand to the edge of the wood and ran it along the side. "There's a draft seeping through the sides, too. It's like the house is—"

"Five to enter, one to stay; the world deceived, a future to pay," a muffled voice whispered in a slow beat from the boarded window.

Jack shot a glance over at Daisy. "Did you hear that!"

"Who was that?" Daisy gasped.

"That's the voice I told you about! You heard it, right?"

"Could it be that thing with the red eyes—the thing that terrorized me at home?" Daisy asked, her heart thumping madly in her chest.

"I dunno," Jack replied, stepping away from the window. "I wonder if—"

"Basement!" the voice hissed.

Jack leaped back, the hairs on the back of his neck standing on end. "Whoa! We need to find out where it's coming from. Let's go around back!"

They rushed down the rickety steps to the side of the house. As they crossed through thick brush, the rear of the house appeared, overlooking an open field. Further out was the tree line that led to the old cemetery a half-mile away.

"Look!" Jack pointed out into the field. "See those double doors out there?"

"Is that a root cellar?" Daisy craned her neck. "That's so creepy!"

"Looks like it," Jack said. "Let's check it out. It could lead to another way inside the house."

"Isn't there a back door?" Daisy said, facing the back of the house. "Never mind, that's boarded, too."

"Let's go!" Jack said, and walked briskly through the open field toward the cellar.

"Is it safe to open?" Daisy asked when they reached the rotted wooden cellar doors.

"Only one way to find out," Jack said, and reached and flipped the latch securing the doors. He gripped the handle to one of the doors and pulled it open, the hinges screeching a warning to the darkness below. "Whoever boarded up the house forgot to lock these doors—ha!"

A cold draft rose from the depths as Jack stepped over the threshold. He clicked on his flashlight and shined it down into the welcoming darkness, illuminating several uneven stairs constructed of decayed two-by-fours that led to the bottom.

"How deep does this go?" Daisy asked, clicking on her flashlight.

Jack shined his light down at the steps. "Looks like five or six feet maybe?" he guessed. "I'll go first and check it out if you want to stay here."

"No way!" Daisy said, grabbing his arm. Her hair fluttered from a sudden gust of wind, and she could feel sprinkles of rain nipping at the
back of her neck. "I'm coming with you."

"Well, come on then," Jack said, and started the descent.

The walls of the chiseled soil around him narrowed with each step. Upon reaching the cellar floor, he shined the light at a pile of broken shelves in one corner. Having no interest in checking it out, he moved on and followed a path several feet to the back wall.

"Is there usually another door inside root cellars?" Jack asked, standing before a crooked section of wood paneling built into the wall of the soil.

"I'm not sure," Daisy said. "I thought a root cellar was just a single room to store things in."

Jack examined a loose handle on the panel. "Maybe this leads to another area for storage. But it'd be cool if it opened to a pathway that goes to the house!" He pulled on the handle, but it snapped off.

"So much for that!" Daisy giggled.

Jack tossed the handle aside. "Yeah. Tells you how old this place is. Hold my flashlight for a sec." He handed his flashlight to Daisy and curled his fingers around a gap between the edge of the paneling and gave a few firm tugs. The force disturbed the ceiling, and dirt sprinkled on his and Daisy's heads as the paneling ripped from the wall.

"Was that supposed to come off the wall like that?" Daisy wondered, shining the flashlights over Jack's shoulder through the doorway.

"Don't think so," Jack said, setting the paneling on the ground and dusting his hands off. He grabbed his flashlight from Daisy and stood at the hole in the dirt wall. "As I thought, another passageway!" He turned back to Daisy. "Ready?"

CHAPTER TWENTY-TWO

Interrogation

S tewart woke to the smell of old machinery with his hands bound at the wrists behind his back. His face was beaded with sweat, and his ribs were sore. A sharp pain surged through his jaw from Reed's fist making contact with his face.

The afternoon sunlight squeezed between the cracks of the wooden walls, dust particles fluttering within the streams of light.

Stewart struggled to stand, then felt lightheaded and stumbled against the wall. Taking deep breaths, he glanced around his surroundings, trying to figure out his whereabouts.

A door closed nearby, followed by the sound of footsteps. Each footfall on the soil was chaotically spaced from the last without rhythm.

"Is that you, Reed?" Stewart spoke through clenched teeth. "You're in a lot of trouble, pal! Untie me!"

The footsteps ceased, and Stewart's eyes gazed at a figure standing a few yards in front of him. He squinted, waiting for his eyes to adjust to the shadowy area where the figure stood.

A chubby man stepped into the light beams penetrating the room. Seconds later, a lantern flickered to life and the man raised the lamp to his face, the light revealing his filthy overalls and big gut. His shirt cuffs were rolled back to his elbows, exposing his hairy forearms. His white beard was stained from tobacco juices. He was a spitting image of a redneck gas station attendant in a horror movie who would give wrong directions to a passerby who would then end up in a slaughterhouse.

Rachael's father! Stewart thought. For several moments, he stared at the man in an uncomfortable silence and noticed him gripping a cattle prod.

The man shifted his weight from one foot to the other then squeezed the trigger to the electric prod, electricity waving between the tips of the metal shock ends. Taking a step forward, the man towered over Stewart.

With no time to react, Stewart was a pancake against the wall. He could feel the man's putrid hot breath on his face as he stared wide-eyed at the tip of the prod held centimeters from his cheek.

"Your name, boy!" the old man grumbled. He grinned a mouthful of crooked, yellow-stained teeth then spat the juices from a wad of chewing tobacco. The colored liquid splashed onto the toe of Stewart's sneaker.

"I'm only gonna ask you one more time," the man continued. *"Who are you?"*

Stewart held his breath and shut his eyes. "Okay—OKAY!" he finally breathed. "My name's Stewart! Now untie me!"

The man gazed into Stewart's fearful eyes. "How long have you been seeing my daughter?"

"Get that thing away from me!" Stewart yelled. Then he realized, how did Rachael's dad know he was seeing her? When did she tell him and for how long had he known? Their relationship was supposed to be a secret!

"It's a simple question," Rachael's father said.

"I don't know what you're talking about," Stewart said, deciding to play dumb. Then he felt the tip of the electric prod pressing firmly against his face. The look in the man's eyes told him he was eager to pull the trigger.

"Last chance," the old man said, his hairy nostrils flaring.

"I told you," Stewart said, cringing. "I don't know your daughter! I've never seen her, and I don't know who she is—you're torturing the wrong—"

Stewart burst a scream when a painful shock shot through his head. "Stop! Stop!" he cried, sliding down the wall and curling into a ball on the ground.

"You're pathetic," the old man said. He stepped to the opposite wall behind him and hung the lantern on a nail. Then, returning to Stewart, he pressed the toe of his boot against the back of his neck. "I'll give you a moment to think about your answer. And when I return, I expect full details as to why you were scavenging around my property and how long you've been seeing my daughter. Your life depends on the truth."

Stewart spit granules of dirt from his mouth and sat up, watching the old man step back into the shadows. He couldn't stand his hands tied behind his back and needed to get them in front of him, so he moved them forward under his butt and slid them past his feet as he folded his legs with his knees drawn against his chest. Now he could work at cutting the duct tape binding them. But how? He brainstormed for a moment, then glanced at the lantern hanging on the wall across from him. Finally, an idea came to him, and he stood with the support of the wall and staggered toward the lantern.

Thankfully, the old man wasn't all that bright leaving Stewart alone in the room with a lantern. "I'm not telling that old dude shit!" Stewart muttered as he grabbed the lantern and lifted it from the nail. He placed the lantern on the ground and used the tip of the nail protruding from the wall to puncture the tape several times. Then he pulled his hands apart as hard as he could, and the tape snapped.

Stewart grabbed the lantern and looked around for a way out. It appeared he was locked in an old mineshaft. He spotted a sloping passageway leading into the creeping darkness. Then, with a frustrated groan, he marched forward, raising the lantern higher as he trudged through the aorta of the earth.

The stagnant path finally came to an end at a closed door. Stewart stood before it, taking in nervous breaths. Finding the courage within, he reached for the knob and gave it a twist, unsure of what he'd find on the other side. He pushed the door open and stood back, the light from the lantern illuminating a new discovery: an extended hallway with walls of sheetrock and linoleum flooring. "This must be part of the house," Stewart said, and pressed on.

Approaching the end of the corridor, Stewart peered around the corner at yet another door. He gave it a slow push open, and a warm draft welcomed him into the dank living room of the farmhouse.

CHAPTER TWENTY-THREE

Tunnel of Terror

Jack pulled the camcorder from his backpack. "Can't forget to capture what's ahead." He also grabbed the roll of gaffer tape from the bag and secured his flashlight to the top handle of the camera. Since he had no camera light, he figured this amateurish rig would suffice.

"Can you even see through that thing in here?" Daisy asked, leery of her surroundings and whipping her head back and forth.

Jack hoisted the camera onto his shoulder, peered through the viewfinder, and pressed the record button. "I can manage," he said. "Although the image is kind of grainy from lack of light, at least our flashlights are somewhat helping." He proceeded through the narrow passageway, shuffling his feet and feeling his way along the walls with one hand.

Daisy grabbed the back of his shirttail as they moved around a sharp turn. She was so nervous, she couldn't keep her flashlight steady.

Jack kicked something, and he stopped short and pulled his face from the viewfinder. Something tumbled down the passageway and ricocheted off the wall with a reverberating *ping*.

"What was that!" Daisy jolted, her hand pressing firmly against Jack's back.

Jack proceeded with caution, spotting a jar snug against the wall up ahead. He peered over his shoulder at Daisy. "Just an empty canning jar," he said.

Daisy let out a sigh of relief. But as they continued through the passageway, she kept glancing back, her flashlight penetrating the darkness
behind them. "I'm afraid, Jack. What if something is following us?"

Jack stopped again.

Daisy's eyes widened with fear, her body pressing against Jack's. "Now what?"

Jack smoothed his hand over roots braiding the sides of the coarse walls like fossilized snakes. "Tree roots."

"What does that mean?" Daisy said, her voice shaky. "We're underneath a big tree? This is getting creepier the further we go!"

Jack hoisted the camera onto his shoulder and zoomed in on the roots. "I don't know *where* we are."

Something groaned through the darkness ahead of them.

"What was that?" Daisy clung onto Jack tighter.

Jack put a finger to her lips. "Shhh! Listen!" He felt something trickle down his back inside his shirt, diverting his attention from the sound. He tilted the camera up to shine the flashlight at the ceiling. Dirt sprinkled from the ceiling like something had passed over them, pounding on the level above.

"Oh my God!" Daisy gasped. "This place better not be caving in on us!"

"I doubt it," Jack said.

"Basement!" a voice pronounced faintly up ahead.

"Someone's down here!" Jack said. "That sounded like the same voice that was coming from the broken window on the front porch!"

"Maybe we should turn back," Daisy whispered, feeling cold goosebumps on her arms.

"No way," Jack said. "If you want to leave, that's fine. I've come too far to turn back now. I want to find where that voice is coming from."

"I'm not leaving," Daisy said. "Just go."

Jack readjusted the camera onto his shoulder, then led the way around another curve.

———

"Now what?" Daisy grumbled when Jack stopped again.

Jack zoomed in on more tree roots dangling from the ceiling like a conglomeration of dreadlocks. "What that hell is this place?" he moaned.

"I'm not going through that!" Daisy insisted. "This is way too weird."

Jack spun around, the flashlight on the camera blinding Daisy. He saw her eyes were brimming with tears. "We gotta see what's on the other side," he said. "If you want, you can stay here, and I'll go through and check it out."

Daisy fidgeted with her bottom lip.

"Look, I know you're scared," Jack said. "But just think, if we're able to capture more stuff about this house on video, we could go down in history as the two who debunked all the rumors."

Daisy blinked, and a tear traced down her pale cheek. "I can't live in fear anticipating another visit from that ghost thing in my room!" she said, wiping her face. "Just go. I'll follow you."

"Are you sure?" Jack's voice pitched. "It won't take me but

a few seconds to pass through, and I'll be right back here before you know it."

Daisy glided past him and hooked an arm around a group of roots. She pulled them back like she was drawing curtains. "I'm sure. You go first since you have the camera. Hurry up because this stuff feels so gross! It's slimy . . . ugh!"

Jack smiled and stepped through and stood on the other side. The walls had opened to a larger area. He lowered the camera and turned around, holding the roots back for Daisy as she made her way through to him.

"Whoa! What is this place?" Daisy asked, waving her flashlight.

"I'm not sure," Jack said, panning the camera back and forth, the flashlight beam fading into the blackness like an abyss.

"What if this is the basement?" Daisy wondered.

"Maybe," Jack said. "I'm not sure if we . . . hey, shine your light over here with mine!"

Daisy crossed her flashlight beam with his. "Is that a ladder?" She squinted.

"It looks like it," Jack said. "Pan your light up it. Does that look like a trap door above it?"

"Yeah, I see it. I think we *are* in the basement! Should we climb it?"

"That wouldn't be a bad idea," Jack agreed. "I don't know where else we could—"

Something rattled in the darkness, and Jack and Daisy whipped their lights in the direction of the noise.

Jack looked through the camera and zoomed in where Daisy was waving her light. "Let's move closer," he suggested. "That sound wasn't too far away."

"Why can't we just see if that door is open in the ceiling above the ladder?" Daisy whined.

"I want to see what that sound was first," Jack insisted, sauntering in the direction where he heard the noise. He picked up something in the viewfinder and whispered loudly at Daisy, "Stop!"

Daisy paused in an instant, having no problem complying with the command.

"Is that . . . a cage?" Jack pressed forward slowly. "Keep your light on it."

Daisy walked alongside him. "I don't think I can take much more of this. Something doesn't feel right."

Jack zoomed in closer with the camera. "Yep, that's a cage!" The autofocus kept trying to adjust, and when it finally locked on the subject, Jack's jaw dropped. "I see something moving inside the cage!"

Daisy dared to take another step.

"We need to get closer," Jack suggested, the camera still shifting in and out of focus. Then, finally, the image became clear again. "You gotta be kidding me!"

"What?" The tone in Daisy's voice pitched.

"I think it's a body!"

Daisy slapped a hand over her mouth. "Tell me you're joking!"

"I'm not kidding," Jack said. "We need to tell Mike about this!"

Daisy had no objection. "Jack, I want to get out of here!"

"Let me get a clearer image first, just to be sure."

"You keep wanting to do more or go further every time something bad happens," Daisy cried. "Why can't you stop being so curious for once?"

Jack concentrated on the body lying on the cage floor as he continued with the baby steps. But before he could steady his shot, the camera glitched, and it lost power. "Oh, c'mon!" He lowered the camera from his shoulder and popped out the battery. "Reach inside the zipper pocket on my backpack and hand me a new battery."

Daisy gulped, too terrified to even take a step closer to where Jack was standing.

Jack raised the dead battery over his shoulder for her to take. "Here, put this in the same place as the other one you give me."

Daisy pointed her flashlight at the battery in his hand. She unzipped the side pocket of his backpack with trembling hands, dug around inside, and pulled out a freshly charged battery, swapping it out with the one Jack gave her.

"Thanks," Jack said, loading the new battery into the camcorder. He hoisted the camera onto his shoulder and pressed record.

"What do you see?" Daisy asked, her eyes on the ground.

"Um . . . whatever I saw before is gone now," Jack said. "It must've moved!"

Daisy tensed, her eyes still on the ground. "Let's go . . . NOW!"

Jack panned the camera along the front of the cage, trying to find where the body or whatever he had seen had moved. "How could it just disappear like that? I don't get it. Maybe something grabbed it and—"

Two pale hands suddenly thrust up from inside the cage and gripped the bars.

Jack stumbled backward when he saw the motion up close in the viewfinder, his heart leaping in his chest.

"Who is that!" Daisy looked up, gasping at the hands.

Jack slapped his own hand over his chest and tried to catch his breath. He slowly panned down with the camera, the flashlight illuminating the prisoner.

Daisy took a few backward steps, her hand over her mouth. Then she paused, and her fingers slid from her lips. "Jack?" she whispered, cocking her head. "Who is that?"

Jack heard her but did not respond. Instead, he spoke to the prisoner. "Hey, you okay?" He thought maybe this was the person whose voice he heard through the broken window, and the sound must've carried up through a pipe or an air vent from this room and filtered into the house.

Silence.

Jack kept the camera on the prisoner, flinching when the person lashed his arms between the bars like a cat reaching out for adoption. Then his head jerked up to the camera lens.

Daisy lurched forward and latched onto Jack's arm.

"Billy!" Jack yelled.

Billy, weak and malnourished, spoke in a garbled voice. "Help me!"

Daisy was speechless, still clinging onto Jack's arm.

Covered in filth from head to toe, Billy looked as though he had shed several pounds. "Jack!" he said, fatigued. "You found me! *Get me out of here!*"

Jack gripped one of the bars of the cage, excited that he had found his friend. "How did you get in here—*why* are you in here? The whole town has been looking for you! *Who did this?*"

Billy's eyes swelled with tears. "I haven't seen daylight in forever!"

"We need to get help!" Daisy finally spoke.

Billy wiped his dirty face. "You know I've always hated riding bikes to this house," he said, life slowly returning in his voice. "Devin Morton and his girlfriend did this! They shoved me down into the root cellar, and before I could sense where I was, the creature snatched me up. I never saw it because it was too dark. But I could smell it. Oh, God. The stench has been stuck in my nose. The thing grabbed me so tight, I couldn't breathe. I guess I passed out because the next thing I remember was waking up in here!"

Daisy's face looked grim. "Creature?"

"Wait, did you say Devin was responsible for this?" Jack asked, unfazed by Billy's mention of a creature. "Why were you hanging around the house if you hate coming here?"

Billy glanced at Daisy. "Yes, a creature," he said with wide eyes. Then, back on Jack, he said, "When you were looking for a way in the house with me and Stewart the night I didn't want to get involved, my comb slipped out of my back pocket when I was running. It was my favorite comb, and I wanted it back! So I went back to look for it. Devin and his girlfriend—and that Kyle kid—came at me from behind the house. I guess they wanted to get high on seeing how scared I'd be if they locked me in the cellar. I tried to run away, but they grabbed me and dragged me to the root cellar behind the house and threw me in."

Jack's face turned red; how dare anyone do this to his friend? "I'm sorry this happened to you. Devin showed up at my house unexpectedly the other day with a sword! He wanted to pick a fight with me. Who the hell shows up at your doorstep with a samurai sword! A gun, maybe. But a sword? That asshole hasn't seen the last of me! But first, we gotta find a way to get you out of here!"

"You'll need something to cut these bars," Billy said. "But y'all aren't safe outside this cage! The creature is in here with us. Sometimes I can hear it breathing. The stench gets worse when it's nearby."

"I didn't bring any tools," Jack said.

"Why don't we go to the police?" Daisy suggested. "They can get him out faster than we can."

"That would be ideal," Jack said. "But I don't want to—" He heard something and panned the camera around the room. "Is there a dog in here with you, too? It sounds like a dog panting."

Billy shook his head. "Not that I know of. It's just me, and that . . . *thing*."

Daisy tensed as the room fell silent. The panting sound ceased.

Jack sensed movement and shined his flashlight over Daisy's shoulder and was stunned with horror when he saw a disfigured *something* looming behind her into the beam of light.

Daisy noticed the fear in Jack's face. "I know that look," she groaned. "Something's behind me, isn't there?"

Jack could only nod.

Billy's eyes were transfixed on the creature. "That's it!" he whispered loudly, stepping back from the bars of the cage. *"Run!"*

Tears cascaded down Daisy's face as she stood vulnerable to what stood behind her.

Jack, frozen with fear, tried to register what he was looking at towering over Daisy. The thing was ugly and intimidating. Its flesh was slimy with a rubber-like texture. Its beady black eyes were sunken deep in their sockets, its nose a single carved hole in the skull. The flesh upon its balding head glistened from the light beam.

The creature snarled, rolling back its lips to bare its elongated razor-sharp teeth dripping globs of mucus.

Daisy felt the warm saliva drip on her shoulders. The stench was putrid. "Jack," she whispered, shutting her eyes. She could feel it sniffing at her neck, followed by its snakelike tongue slithering up the side of her face. She squealed in sheer horror when the beast yanked her and drew back into the darkness like a vampire shunning the sunlight.

Daisy's flashlight took a blow to the ground and expired.

"Daisy!" Jack screamed, reaching out to her a second too late, his flashlight illuminating a dust cloud.

Billy grabbed the bars of the cage and shook them madly. "Get me out of here!" he screamed.

Jack spun around. "Where d-did it take her?" he stuttered at Billy. "Something like that just d-doesn't exist!" His hands and legs were shaking.

Billy stuck his face between the bars. "It's real! And we are both ground beef if we don't get out of here!"

Jack unwrapped the tape securing his flashlight to the camcorder and powered off the camera. He removed his backpack and stuffed the video camera into the bag with trembling hands. Setting his flashlight on the ground pointed at the cage, he took a step and grasped the bars. He shook them in different areas in a fit of rage, hoping to pull one of them loose. Without any luck he tried pulling the bars apart, but he was no Superman. Nothing was working. "I'm so sorry, Billy! I gotta get out of here. But I promise I'll be back for you! You're probably safer in there than me out here."

Billy moved slowly back to the center of the cage with a disheartened look on his face.

Jack felt guilty having to leave Billy and Daisy to fend for themselves. But he didn't know what else he could do. He had no weapons to defend himself.

"Go," Billy finally said softly. "Find something to cut these bars with. And don't come back alone!"

"Trust me, I'll be back for you, Billy!" Jack said, grabbing his backpack and flashlight and shuffling back the way he and Daisy came. But as soon as he made it to the dangling roots in the ceiling, a clatter of metal shattered the stale air. Jack spun around and called out to Billy. "You okay?"

Billy did not reply.

Jack threw his hands in the air. In his mind, he wanted to keep moving, but his conscience wouldn't let him leave without knowing Billy was okay. So he headed back toward the cage, waving his flashlight around the large room.

Approaching the cage, he saw it had collapsed and kicked up a veil of dust. "Billy!" he gasped, his chest tightening, fearing the creature had broken into the cage and grabbed Billy.

The sound of metal clanging caught his attention again, and Jack shined the light at movement around the debris. "Billy!" What he thought was the creature sifting through the rubble was Billy trying to free himself from underneath pieces of the cage. *What destroyed the cage?* Jack wondered.

Jack noticed movement again, but it wasn't Billy this time. He panned his flashlight to another section of the collapsed cage, the light illuminating a pool of blood on the ground. He tilted up his flashlight from the blood to the creature with a metal bar protruding through its abdomen. It must've been going after Billy but instead impaled itself and demolished the cage trying to grab him.

Jack whipped his flashlight over to Billy, who was still flinging pieces of metal off himself. "Billy, you need help?" he whispered loudly.

Billy finally freed himself from the rubble and crawled toward

Jack, his pant leg snagging a piece of debris. His eyes widened with terror at the creature's ear-piercing scream erupting behind him. He ripped a hole in his pants to free himself, then scurried on his hands and knees with a face full of tears.

"Let's get out of here!" Jack said, quickly helping Billy to his feet.

They scrambled to the dangling roots in the ceiling and back through the winding tunnel that led to the root cellar, the sounds of the creature's wails diminishing. Jack and Billy climbed the steps to the cellar doors that Jack had left wide open, and they escaped the underground and stood in a heavy downpour.

At this point, Jack couldn't care less about the rain; he was glad to have escaped alive. Although he still had to return to find Daisy, at least he knew the creature was injured and hoped it stayed incapacitated.

Billy breathed deeply, rain spattering his face.

"Our bikes are around the front of the house," Jack shouted over the storm. "You take Daisy's bike to your house. I'll get help and come back for her. Maybe the creature will be dead when I return." He removed his backpack and unzipped it and pulled out a smashed peanut butter and jelly sandwich. "I know you're starving, but this is all I got."

Billy's eyes lit up. "Thanks, man!" He grabbed the sandwich and devoured it in seconds. "I owe you big time for this, Jack!"

Jack slapped Billy on the shoulder. "Nah, that's what friends are for."

CHAPTER TWENTY-FOUR

At the Door

Tommy and his mother sat at the kitchen table in silence, picking at their Chinese takeout. They had no appetite. Tommy couldn't help but keep glancing at the empty chair next to him where Billy usually sat. He missed his brother so much.

The telephone rang, and Tommy's mother jolted. The bags under her eyes were puffy and dark. Her face was pale, and her lips were chapped. "I can't handle talking to anyone right now," she said.

Tommy got up, pushing his chair screeching across the floor with the back of his legs, and picked up the telephone before its last ring. "Hello?"

"Good evening, this is Detective Gilbert Sanchez from the Rusty Police Department. I'm returning Tommy Crenshaw's call. Is this who I'm speaking with?"

Tommy glanced at his mother swaying in her chair and staring blankly at the walls like a mental patient. He didn't bother trying to get her attention. "Yeah, this is he," he replied into the phone.

"How can I help you?" the detective asked.

"Do you have any leads on my brother?"

"I've been working up the paperwork for the case. We've employed other law enforcement agencies at every level to assist with the investigation. I'm also working on contacting some nonprofit organizations and volunteers to assist as well. Rest assured, I'm gathering as much critical information as possible to conduct an in-depth investigation, beginning within the parameters of the city where Billy was last reported seen. I'm also alerting our station's patrol officers on duty with briefings at every shift. I do understand it's a very tough time for you and your mother. Hang in there, buddy."

Tommy thought that was a lot to take in. Half of the things the detective said went in one ear and out the other. It sounded like the guy was giving him a standardized response to frequently asked questions. "Is there anything I can do to help?" Tommy asked. "I want my brother back! And my mom is worried sick."

"I understand your frustrations and concerns," Detective Sanchez said. "But we have to follow best practice protocols established by the state. You can contact me if you have updates that you'd like to add to the file. Even though we've already conducted interviews with you and your mother, the more information we receive from you, the better we can understand all aspects of the investigation. We can also hold a press briefing if you and your mother are up to doing that on camera to address the general public."

Tommy threw his head back. This wasn't the phone call he was hoping for. "Okay. Thank you for calling back. When should I expect to hear from you again?"

"I'll reach out to you as often as I can, especially with any new leads on the case. However, don't hesitate to contact me directly if you have any questions."

"Okay," Tommy said. "Thank you."

"I know it's tough to do but try and stay positive and get some rest. Good night, my friend."

Tommy hung up and turned to his mother. "Nothing," he said, choking back tears.

His mother slapped her hands over her face and wept.

———

Jack hopped the curb on his bike and rode through the front lawn of his house to the porch. He leaned the Diamondback against the wall and ran inside, peeling off his drenched backpack and dropping it on the floor next to the door. His sneakers squeaked on the tile entry as he hugged around the corner to Victor's room. The door was closed, but he barged in anyway. "Dude, you gotta help me!" he said, out of breath.

Victor slapped down the latest issue of a hot rod magazine on his desk. "You scared the living crap outta me! You ever heard of knocking?"

"Now you know how it is when you do it to me!" Jack panted. He caught his breath and said, "Listen, Daisy's in trouble! You gotta help me!"

"What, did your booger-eating girlfriend fall off her bike and get a booboo?" Victor snickered. He panned down at the carpet in the doorway where Jack was standing. It was soaked from the water dripping off his clothing. "You're ruining my carpet! Where were you that it rained?"

"C'mon, man!" Jack begged. "There's no time to explain. I just need your help!"

"Why should I help you when you never help me?" Victor said. "Go change your clothes and bring back a towel to dry up my carpet. Mom's gonna kick your ass if she sees this! You can thank me later."

Jack tried to keep calm, but he couldn't. Flashbacks of Daisy being pulled away into the darkness kept repeating in his mind. *"Something took her when we were at Whitlock Manor!"* he finally said.

Victor's jaw dropped. "You went back? I was only joking about filming a documentary there. You're such a gullible moron."

Bosco trotted around Jack's legs and entered the room.

Jack stepped from the doorway and intentionally sat at the edge of Victor's bed, petting the dog with shaking hands.

"Are you serious right now?" Victor snapped. "Get your wet butt off my bed!"

"I'm not getting up until you listen to what I have to say," Jack yelled back at his brother.

"Is that a threat?"

Jack took a deep breath and said, "Please. Just shut up and listen. We went back to the house to capture something on video. The front door had a latch and padlock on it, so we found another way through the root cellar behind the house. It led us through some winding tunnels to what we think was the basement of the house."

"Root cellars don't have passageways, dummy," Victor clarified. "It's just a room for storing canned goods and stuff."

"Well, this one has a pathway underground that leads from the field behind the house to a basement or something," Jack said. "Oh, and we found Billy! He was locked in a cage. He said Devin, the kid who came over here with the sword that was looking for me, locked him in the cellar. Then a creature picked him up, and the next thing he knew, he woke up inside the cage."

"Bullshit!" Victor glowered at him. "This is one of your dumb pranks you like to play on me, isn't it?"

"It's not a joke, I swear!" Jack pleaded. "There's really a monster underneath that house! It grabbed Daisy and—"

"Oh, c'mon!" Victor said. "There's no such things as monsters, and you know it! It was probably some dude in a costume scaring y'all. Stop watching those stupid horror movies and you won't have these delusions."

Bosco sensed Jack's frustration and pawed at his leg.

"Really? You watch scary movies, too!"

"But I don't let them get to me like you do," Victor said.

"Victor, you *have* to believe me—something took Daisy! Then it came back and broke through the cage where Billy was locked up, and that's how he was able to escape."

"Then where's Billy if he escaped?"

Jack hung his head. He didn't know how to convince his brother to believe him. "He's on his way home. He took Daisy's bike, and I came straight here to tell you what happened."

"I don't know your friends, except for Daisy," Victor said. "But since you're crying like a baby, take me to where Daisy got lost. Consider this a freebie. *And this better not be a big joke!* I swear, I'll shove your hands so far up your scrawny butt you'll be walking on your elbows."

"Daisy isn't lost," Jack insisted. "She was taken! But thank you for finally believing me! I promise it's not a joke."

"I didn't say I believed you yet," Victor replied.

Jack took a slow, deep breath, then rattled off the requests he had for his brother. "Can you drive your car to the house, and I'll take the motorcycle? And can you bring Dad's shotgun? I know Mom will be in bed soon before she goes to work tonight. And you know Dad, he easily falls asleep in his chair, so it should be easy for us to sneak out."

"Whoa!" Victor threw his hand up at Jack. "Wait a minute. A shotgun? *Are you nuts!*"

"For our protection," Jack explained. "If we encounter the creature, it needs to be killed! You can hide the gun in the trunk of your car and park it at the cemetery. I'll take the motorcycle and meet you there. From there, we can ride the motorcycle to the house. That way, Mike won't suspect anyone is trespassing if he makes his rounds there tonight."

Victor looked at him thoughtfully. "How have you already planned all of this?"

"It just came to me."

"So, what if the monster you say exists is really a person in a costume? If we shoot it, and it turns out to be some homeless dude, we'll be wanted for murder!"

Bosco trotted out of the room when Jack stood from the bed.

"Trust me," Jack said. "I know this sounds crazy, but you'll see for yourself the truth behind Whitlock Manor!"

"I think I might have a better idea," Victor contemplated.

"Oh, yeah?" Jack said with excitement.

"How about we let the cops handle this?"

Jack closed his eyes and breathed. "We can't yet. If we don't find Daisy first, then we can go to the police."

"Dude, what you're trying to do is way out of our league! And bring- ing Dad's gun is too risky. It's a catch-22 if we get caught. We'd be in
serious trouble by the cops and especially Dad! It's a no-win situation."

"Think what you want," Jack argued. "The longer we sit here and theorize what would happen if we got caught trying to save Daisy, the more danger she's in. She's like a sitting duck in the dark. We need to get to the house ASAP!"

"Calm down," Victor said. He slapped a hand on Jack's shoulder and stared him square in the face. "If I find that you're lying to me, you better watch your back for the next two weeks."

"Agreed," Jack gulped.

———

Tommy sat in the living room with his mother watching a re-run of *Mork and Mindy*. People say laughter is the best medicine, so he figured a comedy show might ease their minds off things for a bit.

The Chihuahua suddenly perked up from the sofa, scaring the two cats off Tommy's mother's lap. They launched off the couch and ran to her bedroom.

Looking over at the small dog with the flicker from the television flashing in its face, Tommy muttered, "What's *your* problem?"

Tommy's mother shrugged listlessly. "Something must've startled him," she said, scooping the dog with one arm and pulling it closer to her.

Tommy engaged the recliner and propped his feet up on the footrest extension. He leaned back to get more comfortable and folded his hands in his lap. He was so emotionally drained, his eyes were getting heavy.

The dog cut its eyes toward the front door and barked.

"Tell that thing to shut up!" Tommy roared.

A slight knock at the front door caused the dog to fire off continuous rounds of barking as it soared from the couch.

"Probably another neighbor bringing us food," Tommy's mother grumbled. "I'm not answering it."

Tommy rose from the recliner and stepped to the door, pushing the yapping dog out of the way with his foot. He unlocked the deadbolt and dropped his head mournfully. If his mother was right about a neighbor coming over to express their sympathy, he figured they wouldn't bother them for long if he had a somber attitude. But when he swung open the door, he froze.

"Who is it?" Tommy's mother projected her voice from across the room.

The world around Tommy came to a complete stop.

"Who's at the door?" his mother said with a grumpy attitude, then sprang from the couch.

Tommy spun around teary-eyed and stepped to the side, revealing to his mother Billy sopping wet standing motionless on the front porch, staring back at them like a puppy from a depressing animal adoption commercial.

Sarah gasped like it was her last breath. Full of emotion, she nearly tripped over the threshold as she leaped and threw her arms around her younger son, collapsing to her knees in heavy sobs. She looked up at him like he was an angel sent from heaven and grasped his hand. "Where have you been! I thought you were gone forever!" She reached up and caressed the side of Billy's face. "Look at you . . . I bet you're *starving*."

Tommy grabbed his mother's arms and helped her up. Then, the family threw their arms around each other in tears of joy.

Sarah stepped back, her eyes cutting to Tommy. "Call the detective and tell him your brother is home!"

CHAPTER TWENTY-FIVE

Looks can be Deceiving

The trashy living room in the farmhouse smelled like an unflushed toilet with days-old urine. Torn furniture was carelessly organized and stacked like in a hoarder's house. However, a peculiarly unscathed nineteenth-century loveseat—that would have been more at home in a much cleaner environment—was bunched against the wall, offsetting the room.

A ceiling fan rotating languidly off balance with a broken blade served no purpose in circulating airflow.

This place is a dump! Stewart thought. He peered around a tall stack of leaning boxes, surprised to find a woman knitting in the far corner of the room. She wore an old-fashioned gown with her feet barely skimming the floor in her antique rocking chair. Her glasses were bigger than her face, her eyes magnified behind the thick lenses. Her reaction to his intrusion was dull, like she had been expecting him. She smiled gleefully, set the knitting in her lap, and ceased rocking. A slight breeze blowing through the open window behind her fluttered a discolored valance. She pushed her glasses up and gazed at the boxes where Stewart was hiding. "You must be that fella Rachael told me about," she said with a heavy southern accent.

Rachael's mother, Stewart thought. *She's not supposed to know about me, either!*

"Hmm?" Rachael's mother moaned.

"Ma'am, I don't know your daughter," Stewart said behind the boxes, keeping to his same story. "Why is your family trying to make me confess to something I have no clue about?"

"Sheila," Rachael's mother said. "Call me Sheila." She transferred the knitting from her lap to the end table next to her. "Come out from behind them boxes so I can get a better look at ya."

"I don't think so," Stewart said.

"And just why not?" Sheila said with an edge of disappointment in her voice, leaning forward in the chair.

Peering between the cracks of the boxes, Stewart spotted the back door located a few feet from her. He thought he could dash across the room and escape before Rachael's mother had time to stand up. Then he thought about Reed. He couldn't take the chance of running into that muscle head again.

"Let me tell you somethin'," Sheila said. "Between you and me, I don't mind you being with my daughter. I just want you to be truthful. Her father has always been a hard head. He hates the thought of our daughter goin' steady with anyone. And he ain't ever gonna get over it. But one day, I know it'll happen, and he'll just have to accept it whether he likes it or not!"

"I know he's been strict with her—she's told me," Stewart said honestly. The truth was out. Then, he asked bluntly, "Is she kept locked in her room like a prisoner?"

"She ain't no lab rat!" Sheila barked. "Where we come from, it's custom to seclude the second born from the family."

Stewart stood shocked at her response. "What do you mean *where you come from*? That's not okay to do that to someone, let alone your own daughter! That's psychotic!"

"It's okay." Sheila perked up contentedly. "Tell me, do you love her? Because if you do, feel free to march up them stairs. She's in the first door on the left."

This woman is weird! Stewart thought. *Why is she trying to help me? This has to be a trap!*

Sheila rose from her chair and stood hunched over like she suffered from chronic back pain. "Come out from behind them boxes like I
asked. I wanna get a good look at who I'm talkin' to."

"How do I know you're not going to pull a fast one on me?" Stewart asked. "Your husband and your son both want to torture me!"

"Nonsense," Sheila said. "I ain't that fast no more. I'll be having a chat with Don and Reed later. They ain't gonna lay a hand on you again. I can promise you that."

Stewart peered uneasily behind him at the long hallway from where he had entered, then turned back and looked left and then right. He took a step to his right, out into the open of the living room.

Sheila's smile broadened. "Oh, you're a handsome fella! No wonder Rachael kept quiet about you." She giggled, then her eyes held a dangerous stare on Stewart. She wiped the smile from her face and said in a deep-toned voice, "Heed my words. When you march up them stairs and find my Rachael, take her and run as far away as you can. No questions—just run! You hear me? Run!"

Stewart looked at her funny. "Why do I need to—"

"Nope!" Sheila snapped. "I said no questions. Get up them stairs, and hurry!"

Stewart grunted, hoping he wouldn't regret this, and whisked to the staircase.

———

No matter how cautious Stewart was walking up the rickety steps, each one squeaked. He clenched his teeth, hoping the sounds hadn't attracted the attention of Rachael's father or brother.

He stood at the top of the stairs, staring at three bedrooms branching off the hallway: two on the left and one on the right. *She's in the first door on the left.* He glanced over his shoulder to be sure Sheila wasn't playing a trick and sneaking up behind him.

Tiptoeing to the first bedroom, Stewart reached for the doorknob but paused. He examined the door. The top hinge pin was missing, and the door was dented and chipped in several places, signs of aging and abuse. He grasped the doorknob and pushed open the door, peeking through the doorway before stepping into the room.

The bedroom was clean and well-kept. A twin bed was dressed in wrinkle-free sheets with a couple of pastel-colored pillows stacked neatly at the head of the mattress. In one corner of the room stood a tall wooden dollhouse, highly detailed, consisting of five rooms. It had two winding staircases, a balcony, and several pieces of jumbo furniture. Yet, strangely, there were no dolls.

The sound of grinding metal outside caught Stewart's attention, and he stepped to the window for a look. A couple of flies buzzed around the windowsill when he pulled back the sheer curtains and peeked outside the window at the shed below. Sparks were flying out the opening as if someone was welding inside.

Moments later, Reed stepped out of the shed. He was shirtless, balancing the haft of a double bit axe over his shoulder like a lumberjack. His chiseled chest and abs were sculpted to perfection.

What's this dude doing to keep himself so buff? Stewart wondered. He looked on at Reed, who was leaning and spitting the juices from a chunk of tobacco stuffed in his cheek and glancing around, as if making sure no one was watching him. Then he stepped forward, out of Stewart's line of sight.

Stewart closed the curtains and focused on the closet door at the opposite end of the room, noticing it wasn't shut all the way. The latch bolt was not seated in the strike plate. *Maybe Rachael's hiding in the closet!* he thought. But before he could swing open the door, it crept open on its own.

Stewart slowly backed away, his heart dropping into his stomach.

Bony fingers curled around from behind the door, and Rachael emerged from the closet in a blood-stained white dress, blood oozing from a laceration on the side of her head. Expressing no discomfort, she bared an evil grin, some of her front teeth missing. Her eyes turned wicked, swelling in their sockets and transitioning to solid black.

This was not the Rachael that Stewart knew! Finding himself backed into the far corner of the room, he choked on his words. "Rachael, w-what happened? *Who hurt you?*"

Rachael reached out a gory arm toward Stewart and opened her hand as if to present him with an invisible gift. "You were going to be mine," she said in a strange voice. "I wanted you. I had you. *Then I lost you!*"

Stewart's eyes widened with fear, his palms sweating. *"What?"*

"You were mine." Rachael's voice changed into what Stewart

could only describe as a demonic tone. "I spent years searching for you, but my father denied me the privilege to have you."

"Rachael, what are you *talking* about? This place has poisoned you—your family is nuts!"

Rachael lowered her arm back to her side like something was in control of her body. A deep growl rumbled from within her, raw and raunchy.

Stewart wanted to grab her hand and run, just like her mother told him to do. But he was afraid.

Rachael grabbed the bust of her dress and ripped it in a fit of rage. The torn garment slithered down her curvaceous body and piled at her ankles.

Stewart's eyes landed on her cleavage bulging from her blood-stained bra. Grotesque skin sores covered her torso and legs. Bloody tears cascaded down her face, hinting to Stewart that an evil presence inside of her had a firm grasp on her soul.

"You were . . . to be . . . my first!" Rachael cried. "I could've had this body for eternity."

Stewart stood paralyzed, scrunched up against the wall as he witnessed the gruesome transformation of his girlfriend.

Rachael's arms flailed about like noodles. Bloody foam projected from her mouth and arched across the room, her body convulsing violently. Then the convulsions ceased abruptly, and Rachael's body hunched over in the center of the room like a toy robot whose batteries had died.

"Rachael? Are you okay?" Stewart breathed. He took a step and reached his hand out to her. "Rachael, let me help you. I can take you to see a doc—"

Racheal stood up straight, her flesh incising like a zipper from her navel to the center of her chest. The slit continued up her neck and over her face. Finally, her flesh peeled away and ribboned to the floor, and the true evil of Rachael Eaglecrest stepped forth with a slimy substance dripping from its skeletal figure. The monstrosity grew like an expandable foam water toy, its head nearly touching the ceiling.

The beast staggered toward Stewart on tall legs like stilts with prickly sensory hairs. The arms were excessively long, with huge hands and fingers curled as if they suffered from a muscular disorder. Yet more terrifying still was the head that bared overgrown pointed teeth and glassy black eyes that twitched within deep sockets. Its nose was sunken and hollow.

The creature towered over Stewart, bending over him to intoxicate itself with his human scent. Then the monster's head leveled with his, its breath cold and rancid.

Stewart squeezed his eyes shut, praying the beast would not devour him, because he'd make for a quick snack! Instead, a snakelike tongue glided across his face, and he pursed his lips to block the fluids from seeping into his mouth.

Realizing this may be the end of him, Stewart couldn't leave this world without a fight. His D&D roleplaying character suddenly came to mind, and he proclaimed in his fantasy role's voice, "With a savage cry of barbarity, the almighty Krolk supercharges his stomp and delivers a powerful blow to the beast's ossified foot!" He raised his leg, but before he could smash the creature's huge foot, a voice cried into the room.

"You!" the voice called.

The creature winced and curled into submission.

Stewart eased his leg down and glanced at the doorway.

Reed was standing there wielding his axe.

Luckily for Stewart, the distraction could not have come at a more precise moment. He thought of running and jumping through the window to escape this house of torment, but he couldn't risk breaking a leg from falling two stories.

Reed advanced toward the creature and readied his weapon, the veins in his forearms bulging as he stood in a battle stance. "You turned too soon!" he grumbled fiercely. Then, without remorse, he raised the axe over his head and swung it down with a mighty roar.

The blade sunk into the creature's gut, and it shrilled in pain.

I'm living a true-life D&D adventure! Stewart thought, the scene unfolding in his favor. When he saw Reed raise the axe again to swing it down on the creature, he bolted from the room and ran down the stairs by twos. He leaped from the last four steps and dashed for the back door, vaguely realizing Sheila was no longer in her rocking chair. He busted open the door and hurdled a flock of chickens, then fled toward the fence line behind the old shed.

Stewart's lungs and legs burned like fire as he stopped at what he hoped was a safe distance from the farmhouse. He could still hear the dying shrills of the creature from afar. His mind was beyond blown. He couldn't believe Rachael was not who she appeared to be. "Nothing like that exists!" he said between heaving breaths.

He slipped between the barbed wire fence and proceeded through the area where the dead trees were located, ducking behind a bush near the barbed wire fence to rest.

Peering through the bush, he spotted Don and Sheila climbing up from the ground in the center of the property. "What the hell?" he muttered. It looked like Rachael's parents had come up through a trap door in the ground. The door had been covered with AstroTurf to blend in with the surrounding grass. Stewart continued to watch them as they closed the door and walked around the front side of the house.

"I've had enough of this!" Stewart said, and spun around and ran toward the dirt road. As he closed in on the road, his feet felt funny. They didn't hurt; they just felt . . . numb.

Stopping to rest again, Stewart sat to remove his sneakers, hoping to find it was only pebbles in his shoes that may have been causing the weird feeling in his feet. With one hand on the ground, and one slipping off a shoe, he felt the earth beneath him vibrating. "What now!" he fretted. *"Can this day get any worse?"*

An eerie silence befell his surroundings as if time had stood still. A moment later, a faint warbling noise filled the air. It was the same sound Stewart first heard coming from the metallic object protruding from the earth, only this sound was louder. The deep, steady resonance transposed into an ear-piercing whine like the tone during an EBS announcement. But where was the radio broadcasting this sound?

The vibrations in the ground became stronger, and Stewart could see the earth and trees trembling. "Earthquake!" he panicked.

———

Stewart crab crawled to the nearest tree and leaned against it, slipping his shoe back on.

When the tremors finally ceased, the warbling sound faded, too.

"Unreal!" Stewart said, and diverted his attention toward something moving in the distance. Sounds of leaves crushing with each step echoed in the woods.

Stewart squinted to see if he could make out what it was. "A deer?" he said, and stood and wiped his hands on the seat of his pants. The dirt road was only a few yards behind him, and without any further hesitation, he turned and headed to his freedom.

Behind him, the footfalls were becoming heavier and faster, and he glanced over his shoulder. "No-no-no-noooo!" Stewart double-timed it when he saw Reed closing in on him. The fence line was almost within reach. The dirt road was right there!

But Stewart was not fast enough to slip through the fence in time. Reed caught up to him, grabbed him, and body-slammed him to the ground.

Stewart kicked and squirmed, trying to break free from Reed clutching at his throat. He dug his nails into Reed's forearm, but Reed's strength was overpowering, and Stewart was losing consciousness.

"Join us!" Reed said in a strange voice. "You will thrive. You will seek. And you will consume." The veins in his arms were thickened and discolored.

Stewart's vision was hazy as he desperately gasped for air. Then, everything faded to darkness.

CHAPTER TWENTY-SIX

Sneaking Out

J ack traversed the living room and snuck behind his father, who was sleeping in the recliner as usual. Bosco, lying on the floor next to him, perked up and eyeballed Jack exiting the house through the back door.

"This should do it," Victor said when Jack stepped out onto the driveway. He was making room in the trunk for supplies. "One backpack filled with ammo . . ." He picked up the gun bag off the ground and placed it in the trunk. ". . . and Dad's shotgun."

"I see you decided on the gun," Jack said.

Victor peered over his shoulder at Jack. "I see you finally came out here. Give me your backpack and pull the motorcycle out of the garage . . . and check to make sure it's gassed up."

Jack handed him his bag and hurried to the dirt bike parked near the back wall in the garage. He twisted off the gas cap and peeked inside the tank. "It's full," he confirmed.

"Good," Victor replied. He picked up the gas canister their mother used for the lawnmower. "I'm bringing this in case we need to refuel. With the way you ride the motorcycle, we'll probably need it."

Jack kept his mouth shut. It had been hard enough to get his brother to commit to helping him, so instigating an argument would not be a wise choice right now. He tightened the gas cap on the motorcycle, flipped up the kickstand, and walked the dirt bike out of the garage. He grabbed his helmet from a shelf near the rollup door on the way out.

Victor closed the trunk and walked to the driver's side of the Camaro. "I'll meet you at the cemetery," he said over the roof of the car. "Keep off the streets as much as possible. You don't have a license for that thing."

"Okay," Jack said.

Victor slid into the seat of his car, cranked the engine, and gave it a few revs. The throaty V8 roared to life.

Jack stood confused as to why his brother revved the engine when he wasn't supposed to start the motorcycle in the drive-way. He slipped the helmet over his head, tightened the chinstrap, and walked the dirt bike to the alley.

———

Jack took a different route to try and beat his brother to the cemetery. He turned onto Glenn Avenue and rode through a new housing development, ignoring the posted NO TRES-PASSING signs. He figured rather than scrubbing through the rutted twists and turns, he'd shoot straight across the area and ride over the recently settled foundations.

Brraaap! Jack pinned the 80cc with the throttle wide open. He swerved around PVC pipes protruding from the founda-tions, easing back on the throttle between each plot. Then he gunned it as soon as he hit the next paved surface. Thankfully, none of the wood frames had been constructed yet for the houses.

He was halfway across the housing development when he noticed a white Escort accelerating ahead of him outside the perimeter of the construction zone. Jack maintained his speed but gave the dirt bike more gas between each concrete slab. Then, as he crossed the end lot, he opened the throttle and went for the hole shot in hopes he'd outrun the security vehicle.

The Escort whipped around and cut him off, spraying him with a cloud of dust.

Jack squeezed the handbrake and fishtailed, nearly crashing into the side of the car.

A short and stubby security officer sprang from his vehicle, slamming the door behind him. His hair was slicked back, and he wore khaki pants and a polo shirt. His hawklike face featured penetrating eyes and a beaked nose. "Cut the engine!" the guy shouted at Jack.

Jack killed the engine.

"What were you thinking!" the man shouted.

"You're the one who almost caused an accident!" Jack said in his defense. "You could've killed me! What were *you* thinking?"

"Did you not see me flashing my lights?" The security guard pointed at a pair of handcuffs clipped to his belt. "I have the authority to arrest you for trespassing!"

"You can't threaten me like that," Jack argued. "Do you know Mike Palinsky? One phone call to him, and you're out of a job."

The disgruntled man took a step closer to Jack. "*Excuse me?* You're breaking the law. Do you not realize it's illegal to disobey posted signs? And worse yet, this is private property! The no trespassing signs are clearly visible." He pointed to a sign closest to them.

"I'm not vandalizing anything . . . just passing through,"

Jack stated.

"How old are you?" the man asked. "Let me see your iden-tification. And take that helmet off so I can—"

Jack kickstarted the motorcycle and revved the engine, drowning the security guard's words. All he could see were his lips flapping like in a poorly dubbed foreign film. He gave the bike some gas, kicked up dirt in the man's face, and sped away.

The man, infuriated, spat dirt from his mouth. "You're in for it now, buddy!"

Riding through several neighborhoods, Jack lost the secu-rity guard. By now, if the guy in his Escort was still trying to follow him, he'd be far enough out of his jurisdiction. The man would be violating his legal limitations if he continued pursuit.

Coming up on Jamerson Street, Jack opened the throttle all the way. Brraaap! Although he ignored Victor's warning to stay off the streets, the road to the cemetery was only a quarter-mile ahead. So he continued down Jamerson until he turned onto Cemetery Way, a gravel road that
led to the cemetery.

———

Jack parked the motorcycle at the rusted iron entry gates. The gates were closed and secured with a chain and padlock. Curved letters that read CEMETERY HILL were centered at the top of the gates between two large spikes pointing toward the sky. Beyond the not-so-pearly gates, crooked tombstones scattered about the acreage of overgrown witchgrass with in-tersecting footpaths twisting between homes of the dead. Most of the headstones were unreadable. Surrounding the century-old graveyard, an eight-foot iron fence barely stood the test of time.

Jack removed his helmet and placed it on the seat of the dirt bike. Then he walked over to his brother.

Victor stood leaning against his car with his arms folded over his chest and his ankles crossed. He tapped a finger on the face of his watch. "What took you so long? You're lucky I didn't leave."

"I got stopped," Jack said.

"Huh? Were you riding on the streets like I told you *not* to do?"

"It's all good," Jack said. "I'll explain later. I took quite the detour, so we should probably gas up before heading to the house. And you should move your car further up just in case anyone passing up there on Jamerson spots it."

"Don't be such a fuss," Victor smirked. "Who put *you* in charge? You're still wet behind the ears, bro. And we better not be here very long because I have things to do. We go in, get your girlfriend, and get out. Capisce?"

"What do you have to do that's more important? Flip the pages of your car magazines?"

"That was dumb," Victor said and popped open the trunk. He grabbed the fuel canister and their backpacks and set them on the ground. "Put some gas in the motorcycle and come back."

Jack picked up the gas can and walked back to the dirt bike. He unscrewed the cap to the fuel tank and peeked inside, squinting an eye. The tank was about half empty. After topping it off, he returned the canister to Victor.

"I'm done," Jack said, handing the gas can back to his brother. Then he picked up his backpack from off the ground and slipped it over his shoulders. "I'll be waiting for you by the motorcycle."

Victor loaded the can into the trunk and turned back to Jack. "Wait! You're just going to leave my bag and Dad's gun on the ground?" he asked irritably. "Take it with you, dude. I'm moving my car."

Jack held back a smart remark at his brother and picked up the items. Victor's backpack felt like it was filled with weights. "Jeez, what do you have in here, rocks?"

"Enough firepower to take out an entire city block," Victor replied. He closed the trunk and cranked the engine, then drove toward a conglomerate of dead trees to the west side of the cemetery.

Jack carried the rifle bag in one hand and practically dragged Victor's backpack with the other to the motorcycle. He secured his helmet and waited for Victor to return.

———

Victor strapped his pack and took the rifle bag from Jack. "Move over; I'm driving."

Jack slid back on the seat, his butt hanging over the edge.

Flipping up the kickstand, Victor started the engine, then glanced back at Jack. "Where are we going?" he asked, raising his voice over the idle.

"Take the dirt trail over there." Jack pointed toward the east side of the cemetery. "You'll see it when you get closer. It leads into the woods and ends behind the property about a half-mile."

"How do you know?"

"I've ridden my bike through it with friends many times. You might want to take it a little slow through the woods because the trail gets kind of narrow, and it's probably muddy from all the rain earlier. And watch out for tree branches."

"Great," Victor said, giving the engine a couple of revs. He took off along the fence line bordering the cemetery and stopped when he got to the open field. He eyeballed the trail leading into the woods, then looked up at the sky. Soon it would be dark. "Hey, get the flashlight out of my pack and shine it in front so I can see where we're going."

"But it's not dark yet," Jack said.

"I don't care. Better have it out now. Be prepared! Wait, I forgot . . . you didn't make it all the way through Boy Scouts."

Jack clenched his jaw as he fished around in Victor's backpack for the flashlight. Instead, he pulled out a .38 Special buckled in a leather holster. "What's this!"

Victor twisted around. "Oh, ha! That's Dad's revolver. I brought it for you to use."

"I didn't even know he had this thing!"

"He keeps it in the coat closet on the top shelf, hidden under his cowboy hat. Careful, that thing is loaded."

"You're crazy!" Jack said.

"You should be thanking me. If you run into trouble, how would you defend yourself without a weapon? It's better to have it and not need it than need it and not have it."

Jack carefully placed the gun back into the bag and dug around again, pulling out a green French Military Anglehead flashlight that Victor used in Boy Scouts. He powered it on and angled it over Victor's shoulder.

Victor shifted the dirt bike into gear and eased off the clutch as he pulled back the throttle. The thunderous sounds from the muffler echoed through the trees when he entered the woods.

"It's coming up." Jack tapped Victor on the shoulder a few minutes later. "When you get to the field, keep going straight and head toward the root cellar."

Victor nodded and curved around a large tree.

When they shot out of the woods, Victor slowed to a stop and gazed at the house across the field.

"What's wrong?" Jack asked.

"This place looks sinister! I've never seen it from this angle. Are you sure you want to go back in there?"

"Wait 'til you get inside," Jack said. "You haven't seen anything yet! But if you're having second thoughts, just drop me off. I know what I'm up against, and I think I can handle the thing inside with Dad's gun."

"You've got quite the ego," Victor said. "If I go in there with you, you better hope we don't get ourselves injured or killed! Mom and Dad don't know where we are."

"We'll be fine," Jack assured him.

Victor spotted the doors to the root cellar about fifty yards ahead. "Let's get this over with," he said and cut across the field.

———

Victor parked the dirt bike at the back wall of the house. "The motorcycle will be better off here," he said. "It won't be out in the open for someone to see and then steal."

"Okay." Jack didn't care.

Daylight was fading, and the clouds diffusing the setting sun were making it darker faster.

"Hey." Victor grinned, adjusting his backpack.

Jack removed his helmet and hung it over one of the bike's handles. "What?"

"One dark night when the moon was green, I came around the corner with my turd machine . . ."

Jack smiled. He remembered the little ditty Victor had made up many years ago. He chimed in and sang in unison with him: "Shots were fired, screams were heard, a lady got hit by my flyin' turd!"

Victor fist-pumped the air. "Hell, yeah! That's what I'm talkin' about! Gotta lighten the mood before all hell breaks loose, right?"

"Good timing," Jack laughed as they set out toward the root cellar.

"Are you sure this is the only way in the house without trying the front door first?" Victor asked.

"Yep," Jack said. "The front door is locked, and all the windows on the lower level around the house are boarded up. The cellar will lead us to the basement. Daisy and I saw a ladder that connected to the ceiling in there, which I'm pretty sure was a trap door that opens into the house."

"What do you mean, 'pretty sure'?"

"We never climbed the ladder to find out," Jack said.

"Great." Victor frowned.

Finally, they stood before the entrance to the root cellar. The doors were still open like Jack and Billy had left them.

Victor shined his flashlight down into the gullet and stood contemplating.

Jack clicked on his own flashlight. "Ready?"

"Let's get it over with," Victor said.

They descended the steps like two amateur sleuths embarking on a mission to solve the case of a mystical creature. The passageway leading down into the cellar was warm and damp.

"Grab a box of ammo from my bag," Victor said when they reached the floor. "It's labeled .44 Magnums."

Jack found the box and handed it to his brother. "I thought you were bringing the shotgun."

Victor unzipped the rifle bag. "I changed my mind," he said, inspecting their father's favorite gun, a Henry Big Boy .44 Magnum lever-action rifle with scope. "This thing holds more bullets." He removed the inner brass magazine tube and dropped eleven cartridges into the loading port near the muzzle. Then he replaced the tube and worked the lever to load a cartridge into the chamber. "That's it." He grinned at Jack. "Eleven bullets. Hopefully, it's more than enough to kill this thing you say exists."

"That looked easy," Jack said. "I've never seen Dad use that gun."

Victor slipped the sling carry over his shoulder. "It's fairly new. I know he bought it for the hunting trip with one of his buddies last year. School hadn't let out for winter break yet when he went without us, remember?"

"I guess so."

"Let me show you the gun you'll be using." He turned his back toward Jack for him to retrieve it from his backpack. "Grab it. And don't drop it!"

The old-school six-shooter had a six-inch barrel, clean and shiny. "This looks like a cowboy gun from the old days," Jack said, admiring the weapon.

"It may look old, but it'll get the job done," Victor responded. "And it's always ready to fire." He pointed to the hammer. "The firing pin is this hammer. All you gotta do is point and pull the trigger. And don't *ever* point it at me. You only have six rounds, so make them count. Once you've shot it a few times, you'll get a feel for the recoil and be able to adjust accordingly. And use both hands when you shoot. Don't be acting all macho with it. It's not a toy."

"How do you know so much about guns?"

"When I got my hunting license, I learned a bunch of stuff

during the gun safety class. Dad gave me some pointers, too. If you ever paid attention when we used to go deer hunting with him instead of playing with your toys at the campsite, you could've learned a thing or two."

Jack grasped the gun with both hands and pointed it at the wall. "You said this gun only shoots six rounds. Did you not bring extra bullets for it?"

"I got a boxful labeled .38 Special in my backpack," Victor said. "Put the gun back in the holster, and don't squeeze the trigger in the process. Then set it on the ground over here and step away. I'll show you how to load it."

"Why do I need to go through all that process just to give you the gun?" Jack asked.

"It's called gun safety. I don't want it going off if you handed it to me and pulled the trigger on accident."

"Oh," Jack said. He slipped the gun into the holster and placed it gently on the ground.

Victor retrieved the firearm and unsheathed it. "You'll need to flip out the cylinder, like so, and dump the empty cartridges before you reload," he said, showing Jack how he popped open the cylinder. "Once you load the new cartridges, you're ready to fire again." He secured the gun back in the holster and strapped it around Jack's waist. "Keep it on your hip until you're ready to use it."

"Thanks for the quick lesson," Jack said.

Victor removed his backpack and pulled a box of ammo labeled .38 Special. He retrieved a handful of cartridges and gave them to Jack. "Stuff these in your pocket for when you need them." He glanced around the cellar. "Now lead the way."

CHAPTER TWENTY-SEVEN

Nothing but the Truth

Billy brushed his teeth and looked at his thin face in the mirror. Although safe at home, he was still paranoid about being harmed again and afraid to go back to school. He thought if he told the authorities what happened, it would only make things worse. He feared he'd be threatened and tormented about it at school.

He kept picturing the incident over and over in his mind. Devin, Denise, and Kyle snuck up behind him in the front of Whitlock Manor. Billy had returned to the house by himself to look for the switchblade comb he lost when he fled with Jack and Stewart. He knew it was there because he had it before the cop stopped them on the way home.

But Devin and his friends had other plans for him that day. Devin was still wearing the splint over his nose from when Jack had punched him in the face.

Billy was so excited when he finally found the comb lying in a patch of weeds. He had been looking for it for almost two hours. As he stooped to pick up the comb, Devin asked, "What you got there, chunky?"

Kyle swiped the comb from him and pressed the button on the handle. "Oh, wow!" he said, intrigued by the concept. "You think this toy is gonna make you look pretty after you get your ass handed to you in a fight?"

"Give it back!" Billy shouted.

Kyle ran the comb through his hair. "Not anymore, fatso." He grinned and folded the comb back into the handle. "My brother would *love* this thing!"

Billy tried to grab it before Kyle slipped it into his pocket.

"Not so fast." Denise got in Billy's face. She wanted to play, too.

Billy took a backward step and crashed into Devin. His eyes lit with fear, as he knew no one dared to touch Devin. His imagination ran wild about the things Devin might do to him. He was outnumbered, so his chances were slim if he tried running away.

Devin grabbed him by the throat. "Look here, you little pissant." He gritted his teeth in anger and pointed at the splint on his nose. "Your loser friend Jack did this to me! So I'll be taking it out on you today. Congratulations, it's your lucky day! I want you to send him a message for me." He glanced over at Kyle and Denise and grinned. "Grab him!"

Billy squirmed to get away, but Kyle and Denise had tight grips on his arms.

"Relax, twerp!" Devin barked at Billy. "You'll only make it worse." He squeezed Billy's cheeks, puckering his lips like a fish. "You'll be going off-grid for a while. And when you return—if you return—tell Jack Stinger he's dead the next time I see him. You got that? DEAD! He'll be wishing for a quick death when I get through with him, but I'm not making any promises. In the meantime, you're gonna pay for what he did to my face!"

"What's on your mind, Devin?" Kyle laughed like a maniac.

Devin released his hand from squeezing Billy's face and suckerpunched him, his fist sinking deep into his belly.

Billy doubled over, and Kyle and Denise could barely hold him up.

"Ugh, he's dead weight!" Denise said.

"Take 'im around to the back of the house," Devin commanded. "Follow me!"

Kyle and Denise pulled Billy's arms and dragged him, his heels digging into the ground like an ox-drawn plow.

"How far are we going?" Kyle heaved, beads of moisture running down his face.

Devin pointed at the root cellar in the field behind the house. "See those two doors? Dump him in there. You two are a couple of wimps—my grandma could do this without breaking a sweat!"

"He's dragging his feet!" Denise argued. Her palms were clammy, and she was losing her grip. "Instead of barking orders, why don't you help us?"

"Because my face hurts if I strain too much," Devin responded pitifully.

Billy squirmed, trying to get to his feet.

"Ahh!" Kyle yelped. "He's getting loose!"

Devin grabbed Billy by the shirt collar, forcing him to the ground. "Both of you are a couple of sore losers just like him, I swear!"

Denise shot him a couple of daggers but kept her mouth shut. She knew better.

When they finally made it to the root cellar, Devin swung open the doors. "On three, toss his ass down," he said.

Kyle and Denise looked at each other, both thinking this was not a good idea.

"Do you understand?" Devin yelled at them like a drill sergeant.

"Snap out of it! Go on three—one . . . two . . . *three!*"

For a moment, Billy felt like he was moving in slow motion until his tailbone clipped one of the steps. He tumbled to the floor, ending up on his back. He looked up painfully at the three goons laughing at him from above.

Devin cupped his hands on the sides of his mouth and yelled as a joke to scare Billy, "Come get your dinner!" Then he and Kyle closed the large doors, and Billy was left in the dark.

Billy struggled to his feet. His back hurt, and he was disoriented. He staggered through the darkness and was trying to find the steps that he tumbled down when something growled nearby.

"He-Hello?" Billy called out.

The animal, or whatever he'd heard, grunted from behind. And before Billy knew it, he was grabbed and whisked away into the depths of the cellar.

———

Spitting toothpaste in the sink, Billy reached for a towel and patted around his mouth. Tommy's reflection appeared in the mirror. "Don't do that!" He jumped. "You don't know what I've been through."

"Sorry," Tommy said. "It's gonna take some time getting used to kidding around with you again. I didn't mean to scare you."

Billy stepped around him furiously and stomped to his bedroom, slamming his door shut. He crashed into a beanbag near his window.

Tommy knocked at his door. "You okay in there? I said I was sorry. Forgive me?"

Billy ignored him.

"Hello?" Tommy continued. "Listen, if you need someone to talk to, I'm here for you. I'm a good listener, you know."

Billy sighed and got up to open the door, then he scurried back to the beanbag and plopped down.

"What happened to you, Billy?" Tommy said, sitting on the edge of Billy's bed. "I looked everywhere for you."

Billy closed his eyes, still traumatized. "You wouldn't believe me if I told you."

"Try me," Tommy challenged him.

———

Sarah stood eavesdropping outside Billy's bedroom door. She hadn't been able to get Billy to tell her what happened since he'd been home. She was surprised to hear him talking to Tommy about it. She folded her arms and leaned her head against the trim around the door and listened.

———

"You have *got* to be kidding me!" Tommy was stunned at Billy's story.

"I told you, you wouldn't believe me," Billy reiterated.

"No, no, I believe you," Tommy said. "It's just hard to take it all in."

———

Sarah was in shock at what Billy had told Tommy and didn't know whether to barge in and confront Billy about his story or wait to see if he'd tell her later. If Devin was to blame, the detective on the case should know about it, but she needed more information to state her case. So she continued to listen.

"I ran into that Kyle kid and his two brothers when I went looking for you at The Bowl and down in the sewers," Tommy said. "One of them had your comb—the middle brother, I think. I tried getting it from him, but the idiots got away after they picked a fight with me."

"Kyle goes to our school," Billy said. "He hangs around Devin a lot."

"I know," Tommy grumbled.

Billy fell silent and stared off into space, his eyes unblinking.

"What's on your mind?" Tommy asked.

"That old house," Billy's voice pitched. "It's pure evil! We should burn it down!"

Their mother suddenly barged into the room. "You know there's no such thing as monsters!" she said, raising her voice. "And if any should even exist, it's that Devin kid you talked about. Who is he, and where does he live?"

Tommy rose from the bed. "Mom, relax! He hasn't been home long, and you're already jumping down his throat."

"Stay out of this!" Sarah said furiously. She turned to Billy, her face and neck flushed.

Billy cringed and sank deeper into the beanbag. He looked at his mother and instead saw an image of the creature. "Get away from me!"
he shouted and burst into tears, cupping his hands over his face.

"Whoa!" Tommy said, stepping toward the doorway. "He's really freaked out, Mom!" Then he muttered before slipping out of the room, "I might have to go check out that house."

"I know your anxiety is high right now." Billy's mother knelt in front of him. She took his hand in hers. "But you have to remember that I'm troubled, too. All the things that ran through my head thinking what might have happened to you just about killed me. I never imagined something like this would *ever* happen to you."

Billy wiped the tears from his eyes and sniffed. "I'm still scared about what happened to me. I was living a nightmare, Mom! *A real nightmare!* But thanks to Jack and Daisy, they were brave enough to help me escape." He lurched forward. "Daisy's still down in that basement! She's probably dead!"

His mother wrapped her arms around him, comforting him to quell his stress. "How did your friends know where you were?" She pulled back and cradled his head in her hands, staring him in his reddened eyes. "We'll tell the detective that's working your case about your friend. I'm sure she's okay."

"You weren't there, Mom," Billy said, leaning back into the bean bag. "You have no idea what's living in that house. That thing is vicious! And there could be more of those things."

His mother smiled. "Take as much time as you need to rest. I'll let the detective know when you'll be ready to talk."

Billy released a deep sigh. "Great. He's not going to believe me, either. By the time he hears that Daisy has gone missing instead of me anymore, it'll be too late for a search and rescue over at that old house."

"I'll let him know tonight," his mother promised, and kissed his forehead. "I'm sorry for eavesdropping on you, and I'll give you some space. Now try and get some rest. If you need anything, let me know. Wake me up in the middle of the night if you have to." She stood, smiled down at him once more, and exited the room.

Tommy poked his head through the doorway.

"Now what?" Billy pouted.

"I'm checking it out tomorrow," Tommy said.

"Checking what out?"

"That house."

"No!" Billy exploded. "You'll get yourself killed!"

Tommy tapped his finger on the side of his skull and said, "Don't you worry, I have a plan."

PART THREE

The Haunting of Whitlock Manor

"Because her flesh knows heat, cold, affliction,
I know fire, snow, and pain."

—Ray Bradbury, *Something Wicked This Way Comes*

CHAPTER TWENTY-EIGHT

A Hunting They Will Go

Jack and Victor continued through the twisting passageway from the root cellar. Their flashlight beams danced off the dirt walls in irregular patterns. "Wow!" Victor said. "This is like in the old days where tunnels led to a secret room. Have you gone far enough to find out?"

Jack stopped. "Only to here," he said, waving his flashlight at the roots dangling from the ceiling. "There's a large room on the other side of this—not a secret room, but it's where I found Billy and where Daisy was taken away by the creature."

"It smells like . . . the old tin can to my penny collection," Victor said, waving a hand in front of his nose. "Do you know what else smells like pennies?"

"Copper?" Jack said.

"Blood!"

"Then you're probably smelling the creature's body rotting," Jack assumed. "Hopefully, it's dead, and we don't have to worry about dealing with it."

With his flashlight clipped to his shirt and the rifle's stock resting against his hip, Victor posed like a nerdy action hero. "Then let's go save your girlfriend!" he proclaimed in a cartoonish voice.

Jack frowned. "You better take this seriously," he said. "You'll regret acting like a dumbass."

"Where's your sense of humor, fool?"

"Not in here, that's for sure," Jack said. He grabbed an armful of roots and pulled them back. "After you," he gestured.

Victor gave him a sour look. "Are you trying to use me as bait for whatever's in there?"

"Fine. Come hold this open for me, and I'll lead the way if you're too scared."

Victor stuck his chest out, then stepped and weaved his way through the roots to the other side. "Hmph, where are we?"

Jack caught up to Victor and shined his flashlight in his face. "Keep your voice down!" he whispered. "If that thing isn't dead, it'll sneak up on you when you least expect—"

"Where does that lead?" Victor interrupted, discovering the ladder.

"That's what I was telling you about earlier," Jack said. "I think it leads into the house."

"Then what are we waiting for?" Victor said. "Let's climb it and—"

The sound of clanging metal suddenly pinched the stale air.

"The creature!" Jack whispered loudly.

Victor spun around with his rifle at the ready. "I don't see anything. I bet it was the house settling, so calm down."

Jack waited for a moment but all was quiet. "I guess let's check out the ladder." He changed his mind and started for the ladder but proceeded too fast. He lost his footing. "Whoa!"

BANG! The muzzle flash lit up the room for a split-second.

"What the hell, Jack!" Victor yelled. He unclipped the flashlight from his shirt and shined it around the room. "You okay? Did your gun discharge on accident?"

"I'm okay," Jack said, dusting himself off. He stooped down and picked up a busted flashlight, holding it up in Victor's light. "I almost rolled my ankle on this."

"Whose is that?" Victor wondered. "And why was your finger on the trigger? Where's the gun?"

"The flashlight is Daisy's," Jack said. "She dropped it when the creature grabbed her. And my gun is over here. It went off when it hit the ground as I slipped."

Victor followed Jack a few feet to where the revolver had landed.

"You could've killed yourself . . . or me!" He picked up the gun and flipped out the cylinder, dumping the cartridges into his hand and tossing the empty round. Then he inspected the weapon. "There's a scratch on the cylinder. Dad's going to be pissed!"

"Sorry," Jack said softly.

"Hand me another round," Victor said.

Jack dug in his front pocket and pulled a single cartridge, giving it to his brother.

Victor reloaded the .38, closed the cylinder, and sheathed the gun back into Jack's holster. "Why did you have the gun out in the first place? Keep it on you *until* you actually need it."

"You said to always be prepared," Jack said. "I thought the creature was going to show up, so I was being proactive. I didn't know it was going to fly out of my hand!"

"That's the thing; you never know," Victor said, shining his light around the room. He picked up something shiny in the distance and walked toward it, finding the pile of debris from the cage that had collapsed. "What's all *that*?"

Jack slipped Daisy's flashlight into his back pocket. "That's the cage where we found Billy. It also collapsed on the creature, so it's probably still piled on top of it." He stopped suddenly.

"Oh, no!"

"Now what?" Victor said.

"The sound we heard—that clanging noise before my gun went off—it may have been the creature moving around! It could still be alive!"

Victor stepped closer to the mangled cage. Many of the bars were bent and twisted, some snapped in half with sharp edges.

"Don't get too close," Jack warned, scanning the area with his flashlight, looking for the injured (or dead) creature.

Furthest away from them, a piece of debris moved. Jack whipped his light toward the direction of the movement. "There!" he pointed. "It's right there—the creature!"

Victor finally witnessed the beast lying on the other side of the busted cage, curled in a fetal position surrounded by a pool of blood. "I see it!" he confirmed. "My God, Jack, I can't believe it. You were right!"

"I told you!" Jack said.

Victor moved to the side for a better look. "It looks like it must have impaled itself and crawled away to die."

"I know," Jack said. "It's like something you'd see in a movie, isn't it?"

"It looks like a Chupacabra—a *dead* Chupacabra!"

"Can you believe that thing grabbed Daisy!" Jack said. "I don't think it has moved since I came home to get you. That means Daisy could still be alive in here somewhere!"

"How do you know there aren't any more of these ugly bastards still lurking around?" Victor said.

"I don't. And I hope there isn't, but if there are, then Daisy could be—"

Suddenly the creature's bloody arm reached up, and like a toy robot hand grabber at an amusement park gift shop, its oversized hand opened and closed.

Jack struggled for his revolver.

Victor cocked the lever to his rifle and aimed it at the monster's head. He breathed in and exhaled slowly, then squeezed the trigger.

BLAM!

The creature's arm dropped like a dead fly when the projectile drilled through its skull.

"That oughta do it," Victor said, backing away. He turned to Jack, noticing his revolver still in its holster. "Too scared to draw your gun now?"

"My reaction time wasn't as fast as yours," Jack responded.

"That's a good thing," Victor chuckled. "At least I didn't have to worry about you accidentally shooting me."

Jack held his hand out. "Look, I'm still shaking."

Victor slipped the gun sling over his shoulder. "Why? I wasn't scared, and you've already been here before."

"So?"

"So . . . " Victor pointed his flashlight in the direction of the ladder. "Let's get to that ladder."

Jack glanced back at the creature and stared at it, looking to be sure it wasn't going to move again. Then he moved on.

———

Upon reaching the ladder, Victor decided he'd go first, so he clipped his flashlight to his shirt and started the climb. He went up ten rungs to the top and pushed up on the trap door in the ceiling. It wouldn't budge. Then he tried banging on the door with his fist. Nothing happened.

"What's wrong?" Jack pointed his flashlight up at his brother.

"It's locked," Victor replied from above. He unclipped his flashlight and shined it closer to the trap door. "Oh. There's a latch." He reached for the fastening, gave it a vigorous twist, and then pushed up on the door. The door flipped up and over, banging against the floor above him.

Jack watched Victor as he climbed through the hole in the ceiling and disappeared. Seconds later, Victor peeked his head down through the opening.

"All clear!" Victor said. "Get up here."

Jack climbed the ladder, and when he made it to the top, Victor reached down through the opening and helped pull him up.

"I guess you were right again—looks like we're in the house," Victor said, closing the hatch behind Jack. A pile of dust swooped up from the floorboards like a thick mist and lingered in the air. "This place is pretty creepy. And it smells like mildew."

Jack coughed and waved the dust out of his face. "This is only one room. Wait 'til you see the kitchen!" He scanned the room 360 degrees then shined his light down on the trap door. The old, ugly rug that he and Daisy discovered when they first explored the house was bunched up on the floor next to the hatch. "This was covering the trap door the whole time?" he said.

Victor threw him a dull glare. "So?"

"So! If only we had moved it, we could've found this trap door a long time ago! And we could've found Billy quicker instead of wasting our time through the tunnel."

"You still would've run into that monster down there," Victor said. "It is what it is. So where do we go from here?"

Jack pointed his flashlight toward the adjacent room. "The

great room is in there. Beyond that is the kitchen, which I haven't gone through yet."

"Lead the way," Victor said, lightning flashing through the upper window above them. "If anything sneaks up behind us, I got your back."

CHAPTER TWENTY-NINE

Unfinished Business

Whitlock Manor was taking a beating from the pouring rain. It was the fiercest storm Jack had seen since he'd been around the house. Water seeped through the boarded windows, trickled down the walls, and dripped between the slats in the floorboards. Then, a deafening thunderclap rattled the walls.

The kitchen looked as if it had been destroyed by a tornado. Rubble was scattered everywhere. Rainwater gushed down dislocated cabinets like a vintage water feature and emptied into a wide gap near the center of the floor.

"This is new," Jack noticed.

Victor stood in awe at the obstacles that lay ahead of him. "What the hell happened here?"

Jack shined his light through the kitchen and into the den area at the adjacent staircase. "We need to get to those stairs. Daisy could be trapped somewhere on the second floor."

"You didn't mention anything about wading through a flood," Victor said.

"It wasn't like this the last time I was here. This is also where we saw the ghost with the red eyes."

"You mean the thing I saw on your videotape? I thought that was staged!"

"Nope," Jack said. "It was real. I saw it with my own eyes. And the camera doesn't lie."

Victor observed the pattern of water flowing to the hole in the floor.

"One wrong step, and you could either break an ankle or get swallowed up in that drainage to who knows where it goes." He turned to Jack and asked, "Is there not another room we can pass through to get to the stairs?"

"I don't know." Jack frowned. "Are you telling me that you're afraid of a little water? You could take your shoes and socks off and wade through it if you don't want to get them wet. It doesn't look deep."

"Are you kidding me!" Victor retorted. He glanced around the area. "Look at this place. I'm not risking stepping on a rusted nail or broken glass or getting bit by a snake."

"You got any other suggestions?" Jack asked.

"Look for something dry, like a piece of wood we can use to bridge over the water."

"Dude, I'm not afraid to get a little wet or dodge a water moccasin. I say we walk through it."

Victor huffed. "Be my guest. I'll wait here and see if you make it across. If you fall on your ass, I'm not rescuing you."

"Some brother you are!" Jack snapped. "The water's not going to hurt you."

Victor shoved Jack aside with a twinge of envy. "I was joking, moron. I'm not afraid." He placed a foot in the water and tested the depth. The water barely flowed over his shoe.

Jack intimidated him with a slight push.

"Don't do that!" Victor retracted his foot from the water. "Test me like that again, and I'll kick you into next week."

"Ooooh, I'm scared," Jack said. "First, you doubted me, and

now you suddenly change your mind. Quit fearing a little water, dork! Now I know why Mom told me you used to always cry before your swimming lessons."

"Not true, doofus," Victor said. "You were still a swaddled little turd in a stroller those days. And for the record, the swim instructor threw me in the deep end the very first day, and I sank to the bottom of the pool before the jackass finally dove in and pulled me up."

Jack couldn't help but grin. "You could've at least tried to tread water."

Victor had no comment, probably because Jack was right. But they were getting nowhere arguing.

Splashing through the water in the kitchen and climbing over piles of rubble, Jack eyeballed the water funneling down into the hole in the floor. It looked as if the hole was manmade, the cutout perfectly round with a smooth center edge. It looked deep.

Lightning lit up the kitchen through a window up high, and another thunderclap rumbled the house.

Victor slipped and almost fell, his shoe punching a hole in the floorboard. "Whaaaa—Ninja skills!"

"You almost bit the dust!" Jack laughed.

"Yeah, this place is full of it, too," Victor joked. "And don't forget that you owe me for getting me into this little adventure of yours."

Jack chuckled. "I'll buy you a frozen toe from the ice cream truck next time it comes down our street! The one with the green gumball you like because it reminds you of your swollen ingrown toenails."

Victor brushed his words away with a flip of his middle finger.

They leaped over a gap in the floor that separated the kitchen and the next room with the staircase.

"Hey, there's a back door," Victor said, adjusting the rifle slung over his shoulder.

Jack stepped between him and the base of the staircase, and Victor turned to him and said, "Could we not have broken in through here to save us from having to climb through all that mess? You know, like you said in the room with the rug you found covering the trap door."

"Very funny," Jack replied. "But all joking aside, isn't the motorcycle parked right outside? I think the door is boarded up from what I recall."

"I think it's around the corner, yeah," Victor said.

Turning back to the staircase, the brothers examined the tall frame that spiraled up like a child's slinky toy. An undisturbed thick layer of dust covered each step. The handrail and spindles were sadly rotted,
crippled over time.

"Well?" Victor paused and gestured at the stairs. "Shall we choose death?" Then he turned and gestured at the back door and said, "Or shall we choose freedom?"

"I know where *you* want to go," Jack said. "You're more than welcome to wait outside if you want to be a—"

A door slammed upstairs, and Jack and Victor turned to each other with fixed stares.

"Daisy!" said Jack. He placed his foot on the first step, and the squeak was immediate and loud. Then, assuming it would hold his weight, he applied more pressure, avoiding grabbing the handrail because it looked too fragile.

Victor shined his light on the next step. "Get your butt up there and rescue your girl. I'll wait here. If you make it to the top without falling through, I'll come up."

"Gee, thanks a lot," Jack said, and proceeded up the stairs.

———

The brothers stood at the top of the staircase, Jack shining his light down the hallway on his left while Victor looked to the right. The two bedrooms and bathroom Jack noticed mirrored the two bedrooms and bathroom Victor also saw on his end.

At the end of the corridor that Victor peered down, he discovered another window which was not boarded. Tilting up his flashlight, he saw the ceiling was buckled due to excessive water damage. "Looks like we're not going this way," he concluded. Then he turned and shined his light at the three closed doors at the opposite side of the corridor. "Any idea which one of these we heard slam shut?"

"I have no clue," Jack said.

Victor pointed at the staircase directly in front of them that was recessed in the wall and barricaded by cobwebs. "Where does that lead to?"

"I would imagine the third floor," Jack quipped.

Victor closed his eyes for a second, refraining from knocking Jack upside the head. "Smartass."

"You asked," Jack said.

Victor glanced down the hallway with the three doors again. "Let's see what's in these rooms before we head to the third floor, shall we? I'll take the first door on the left, and you can take the one on the right."

"I don't think so!" Jack rejected with an edge of fear in his voice. "We need to stick together."

"Dude, we can cover more area if we split up."

"No way!" Jack said through clenched teeth.

"Hey, I'm only trying to make things a little easier for us so we can find your girl and get out of here."

The sound of another door closed.

Victor reversed his direction back to the other staircase. "That came from the third floor!"

"You go first this time," Jack said.

"We're playing this game again, huh?" Victor chuckled. "Why don't you shout for your girlfriend from here and see if that was her before we head up?"

Jack thought he had a good idea and walled his hands to the sides of his mouth. "Daisy! Was that—"

A monstrous voice overpowering Jack's shouting echoed through the house. "Five to enter; one to stay!" it called out.

Victor drew in a breath. "Was that her!"

"It sounded like the voice that I heard on the front porch!" Jack said.

"Then I take it that wasn't your girlfriend," Victor said.

"Stop saying she's my girlfriend!" Jack snapped. "Just because she lives on our street doesn't mean she's my girlfriend."

"Well, pardon me!" Victor smirked.

Jack stepped to the staircase and swatted at the cobwebs like a spaz. "We need to find where that voice came from," he said, still waving his hands to clear the thick webbing so he could make a clean pathway up

the stairs. He turned back to his brother. "Are you coming?"

Victor bit at his lower lip. "Something doesn't seem right."

"What do you mean?" Jack asked.

"The spiderweb," Victor said.

Jack threw his arms in the air. "What about it?"

"Dude, think about it," Victor said. "If your friend is up there, that spiderweb should not be stretched across the width of the stairs, because if she ran through it going to hide, it would have been broken up. Do you think a spider magically spun another web that quick? And did you happen to notice any footprints on the spiral staircase we took coming up here from the first floor? All those steps were caked with dust! Does that not register as odd to you?"

He has a point, Jack thought. But as hardheaded as he was, he said, "What if there's another way up here—like there might be more stairs in one of the rooms we haven't checked out yet?"

"I don't think so," Victor said clearly. "This feels like a trap. I can't handle this supernatural stuff like you."

"Jaaaack," a voice suddenly called out.

"Oh, now that was definitely Daisy's voice!" Jack said. He turned and made his way up the stairs, breaking through the thick spiderweb. Daisy's busted flashlight he had stuffed in his back pocket flipped out and tumbled down the steps.

Then: *BLAM! CLICK . . . BLAM!*

Jack tripped at the top of the stairs. He spun around and saw Victor leaning over the balcony aiming his rifle at the ground floor. "What are you shooting at!"

BLAM! CLICK . . . BLAM! CLICK . . . BLAM! Victor shot a few more rounds, then darted up the stairs toward Jack. *"RUN! RUN!"*

"What were you shooting at?" Jack said with his back pressed against the wall, giving room for Victor to stomp past him.

"Move!" Victor yelled. "That thing from the basement is still alive! It's coming up here!"

"What!" Jack drew his revolver.

Victor pivoted on his heels and aimed his rifle down to the second level, his chest expanding and contracting rapidly. "Why is that thing not dead! I shot it in the head, remember?

Even the rounds I just shot didn't faze it! How in the hell is it still alive?"

A mighty roar cut through the darkness below them.

Jack's hands trembled, but he kept a solid grip on the revolver.

"Get ready," Victor warned, peering through the scope and lining the crosshairs at the top of the spiral staircase below. "As soon as you see it, aim for the head! Then keep firing and make every shot count!"

"I'll try," Jack said nervously.

The creature pounded up the spiral staircase, grunting on each step like an aggressive bull.

"Here it comes!" Victor said.

A streak of lightning flashed through the upper window behind them, illuminating the tip of the creature's head. The first-floor staircase suddenly gave in, and the monster dipped out of sight. The top tread of the stairs pulled away from the second floor, and the whole thing crumbled to the ground like a domino effect.

Victor looked over at Jack, stunned. After the deafening crash diminished, he descended to the second floor.

"Wait!" Jack pleaded. "What are you doing?"

Victor approached the broken edge and peered over at the creature below, buried underneath the rubble. Its arms and legs were twisted pretzels with compound fractures.

Jack found himself rushing down the steps to his brother. He holstered the revolver and looked down over the ripped-away edge, his flashlight spotting the creature. "Shoot it again!" he said. "Just to be sure. Like in the movies, you need to kill it again after it's dead."

"You mean a double-tap?" Victor said. He peered through the

rifle's scope and scanned the debris for a clean shot, but the thick cloud of dust billowing up from the rubble obstructed his view. "I can't see anything with all that dust kicked up."

Jack threw his head back in frustration. He pointed to where the spiral staircase should have been. "How are we supposed to get down from here now?"

Victor slid off his backpack. "We'll figure something out," he said in a calm manner.

Jack looked at him, puzzled. "Now what are you doing?"

Victor unzipped the bag. "Reloading."

CHAPTER THIRTY

Corridor of the Dead

D aisy woke with her body aching and the smell of mildew making her nauseous. *Where am I?*

She felt for her backpack that was not there. Her memory was a haze, and it took a few moments to realize she had separated from Jack.

The back of her shirt was damp and reeked of a tangy odor, like the sulfur-produced bacteria from saliva. She'd peel her shirt off and crawl around in her bra if she had to just so she could get rid of the stench.

"Jack!" she called out, her voice scratchy and dull. The room absorbed the sound of her voice.

No response.

Daisy pulled her knees to her chest, rolled back on her tailbone, and rocked to and fro, tears rolling down her cheeks. "This can't be happening!" she sobbed. *"Please let this be a dream!"* She was lucky the creature whisking her away hadn't killed her, although the incident had been merely a blur to her.

I need to find a way out of here! She didn't want to become the highlight of the five o'clock news as another kid gone missing or her picture on the back of a milk carton. So, rolling onto all fours, she crawled, almost mechanically, waving a hand blindly in front of her in hopes of feeling a wall. But the darkness was swallowing her up, and she thought she was merely crawling in circles.

"Jack!" Daisy cried again. "Are you in here? *Help! I'm scared!*"

Something in the room suddenly caught her eye, and she ceased crawling. The image vanished as soon as she turned toward it. *The red eyes!* She held her breath and remained still, waiting to see if the eyes would appear again. The anxiety was causing strong palpations in her chest, and she could hear her heart drumming in her ears.

The eyes finally appeared again, this time in front of her.

A scream rose in her throat, only to be drowned out by a voice projecting through the room or pit she was trapped in.

"Faaaaallooooow," the voice hissed, and the eyes moved closer to her.

Daisy dug her fingers into the ground, as there was nothing that she could grip to brace herself for what she thought the entity might do to her. "Somebody help me!" she shrieked. "Help! Please!"

The voice hissed again, this time with more emphasis. *"Faaaaallooooow!"*

What? Is it trying to help me? She could see the outline of the wraith's cloak fluttering in midair like a dead ferryman awaiting payment to guide her into the unknown.

Daisy stood unsteadily, her legs as weak as a fawn attempting to stand for the first time.

The entity moved backward.

Daisy took a small step forward.

The glowing red eyes moved back again. And as Daisy took more baby steps toward the apparition, the eyes kept moving yet further.

Her hands finally touched a dirt wall, and her fingers naturally gouged into it, the muck seeping between them and clumping underneath her nails. Then, wiping her hands on the seat of her pants, she rounded a corner where she saw the apparition had turned. The entity *was* helping her! But where was it leading her?

Her fingertips glided along the dirt walls on either side of her, the passageway narrowing the further she walked. This *had* to be the way out!

Then, she noticed a flickering light ahead. A light at the end of the tunnel? Perhaps there was hope for her yet!

The red eyes swooped up the tunnel and disappeared into the wall without a salutation, its deed fulfilled.

Daisy paused briefly, waiting to see if the apparition would appear again. It didn't, so she kept on down the tunnel, her eyes focused on the light up ahead. She moved quicker, feeling more confident in herself and hanging on to the hope that she would finally escape this evil place.

—————

Is that a doorway? Daisy thought intuitively, approaching with caution. What she thought was the end of the tunnel, and her way out, led into another room—a smaller room.

She paused outside the crooked doorway etched in the earth and peered inside the room. The dank smell of the earth was more pungent here.

Garments lay piled in one corner of the room like dirty laundry. Across from the clothing was a decrepit table leaning against the dirt wall, coated with cobwebs and a pattern of lit candles stair-stepping stacks of old books. An overturned brass urn spilled shriveled stemmed flowers, and a peculiar wooden object the size of a softball rested on a velvety pouch.

Someone lives here! Daisy thought. She stepped into the room and picked up the wooden spherical object, which for some reason seemed to be significant. She blew off the dust then cupped it in her hands, studying it curiously. It looked like a mechanical puzzle of some sort; its parts could slide, twist, and interlock with other pieces.

"What is this?" she muttered, her fingers gently tracing its irregular parts. Something shiny was inside it; she could see it between the slits. Her fingers worked the pieces while flipping the object this way and that. She was never good at solving puzzles, but this one was fascinating. What tempted her even more in trying to figure out the contraption was the reward it offered inside. Could the thing even be solved?

"How does this work?" she said, frustrated. She began sliding and twisting the pieces aggressively. "Open up, you piece of—"

CLICK!

Her eyes lit up.

The object began twisting robotically on its own from tiny gears churning inside, and the top sprang open like a jack-in-the-box. Then the face of the puzzle swung outward in a smooth motion like French doors.

Daisy held the object in the palms of her hands at eye level, peeking inside at something moving behind a dangling piece. She reached her fingers into the gadget and was able to flip the piece up and push the tips of her index and middle fingers further in.

The object felt fuzzy. *A stuffed animal!* she thought excitedly. Her two fingers pinched the toy, and she carefully pulled it out.

Her big smile was instantly wiped off her face when several long, hairy legs expanded in her hand. She shrieked and leaped back, dropping the puzzle at her feet. But the live tarantula she thought she had flicked from her hand had clung to the underside of her wrist!

Daisy twisted her wrist, and the eight-legged creature crawled up her arm faster than her reflexes and perched atop her shoulder. She froze and held her breath. She couldn't allow it to crawl to her head and get tangled in her hair! So, she surprised it, moving her hand slowly up her chest and quickly flicking it off her.

The spider flew against the wall behind her and landed on the ground with a soft thud, only to crawl back to her.

Daisy shrieked and hopped around the room to evade the arachnid climbing up her leg. Her anxiety level skyrocketed. Now she was feeling phantom pricks like a cluster of baby spiders were dispersing up her arm. She rubbed her arm and kept feeling at her hair, but she could not find where the stealthy tarantula was hiding.

The puzzle she had dropped twitched. *Oh, you went back in there*, she thought and crept toward the gadget. She gave it a swift kick, and it spun through the air and smashed against the wall. The puzzle broke apart, spilling a black orb the size of a tennis ball that rolled to her feet.

The tarantula crept out of the damaged shell that was the puzzle and scuttled under the table.

Daisy glanced down at the orb, then over at the spider hiding behind a table leg. She scooped up the sphere and stepped back, fearing the spider would run after her again. But it never budged.

Cradling the sphere in her hands, Daisy was mesmerized by

its smoothness. It was shiny, and she could see her reflection in the object. As she held it up, a blue light reflected from the center like the dye against the window of a Magic 8-Ball. "Is this a crystal ball or something?" she wondered. "This must be worth a lot of money!"

Daisy glanced at the spider underneath the table, making sure it was still a good distance from her as she inspected the sphere.

Dirt sprinkled down the back of her shirt, and she jumped, thinking it was another spider. Behind her, the wall was vibrating.

What began as granules coming down from the ceiling became a conglomerate of chunks of dirt falling in heavy intervals. Then the wall mysteriously opened—a hidden door rather—and an older woman appeared at the secret doorway wearing an ugly, raggedy sleeveless dress. Her silver hair was long and wiry. Her crispy-looking nose was bumpy with a prominent curve in the dip like the old witch imagined by the *Hansel and Gretel* fairytale.

Daisy's jaw sprang open as she realized the woman was someone she knew. "Ms. Bagleweed?"

"Delanore," the old lady's voice crackled. "Call me Delanore."

———

"What's the cafeteria lunch lady doing here?" Daisy mumbled when Delanore Bagleweed stepped through the secret doorway. "The rumors were true! An old lady *does* live in this house!"

Delanore clasped her hands together in front of her and said in a sweet voice, "I see you solved the puzzle ball and met Gerald."

"What is this?" Daisy held up the orb. "And who's Gerald?"

Delanore's eyes cut to Daisy's feet. The tarantula had snuck up next to Daisy with its front legs propped up on her shoe.

Daisy yelped.

"It's okay!" Delanore assured her. "He won't hurt you. He's thanking you for setting him free!"

"I hate spiders!" Daisy cringed.

Delanore made a strange hand gesture at the arachnid. Like an obedient pet, the spider scuttled back underneath the table. "The orb you possess is unique," Delanore said. "Keep it close, and don't let it out of sight." She nodded over at the table. "Do you see the pouch on the table where you picked up the puzzle ball?"

Daisy turned her head toward the table, then back at Delanore.

"Take the pouch and place the orb in it for safekeeping. Its powers are strong and must be hidden from view."

"I'm not going near that table with the spider under there!" Daisy snapped.

"He's harmless," Delanore said.

Daisy looked at the velvet pouch on the table again, confused as to why she had to grab it. She fixed her eyes back on Delanore. "What's so powerful about this thing? It's just a glass ball."

"The orb of light has claimed you as its keeper. Its power has unlocked your abilities to break the curse of the underground."

Daisy stared at her. "What abilities?"

Delanore smiled. "Keep the orb close," she repeated. "It must be protected in the pouch when not in use, for it possesses many wonders beyond your control."

"What kind of power can this produce?" Daisy asked.

"Please, take the pouch," Delanore insisted, ignoring Daisy's question.

"Tell me how I can get out of here first," Daisy tried to bargain. "I've been trapped down here for so long, my mother is probably worried sick about me!"

"It's important that the orb be protected first," Delanore said. "Protect it by placing it in its pouch, then I shall show you the way out."

Irritated, Daisy sighed and reached for the pouch on the table, making a quick grab before the spider had a chance to move. She inserted the orb at the lip of the bag, thumbed it down inside, and then pulled the strings taut. "There," she said. "Now, how do I get out of here?"

Delanore nodded toward the table again. "Take the lantern and the book of matches from underneath the table," she said.

"I got as close to that spider as I'm going to get," Daisy fretted. "Do you have a bad back? Why can't you get them? This is your place, isn't it?"

"You need not worry about Gerald." Delanore grinned. "Take the lantern and matches. You'll need light to see your way out. This is your destiny. I can only guide you."

Daisy rose on the tips of her toes, thinking if she wanted to get out of this place, she needed to overcome her fears. She dove under the table, an arm's length from the spider, and grabbed the lantern and box of matches as quick as she could.

Gerald never twitched.

"Good," Delanore said. "Give the lantern a few pumps and hold a flame underneath to light it."

Daisy dusted off the lantern. She had never used one of these before. Trusting Delanore was an expert, she pumped it a few times, pressurizing the fuel tank. Then she struck a match and inserted it into the globe.

WHOOSH! The mantles burned to life.

"Time is running out," Delanore warned. She pointed to the doorway from which she had entered. "The passage beyond is partly your way out. When you discover the green light, you'll be instructed where to go from there."

"What do you mean?" Daisy wanted clarification. "I can't just walk out of here like the way I came?"

"Get to the light, and you will understand." Delanore gestured toward the doorway. "And remember, don't lose sight of the orb!"

Since the orb was too big to fit in her pockets and she did not have her backpack, Daisy tied the pouch around her wrist to keep it secure.

As she stepped through the doorway, she turned back to Delanore and asked, "Was it you that led me to this room—the red eyes?"

"That must've been William. He slips down this way sometimes."

"William Whitlock?" Daisy's eyes widened.

"Yes," Delanore replied, pointing at the ceiling. "He's the original owner of Whitlock Manor above us."

Daisy thought about the articles at the library when she and Jack researched the history of Whitlock Manor. Delanore must be related to William Whitlock! She turned and held up the lantern, the light illuminating the outer walls of a sewer pipe with a hole that looked like it had been blasted with an explosive.

Daisy turned back once more and discovered Delanore had disappeared. "Hello?" she called through the doorway. She gazed at the table and saw the spider was gone, too. "I must be losing my mind!" She spun around and stepped through the etched hole in the side of the sewer pipe.

Standing in the pipe, Daisy looked left, then right. "Which way do I go?" she said, her voice carrying through the tunnel. She noticed water trickling down the center of the pipe, so she followed it to the right.

———

The reverberations from Daisy's footsteps pinged through the sewer system, which stunk of hydrogen sulfide and ammonia.

After several minutes of winding through twists and turns, she stopped and threw her arms against the walls of the tunnel for leverage, catching herself from falling over the edge at a four-foot drop-off.

The vast area below flowed into a cave-like opening. Rocks spiraled in a pattern along the outer edges of the entrance like a mouthful of teeth.

Daisy squatted on the lip of the pipe. Then, setting the lantern down next to her, she dangled her feet over the edge. The corners of her mouth were crusted from dry saliva. She could feel the sweat rolling down her back and armpits, getting a whiff of the warm, smelly draft billowing through the pipe behind her.

She knew she couldn't stay in one place for too long because the lantern would eventually run out of fuel, unless carbon monoxide poisoned her first. She eased herself down the four-foot drop, then grabbed the lantern and started toward the mouth of the cave. Raising the lamp at the cavity, Daisy saw the inner circumference was shaped like a funnel. The further she'd walk through it, the narrower the walls and ceiling would become. *A claustrophobic nightmare!*

———

Tree roots pushed through the walls, making it more difficult for Daisy to walk as she had to turn sideways and squeeze through a thin passageway. But she had to keep moving to avoid getting stuck.

She extended the lantern out in front of her, freeing up some room to walk. Unfortunately, the light was heating up the tight space like an oven and her face was getting hot.

Finally, she forced herself through the cramped space and stumbled into a wide-open area. Then, she saw the light.

Meet me at the green light, Daisy recalled Delanore telling her. Hoping she wasn't hallucinating due to lack of oxygen down here, she started toward the light, the walls closing in again.

As she moved through another confined space, something snagged on her shirttail, and she paused to untangle a root protruding from the wall. "What the—"

Dirt cascaded down the wall and sprinkled onto her shoes, slowly filling the corridor. Daisy set down the lantern and grabbed at her shirt, ripping it free from the root. Then she scooped up the lantern and squeezed from the thin walls filling with dirt and into another open area.

Behind her, the walls crumbled and filled the pathway from which she came. She leaped forward just before the implosion came down on top of her, blocking her way back.

An unpleasant odor rose from a unique cocktail of contaminants mixed with the dirt that had collapsed. Daisy turned and scurried away from the walls. The air was getting thinner. She set the lantern down and slapped her filthy hands over her face and wept. "I can't do this!" Her lips trembled. "Why did I even *think* about coming back to this place! How could I be so stupid? *I'm going to die here!*"

Looking up, Daisy sniffed and wiped her face with the sleeves of her shirt. The green light was more prominent up ahead. She was getting closer to ending this nightmare—she hoped.

Daisy grabbed the lantern and pressed on, her legs killing her and her back sore.

A low, grumbling sound slithered up from the area that had caved in behind her, and Daisy paused and looked back in the direction of the sound. Dirt from the ceiling dotted her face from the vibrations of the rumbling noise. *Oh my God, it's happening again!*

Then, bursting through the backfill, a wave of dirt pushed along the ground and rolled toward Daisy. Daisy tripped over her own feet trying to flee and shrieked as she took a fall, the lantern flying from her grasp. Unable to get up in time, she saw that the object pushing the dirt in her direction looked like it was going to run over her. She braced for impact.

A rectangular object burst through the moving dirt and crushed the lantern before finally losing its momentum and halting inches from Daisy's feet.

Daisy found the strength to stand up. Thankfully, the green light from the area behind her offered enough light for her to see. She glanced down at the object—a coffin that had tipped onto its side. The lid sprang open, and the brittle frame of a corpse flipped out. The skull detached from its spine and rolled onto Daisy's shoe, greeting her with a gaping jaw.

Daisy screamed and kicked the skull, sending it streamlining back into the casket. Then her eyes locked on another casket lined up behind the one that had flipped open. And from above, more coffins protruded down through the ceiling like bats in a cave.

Daisy was suddenly breathless. *I'm trapped underneath the cemetery!*

CHAPTER THIRTY-ONE

Spaces Between Time

Daisy moved toward the green light, fearing the ceiling would cave in as she progressed through the tunnel. She pictured the cemetery above her becoming a giant sinkhole with caskets raining down on top of her if she didn't find her way out of here in time.

The passage curved slightly to the left at a downward slope. The light ahead was getting brighter.

Her feet slipped on the damp ground, and she stumbled forward through another stretch of tunnel, throwing her arms out against the walls to catch herself from landing flat on her face.

Finally, she spotted the light source as she came around the bend, and the area opened to a vast chamber. Green light pulsated subtly around the place, and the dirt walls and ground were surprisingly smooth. There were no doorways or other sections of tunnel that branched off.

"This is what I've been working toward?" Daisy said. "A dead end!"

She was at least enthralled by one feature in the room—a spinning ball of green light suspended between two prongs. The U-shaped bars of metal resembled a gigantic tuning fork. There had to be a reason for this thing to exist, being at this very distinct location. So maybe there was still hope for Daisy yet.

She approached the object slowly, being cautious of her surroundings as she stepped further into the room.

It was mesmerizing, the light, and she could feel the energy from it pulling her magnetically, reeling her in as if a gravitational force was in control. Daisy barely had to take a step; the energy within the room was guiding her toward the light.

Then, the familiar voice. A whisper.

Daisy froze, not of her own accord, but like she had lost all functions of her motor skills. As if in a coma, all she could do was listen, unable to react to anything physically.

"Five to enter, one to stay; the world deceived, a future to pay," the voice said.

Delanore!

"Unlock the orb of light and break the curse of the underground," the voice continued.

The orb in the pouch tied to Daisy's wrist began glowing through the fabric, pulsating a blue color to the rhythms of the green light in the room.

"Hear the sound of my voice, follow it to enter the realm, for it is here that you shall adopt a new strength and walk the earth to eliminate a hidden threat. Fear not, you'll be unseen, but your presence will be known. Your powers are greater with four."

The green light suddenly faded, and the room fell into total darkness. Although the source was not controlled by a power supply, Daisy could subconsciously hear it shutting down like heavy machinery. Still in a transfixed state, she felt like she was balancing between the spaces of time. Like in cartoon physics, there was no gravity until she looked down, then she'd drop into a freefall. But she never looked down.

Her mind shielded her thoughts and focused strictly on the future as her paralyzed body encroached upon an unknown destination.

Then, appearing against the blackness, a twinkling star blinked. Daisy wanted to reach out and touch it, but the illusion molded itself into the shape of a person. And she heard that same, riddled voice speak to her again: "The force of an army you must acquire. Gather the alliances that you desire. The power of light you shall receive. Once complete, return to me."

A bolt of lightning zapped from the entity, creating a forcefield around her.

The green ball of light suspended between the prongs in the underground reappeared, and Daisy felt her body drifting toward the light. Streaks of multi-colored lights stretched past her, and she was launched into a warp speed, her body catapulting through the universe.

I'm on my way to heaven! Daisy's subconscious mind celebrated.

The colored lights zipping past her abruptly faded, and Daisy found herself surrounded by darkness again. The feeling of claustrophobia was settling in, her arms and legs still unable to move. Her lungs burned for oxygen, and the taste of soil lingered in her mouth. Was she returning to a state of consciousness?

A swift burst of energy shot through her system, forcing her to finally move her extremities. She felt trapped within a compact space, the area tightening all around her as she gasped for breath. Muffled squishing sounds filled her ears.

Daisy's head felt like it was going to explode. Then her eyes opened and burned, still only seeing darkness. *I'm blind!* she thought as her arms and legs propelled faster and faster through a dry yet grainy substance.

Her hands pushed up through the earth, and her fingers stretched upward toward the sky. Then, angling her hands down on top of the dirt and pulling herself up, Daisy rose out of the ground like a zombie digging itself from the grave.

She spat out a mouthful of dirt and took a long, deep breath before collapsing on her back, weeping and wiping her eyes.

That first intake of oxygen felt so good!

MONDAY, MARCH 20. 8:05 AM

Amidst the dilapidated cemetery, Daisy saw it as the most beautiful sight she had ever seen! And the golden threads of morning light made it all more fascinating.

She sat exhausted as a gentle breeze nipped at her goose-flesh. Her clothes were filthy, her hair was a tangled mess, and her fingernails were caked with dirt. She was a dirty rag doll.

She slapped a hand over her mouth. "I just dug myself from a grave!" She looked at her hands, all scraped and filthy. "Impossible! This *can't* be real!" But seeing the pouch holding the orb still secured around her wrist convinced her otherwise. Her wrist was sore from the string rubbing her flesh raw.

Daisy glanced around at the ancient gravestones and monuments surrounding her. It felt like several days had transpired since she was trapped in the tunnels beneath Whitlock Manor.

Her eyes followed the spiked iron fence that bordered the cemetery to the tall gates with the CEMETERY HILL lettering arced across the top. Then she glanced over to the far side of the iron fence, spotting a Camaro beneath a shaded tree. "That's Jack's brother's car," she said. "Yes! Help at last!"

Daisy stood and stretched. Then she followed the foot trails that weaved between the headstones and limped toward the gates. She grabbed the gates and pushed and pulled madly, but the heavy chain and padlock securing them would not allow her to escape. "No!" she shouted angrily, and walked to the other side of the fence where Victor's car was parked.

She put her face between the gaps in the fence and shouted, "Victor! It's me, Daisy. Help!"

Not getting a response, she tried to see through the back window of the car if Victor was inside, but the windows were tinted too dark. "Victor!" she cried out again. "Help!"

No response.

Daisy pushed away from the fence. *When will this streak of bad luck end!*" she howled, pulling her hair in a fit of rage. "Why does everything always happen to *me!*"

She limped back to the entry gates again and violently shook them as hard as she could, the chain rattling loudly. She drew in air and let out a piercing scream that burned her lungs. Then, as she released her grip from the gates, an electrical current zapped from her fingertips! The electric discharge danced around the parameter of the gates and outlined the letters along the top.

Daisy backed away a considerable distance and glanced down at her hands. Thin streams of smoke rose from her fingertips. Strangely, she felt no pain.

She glanced back up at the gates and saw sparks flying amidst heavy sounds of crackling, the electrical currents charging the gates.

Daisy stepped further back, keeping an eye on the gates. And moments later, the gates blew from their hinges! They soared through the air, end over end, landing in the trees. The vibration from the blast was so powerful, it shook the ground and triggered the Camaro's anti-theft alarm system.

Daisy stood baffled. *The power of light you shall receive*, she recalled Delanore's voice. Then she thought, *Is this my new ability she was referring to? How did I do that?*

A smile stretched across her face, and she walked out of the cemetery.

CHAPTER THIRTY-TWO

Jack Sees the Future

*P*REVIOUSLY - *SUNDAY, MARCH 19. 7:52 PM*
    A mournful silence fell on the third floor of Whitlock Manor. Only one room occupied this floor, and Jack's and Victor's light beams met at its rotten door.

"I bet this is the door we heard closing," Victor said. He looked down and saw green light pulsating like Morse code underneath the door, then turned to Jack and said, "What's going on in there, a disco party?"

Jack shrugged.

Victor pressed his ear against the door. "I don't hear anything," he said, and took a step back.

Jack grasped the doorknob and pushed the door open, giving it an extra shove with his foot because it dragged the floor. He and his brother stood in awe as a green light from the room reflected from them in a photoelectric effect. But more peculiar was an old woman with long silver hair, sitting in a meditation pose on the floor facing a window with her back turned to them. A green, pulsating halo outlining her body illuminated the room.

Jack cut his eyes at Victor. "You're seeing what I'm seeing, right?" he whispered.

Victor nodded, then shined his flashlight on the old woman.

He leaned into the room, trying to figure out what the woman was doing. "Is she conjuring a spirit or something?"

Jack grabbed Victor's arm. "Get back! What if she turns around and has a demon face? You know, like in the movies when the camera dollies in behind a little kid, and he turns around with a bloody skeleton-looking face and scares the crap out of you."

Victor rolled his eyes. Then, leaning to Jack's ear, he whispered, "What's in her hands?"

"I don't know," Jack whispered back. "But hold this for me." He handed his flashlight to him and peeled off his backpack.

"What are you doing?" Victor said.

Jack unzipped his bag. "I want to capture this on video!" He pulled out the camcorder and powered it on. Then, hoisting it onto his shoulder, he crept into the room to get a better shot.

"I don't think that's a good idea, bro," Victor warned.

Jack pressed the record button and peered through the viewfinder, zooming in on the old woman from behind. He panned down at her midsection. "It's a ball spinning in mid-air!" he said out the side of his mouth. "This is some crazy witchcraft!"

The woman finally spoke. "Come in." Her voice pinched the air.

Jack lowered the camcorder and glanced back at Victor, slack-jawed.

Victor set the flashlights on the ground to where he could still keep the woman lit. Then he low-readied his rifle and cocked it, loading a cartridge into the chamber.

"I've been expecting you," the woman said. She lifted her hands, and the glowing sphere rose, spinning faster and faster in the air. The shape expanded into a vortex hovering before her.

Jack continued with the recording. *This is good stuff!*

Victor peered through the scope at his target, lining up the crosshairs to the back of the old woman's head.

"Come closer," the woman insisted in a nonthreatening tone. Then she chanted her riddle. "Five to enter, one to stay; the world deceived, a future to pay."

The words sent chills down Jack's spine. "*You're* the one who I heard whispering through the window on the front porch!" he said, trying to keep the camera steady. Then, remembering the research he and Daisy conducted at the library regarding Whitlock Manor, he asked, "Are you related to William Whitlock?"

The old woman turned her head slowly like a possessed porcelain doll. She smiled into Jack's camera, her face filling the frame.

"Ms. Bagleweed!" Jack flinched. "What are *you* doing here?" He turned to Victor, his eyes wide.

But Victor was too concentrated on keeping the woman in his line of sight through the scope.

Ms. Bagleweed's body twisted at the torso 180 degrees, and she glared at the boys with a creepy smile.

Jack's eyes widened, expecting to see the woman projectile-vomit pea soup across the floor.

"Receive the powers of sight and fire." Ms. Bagleweed busted out another riddle. "The force of an entire army you must acquire."

Victor steadied his rifle. "She's nuts!" he said. "How is she doing this and not in serious pain right now?"

Jack zoomed out at the woman gesturing toward the vortex

with half her body turned toward him. "Step into the light to reunite," she said.

Victor peeled his eyes from the scope and stared at Jack in confusion.

Jack zoomed back in on Ms. Bagleweed and asked, "Reunite with who, our dead relatives?"

"Dude, is this for real?" Victor said. "This is some really strange poltergeist sh—"

"Your friend waits for you!" The woman projected her voice.

"Daisy?" Jack said. "Where is she! If you did something to her, I'll—"

"Enter the realm," the woman interrupted again. Then, another riddle. "Fear not, you both shall be unseen, but your presence will be known."

"Jack, this woman is not the cafeteria lady that we know!" Victor said. "She's got to be a demon or something. So help me, if she starts turning into something wicked, I'll put a bullet through her brain!"

Ms. Bagleweed frowned, and her body untwisted like a corkscrew as she stood and faced Victor. Apparently, the barrel of a gun pointing at her head did not faze her. She gestured toward the vortex again. "This is the exit you seek!"

Victor dared her to take a step toward him.

Although she looked like the Ms. Bagleweed that Jack knew, he figured this was not her. The lunch lady was kind and spirited, never demanding.

Victor lowered his rifle. "Screw this place. Let's get out of here!"

"What?" Jack said. "We can't just leave after we've come this far!"

"You really want to jump through that . . . that whirlwind thing and die?" Victor said. "This is all too bizarre, man." He slung the rifle over his shoulder and added, "My gut tells me this is something we should not be messing with. I mean, killing that creature back there was proof that evil exists! This woman could turn into something worse! I'm sorry about Daisy, but we have to do what's right."

Although Victor's theory made sense, Jack didn't want to accept it. "Okay," he said finally, feeling guilty that it was his fault for pulling Daisy into this ghost hunt in the first place. "Let's go."

———

"What do you think she meant by that thing being our only way out?" Jack asked Victor as they stood outside the doorway.

"Who knows and who cares," Victor replied. "The only thing I *do* know is we need to jet before she decides to come out of her frozen trance back there and starts chanting more stupid riddles."

They started back to the stairwell, but a funny feeling overcame Jack. "I think we should go back," he said.

"Don't be stupid!" Victor snapped. "You can go back if you want—maybe throw something in that portal and see what happens if it makes you feel any better. But I'm getting out of here, end of story."

Jack's eye caught something extending up from behind Victor, like a long prickly stick. Then another one reached up over his shoulder and curled down in front of him to his chest. "Look out!" Jack yelled and drew the .38.

Victor ducked out of the way before he got shot. "What did I tell you! Don't be pointing that thing at me!" He spun around to see why Jack had pulled his gun on him.

Climbing the staircase was a gigantic human-sized spider! The hairs on its long legs sensed the floor and stood in a defensive pose, taller than Jack and pointing its furry abdomen toward the ceiling. Teardrops of venom accumulated at the tips of its fangs.

Jack shot at the spider and missed, the gun nearly flying out of his hands from the kickback. How could he miss something so huge and only a few feet away!

The spider raised its pedipalps and slammed them down, then it speed crawled toward him.

Victor took a shot, penetrating the animal's abdomen and stopping it in its tracks. He cocked the lever, ejecting the shell, which also loaded the next round into the chamber. He fired again and hit near the same area, pus-like fluid leaking from the wounds.

The spider dipped its abdomen, then rotated toward him.

"Run!" Victor shouted at Jack, cocking the lever. "I'll hold it off!"

Instead of bolting down the stairs, Jack ran back to the room with the portal.

"No! Downstairs! Get down—"

The spider inched forward, then hesitated, as though waiting for the best opportunity to leap and tackle Victor. But Victor was too quick for its thinking and fired another shot, hitting its eye.

The spider crawled backward, waving its pedipalps madly.

CLICK. BLAM! Another shot, and the animal fell forward onto its cephalothorax, its abdomen shooting straight up.

"Down for the count!" Victor said, then ran after Jack.

Curling its legs underneath the abdomen, the spider shrunk.

Not because it was dead, but the spell cast upon it was reversing. Reduced to the size of a fist, Gerald scuttled across the floor after the boys.

———

Jack was standing in front of the vortex when Victor stormed into the room, the woman still frozen in the same position.

"GO! GO! GO!" Victor screamed. The spider was hot on his trail!

Jack had no time to react before Victor came up on him fast and shoved him into the portal and dove in behind him.

———

The two brothers tumbled through the void, streaks of multicolored lights zipping past them. Seconds later, time stopped, and Jack and Victor floated in an empty space of darkness.

Then, out of nowhere, a burst of light exploded into a cosmic inflation and faded, like the universe had taken their picture with a camera flash.

The canvas of space was filled with brushstrokes of shapes and colors. Then, rotating beneath Jack and Victor, a 3D model of the interior of Whitlock Manor came into view and they were consumed back into the house of hell.

———

MONDAY, MARCH 20. 9:02 AM

Jack and Victor found themselves lying in the foyer, sunlight creeping through the cracks around the front door.

"What happened?" Victor said groggily and sat up. "I feel nauseous." He glanced over at Jack lying on the floor a few feet away. "You good? You look like how I feel!"

Jack sat up. "Yeah, but a little dizzy." He felt nauseous, too. If only he had an alcohol swab to sniff, it would ease the queasiness—something he learned from his mother.

"How is it daylight?" Victor wondered, seeing sunlight spilling through the upper window. He grabbed for his rifle that was not there. "No! Where's the rifle?"

Jack grabbed at the empty holster on his waist. "The revolver's gone, too! We must've lost them during the teleport."

"That's just great!" Victor said. "Even if we survive this, Dad's going to kill us!"

"Hey, look on the bright side. Dad can replace his guns, but he can't replace us," Jack said, unconcerned. He felt for his backpack, thankful that it was still there because his camera was inside it. He knew the footage on the tape couldn't be replaced. If the camera were lost, no one would believe what he and his brother had experienced. "At least we have our packs and the ammo."

Victor stood and dusted himself off. "Yeah, but what good is ammo without weapons?" He extended a hand to Jack and helped him up, then he turned and tried opening the front door. But it wouldn't budge, like it was locked from the outside. "Oh, I'm not letting this shithole of a place win!" He kicked as hard as he could at the door, and it flew open, the padlock on the outside ejecting through the air and bouncing and skidding across the porch.

The brothers stepped outside.

Glancing around from the porch, Jack shaded his eyes from the sunlight peeking over the horizon. "Hmm."

"What?" Victor said.

"It's not raining."

"So?"

"It always rains when I'm here. It was raining last night, re-member?"

"Okay?" Victor smirked. He peered over the railing past the front yard. "Hey, is that Mike's car out there?"

"Seven-thirteen is his unit number," Jack said. "Is that the number on the car?"

"Um, yeah," Victor verified. "He must be scoping out the place." Then he said feverishly, "Oh, man! We need to get to the motorcycle before he confiscates it!"

The brothers flew down the rickety steps and rounded the side of the house, sloshing through mud and tall grass. But be-fore they could make it around the backside, Jack stopped as a sharp pain surged through his head. He slapped his hands over his face in agony. "Ahh!"

Victor turned around. "I thought you said you were okay," he said, frowning. "What's wrong?"

Jack leaned forward and moved his hands over his knees like he was about to puke. "My head," he said, removing his backpack. "It's killing me! It's like a migraine or something. I need to—"

"Dude, don't die on me!" Victor said, only half teasing.

"What the hell!" Jack said. "I just saw Stewart! He's in trou-ble!"

Victor looked at him strangely. "Who?"

"My friend Stewart."

"Okay, what do you mean you just saw him? Where is he?"

"I don't know," Jack said. "Everything was so bright. It looked like he was being tortured! Oh, man, I can't stop seeing it!"

"You're talking out of your head, dude," Victor said. "You're not making any sense."

"I don't know." Jack's voice softened, the pain in his head finally subsiding. "It was weird."

"That's some crazy talkin', man," Victor said, helping Jack with his backpack. "That portal we traveled through must've messed up your brain!"

"You went through it, too," Jack reminded him.

"I know, and I hope nothing happens to me," Victor said. He peeked around the corner at the dirt bike, making sure the coast was clear. Then he glanced back at Jack and said, "Time to go!"

CHAPTER THIRTY-THREE

Tommy's Close Encounter

Tommy Crenshaw coasted on his bike down Cemetery Hill, balancing a wooden baseball bat over his handlebars. His pockets were stuffed with a handful of M-80 firecrackers and a cigarette lighter, leftover from last year's Fourth of July. If what Billy had said was true about a monster dwelling within Whitlock Manor, at least he wouldn't be empty-handed when defending himself. But he knew monsters weren't real, so there was nothing to worry about, at least so he thought.

It had been several years since he had seen Whitlock Manor. There had never been a reason for him to go near that place, primarily since he'd heard the rumors about it being haunted.

Rounding the cul-de-sac, Tommy saw a patrol car and squeezed the handbrakes, his bike skidding to a halt. He nonchalantly peeked into the passenger side window as he got off his bike, and after finding no one inside, walked his bike to a nearby tree. He leaned the bike against the tree and headed up the sloped pathway toward the house with his baseball bat. He was never interested in baseball; he just remembered the bat being in the garage for several years, propped up in the corner. His father had bought it for him when he was younger in hopes that he'd try the sport and stick with it well into high school.

But when Tommy got his first bicycle, everything his father had hoped for had changed. BMX racing was instantly set on his mind, and no other sport seemed as exciting.

Ascending the rickety stairs to the front porch, Tommy sensed an ominous vibe about the house. First, he noticed the door was ajar. *That cop must be in here,* he thought. Then, as he proceeded to inspect the busted door latch, his foot kicked the padlock across the decking, and it slid to the other side underneath the motionless swing.

Pushing open the creaky door with a firm grip on the bat, he stepped into the house. "Hello?" His voice carried through the foyer. The smell of rot lingered in the air, and he cupped a hand over his nose and mouth. "Ugh! This house is *rank*!"

Tommy had never seen such a decrepit place. As he looked around, something caught his eye when he turned the corner into the next room. Footprints.

"Hello?" he called again, knowing he was probably not alone in the house. "Officer?"

Tommy followed the prints, tracing them across the room that led to the trap door. He also noticed the bunched-up old rug but was not concerned about it. Instead, he pulled open the secret door in the floor . . . and was greeted by darkness.

"There's no way I'm going down there without a flashlight," he said. "I *knew* I should've brought my light!" He closed the hatch and traversed the other half of the room but stopped short. He didn't want to go beyond the edge of light streaming through the slits of the boarded windows that illuminated this part of the house.

"The root cellar," he remembered. Billy had talked about it being located around the back of the house. "Maybe I'll have better luck finding answers there."

As he spun around to head back toward the front door, he could've sworn he saw something move in the room. The cop? If so, why hadn't he acknowledged his call? Tommy stared at the dark shadows in the far corner, his palms sweating from gripping the baseball bat. He blinked several times, making sure his eyes weren't playing tricks on him.

Without warning, a cloaked figure shot across the room, coming at him fast. Watching it hovering inches in front of him, Tommy thought it was someone's jacket on a pully system, ziplining across the room as a prank to scare him. But who could have been the mastermind behind such a trick?

Devin Morton came to mind. *Yes*, Tommy thought. *Devin would definitely do something like this!*

As a test, to see if someone was baiting him, he took a step back and swung at the figure. He expected the bat to knock the jacket clear across the room, but it whooshed through the entity, slicing only thin air.

The baseball bat slipped from his sweaty hands and twirled like a rotor blade across the room, striking a hole in the opposite wall.

The apparition suddenly thrust at Tommy, then pulled back as if it were taunting him. At the same time, Tommy caught a glimpse of its lifeless, gray-toned face deep within the hooded cloak. Its lips were pursed, and its dreadful red eyes glared at him like a pair of hot embers, the lining of its cloak rippling in midair like small waves. Then, it spoke. "Tommy," it hissed.

Tommy's skin crawled. How did it know his name? There had to be someone playing a joke on him. Ghosts don't talk! At least not in a clear, audible voice like what he had heard.

He remembered the firecrackers stuffed in his pocket. Maybe the blast from one of those might counter-scare whoever was trying to frighten him. He fished nervously in his pocket and pulled out the cigarette lighter and an M-80. A few other firecrackers spilled from his pocket and bounced onto the floor. But there was no time to scramble and pick them up. Instead, Tommy needed to light the fuse, throw the explosive, and get the hell out of there.

He flicked the lighter repeatedly until, finally, a solid flame. He lit the fuse, held the firecracker for a couple of seconds, then tossed it at the apparition and ran. But he forgot about the trap door and tripped over it.

BOOM! The explosion occurred in midair as Tommy hit the ground, the powerful blast making his ears ring.

The entity faded like smoke clearing the room.

Tommy's attention diverted to the trap door springing open at his feet, and he crawled away just as two black arms grew out of the hole and slapped down against the floor. "Shit!" he screamed, backing into a wall.

His eyes were transfixed on Mike Palinsky rising from the floor, the officer's head angling left, then right, before making eye contact with him. Tommy scooched on his butt across the floor, his back gliding against the wall.

Moving robotically, Mike struggled to stand and staggered toward Tommy, reaching an arm out toward him.

"Hey, you're Officer Mike, the one that hands out those Dallas Cowboys cards," Tommy said, getting to his feet.

"Get out!" Mike warned Tommy, blood ejecting from his mouth like he had been punched in the jaw by an invisible force.

Tommy dodged the blood from spraying on him. "You okay?"

Mike collapsed to his knees then glanced up at Tommy, trying to respond, but only gurgling sounds came out of his mouth.

Standing in shock, Tommy was unsure of what to do.

Then Mike pointed toward the foyer, and Tommy peered over his shoulder to see if something was behind him.

Still unable to get a word out, Mike bared his teeth and clenched at his throat.

Tommy didn't know if he was having trouble breathing or just upset that he couldn't talk. "I'll get you some help!" he said anxiously and rounded the corner into the foyer and headed for the front door.

But the door was closed. He didn't remember closing it behind him when he entered the house. Maybe the wind had blown it shut?

He reached for the handle and gave it a tug, but still, the door wouldn't budge. Trying again, he pulled with more strength. It was like the door had been welded shut!

Tommy pounded on the door with his fists. The latch was busted on the outside, so how could anyone have locked the door within the short time he had been in the house?

Then he remembered the baseball bat. He could run back and get it to break down the door! But when he turned to head back into the room where Mike was, to retrieve the bat, he threw a hand up, shielding his eyes from a pulsating bright light. Squinting between his fingers, he witnessed the silhouette of a person walking toward him. "Is that you, Officer?" he asked.

"Five to enter, one to stay; the world deceived, a future to pay," a voice pronounced.

"What?" Tommy said. "Who are you?"

"Enter the portal to reunite with the immortal," the voice continued. "To flee is your ability."

Tommy lowered his hand, his eyes adjusting to the light. "You've got to be kidding me!" he said. "You're the cafeteria lady at Remington High! What are you doing here?"

The woman smiled, her eyes snapping up at him. Her hands moved in circular motions around a free-floating orb of light. She raised her arms, and the sphere moved behind her, stretching and transforming into a portal that suspended in midair.

Tommy's heels pressed against the door. "This can't be real!" he said and tried once more to open the front door. He pulled on the handle with all his might. "Let me out of here!"

Ms. Bagleweed's voice escalated over his, and she pointed at the rotating black hole. "This is the way to the freedom in which you seek."

Tommy spun around with his back against the door. *"This isn't real!"* he repeated, fighting to control his fear.

Ms. Bagleweed glanced at his feet. "Perhaps Gerald can be of some assistance?"

"Gerald?" Looking down, Tommy saw a tarantula move onto his shoe, its hairy legs settling over the laces. "Eww!" His reflexes were quick, and he kicked at the spider, sending it flying over the woman's head. It landed on the floor behind her.

Ms. Bagleweed gestured toward the portal again, her face without expression. "Evil is on the rise. You must enter the light!"

Tommy's eye caught Officer Palinsky glaring at him from afar, careening around the corner behind the cafeteria lady. He couldn't tell, but it looked like the cop's face was . . . peeling? His appearance seemed to have degraded within a matter of minutes.

"This house is possessed!" Tommy said, believing every word he just said. He was tempted to take Ms. Bagleweed's advice and jump through the portal since he had nowhere else to go. The door was locked, and Mike looked like he was changing into something he didn't want to stick around and see. But what would happen if he entered the portal? Did it lead into another dimension, would it transport him into another room of the house, or would he be disintegrated immediately upon entry? Could he trust an old woman from school who was the sweetest person he knew but appeared to be some kind of sorceress in this house? None of this made sense!

Mike stood with his legs apart, trying to hold his balance. His body jerked into seizure mode, twitching so violently that a mixture of foam and blood bubbled up from his mouth and splattered on the walls. The officer hunched forward, and his shirt ripped straight down the middle of his back. Even his pants were ripping down the seams. The cop was growing out of his uniform, his arms flailing about madly like wet noodles! Then, when he seemed to have control of himself again, his eyes blinked open. They had grown twice their size, enlarged as glassy black ovals.

"Screw this!" Tommy yelled, taking a chance and leaping into the portal.

CHAPTER THIRTY-FOUR

The Four

Ten Minutes Earlier.

"What is this?" Victor said, observing the back wheel of the dirt bike.

"Is this a disc lock? Who put this on here!"

"I bet Mike booted it!" Jack said. "He knows I'm not supposed to be around this place and probably put a lock on it so we couldn't get away. I bet he's looking for us!"

"Well, we don't have any tools to get it off. An angle grinder could cut right through it if we had one."

Jack stood with his hands on his hips. "I guess we're walking back to your car," he sighed. "Can't we go to the hardware store and buy the tool we need, then return to cut it off?"

Victor kicked at the lock, cursing at it. "I don't want to have to do that, but I guess we have no other choice. This thing is a piece of—"

BOOM! The sound of a muffled blast diverted their attention from the motorcycle.

"That sounded like a gunshot!" Jack said.

"From inside the house," Victor added. "I wonder if Mike shot at that creature! *Does that thing not die?*"

"Should we see if he needs help?" Jack suggested.

"No!" Victor said. "We barely escaped death the first time,

so why put ourselves in danger again? Besides, we have no weapons, remember? If he was smart enough and called for backup, I'm sure he'll be okay. That also means we need to get out of here before they arrive. I can return later with a friend to help me load the motorcycle in the back of his pickup."

"Okay," Jack agreed.

They hurried across the field behind the house, the morning sun hanging over the horizon in the cloudless sky. Jack was still amazed that he hadn't seen a dark cloud circling over them.

Upon their approach to the pathway that led into the woods, Victor spoke his mind. "Never again will I come near this place. That house needs to be bulldozed!"

Jack paid no attention to his brother's ranting. Instead, he walked with his head hung low, thinking about Daisy. But when Victor's rambling faded to silence, he spun around to see his brother at a standstill. "What's wrong?"

Victor cupped his hand behind his ear. "Do you hear that?"

Jack stood still for a moment. "Hear what?"

"Exactly!" Victor said. "No sounds."

"So?"

"I haven't heard a dog bark or an animal scurrying about. No birds chirping. Not even the sound of an airplane flying overhead."

Jack gave another listen. His brother was right. But he didn't think the silence around them meant anything. He wasn't worried, and frankly, he didn't care. "Dude, we are in the middle of nowhere. Why would dogs be barking out here? Coyotes, maybe, but they usually come out at night. And maybe airplanes are flying too high for us to hear them."

Victor scratched at his forearm. "You can hear things out in the middle of nowhere, you know."

"If a tree falls in the woods and no one is around to hear it, does it make a sound?" Jack laughed.

Victor gave a fake smile, still scratching at his arm.

"Did you get bit?" Jack asked.

Victor shook his head. "I dunno, but it itches like crazy!" He dug his nails deep into his skin, and his hand suddenly cramped. *What the hell!*

The pain surged in his wrist, and he uttered a sharp scream and collapsed to his knees, cradling his arm against his chest.

"Victor!" Jack yelled, running to his brother. "What'd you do?"

Victor winced at a sharp pain shooting up his arm. "I think I pulled a muscle," he said, removing his backpack. "My arm feels like it's on fire! *What did that portal do to me!*"

Jack knelt beside him in a panic. "What can I do to help?"

"Make the pain go away!" Victor said between clenched teeth.

Jack realized this was serious because his brother was no actor. If this really had been for show, it was an Oscar-worthy performance!

Victor rocked back and forth as if it would help to nullify the pain.

"Dude, um, your skin is sizzling!" Jack pointed.

"Shut up!" Victor mumbled. "This is serious; my arm really *is* killing me!"

"I'm not joking!" Jack said. "Look at your arm!"

Victor glanced down. The flesh on his arm was blistered as if a bucket of acid had been poured over it. Globs of thick, puss-like fluid dripped in elongated strands from his hand and forearm. Yet, strangely, there was no blood! He wiped the distress off his face and breathed deeply. "My arm just went numb!" he said.

Jack was too shocked to think of what to do. Walking to get help was out of the question because it was too far. The only thing he thought might be useful was a tourniquet. He could use his shirt. But then he thought, *Victor's arm isn't bleeding, so what's the use?*

Victor looked up at him with teary eyes. Although he no longer felt pain, his left hand was shriveling, melting into a pasty substance that seeped between the fingers of his other hand holding the stump of his wrist. "Jack!" he cried. "I'm melting!"

Then, like a stop motion animation, the stump of Victor's wrist self-cauterized, and within seconds, it was scabbed over.

Victor snapped his head at Jack. "That thing we teleported through, I'm telling you it did something to us!"

"I don't know, maybe," Jack said. Then he asked, "Can you walk?"

"I can try." Victor wobbled to his feet.

Jack grabbed his brother's backpack and helped him up. "Mom and Dad are going to flip out when they see you like this. And they'll want to take you to the hospital."

"Ya think?" Victor said, his face turning pale. "You know, it's a long walk back to my car. I hope I can make it without passing out. I'm feeling kind of lightheaded."

Jack knew he wouldn't get very far with Victor leaning on him like this. It was a half-mile walk to the car. He had a better idea. "Why don't we walk back to the house and check around front to see if Mike's car is still there? Maybe we can use his radio and call for help. It beats having to walk so far to your car!"

"That's the best idea you've had all day!" Victor said with a bit of a smile. "Let's check it out."

———

"Hey, that looks like Tommy's bike!" Jack said, spotting the bike leaning against a tree. He stopped for a quick rest. "Is he here, too?"

"No idea," Victor said.

Jack spun to Victor from inspecting the bicycle, his jaw slightly unhinged. "You know what? What if that gunshot we heard was Mike shooting at Tommy!"

"I doubt it," Victor said. "Worry about your friend later. We need to get home before some other part of my body decides to disintegrate or fall off. What if I have leprosy? I'm gonna look like the Toxic Avenger!"

"Come on, you don't have leprosy!" Jack sneered.

Finally making it to Mike's cruiser, Jack extended his arm in front of Victor.

"What's with you!" Victor groaned. "You almost hit me in the face!"

"I thought I saw someone moving around inside the car!" Jack said. "Do you think Mike's in there?"

"Yell his name and see if he rolls down the window or gets out," Victor suggested.

"*You* yell his name," Jack insisted. "If he shot Tommy, we could be next!"

"But if he didn't, he can help me!" Victor said.

The driver's side door sprang open, and Jack saw a pair of filthy-looking shoes landing on the ground underneath the door. He gasped when Daisy's head rose over the door frame. "Daisy!" he shouted, dropping Victor's backpack.

"Jack!" Daisy cried. She ran to him and threw her arms around him, weeping into his shoulder.

"You're safe!" Jack squeezed her tightly. But before she could respond, he leaned back and lifted her chin, staring passionately into her teary eyes. He looked beyond the dirt smearing her face and dove in for a kiss.

It took a near-death experience for Jack to have finally made a move on her. He had bottled it up for too long, yet he thought it was well worth the wait. Every nerve in his body was electrified. He could sense her soul finally recognizing his, for she did not hold back. Her tongue lashed madly in his mouth as she gripped her arms tighter around him, holding him as if never wanting to let go.

Victor shuffled his feet to get their attention. "Did you forget that I'm dying here?"

Daisy took a step back, embarrassed.

Jack turned around, his eyes catching a glimpse of Victor's deformed arm. And before he could make a crude comment, the radio in Mike's car buzzed, and dispatch squawked through the speaker.

"Central to 713."

Daisy glanced back at the vehicle. "I saw this police car here on my way home," she said. "I stopped to see if I could get help, but the cop wasn't inside or anywhere to be found. I'm surprised the door was left unlocked. People have been talking a lot through the radio, trying to get 713 to respond. I wasn't sure how to work it, so I just sat and listened while I waited to see if the cop would come out of the house."

"How long have you been here?" Jack asked.

"Maybe ten minutes," Daisy replied.

The dispatcher's voice crackled through the radio again. "Seven-thirteen, backup has been deployed to your location."

Hearing the dispatcher's voice made Victor more anxious in calling for help, so he stepped to the vehicle and slid into the driver's seat. He grabbed the transceiver with his good hand and depressed the button to talk. "Please help! Send EMS to Whitlock Manor on Cemetery Hill *STAT!*" He released the button and listened for a response.

Only the sounds of different radio frequencies buzzed in return.

Victor spoke into the transceiver again. "Can anyone hear me? We are in danger, and I've been injured! Do you copy?"

Jack stood outside the car door, holding Victor's backpack as Daisy clung onto his arm. "Maybe the volume needs to be turned up or something?"

Victor checked. "It's turned up," he confirmed and tossed the radio on the dash.

"At least they're sending backup. Here, take your bag," Jack said and leaned over his brother's lap, tossing the bag onto the passenger seat.

Daisy leaned in close to Jack's ear. "What happened to your brother's arm?" she whispered.

"I heard that!" Victor said. "No need to be discreet. Go on, Jack. You know you want to tell her."

Jack took Daisy's hand into his. "Something really strange is going on."

"You're telling me!" Daisy said. "I just dug my way out of a grave!"

Jack jerked his head back. "Huh?"

Victor cut his eyes up at her. "Now this, I gotta hear!"

Daisy raised her hands and wiggled her fingers. "I'm not sure how, but I can shoot lightning from my fingers!"

Victor stepped out of the vehicle and showed his disfigured arm to Daisy. Since she was sharing strange stories about herself, he could, too—like battle scars. "Something is eating my arm, but I have no feeling in it. And Jackie boy here can predict the future. I'd say we all are feeling something in common—some sort of connection?"

"I can *see* things, not predict the future," Jack clarified. "There's a difference. I saw Stewart was tied down somewhere. That tells me that he must be in trouble."

"I believe you!" Daisy said. "Based on everything that I've been experiencing the past twenty-four hours, there's no doubt in my mind that you saw him."

Jack noticed the pouch tied to her wrist and reached to feel its soft texture. "What's this?"

Daisy jerked her arm away. "It's an orb I got from Delanore—you know, Ms. Bagleweed, the cafeteria lady? I'm supposed to keep it safe for when I seek the light to break—"

"You ran into her, too?" Jack interrupted.

"Yeah," Daisy said. "And I found out she lives in a chamber underneath the house! Remember those red eyes we saw when we first explored the house together?"

"How could I forget?"

"There's this portal thing down there that's located directly underneath the cemetery," Daisy continued. "I went through it and found myself digging out of someone's grave!"

"So, the rumors at school must be true!" Jack said. "The old lady people claim to have seen must be Ms. Bagleweed!"

"Delanore," Daisy said.

"Whatever," Jack said. "I never knew her first name was Delanore."

"That's because she's addressed as Ms. Bagleweed at school,

dummy," Victor butted in. "Who calls their teachers by their first name? That's just rude."

Jack noticed Daisy's hair flutter from a gusty wind that swept through. He wondered if another storm was brewing, but when he looked up, there were still no clouds. Then he glanced behind him at Whitlock Manor.

"Great, now what?" Victor said, noticing Jack's sudden stare.

"Is that what I think it is?" Jack said.

Daisy turned around and faced the house with Jack. "If you're thinking what I'm thinking, it's a portal!"

Victor peered curiously around Jack and Daisy at the house in the distance. "But it's different! It's upside-down. How is that possible!"

The familiar phenomenon rotated like a tornado funnel pointing toward the sky instead of to the ground. Then, like shaping clay on a potter's wheel, the reversed whirlwind sculptured Tommy into existence! Finally, lightning flashed around him, and the portal disappeared.

Tommy appeared disoriented, looking at his hands and patting himself on the arms and legs as if making sure he wasn't dreaming. He stood a few yards from the front door of the house.

"Who is that?" Daisy asked.

"That's Billy's older brother!" Jack said. He turned to Victor. "At least we know Mike didn't shoot him!"

"Told you," Victor said.

Tommy spotted his bike leaning against the tree where he had left it. And when he saw Jack, Victor, and Daisy hunched around the police cruiser, he took off toward them. "Hey, I was just inside that house!" he said when he met up with them, pointing back at the mansion.

"Welcome to the 'I'm so confused club!'" Victor grinned, waving the stump of his arm like there was nothing wrong.

A crazy thought triggered in Jack's mind. "I think I know what's going on!" he blurted.

Everyone looked at him like cats snapping their heads to a noisy wrapper, intrigued at what he had to say.

"Do y'all remember the riddle Ms. Bagleweed—"

"Delanore, apparently," Victor said.

"Whatever!"

"Are you referring to the five to enter riddle?" Daisy asked.

"Yes," Jack replied.

"And one to stay," Tommy chimed in.

"That's it!" Jack confirmed. "What if the five to enter is us? We've all been inside the house, right?"

"But there's only four of us here," Tommy said. "Didn't my brother go inside the house, too? That would make five . . . five to enter."

"Billy was underneath the house in the basement," Jack said. "I don't know if he was actually *in* the house."

"Then who's staying?" Victor asked, confused. "Who's the fifth? She said there were five to enter and one to stay. Would that make six total? Or is it five to enter, and one of those five stays? Who's staying? I sure as hell am not!"

"Who's on first?" Tommy joked, referring to the Laurel and Hardy skit.

"Not funny," Victor responded.

"Maybe the fifth person is Mike," Jack said. "He's got to be inside the house!"

Tommy shook a finger at him. "That's true! I saw him in the house, changing into something disgusting. Whatever was happening to him, I didn't stay to find out. Ms. Bagleweed—Delanore, I guess—insisted I enter the portal to reunite with . . . the immortals? Whatever was meant by that riddle, I chose to enter and ended up here with you guys."

"So, what does that mean?" Daisy asked, her voice scratchy. "Was she referring to us? We aren't immortal!" She held up the pouch tied to her wrist. "She also said I'm supposed to keep this with me at all times when I seek the light to break the curse of the underground. I didn't understand what she was talking about. What would that have in connection with the five to enter riddle? And what about the second part of that riddle? The world deceived, a future to pay?"

"Maybe when the other cops get here, they can shed some light on the situation," Jack said. "I never paid attention to the other half of her weird brain-teaser."

Victor glanced at him, cradling his deformed arm. "Dude, our backpacks!" he said. "My bag is full of ammo. If they search it, the only light they're going to shed is at the station when they take us downtown to explain ourselves!"

"I didn't think about that!" Jack said. "Should we hide somewhere? Then again, you still need help with your arm! Or maybe we watch and see what they do first when they get here then approach them like we were just strolling through the area."

"Yeah, that's a good idea," Victor said sarcastically. "Where are we going to hide our backpacks?"

Jack's eyes scanned the area. "I don't know," he said, then glanced at Tommy's bike against the tree. "We can hide them behind Tommy's bike over there, and when it's safe, we show up like we were just walking through the area."

Victor grabbed his bag from the passenger seat and got out

of the vehicle. "I'll meet you over there," he said and ran to Tommy's bike.

Jack shrugged at Daisy and Tommy.

"How is he not in pain?" Tommy asked. "It looks like his hand was in a fight with a meat grinder!"

"Beats me," Jack said. "I'm just as puzzled as you are about what's going on. It seems we're trapped in an eternal nightmare that we can't wake up from."

They caught up with Victor standing behind the tree and watched together for the cops to arrive. Feeling the pouch around her wrist move, Daisy stepped away from the boys, her back turned discreetly, and opened the velvet bag to peek inside. The orb radiated an eye-catching bright and delicate blue glow that reflected off her face. Her eyes widened with wonder, and she reached in the bag and removed the orb, holding it in her palm with her fingers splayed out.

Tommy took his eyes off Mike's cruiser and peered over at the mansion. "Hey!" he shouted, pointing at the third-story window. "Look up there . . . what *is* that!"

"Is that Ms. Bagleweed?" Victor wondered. "I mean Delanore—shit!"

The orb in Daisy's hand twitched again, and she grasped it before it rolled off her fingers. "Um, guys?" She rejoined the group. "I don't know what's happening, but this thing is going crazy."

Jack, Victor, and Tommy crowded around her for a closer look.

"Get rid of it," Victor said sharply. He took a backward step in his own defense. "It looks like it's about to explode!"

Daisy glared at him like he was crazy. "I can't. I was instructed to protect it!"

"I know, but protect it from what?" Jack asked.

"That old woman has supernatural powers like she's controlling all the weird stuff going on inside that house," Victor said, jumping to conclusions.

Tommy pointed toward Cemetery Hill. "The cops are here! I just saw lights flashing at the top of the street."

Daisy looked at the orb, then at Jack.

Jack eyed her questioningly.

Daisy frowned, then threw the orb as far as she could into the yard. The globe hit the ground without a single bounce and shifted around in the tall grass like an excited gerbil in an exercise ball.

Sounds of a window shattering split the air, and everyone looked up at the house. The creature Jack and Victor thought they had killed dropped from the third-story window and landed in the front yard with a thud. It hunched low to the ground like a cat sneaking up on its prey, opaque liquid seeping from the bullet wounds.

"I thought the staircase crushed that thing when it collapsed on top of it!" Victor said. "Did its wounds just magically heal? How is it still alive!"

Jack instinctively reached for his revolver that was not there. "Oh, crap! No weapons!"

Daisy quickly moved behind him. "That's the thing that took me away when we found Billy in the cage!"

Tommy backed away slowly. "Not today, Satan!" he yelled, then turned and darted up Cemetery Hill.

Daisy's hands went up. Bolts of electricity zapped from her fingertips, the lightning arcing through the air and striking the creature, paralyzing it.

Victor shunned the electricity and raised his deformed arm

when a fireball launched like a Roman candle firework from the stump of his wrist. "Holy cow!"

Like a burning projectile flying from a trebuchet, the fireball collided into the creature with an explosion of sparks and flames, sending the beast soaring through the air at least thirty yards back.

Victor stared in awe at a thin stream of smoke rising from the stump of his wrist. "My arm is a gun!" he said. "Unreal!" He twisted his arm upward and watched as the hole in the stump closed like the contraction of a jet engine's propeller nozzle on an afterburner.

"What just happened!" Jack stood, amazed. "How'd you do that?"

"I don't know, but that was so cool!"

Daisy shook her hands, trying to speed up the process of making the short electrical currents dancing between her fingers fizzle out. Then, looking around, she asked, "Where did Tommy run off to?"

Behind them, a grassfire spread rapidly toward the house.

"Did I do that?" Victor grinned. "Oh, I hope this place burns!"

"There!" Jack pointed at the top of the street of Cemetery Hill. "Is that Tommy?"

"How did he get that far so fast?" Victor wondered.

"New abilities." Daisy smiled.

CHAPTER THIRTY-FIVE

What Lies Beneath

Black smoke billowed halfway up the street. The fire spread aggressively around the house, dead grass fueling its path. It was only a matter of minutes before Whitlock Manor was engulfed in flames.

The police cruiser pulled up next to Mike's vehicle, and Officers Rick Silvestrie and Joe Milberry stepped out. Rick hung back to contact dispatch as Joe proceeded to investigate Mike's squad car.

"710 to dispatch," Rick said through his shoulder radio.

"Go ahead, 710."

"Unit 713 equipment located. Standby for location of officer. We have an 1171—dispatch fire department *STAT*. Class A at the old abandoned house on Cemetery Hill Road. 3939—requesting immediate backup."

"Cemetery Hill Road, copy. Backup en route. Send update on officer ASAP."

"Copy that," Rick replied.

Joe popped up from searching Mike's vehicle. "I hope Mike's not in that house. Fire rescue needs to get here immediately!"

"They're inbound," Rick said, watching the fire eat its way to the house. His eyes followed the black smoke rising overhead, then to Whitlock Manor, and he muttered to himself, "Damn, I'd check inside the house for you, Mike, but it's just too dangerous to cut through the yard that looks like the pit of hell!"

"What the hell happened here?" Joe frowned.

"I don't know, but I'm glad this place is finally burning down," Rick sneered. "It's been an eyesore for too long."

"Yeah, it *was* kind of creepy!" Joe agreed, leaning back inside Mike's car to continue searching for clues. He remembered when Sergeant Lewis first assigned Mike patrol duties on Cemetery Hill. Almost two years ago, a slew of reports came in about kids trespassing on the property. However, Mike was persistent with the assignment, and not a single trespassing complaint had come across the sergeant's desk since.

Joe shook off the memory and walked around the vehicle.

Rick joined him behind the car, and they popped the trunk.

The teens stood in awe, wondering why the officers hadn't said anything to them yet. Was the smoke too thick for them to have even noticed them standing off to the side?

Daisy discovered the orb had rolled over a patch of dead grass yet to have been touched by flames.

Jack and Victor paid no attention to the object. Instead, they were preoccupied with watching the cops, anticipating when one of them would make his way over for a chat.

Tommy crept up behind them. "What did I miss?" he asked. Somehow, he had avoided being seen by the two officers on his way back down Cemetery Hill.

Victor spun around, startled.

"Hey!" Jack said. "Why did you leave us? We could've used your help!"

"Sorry, guys, but something happened that was out of my control," Tommy said. "I can teleport! I don't know how, but when I took off running, I saw lights flashing all around me. And the next thing I knew, I was at the top of the street!"

"You can teleport?" Jack chirped.

Victor was not convinced. "You sure about that? We would've noticed the portal."

"There was no portal," Tommy said. "It just . . . happened."

"Hey," Daisy intervened, regrouping after she had discreetly stepped away to retrieve the orb. "I think we need to let these policemen know what happened here."

"I thought you got rid of that thing," Jack said.

"My gut keeps telling me to keep it close like Delanore said," Daisy replied, inserting the orb back into the pouch. She tied the bag closed and looped the string around her wrist. "I don't think this thing is a bomb like y'all think. I'm keeping it with me." She peered over Jack's shoulder.

"What's wrong?" Jack noticed her attention distracted.

Flashing lights appeared diffused by the dark smoke at the top of Cemetery Hill. "Looks like the show's about to start," Daisy pointed.

Jack spun around at the same time as Victor and Tommy.

"We better talk to those officers before this place gets crowded," Jack suggested.

Victor shrugged. "I'd rather not. What are they going to do if they find out my arm is a weapon of mass destruction? They'll take me in, and I'd have scientists from all over the world questioning me, and I'd become a human lab rat!"

Flashing lights atop Cemetery Hill penetrated through the smoke. Emergency vehicles headed down the street.

"If we're gonna talk to them, let's do it now," Jack said and proceeded to the officers.

Victor grumbled at Jack, but followed him anyway.

Joe and Rick were leaning halfway in the trunk when Jack walked up to them. "Excuse me, Officers? We were here when the fire broke out, and we know what—"

The cops stepped back from the vehicle, ignoring Jack like he wasn't there. Joe glanced up at the smoke-filled sky, then back at Rick. "Move our vehicle to a safer distance. The fire trucks coming in will need room to park. I'll radio for a wrecker to tow Mike's cruiser to the station for further investigation. The fire is our priority right now."

"Copy that," Rick said.

Jack and the gang stood dumbfounded. "Sooo, are they ignoring us, or do they really not see us standing here?" Jack said.

Fire engines finally rolled in and everything was happening in fast motion. Firefighters hopped out of their trucks and went to work pulling hoses and equipment from compartments. However, none of them seemed worried about the teens being on the scene and didn't even attempt to get them to move to a safer distance.

During the organized chaos, the incident commander observed what his team was dealing with and approached the captain on site. "This is a fully involved fire. Stand down internal access for now. I'll get some tankers on the backside of the house to start hosing."

"Copy that, brother," the captain confirmed.

"This is nuts!" Tommy thundered.

"I think I know what's going on," Jack said. "Let's get out of people's way and head back to where Tommy's bike is, and I'll explain."

———

"So, what's up?" Victor said when they reconvened.

"I think we're dead!" Jack said bluntly. "I mean, look at us. We have these weird powers, and look how close we are to the flames eating up the house! Shouldn't we be feeling the heat giving off and the smoke burning our lungs? And no one sees us!"

Victor grimaced. "Huh? How are we standing around in the middle of all this chaos if we are dead! Shouldn't we be reuniting with our relatives?"

"I don't know," Jack said. "It's not often that I die. So maybe we're trapped between life and death?"

"Like lost souls!" Daisy added.

"But everything looks and feels normal," Tommy said. "I mean, we are still competent, walking and talking to each other like normal everyday life."

With his normal hand clenched into a fist, Victor threw a jab at Jack's arm, catching him off guard like he did sometimes before school. "Did you feel that?"

"OUCH!" Jack rubbed at his arm. "Yes—asshole."

"Then we aren't dead!" Victor said.

Daisy grabbed the pouch around her wrist. She felt a slight vibration coming from the orb again. When she opened the bag, the globe was glowing purple. First, it was blue, and now purple. *What do the colors mean?* she wondered.

"What is it?" Jack asked curiously.

"It's moving again," Daisy said. "Something's not right— the last time this thing had a mind of its own, that creature showed up. Now it's a different color." She removed the orb and showed the group.

Jack was amazed at its wonder and luminous quality. But its splendor seemed to have a subtle premonition of something that was yet to come. "That thing must be some sort of—"

An explosion erupted from the house, and debris rained into the street.

"Fall back!" the incident commander shouted.

A second explosion occurred, this time from behind the house.

"The motorcycle!" Victor said. "I bet that's what just blew up behind the house!"

The fire finally reached Whitlock Manor, burning it rapidly like the place was made of straw.

"Look!" Jack pointed. "Is that . . . the creature getting up?"

"It's unstoppable!" Victor raged.

"That's not the creature," Tommy said. "The first explosion came from the front of the house. Look at the huge hole where the front door used to be! That's the cop coming out of the house!"

"Mike?" Jack said. "No way!"

"Holy crap, that *is* Mike!" Victor said.

Mike Palinsky, consumed in flames, leaped through the hole blown through the front of the house and ran down the front yard to the curb.

First responders stared in horrified disbelief as Mike just stood there, seemingly immune to the pain. The fire encompassing him extinguished to wisps of sporadic bluish flames around his charred body. All eyes were on him, his frame scorched like he was one massive piece of human charcoal. Yet, he remained stout, surveying the first responders gathering in the distance.

A couple of ambulances arrived and parked near the tanker.

The fire captain cautiously approached Mike. "Hey, buddy, everything's going to be okay," the captain said calmly. "What's your name?"

Mike was silent, his stare still fixed on the crowd. Behind him, the popping and sizzling sounds of Whitlock Manor burning were like the ambience at an out-of-control bonfire.

"Can you hear me?" the captain asked, stepping closer.

Mike's face was an ember of bubbling flesh, his eyes solid black. He moved his head slightly and gazed into the captain's eyes, staring deep into his soul. Then, in a soft-toned voice, he said, "You're too late."

The captain had no time to react when a stream of fire projected toward him from Mike's gaping mouth. The captain fell and screamed as he rolled on the ground in a ball of flame. But the flames weren't extinguishing!

Several EMTs rushed to his rescue and threw fire blankets over him. Then they dragged him to a safe distance where they could render first aid, all the while keeping an eye on Mike in case he tried lighting them up, too.

"Unreal! Mike's burnt to a crisp yet still alive!" Jack babbled, watching in horror with his friends.

Although she was terrified, Daisy could not interact with her friends. She was too busy trying not to drop the orb. The thing was going crazy like it was possessed! It cycled through different colors and was rolling around in her hands.

A half dozen squad cars moved into position, forming a barricade between Mike and the first responders in the street.

Rick and Joe were on the front line, their weapons drawn over the hood of their vehicle.

"Is it just me, or does that look like Mike Palinsky?" Rick said out the side of his mouth.

Joe studied the crispy perpetrator more thoroughly. He *did* appear to have the same stance and proportions as Mike. "If it is Mike, how could he survive those burns! Look at the glowing embers in his arms and legs. He's burning from the inside out!"

"Should we radio the sarge for a crisis negotiator?" Rick suggested. "If he's gone mental, who knows what else he might do."

"I'll talk to him, see what I can do first," Joe said. He reached inside the vehicle for the siren controller, switched it to the microphone setting, and grabbed the transceiver. His voice projected through the speaker mounted behind the front grille of the cruiser. "Mike Palinsky!" he said, leaning over the hood of the car. "Please stand down! We can see you're upset. Let's end this peacefully and get you some medical assistance. We can help you!"

Mike surveyed the growing number of police gathering behind the cruisers with their weapons drawn. The rage in him was building again.

Although he was no crisis negotiator, Joe knew there was no time to wait for one to arrive on the scene. So he continued to try and lower Mike's emotions. "Mike, you are seriously injured and need medical attention. Do you think becoming violent is going to solve this situation? How do you think your family will react? Let's end this peacefully, brother."

Mike stood motionless, showing no remorse. Then he homed in on Rick and Joe.

Joe held the transceiver away from him and glanced at Rick, whispering, "What's he doing?"

Rick shook his head slowly.

Mike took a step forward and raised his arms.

"He's surrendering!" shouted another officer standing adjacent from Joe.

Joe spoke into the transceiver. "Mike, can we approach without harm?"

Mike suddenly went into convulsions, his body shaking violently—so violently, his burnt flesh cracked like a chocolate shell and then glided off his frame like a charred layer of melted marshmallow, revealing incandescent muscle and tissue.

Gasps fluctuated within the crowd.

In a matter of seconds, Mike grew to twice his size, his bones cracking and his tendons snapping. Finally, his head split open, giving way to the grotesque creature's face to push through. The monster ripped from its human costume and ejected fire from its mouth and into the crowded street.

The fire sprayed out like a flamethrower sweeping side to side. Although Rick and Joe had ducked when the flames came their way, the burning fuel penetrated their vehicle's gas tank, and the car exploded—Rick and Joe unable to flee in time.

One police officer, unaffected by the blast, ran for cover like he was expecting a chain reaction from the explosion. Then, trying to be a hero, he returned to open fire on the creature only to be doused by flames.

The crowd became a mass hysteria of screams and panic as people fled up Cemetery Hill to avoid the creature's path of destruction.

Barreling down the street in his unmarked vehicle and swerving between the crowd of retreating first responders, Sergeant Lewis Dickson skidded to a halt behind the barricade of his department's cruisers. He threw open his door and leaped from the vehicle, drawing his firearm and joining his comrades in the fight. "Good God almighty! What is that thing?"

"Mike Palinsky, sir!" a police officer next to him yelled over the gunfire. "It just stepped out of his skin like an exoskeleton!"

Lewis stared at the officer. "Like a body snatcher?"

"I guess so." The officer shrugged.

The heat emitting from the creature was so hot, shots fired were exploding before penetrating it. It looked like an invisible forcefield surrounded the monster, bullets unable to touch it.

The monster advanced toward the firing squad with smoke rising in thick succession from its blazing stature. It paused before the barricade of police vehicles, a slew of bullets disintegrating in midair.

"Call the National Guard!" a voice pleaded amidst the gunfire.

The creature bent slightly at the knees and balled its clawed hands before thrusting its chest out and throwing its head back, releasing a mighty roar that shook the earth and knocked half the squad off their feet.

Even the teens watching from a distance felt the vibrations.

Daisy was still struggling to keep the orb from rolling out of her hands when Victor noticed something odd happening to Whitlock Manor. "Look!" he shouted.

If Daisy looked up, she'd lose her grasp of the orb. But Jack and Tommy turned from the chaotic scene, and their eyebrows shot up in surprise. The foundation around the mansion had split outward in multiple directions and a pulsating green glow emitted from the cracks like exposed magma flowing underground.

"What's happening!" Tommy said.

A tremor underneath the house increased until it created a massive sinkhole. Whitlock Manor (with its mysterious past) collapsed like a house of cards. It was swallowed into the earth, and a burst of green light radiated up from the crater.

"Let's get out of here!" Victor demanded.

Jack grabbed Daisy's forearm as he turned to run.

But Daisy resisted.

"Daisy, let's go!" Jack panicked.

Daisy's eyes were affixed to the orb's new pale glow. The object was calm as she gazed at its pulsating rhythms. She tuned out everything around her, including her friends.

"What's wrong with her?" Victor turned back. "C'mon, Jack, we need to go!"

Tommy snapped his fingers in her face. Daisy didn't remove her eyes from the orb.

"It's retreating!" a police officer shouted.

Still unscathed by the firepower used against it, the creature spun to face the teens in the distance and snarled.

Victor saw it staring at them. "It sees us!"

Jack tugged on Daisy's arm again, but he couldn't drag her away if he wanted to. It was like her feet were cemented to the ground. "Daisy, snap out of it!" He turned to Victor. "Can't you use your arm cannon on that thing?"

"I don't know how I triggered it the first time!" Victor said, squeezing around his deformed arm for a mechanism that would shoot another fireball.

"It's coming this way!" Tommy screamed.

The beast broke from the standoff and stomped up the slope toward the teens like a charging bull.

"No one goes after it." Sergeant Dickson's voice split the silence after the ceasefire. "NO ONE!"

"Holy crap!" a police officer erupted. "Where did the house go?"

The creature let out another bloodcurdling roar as it came after the teens, its rage reaching its full potential.

Victor quickly aimed the stump of his wrist at the beast. "Maybe my mind controls this thing," he said and cringed like during an unsuccessful bowel movement. He anticipated the blast, but nothing happened.

The creature sprung in the air, its elongated arms reaching out, its oversized clawed hands in position to snatch Tommy from the group.

"No!" Jack felt his heart drop.

The power of the orb coursed through Daisy's veins. She finally snapped out of her trance, clutched the object in one hand, and raised it above her head. The globe blinked like a beacon, and a bolt of lightning shot up into the sky. A shower of sparks rained down over the teens, creating a forcefield that arched over them like a half bubble.

Flailing its arms and legs in midair, the creature crashed into the shield, and a current of electricity forced it against the protectant wall like a magnet. Then, a massive accumulating surge of energy blew the spastic beast to kingdom come, bits and pieces scattering across the lot.

Lightning danced between the teens inside the forcefield like in a plasma globe lamp. It was not harmful, but they remained still and held
their stance until the electrical currents dissolved back into the orb.

Then, sighs of relief.

———

"Did that orb thing just do that to protect us?" Victor said.

"It saved us!" Jack cheered.

Tommy glanced around the forcefield wondrously. "Do you think it's safe to walk through without getting zapped?"

Daisy lowered her arm and slipped the orb back into the pouch.

"I'm not sure about walking through it yet. I could feel the orb's energy inside me. It was like when you need to throw up. Bad analogy, I know. But it was a weird feeling like that."

"Why didn't your arm cannon thingy work?" Jack asked his brother.

Victor inspected the stump of his wrist, twisting it to and fro. "I dunno. I guess I'm out of firepower? Maybe it needs to be recharged or something."

"Check it out!" Tommy said excitedly. "All those cops are walking straight for us. Do you think they see us?"

"I don't know," Victor said. "Is this bubble visible to them?"

"I can't believe Mike turned into that thing!" Jack blurted. "Has it been inside him all the years that we've known him? It makes you wonder who else we know might be one of those things! Or anyone we've encountered in our lives!"

Daisy stared in the direction of the officers advancing toward them and cupped her hand over her mouth. "Oh, no!"

The officers were suddenly thrown backward from an invisible force like they had stepped on landmines. Some guys backflipped in the air and landed on the hoods of law enforcement vehicles, while others dropped straight to the ground.

Daisy quickly looked away. She'd seen enough carnage for one day.

The fire was still consuming everything around the area. The green light glowing from the sinkhole where Whitlock Manor once stood had become more prominent. And to add to all the chaos, the ground surrounding the crater started ballooning.

"Guys, look!" Tommy said, noticing the phenomenon first.

More cracks appeared, extending all the way up Cemetery Hill. The fire trucks, ambulances, and police cruisers sank into the crevices of the earth. Even the cops who took a hit to the ground were falling into the canyons.

"This is Armageddon!" Victor said. "We're all gonna die!"

Daisy frantically unsheathed the orb and held it in front of her. It was vibrating again and cycling through different colors. "You've got to be kidding me! I don't get it."

"What's happening?" Jack said nervously.

"Enough of this already!" Tommy cried. "When do we wake up?"

A heavy mist seeped from the crevices in the ground surrounding the teens, releasing pressure from the earth. Then the soil erupted and spewed a thick green lava-like substance that splattered over the forcefield, still protecting the teens.

Something was rising from underneath the earth! Punching through the floor of the crater where Whitlock Manor once stood, a massive shuttle hovered above the surface, its engines revving to a high-pitched scream. The ship yawed then eased to the fractured ground with its heat shields cycling through colored patterns in sync with the orb's flashing lights.

"The world deceived, a future to pay." Daisy grinned slightly, finally understanding the second part of Delanore's riddle. And now she knew why she needed to protect the orb.

PART FOUR

The World Deceived

"If time travel is possible,
where are the tourists from the future?"

—Stephen Hawking, *A Brief History of Time*

CHAPTER THIRTY-SIX

Stewart's Experiment

Stewart's eyes blinked open to a dimly lit room. He felt weak and cold. The last thing he remembered was being choked by Reed, pinned to the ground where he couldn't get away.

Sounds of movement constantly whisked by him, a subtle breeze touching his face upon each pass. Or was it someone's breath? *How did I end up in the hospital?* he thought. *Oh my God! Reed must've left me for dead!*

He heard ticking noises.

TICK! TICK! TICK! The annoying sounds were like fingers snapping during a poetry slam. He wanted to cover his ears but could not, because his arms and legs felt restrained.

Something slithered inside his leg, moving steadily to his inner thigh and up his groin like a snake. Although he felt no pain, his heart pumped madly in his chest, yet his breathing was slow and controlled.

Another set of lights flickered on in the room, and Stewart blinked a few times for his eyes to adjust. He shifted his head left then right, his neck stiff as a board, and counted four transparent tables lined in rows on either side of him. Who knew how many were behind him; Stewart couldn't tilt his head back enough to see. When he tried raising his head, it felt like he was lifting a sack of rocks, and it fell back against the table, causing an otherworldly wail that reverberated in the room. *A plastic table?* Frustrated, he squeezed his eyes shut and hoped this was just a dream.

Taking slow deep breaths, Stewart opened his eyes again. He looked straight up and noticed his reflection against a mirrored ceiling this time. He was naked on a see-through table with wires attached to his chest. Fluid from an IV bag dripped into a vein in his hand, and ventilator tubing was stuffed down his throat. The flesh from his arms and legs was peeled back, exposing his muscles and bones. *Oh my God!* Had he awakened in the middle of an operation?

Squishing and sucking noises added to the ticking sounds from the machines hooked up to him like a droid on a charging port. He wanted to scream, but only his eyes could do that for him. He blinked a tear that rolled down his cheek and curled under his chin. There it rested until the next breeze whooshed by to dry it up.

He closed his eyes again.

———

"Wake up," a raspy voice said near his ear.

Stewart could see someone standing next to him in his peripheral. His neck was too sore to move. The reflection of himself in the ceiling was gone. The mirror had fogged up. It was getting warmer in the room now.

He tried to speak, or at least moan to get their attention that he was alert and to please, please not hurt him. He'd heard the horror stories about comatose people who sometimes could still hear and feel but couldn't respond, like they were trapped deep inside their own bodies trying to get out. Stewart hoped this wasn't the case for him.

A head suddenly slipped into view, inches from his face. It startled him, although he could not flinch, as the only muscles he could control that reflexed from the scare were his eyes. The head, too close for him to focus on, hovered over him like it was concentrating on him, contemplating on what to do. The odorless breath was warm and heavy against his face. Then the head pulled back slowly, and Stewart screamed bloody murder in his mind.

The creature was massive! It was at least twice the size as the one he saw Rachael transform into. Its textured amber flesh glistened beneath the LED lights in the room. Another head slipped into view. And then another one, for a total of three that looked like snakeheads swaying in hypnotic rhythms.

I'm in hell! Stewart thought. *This is my place of eternal torture? What sin did I not repent that landed me here? Wait! I'm supposed to be judged in the presence of God. Did I miss something?*

One of the heads glided smoothly toward his face and gazed into his twitchy eyes. "Thou shalt destroy and conquer," it said, the voice having a familiar tone to it.

Rachael's father! Stewart thought. *Please don't hurt me. I'll do anything!*

The second head maneuvered toward Stewart's face, pushing the first head away. "Clear the way for our existence," it cackled.

Again, Stewart knew the voice. *Reed!*

The third head, noticeably female, slipped in between the other two snakelike heads. "The rewards shall be plentiful!"

Of course, Stewart thought. *Sheila! The whole family fused together as one huge beast!*

The heads grinned in unison, exposing their pointed teeth

as sharp as razors.

The conjoined Eaglecrest family (minus Rachael) raised an oversized clawed hand, and the three heads spoke together. "Rise!" they demanded strongly.

And without hesitation, Stewart suddenly sat up and swung his legs over the side of the table. His feet planted firmly on the ice-cold floor. How he did this, he had no clue. Either he was under a spell or he was being controlled like a puppet. How could he sit up after being paralyzed for who knows how long?

He checked out his arms, legs, and other parts of his body. The gashes he had seen in the reflection earlier were healed. Whatever was in the IV that dripped in the vein in his hand must've been some powerful steroids because his arms and legs were bulging with firm muscles. Even his chest was chiseled. He had *never* maintained toned muscles in his life. There were no stitches and no scars anywhere; his skin was clean and smooth.

"*Rise!*" the creature's three heads spoke in unison again.

Inspecting his enlarged hands, Stewart stood, amazed at his transformation. He felt as if he was born again. But this wasn't his body! His hands curled into tight fists, and he bared his teeth. "What did you do to me?" he snarled.

One after the other, the creature's heads craned toward him, each one taking turns to speak, sharing words to complete full sentences. "You're feisty . . . right out of . . . the gate, I see." The heads repositioned and repeated the pattern of movements again. "Repeat . . . after . . . me."

Stewart stood silently in attention, his body stiff and straight, his feet together, both arms at his sides.

"I . . . am . . . invincible!" the snakelike heads came at him one at a time.

"I am invincible," Stewart repeated.

———

The earth around Eaglecrest Farm inflated like a hot air balloon, causing livestock to tumble down the expanding hillside. Trees pulled away at their roots, and structures around the land collapsed. The farmhouse was last to implode; everything was demolished.

Chunks of soil slid from a massive silver object ascending from underneath the ground. The ship hovered silently above the crater from which it had lain dormant for centuries. The metallic sphere that Stewart had seen poking from the surface of the earth was erected atop the spacecraft like an antenna.

A sandstorm of dirt stirred up underneath the ship as it slowly dipped and kissed the floor of the crater. Then it ejected like a gravitational slingshot across the sky.

Stewart was onboard that flight—destination unknown.

CHAPTER THIRTY-SEVEN

Final Goodbyes

The ship's engines leveled to padded hums.

Daisy heard crackling noises coming from the orb. "Guys, listen to this!" She held out the object, and everyone gathered around it.

A woman's voice—calm yet authoritative—announced through the orb like it had a built-in speaker: *Chosen ones! You have broken the curse of the underground. Bring peace and prosperity before a new colony emerges. The extinction of mankind is near. Enter the portal to your loved ones. Return at the sound of the trumpets. The fate of humanity is in your hands.*

The orb's light faded.

Daisy held the globe close to her mouth and spoke to it, thinking it was a two-way radio. "Hello? Can you hear me? Delanore?"

"So, we're getting a free pass to go home?" Jack asked.

"It sounds like it to me," Tommy said. "I can't believe we're witnessing an alien invasion! Look at the size of that spaceship! Tell me this isn't a dream."

"Whatever is inside that ship is communicating to us through the orb," Jack said. "It sounds like we've been allowed to say goodbye to our families before heading off to war!"

"Like a draft," Victor said. "But with aliens!"

"What are we fighting?" Daisy asked. "I didn't sign up for this!"

"None of us did," Jack said. "But would all of this have transpired if we didn't break into the house? Or walked the tunnels of the underground? Or returned to save Billy? The pieces are coming together. That old house was just a decoy to hide the ship, alluring us to awaken the beast! And I bet that orb thing you have was the key to unlocking the beginning of the destruction of the world!"

Tommy snapped his head toward Jack. "What happens if we don't return from saying our goodbyes to our families? It feels like we're prisoners to whatever is on that spaceship, and this is our one phone call!"

"Your guess is as good as mine," Jack said. "Maybe we can try to bring our families back with us? What's going to happen to them if we don't?" He strained his head up at the forcefield arching over them. It was vanishing, fading like the afterglow along the horizon. Then they stood in a vulnerable position, surrounded by destruction, fire, and a spacecraft. The apocalyptic world around them did not seem real.

Glancing around the desolation, the teens noticed the remaining first responders who had retreated to the top of Cemetery Hill and had not fallen into the crevices of the earth were motionless. They were staring up at the hovering spaceship as if hypnotized by its slow rotations.

"That's eerie," Victor said. "We know none of those people can see us, so getting help from them will be pointless." He turned to Jack with a slight grin. "I guess you were right, little bro! We are either stuck between space and time or we're dead. My arm doesn't naturally shoot cannonballs like this in the real world!"

"Nor would we have any other of these special abilities," Jack added. "Maybe we *are* living in an altered universe or a virtual reality."

"Wait!" Tommy's voice boomed. "Are we like superheroes?"

Before anyone had a chance to respond, a violent burst of light appeared, quickly forming into an expanding circle of glowing mist before them.

Daisy grabbed and squeezed Jack's hand.

"Wow! Is this the portal?" Victor said. "It looks different. I suppose we don't have any other choice but to step through."

"Maybe it's our ticket out of this nightmare, and we finally wake up," Tommy hoped.

"How long will it stay open before it closes and we miss the opportunity to save ourselves?" Jack said. "Then again, what will happen if we
don't enter? It's another catch-22!"

Everyone's eyes spoke for themselves. And one by one, they stepped through the portal, hoping they were making the right decision.

———

The portal loomed briefly in the front lawn of Tommy Crenshaw's house. Tommy dropped from the hole in the air and rolled in the grass, breaking his fall. He got to his feet, brushed himself off, and headed for the front door.

"Hmm," he pondered, noticing the door was left ajar. Did someone break in? He pushed it open and stepped cautiously into the living room.

The house was quiet. He expected his mother to be clanging dishes around in the kitchen. But, instead, he could hear the shower running in her bathroom. *I'll surprise her when she gets out,* he thought.

The cats and dog must have migrated to her bedroom or found a good hiding place because they were usually on the sofa whenever he came home.

Something felt out of place.

Tommy proceeded upstairs to Billy's room. Seeing that his brother's door was closed, he knocked softly before pushing it open. A cool breeze blew through the opened window as he approached the side of the bed. "Billy, are you awake?" he said, grabbing the corner of the bedsheet. He peeled it away and smiled at Billy, sound asleep. He looked too peaceful to be waking him up. "Get your rest," Tommy whispered and pulled the sheets back over him. "I'll come back for you."

Scurrying downstairs, Tommy decided to check on his mother. Like the front door, her bedroom door was slightly ajar, and he could hear the shower running. *She usually closes this door when she's in the shower,* he thought as he peeked into the room. "Mom," he said.

No response.

He traversed the bedroom and stood outside the bathroom door, calling out to her a little louder. "Mom!"

No answer.

Tommy stepped into the bathroom and paused in front of the shower curtain. "Mom, are you okay?" he roared. He grabbed the edge of the curtain and slid it open slowly. His heart dropped when he stared down at his mother curled on the floor of the shower, the high-pressured water from the multifunction showerhead beating down on her lifeless body. "NO!" Tommy boiled over the threshold of the shower.

Blood gushed from the vertical slits in his mother's wrists, the razorblade she used lying next to her. Her eyes stared up with her mouth gaped open and her lips the color of blueberries.

"Why!" Tommy cried angrily. He pressed his forehead firmly against his palms, the water jetting from the showerhead misting the back of his neck. "Why did you give up! You were doing so good!" He struck a fist against the tiled wall.

He reached to shut off the water then closed the shower curtain. Then, as he turned to exit the bathroom and retrieve the telephone to call 911, he noticed a handwritten note taped to the mirror above the vanity. Tommy looked at it warily and yanked it off the mirror, reading the message with tearful eyes:

Sons,

I'm sorry you had to find me like this. I don't know what else to say, but I'm sorry for the way I acted around you two for so long. Please understand it wasn't me. It was the alcohol—the monster coursing through my bloodstream daily and nightly due to the death of your father. I don't think I would have ever gotten over it! Your father meant the world to me and losing him felt like my soul had been ripped out. Your father had a great career; he was a great lover and an absolute gentleman. Then he was stripped from our lives! It hurt me so bad, and I dipped too far in the bottle to have been able to resurface with a new life. Moving forward was just too hard for me.

Thank you for standing your ground and expressing your feelings regarding how I was acting recently. This kind of "woke me up" from the hellish nightmare I was living. I couldn't continue having that gut-wrenching feeling of anger balled up inside me all the time.

Tommy, please look after your brother. You two are insep-arable and will both live successful lives! I know you never liked the dog and cats, so I left the front door open for them to run out in hopes they could find new homes. I know, that was kind of mean, but it's for the best because I know you wouldn't like taking care of them.

In my closet is a safe containing everything you need for settling things, like the deed to the house, my will, and some cash and other things (39:18:24 is the combination). I'm going to miss you both, but I am looking forward to the day we meet again. Please take care of each other and make good decisions in life. DO NOT take the path I went down! I love you, boys.

Love, Mom.

Tommy choked back tears as he folded the note and stuffed it in his pocket. "I love you too, Mom," he mumbled, then headed for the safe in his mother's closet.

———

Daisy's teleportation through the time continuum was not as rough as her first experience. Like Tommy's return home, the portal burst into existence in front of her house.

She sat in her filthy clothes at the kitchen table drinking a glass of water, staring at her mother's half-smoked cigarette still burning between the teeth of an ashtray. It hadn't been emp-tied for days. Crumbs from a toasted bagel were all that re-mained on a dinner plate. She waited in the kitchen, knowing her mother would soon return because she knew her mother never wasted a lit cigarette.

A few minutes turned into ten minutes, and Daisy figured she had no time to keep waiting. So she dabbed the cigarette out in the ashtray, twisting and pressing it until it was fully extinguished. Then, standing from the table, she picked up her glass and grabbed her mother's plate, submerging both in the sink. Although she noticed the sink had previously been filled with soapy water, the suds had already dissolved. This indicated her mother had prepped the sink for washing dishes long ago.

After washing and drying the dishes the old-fashioned way, Daisy dried her hands with the dishtowel and headed down the hallway to her mother's bedroom.

"Mom?" she said softly at the doorway. Her mother's bedroom was dark from the blinds and curtains being closed. Her mother rarely had them closed unless she was feeling ill.

Daisy staggered toward the window, drawing the curtains and twisting open the blinds. Then she peered down at the bed. Her mother was sleeping. She smiled at her and kissed her on the cheek. "I'll see you later, Mom," she said softly. "I'll see you later."

———

The third portal appeared in the empty field behind Jack and Victor's house. The two brothers stumbled out of the vortex and hightailed it home.

When they made it to the driveway, they took time out to rest. Victor sat on the rear bumper of their father's van while Jack leaned against their mother's Fifth Avenue.

Setting his backpack on the ground, Victor stood thinking how much trouble he and Jack would be in for loading the bag with their father's ammunition. On top of that, he was still kicking himself for losing the rifle and the old revolver. He and Jack were about to be grounded for months!

Jack crossed his ankles and tipped his head up toward the sky, wondering what would happen to them when they returned through the portal. Something told him the situation they'd come back to wasn't going to be pretty.

Wincing at the sun glaring him in the face, Victor grabbed his bag and moved to the gate. "Let's get Dad's butt chewing over with," he sighed. "I won't be surprised if he makes us bend over and touch our toes while he whips us with his belt! And when he finds out what happened to Mike, he'll go nuts!"

"That's if he believes us," Jack said. "I didn't see any news vans or reporters out at Whitlock Manor. Did you?"

Victor shook his head no and swung open the gate.

They quickstepped through the yard to the enclosed patio, hopping over landmines that Bosco had planted. Their mother was usually consistent at picking up his turds, but today she was slacking. Although Jack had promised her he'd do his part and pick up after the dog, she still enjoyed doing it herself. It gave her peace of mind knowing the backyard was well-kept.

Jack opened the back door, and Bosco ran to him, wagging his tail madly. "Aw, you missed me!" he said, kneeling and rubbing the puppy behind the ears.

Victor shifted around them and stepped into the house, setting his backpack on the kitchen table before trotting off to his room.

"Go potty!" Jack commanded Bosco, and the dog frolicked to the yard. He stood at the edge of the patio as Bosco did his business and looked up at the sky. It had a shade of pink with black smoke spreading across the horizon in the direction of Cemetery Hill. The colors reminded him of the old-fashioned Neapolitan coconut slice candies he used to get at the candy store when his family visited their grandparents in Mississippi.

His daydream was cut short when emergency service sirens

screamed in the distance. Assuming it was more first responders arriving on the scene at Cemetery Hill to confront the phenomenon, he knew they would be in for a big surprise. He
watched as Bosco pointed his nose in the air and sniffed the
wind. Jack could smell it, too. The odor was like gases and com-
pounds produced in decomposition. *Rotting flesh.*

Victor rushed back out onto the patio. "Hey, any clue
where—" He pinched his nostrils closed. "Eww! What's that
smell!"

"I don't know," Jack said. "Maybe it's your upper lip!"

"Haha, very funny. Anyway, have you seen Mom or Dad?"

"You already know their cars are parked in the driveway, so
they gotta be around here somewhere, duh. Did you check
their bedroom?"

Victor stared at him blankly. "Um, that never dawned on
me. *No shit, moron!* I peeked inside, but I didn't see them."

Jack called Bosco into the house. Then he glided past his
brother standing at the doorway. He entered the kitchen and
dug in his jeans pockets, pulled out the few cartridges he had
left from the lost revolver, and piled them next to Victor's backpack on the table. Then he advanced to his parents' bedroom
and crept open the door, Victor right behind him.

Jack flipped on the light switch and peered around the wall
extension at the bed. His shoulders dropped with a sigh of relief.

Victor leaned in through the doorway.

Their father was in bed with his arm around their mother.
Both were sleeping.

Jack and Victor approached their parents, watching their
chests rise and fall. "Can't believe you didn't notice them in
bed," Jack mumbled to Victor.

"Shut up," Victor said. "It was dark in the room, and I didn't flip on the light. Should we wake them? Do you think we're even allowed to bring them with us?"

Jack shrugged. "I say we pack whatever we need, then wake them up. If we get them now, Dad might try to hold us back from leaving the house."

"Two for two." Victor pointed at Jack with a grin. "You're on a roll!"

CHAPTER THIRTY-EIGHT

The Calling

Victor turned on the television in the living room and plopped down on the couch. "What do we do now?" he asked Jack, anticipating waking their parents soon.

"What's your gut telling you?" Jack asked. He took a seat in his father's recliner, and Bosco jumped in his lap when he propped his feet up on the footrest.

"To wake up Mom and Dad," Victor replied. He looked at Bosco strangely. "What's that dog's problem? I've never seen him jump in Dad's chair before."

"I don't know," Jack said. "He's acting weird like he's scared of something."

Victor's attention diverted back to the television, and he flipped through more channels with the remote, trying to find a clear signal. "I didn't think this was supposed to happen with cable TV," he said. "Why are the stations all staticky?"

Jack petted Bosco and tried to make him lie down, but he resisted. "Have you not been fed?"

"Get 'im a bone," Victor suggested.

Jack retracted the footrest to the recliner, and Bosco jumped down. Jack rose and checked the bowls on the kitchen floor for food and water as Bosco circled frantically around him.

"Hey! Calm down." Jack raised his voice. "I'm feeding you!"

He stooped to pick up an empty bowl but suddenly doubled over and fell onto his side without warning.

Victor heard the metal bowl clang and wobble on the linoleum. He jumped up from the sofa and peered over the kitchen island.

Jack's knees were drawn to his chest in a fetal position, and his body was twitching.

Victor tossed the remote onto the sofa as he darted to the kitchen. It bounced off the cushion and landed on the floor, the battery compartment snapping open and the batteries spilling out.

Jack pressed his hands against his temples like he was suffering a migraine. "The visions!" he cried. "They're coming again!" He threw his head back, his eyes tightly shut. He could see strobe lights behind his eyelids that were painfully picking at his brain.

Victor pushed Bosco away from Jack. He almost lost his other hand doing so as Bosco snapped at him and bared his vicious little teeth. It was more cute than ferocious.

Like a flashbulb from a camera, Jack saw a glimpse of what was yet to become of mankind. It was a first-person view of wastelands, like so many science fiction movies that depicted what would happen during the apocalypse. To his right was a spacecraft hovering inches above the ground, and he approached it. The closer he got, the more transparent the ship's hull became. Finally, he could see right through it!

Everything around him began shaking like it was the mother of all earthquakes. Then the image blurred, and Jack opened his eyes to Victor nudging him.

"I didn't think you were coming out of that one," Victor said, relieved.

Jack cupped his hands over his face. "I think I just saw the end of the world!"

"What!" Victor jerked back.

Bosco licked Jack's face and sat staring at him, ensuring he was okay. Then he snapped his head toward the back door and growled.

"What is it, boy?" Jack said, turning to look at the window in the back door. He noticed there was no trace of pink in the sky anymore. Instead, it looked like civil twilight outside.

Victor helped Jack to his feet. "You okay?"

"I think so," Jack said. "The effects wore off quicker than last time."

"Your body must be getting used to it," Victor told him on their way to the back door. "Like my arm. I have no pain, I just can't grab anything. But I get these phantom sensations sometimes that feels like I'm moving fingers that I don't have."

"So weird," Jack said as he opened the back door to check out the view of the sky.

Bosco ran between his legs and zoomed through the enclosed patio out into the backyard, barking and howling nonstop.

A gray film blanketed the sky with a creepy stillness in the atmosphere. The air smelled of sulfur, the sun a giant smudge in the sky like a Bob Ross oil painting.

"We need to wake up Mom and Dad!" Victor demanded and dashed back into the house. He stood at the side of their parents' bed and shook their father's shoulder. "Dad, get up!"

Jack appeared at the doorway with Bosco. "What's wrong with them?"

"They won't wake up!" Victor said.

Bosco whimpered and pawed at the foot of the bed. He was

still too short to jump up onto the mattress without assistance.

Jack hurried to their mother's side of the bed and tried waking her up. But, like their father, she wouldn't respond. "Check Dad for a pulse," he told Victor, grabbing their mother's hand and applying just enough pressure to her wrist with the tip of his index and third fingers, just like their mother showed him long ago. "Mom has a pulse. So why isn't she waking up?"

"Dad's got a pulse, too," Victor said. "And he's breathing. But it's normal for Dad not to wake up easily because he always sleeps like a rock."

"And Mom sleeps like a cat," Jack told him. "She usually wakes up to anything!"

Tornado sirens began blaring outside, and Jack raised his eyebrows at Victor. "The sky is falling!" he said, panicked, and ran out of the room.

Bosco was right behind him until they got outside in the backyard, where the little dog rushed off to the gate, digging underneath the panels, trying to escape.

Victor caught up to Jack outside and glanced over at Bosco wildly flinging dirt. "Now what's his problem?"

Jack craned his head back and admired the massive cumulonimbus cloud swirling above them. Then a gust of wind whooshed through the backyard, nearly knocking him and his brother off their feet.

"We better get back inside!" Victor shouted over the brewing storm. "This is getting worse by the minute!"

Jack recalled the voice from Daisy's orb mentioning to return to the portal when they heard trumpets. "Wait!" he yelled.

"What now?" Victor said, wondering what else could possibly happen.

"The trumpets!" Jack reminded Victor. "Delanore told us to

return to the portal when we heard the trumpets."

"So?" Victor said.

"So, the tornado sirens could be what she was referring to as trumpets!" Jack ran to where Bosco was digging at the fence and scooped him up. He returned to Victor and said, "We need to get back to the portal!"

"Leave the dog here," Victor suggested. "He'll just get in our way."

"No!" Jack retorted. "He's coming with us! Who knows how long Mom and Dad are going to keep sleeping. He won't survive! Who will feed him? Let's go!" He ran for the gate with Bosco squirming in his arms.

Instead of arguing—as there was no time for that anyway—Victor whisked ahead and opened the gate. Together, they ran into the field behind the house and stopped before the portal.

Jack tightened his grasp on Bosco. He'd be one sad kid if he lost his dog. He nodded at Victor and stepped into the portal.

And Victor leaped through immediately after him.

The brothers and their dog were sucked weightlessly through a trippy transparent tunnel with flashing lights and swirling mist before total darkness finally encompassed them. Then they spun head over heel through the silent void, Jack keeping a firm grip on Bosco.

It seemed like an eternity before an expansion of bright light finally appeared. The teleportation was similar to what Jack and Victor had experienced before. They felt themselves free-falling, gravity pulling them down quickly. However, there was no house below them that they would drop into this time. So they kept falling, and falling, and falling.

———

Jack woke to a blurry image of Daisy's face pulling away from his. He licked his moistened lips and tasted . . . strawberries?

"Get a room," Victor's voice echoed.

"You must've bumped your head when you spilled from the portal," Daisy said, dabbing the corners of her mouth with the tip of her pinky finger, thinking her strawberry lipstick had smeared. She wore a loose-fitting blouse and a tight pair of jeans. Her hair was straight and silky smooth. She had freshened up when she was at home.

"Why are you dressed up so nice?" Jack asked. "You look gorgeous! And you smell good, too."

Daisy blushed and smiled. She helped him sit up, then leaned in and kissed his forehead.

Jack winced at the knot on his head.

"What a wuss," Victor said. "I walked right out of the portal with no problem. And so did the dog!"

"Bosco!" Jack perked up. "Where is—"

Bosco wiggled his way into his lap—disrupting Daisy's affection toward him—and licked his face.

Daisy giggled and stood to join Victor, Tommy, and Billy crowding around Jack.

Jack patted Bosco on the head, thinking how lucky he and the dog were to not have been separated during the teleport. He was surprised to see Billy had joined the group as well. "Did I click my heels three times or something? How did *you* get here?"

"Very funny," Billy chirped, reaching down to pet the dog. "I was wondering how long it would take for you to notice me here."

"Apparently not long," Jack said. He finally got to his feet and gave Tommy and Billy a fist bump, then swiftly punched

Victor in his good arm, catching him off guard just as he did to him. He faced Daisy and gave her a hug, taking a whiff of her soft hair. Then, stepping back, he glanced around the room, wrinkling his brow. "Where are we?"

Bosco trotted off, sniffing the ground like a K-9 hot on the trail of a perpetrator. He already seemed accustomed to the place.

"We teleported into the spaceship!" Daisy announced.

Jack's eyes lit up. "What? No way! How?"

"Yes, way," Victor said sharply. "And we've already met the crew while *your* lazy ass was knocked out on a ten-count."

Jack frowned. "What crew?"

"The ones in the control room," a familiar voice answered behind him.

Jack spun around. He wasn't sure if he should be happy to see Delanore Bagleweed, or fear that she was hunting him down for squeezing too much ketchup on his fries.

"Welcome aboard, Jack Stinger." Delanore smiled, several people behind her moving about in front of a window the size of a movie theater screen that overlooked a breathtaking view of deep space.

Delanore clasped her hands together with a broad smile.

Jack was at a loss for words. "How did you—"

"Get here?" Delanore finished.

"Yeah."

"It's a long story, but I'm excited to share it with you during your travels."

Jack's eye twitched. "Travels?"

"Yes," Delanore said. She gestured for him and the group to follow her to the large window. The crew keeping the ship operational paid no attention to the teens entering the control room.

Delanore pointed to the far corner of the window at Earth floating in the infinite darkness of space. "We'll orbit a few days before we reenter the atmosphere," she said. "What you're looking at is not Earth, but another planet many light-years from your home that scientists there have yet to discover. The technology on your planet cannot capture this greater distance."

Jack was flabbergasted. "What do you mean?"

Victor thumped him upside the head. "Let her finish, numbskull!"

Delanore cleared her throat and continued. "The planet you're looking at is called Obuathea. It means *Mirror Earth* and resembles much of your home. But Obuathea is hundreds of years ahead of your time. It's where you will call home for now—the place where your training begins."

Victor leaned toward Jack, distracting him from the orientation. He gestured his normal hand at the side of his head to simulate an imaginary explosion. "Mind-blowing, isn't it? But do you wanna see something *more* bizarre? We noticed this while you were knocked out cold."

"Do I really want to know?" Jack whispered, cutting his eyes at him curiously.

As Delanore continued spilling more information about the planet, Victor waved his good arm at her, and his hand passed through her body. "Hologram." He grinned. He gestured toward the ship's working crew. "They're *all* holograms, bro! Crazy futuristic stuff, isn't it?"

The holographic image of Delanore cut her talk short and faced her rookie cadets. "Meet me in the mess hall located down that hall and around the corner," she ordered, pointing behind the teens. "I'll debrief you there. In the meantime, grab something to eat. I know you have questions, and I'll be happy to answer them. Make haste, for we don't have much time!"

The hologram glitched and fizzled out like an old, boxed television
powering off. A small dot remained stationary in midair before it slowly dimmed then disappeared.

The crewmembers at the command center also signed off, their images blinking into synchronized particles.

Hanging in a geo-synchronous orbit inside a futuristic spacecraft beyond their wildest imaginations, the teens stared at each other in mass confusion.

"What just happened?" Victor broke the awkward silence.

"I've never known such advanced AI even existed!" Tommy said. "I could see her as a synthetic or some other tangible material. But a transparent image that looks just like you and me? Unbelievable! Where are all the lights and cameras to create such a system?"

"This planet she's talking about, how do we know if there's oxygen or gravity on it?" Jack wondered. "And is it colonized?"

"No clue," Victor said. "I'm still freaked out that we are in space! What the hell, man!" His eyes moved to Jack's feet. "Oh, and check out your shoes."

Jack glanced down and noticed his sneakers had been replaced with futuristic high-top shoes. He reached down and touched them. They were oddly squishy and firm at the same time. But they were comfortable. He was amazed that he could pull on the toes of the shoes to stretch them out and push them in to readjust to his feet again. There were no laces or Velcro straps. The shoes molded to his feet automatically.

"Gravitational force shoes," Victor said. "These things are

badass! But don't take them off, or you'll start floating."

"This is cool!" Jack smiled. "How do they work?"

"Who knows," Victor replied. "Maybe the soles are magnetic or something?"

Daisy admired Jack's enjoyment of his new kicks. But, of course, she and everyone else wore them, too. She wasn't as thrilled as he was. To her, they were just another pair of shoes. "Do you want to see something else that's really strange?" she asked Jack.

Jack smirked at her. "Like all of this isn't strange already?"

Daisy pulled the orb from the pouch still tied to her wrist. It was a dead light now, restored to its original state when she first discovered it inside the round wooden puzzle. It looked like an oversized black pearl. "Ever since we've been on this ship, the orb has been dark," she said, saddened that it no longer changed different colors.

The group huddled around her, anticipating the orb to light up.

"Did you solve its riddle?" Jack asked. "What was the light you were to seek?"

Daisy shook the object like a fortune-telling Magic 8-Ball. "No," she said with disappointment, and slipped the orb back into the pouch.

Bosco returned and dropped a bone at Jack's feet, then sat panting with his tongue hanging out the side of his mouth.

"Hey, buddy! Where did you get that bone?" Jack said. He looked at Bosco peculiarly. Something about the dog was different. "Have you grown?" He turned to his friends. "It looks like he's grown twice his size! How did he suddenly have a growth spurt? And how is he not floating if he isn't wearing anti-gravity shoes like us?"

"He *is* bigger!" Victor confirmed. "I bet he got the bone from where we are supposed to go and eat. And no clue about how he's clinging to the floor. Ask the glitchy old woman when we see her again."

Bosco barked, snatched up the bone, and trotted off.

"I think he's trying to tell us he's hungry," Victor said. "And so am I!"

"That makes two of us," Tommy chimed in.

"Three," Billy added.

"Then let's find the mess hall and eat!" Victor said.

Daisy grabbed Jack's hand and pulled him close. "Stay here with me," she whispered, slipping her arm around him. She leaned her head on his shoulder and gazed out the large, fused silica glass window at the new Earth. "Can we just spend a moment together without anyone else around?"

Jack didn't argue. "I don't see why not." He smelled her hair again and closed his eyes, lost in the moment with her fresh scent intoxicating his senses.

Bosco's bark suddenly echoed in the room.

Frustrated at him for interrupting an intimate moment, Jack bared his teeth at the dog. Then he turned back to Daisy. "I think he's trying to tell us to—"

Daisy stopped him mid-sentence with a sensual kiss, her lips locking with his. Their heavy breaths welcomed wild desires.

Jack's hand moved slowly to her thigh, then glided up her body and curved to her chest, her moans accelerating as his hand edged her breast.

Daisy's hand met with his, and they interlocked fingers. "Not here," she whispered fervidly, and the intense moment ended with a few more wet kisses.

Jack and Daisy turned from the gigantic window and walked

hand-in-hand out of the control room. Passing Bosco sitting and waiting for them by the hall, Jack patted him on the head. "C'mon, boy."

Bosco tilted his head, then scooped up his bone and scurried down the hall. With his head held high, he left a trail of bright green paw prints that faded one after the other.

CHAPTER THIRTY-NINE

Information Overload

The bay door of the mess hall swished open after everyone finished their meals, and the three-dimensional image of Delanore whisked into the room.

"What's going on, and *what* are you?" Tommy spoke for the others, who were all eyeing the holographic light source as it moved in the room. After finding out Delanore was just a floating image, they could see now how she differentiated from a human. The outlining of her body contained a thin blurred line barely noticeable only if you were looking for it.

"One moment," Delanore said, putting Tommy's question on hold as if she were a machine compiling the information. Then she turned to Daisy and asked, "Do you still have possession of the orb?"

Daisy gave a slight nod.

Delanore extended her arm, palm up. "Please place the orb in my hand."

Daisy removed the orb from the pouch, held it above the holographic hand, and released it. The sphere floated, making it appear like the image of Delanore was holding it. It was an incredible illusion! "Why did you have me protect it?" she asked, not wanting to give it back. She pocketed the pouch. "It has some crazy powers! How does it work?"

Delanore raised the dark orb to eye level. "You broke the curse of the underground!"

Daisy shifted her head inquisitively. "You said that before. What exactly do you mean?"

Before Delanore could answer, Billy yelped and stood up in his chair. "Jesus! Where did that come from!" he shouted, pointing at something moving underneath the table.

Jack, Victor, and Tommy darted gazes at a tarantula scuttling across the floor before pausing at Delanore's feet.

"I thought that thing died when the house imploded!" Victor said.

"Gerald!" Daisy shrieked.

Delanore stooped, and the orb followed her down to the spider. The arachnid climbed on the globe and settled at the top, its exoskeleton camouflaging with the spherical object.

"Is that thing real?" Victor asked.

Delanore gave a warm smile. "He is," she said. "And he shall guard the orb until it is needed again." She moved to the corner of the room, the orb with the spider frozen on top floating alongside her. She waved a hand at the wall like she was casting a spell, and a hidden compartment opened. Then, as though with a mind of its own, the orb floated into the partition.

"All a mind trick," Tommy mumbled, convinced that none of what he was seeing was real.

"Now, where were we?" Delanore said, returning to the group.

Billy eased back into his seat.

"You were going to tell me how I broke the curse of the underground," Daisy reminded Delanore.

"Oh, yes!" Delanore's holographic eyes wrinkled. She paced the room like a professor giving a lecture. "Only the touch of a chosen one could have called this ship from the earth by controlling the powers of the orb," she clarified.

"Wait . . . *what?*" Daisy said. "How?"

"I've searched for centuries to find the one who can unlock the magic of the orb," Delanore said. "When you found your way to my chamber underneath the house and solved the puzzle to unlock it, you became bearer of the orb. It's an ancient jewel discovered from another planetary system long before Earth's and Obuathea's time. Its powers can control a single universe. But it requires a special light to unlock its full potential and save your planet. Creatures all over your world have disguised themselves as your kind."

"I don't buy it!" Victor blurted.

"We have yet to determine where the creatures came from," Delanore said, ignoring Victor's thoughtless remark. "However, we know they have been plotting ways to wipe out the human species. We think their intent is to hijack Earth so they can house powerful weapons and strengthen their armies to destroy Obuathea."

Victor looked Delanore up and down. "So, how does *this* work?" he asked, gesturing his hand wholly at the holographic image before him.

"I'm operating the three-dimensional image from a control room on Obuathea."

"Ah, the woman behind the curtain," Tommy smirked.

"We know the creatures on your planet are searching for the orb," Delanore said. "If they gain possession of it, they can unlock a portal to a new realm and call upon other evils to take over other lifeforms in the universe that we have yet to discover."

"So, the creatures are like an infestation of the universe,"

Victor guessed.

Jack had a question he couldn't resist getting off his chest. "How is it we have these special powers that are impossible to achieve in reality?" He pointed at Victor's arm. "Like my brother's arm, for instance. He can shoot fireballs out of it! How does that happen? I've also noticed people can't see us. Are we stuck between reality and the spirit world?"

Bosco grunted as if he understood Jack and eased his chin onto his lap. He looked up at him with the whites of his eyes, his brows fluctuating, begging for another scrap of food.

The others suddenly became restless around the table, knowing Jack's theory could be true. They were all just kids and still had their entire lives ahead of them—they didn't have time to be trapped between worlds.

Tommy shot up out of his seat. "If you're controlling this . . . this holographic video . . . *thing*, where are the projectors? Enough with all the magic tricks and witchcraft, or whatever. This is a whacked-out mind trick, and we're enclosed in a simulator with fake backgrounds and fake images like you! Am I right?"

"Your minds have not been hacked," Delanore clarified, "and you are not having an out-of-body experience if that's what you are thinking. I needed to disguise myself on Earth as this hologram to lead one of you to the orb and the rest to train into warriors."

"Five to enter and one to stay!" Daisy interrupted. "I stayed underneath the house and discovered and solved the puzzle to release the orb!"

Jack glanced at her and smiled. "So, the whispers through the broken window were calling for *you*, the bearer of the orb—the one to stay!"

Delanore winked at Jack and continued. "The creatures cannot harm a digital representation. Therefore, I can move about like a spy, communicate with others, and even have the capability of changing my image into something different. But the program is not able to vanquish anything. What you are seeing is a computerized image made up of thousands of powerful microscopic electronic chips. They all function as cameras, projectors, lights, and sound—technology."

Tommy breathed deeply. "I feel like I'm in an advanced physics class or something. All I want to know is why we were transported to this ship and what the plan is for us."

Victor raised the stump of his severed hand and added, "And will I *ever* get my hand back?"

"You still haven't explained why you chose *us*," Jack broke in. "What did we do to deserve this draft pick?"

"Such curious minds you all have!" Delanore smiled. "My species, like your species, are creatures of habit. Even though Obuathea is many light-years away from Earth, we have concluded that both planets were created simultaneously and share the same features, based on years of scientific studies. We go about our business just as you do, only we mirror your lives! I'm sure you've heard the saying that everyone has a twin?"

Jack perked up. "I knew it! I *knew* everyone had a twin somewhere! I remember seeing my twin at least twice, from a distance. I saw myself in the grocery store once while shopping with my mom and again at a Luby's cafeteria several years later. But I never went up to them because I thought it would've been awkward talking to myself!"

"I've heard people mention it, but I've never run into my twin," Tommy said.

"Me, too!" Daisy chimed in.

"Not me," Victor said, slouching in his chair.

Billy had no comment.

"Every person on Earth has a twin, or a twin of twins, triplets, et cetera," Delanore continued. "Your twin lives on Obuathea!" She turned to Jack. "When you saw your twin, you initiated the first sequence of a déjà vu experience. In other words, you shared a split-second thought with your twin on Obuathea; therefore, your mind depicted yourself standing before you. What you *thought* you had experienced is a true phenomenon because you share the same brain waves as your twin. We are still learning how and why these connections exist between the two planets."

Eyes around the table were vacant, and minds were blown. But the teens wanted to know more.

"Earth is soon to fall to its doom if we don't stop the hidden evil that's making itself known into your world," Delanore said. "For centuries, they have been disguised as your own species. These creatures are what we call Adrotomytes, and they exist amongst your friends, colleagues, and even your family! The evil must be stopped before it spreads to our world! One breakthrough episode of telepathic communication between an Adrotomyte on Earth and one of our species on Obuathea can lead to the transformation process on our planet."

"The world deceived, a future to pay!" Jack said.

"Body snatchers!" Billy exclaimed.

"Mike!" Jack added, eyeing Victor. "We knew Mike for years. But holy cow! He was never human?"

Delanore regarded him keenly. "As stated, many creatures have been living amongst you for centuries. Now that they are coming out in the flesh, so to speak, Earth is seeing its end of days. But that's where all of *you* come in. You were monitored closely at school, picked explicitly from the crowd. Other holographic images like me are stationed in other parts of your world, searching for people who could protect the earth from a total takeover.

"Finally, after centuries of seeking the right people to carry out this daunting task, it is your generation that seems fit for the job. With your combined abilities, you can defeat the Adrotomytes and restore peace on Earth, thus saving Obuathea."

"What peace?" Victor said.

"Why can't the military wipe out the Adro-whatever-you-call-them?" Tommy asked.

"Your military does not have the advanced weaponry needed to take them out alone," Delanore said. "With our technology, we've found a way to implement weaponry into your bodies, to fuse with your tissue. This way, we can work together, with the same powers, in destroying the Adrotomytes! All of this will make more sense once we land on Obuathea."

The room fell silent, and since there were no more questions, Delanore took the opportunity to explain each of their abilities, beginning with Jack. "Jack, you've been given the gift of sight. Your unique vision can foresee the enemy's next move. I also see you as a leader with great strength." She rotated to Daisy. "Daisy, your power of electricity can stun the advancement of the Adrotomytes. I also see you as a voice for others, so your vocals shall also be enhanced. Additionally, know that you are the only one who can possess the power of the orb, and you will be trained on how to use it."

Daisy scratched her head, unsure of what Delanore meant by enhanced vocals. Would she become a leader since she would have possession of the orb? Or would she be able to scream like a banshee to ward off creatures?

Shifting to Victor, Delanore said, "With your firepower, Victor, you can destroy the hives where Adrotomytes dwell beneath the surface before their transformation. When the creatures roam the underground, they are known as scouts. I also see that you are manipulative. You'll be able to master hypnosis and inflict confusion upon the enemy. You shall learn this secondary power on Obuathea."

Victor stared at her in awe.

Next, she gestured a hand at Tommy. "Tommy, with your speed, you can outrun any Adrotomyte. Time is on your side; therefore, you will also master the ability of teleportation to sneak attack the enemy."

Tommy nodded in satisfaction.

It was Billy's turn next. "I'm delegating you, Billy, in mastering the controls of a new ship that's awaiting your skills on Obuathea!"

"Cool!" Billy came alive. "What about my secondary ability? Do I get one?"

"Not at this time," Delanore said.

"You're the getaway driver!" Tommy laughed, the others chuckling at his remark.

Delanore did not forget about Bosco. She moved to the end of the table, kneeling beside him.

Bosco lifted his head from Jack's lap with his ears perked.

"And you, my cute furry friend," Delanore said, smiling, "your paws shall light the way in the darkness." She peered up at Jack and said, "You'll see a growth pattern developing in your companion. Keep him close, for he can protect you with a strength you have yet to see!"

Jack smiled, then asked Delanore, "What about our friend

Stewart? I've had a couple of visions of him being tortured! Why hasn't he been chosen like us? What is my vision of him telling me?"

"I'm sorry, but the Adrotomytes may have turned your friend into one of them. It could be possible to save him, but I fear it may be too late."

Jack gaped at Delanore, but before he could respond to this shocking revelation, Tommy spoke.

"Wait a minute!" he said, sitting up. "How did we even acquire these powers in the first place? I've never been a sprinter, so how does my ability of speed relate to me?"

Delanore moved to the opposite end of the table where Tommy was sitting. "The powers you possess were merged into your system during the teleportation sequence when you entered the portal," she said. "They have nothing to do with your natural capabilities. Therefore, you still need to learn the powers to perfect them."

"Sounds like we've become victims of witchcraft." Tommy sank back in his chair.

Billy slapped a hand to his face. "If you've called upon us to take out these creatures, then why was I locked in that cage and not killed by the thing roaming the underground? How was it smart enough to even build that cage! It sounds to me like I was the one who was to 'stay,' and not Daisy!"

"That Adrotomyte was a scout," Delanore said. "And the cage was previously constructed. The creature used it to keep you nearby when it was ready to transform. Most Adrotomytes are not that intelligent to do something like that. During the early stages, the creatures roam deep underground like gophers until they are ready to proceed to the next phase. That's when they advance closer to the earth's surface, and lie in wait to pick its host. The scout you encountered managed to prowl beneath the house with its evil presence possessing the structure, and at the same time, conjuring up a spirit. In the final stage, they require a body, or a host, to roam above the surface. Without a host, the earth's atmosphere quickly decomposes the creature from the inside out!"

Daisy's eyes lit up. "So the house really *was* haunted!" She smiled at Jack, finally knowing the answers they had longed for about the haunting of Whitlock Manor. She focused back on Delanore. "What happened to the spirit of William Whitlock since the house was destroyed?"

"I had a close encounter with a ghost before I ran into Mike in that old house!" Tommy interrupted. "Are you referring to the thing with the red eyes?"

Daisy nodded with a slight smile.

"I was able to communicate with the entity, Mr. Whitlock, through EVP transmissions built into my system," Delanore said. "I do not know what has happened to the spirit now that the house is gone. I have lost signal. Perhaps he is no longer trapped between worlds!"

"That explains the visit to my house!" Daisy breathed. "You sent it as a messenger to reel me into Whitlock Manor, where you wanted me to discover the orb!"

"You are clever." Delanore smiled broadly.

"Vampires!" Victor busted out randomly.

"Excuse me?" Delanore whipped her head over to him.

"I'm referring to the creatures. You mentioned without a host, the earth's atmosphere decomposes them from the inside out. Vampires turn to ash in the sunlight!"

"No," Delanore disputed. "Adrotomytes are an alien species that act as parasites, living inside their hosts."

"So, you're saying when I was trapped inside the cage, that monster was preparing for me to become its host so it could escape the underground?" Billy said. "And where were *you* when you could have set me free? This ship was beneath me the whole time!"

"Oh my God!" Daisy jerked back in her chair, her reaction sidetracking Delanore. "That thing was probably going to use me as a host, too! If it didn't get to you first, Billy."

"But it chose Mike since it was injured, and we all escaped!" Jack said. "Victor and I thought we killed it, but I guess Mike must've found it injured underneath the rubble of the collapsed staircase and it performed the transformation on Mike!"

Delanore seemed entertained by their assumptions. "Exactly! The creature possessed him and fused with his body before it could die from its injuries."

"But I initially shot that damn thing in its head!" Victor said. "Why wouldn't that be instant death?"

"Its weakness is its heart," Delanore explained. "After an Adrotomyte picks its host and makes the transformation, the exoskeleton from its original state releases a final burst of energy—much like the surge of energy released within a human before natural death. The Adrotomyte's shell is capable of roaming around aimlessly for a short time before finally coming to rest."

"That explains why the creature burst through the upper window when Victor and Daisy combined their powers to finally destroy it!" Jack said, perking up. "It was an exoskeleton!"

Delanore smiled.

Victor sighed. "So, all the ammo I shot at that thing was wasted because I missed its heart?" He slumped in his chair. "Wow! Now I feel sorry for Dad losing his longtime friend!"

"What about our families and friends that we left behind?" Jack asked. "Are they safe?"

"Your immediate families are in a deep sleep. When the orb formed a protectant barrier around all of you, its powerful radiant scanned your DNA to pinpoint your bloodlines. The orb absorbed the information, and through telepathic force manipulation, it pinpointed your families and hypnotized them into hibernation. Your families will remain asleep throughout your time away. When they awake, they will have thought they only slept through the night. They require no food or water, for their body functions have slowed, tricking them from the lapse in time."

"The electricity bouncing between us!" Jack turned to Daisy with wide eyes, recalling the lightning ricocheting within the forcefield that protected them from Mike as a creature.

Still not convinced about all of this, Victor pursed his lips and then asked, "How are only the five of us—"

"Six." Jack cleared his throat. "You left out Bosco!"

Victor rolled his eyes, then continued. "How are the five of us and

our pet going to save the world?"

The holographic details of Delanore's eyebrows elevated. "You all seem frustrated. Getting some rest will help you recharge, and we can continue this discussion later. There is still so much to learn in very little time. On that note, let me show you to your pods. You will rest there until we begin reentry into Obuathea's atmosphere in a few days."

Victor glanced around the table at the others. *Pods?* he mouthed.

CHAPTER FORTY

Dream a Little Dream

The teens and Bosco followed the hologram down a long corridor, LEDs lining the ceiling coming to life upon sensing their movement. The dim light illuminated separate chambers branching off the hall that housed multiple upright pods or some form of biological incubators. A silicone-like substance domed over the front side of each pod. Inside were motionless figures that resembled embryos within protective membranes. And floating inches above the floor in front of each pod were neatly folded garments apparently belonging to the subjects hibernating inside.

"Hmph." Victor regarded the incubators with a faint frown upon passing them.

Jack was so interested in the objects, he wasn't watching where he was walking and nearly tripped over Bosco. "Oops! Sorry, boy," he said. Then he muttered, "How did debunking a haunted house suddenly lead to *this*?"

Daisy was overwhelmed by what she was seeing. "I have no idea!" she replied while passing the strange chambers.

The group finally reached a set of bay doors that swooshed open to a room filled with dozens more pods lining the walls.

"You'll rest here," Delanore said. Then, pointing at each pod individually, she explained, "Each pod is programmed according to your ability. From right to left, your pods are designated in the following order: Billy, Tommy, Victor, Jack, Bosco, and Daisy."

Victor eyed the pods dubiously. "Is this safe? How do we know these things won't disintegrate us or melt us into plasma!"

"Trust me, they are perfectly fine," Delanore assured him.

"I'm not a fan of someone who says to trust them," Tommy said.

"How do we get in these things?" Billy asked. "They look sealed."

"First, you must enter the pods unclothed," Delanore instructed. "Keep your gravity shoes on and fold and leave your garments in front of your assigned pod so you can change back into them when you awake. After unclothing, stand in front of your pod in the tiled square. Your backs should face the skin of the capsule."

"Skin?" Tommy cringed.

"Yes, the transparent astrodome," Delanore clarified. "When you lean back, your body will glide into the pod effortlessly. Do not fight the entry! You'll experience a smoother transition into sleep if you keep relaxed. Then, as you sleep, the advanced techniques of your abilities will come to you in your dreams, where you will later master them on Obuathea.

"Finally, once we land on Obuathea, the pod will wake you. Step out, reclothe, and wait for me here for further instructions. I look forward to meeting you all in person soon. Sleep well, my friends!"

The projection of Delanore saved no time for questions. Instead, it glitched and fizzled out to a small, stationary dot in midair, then slowly dimmed and disappeared.

"Wait!" Daisy reached out, but she was too late.

Everyone stood momentarily in silence, suspicious about the pods and whether they were safe.

"I'm not taking my clothes off!" Victor said.

"At this point, I don't think we have a choice," Jack assumed. "Where else can we go? We're in space!"

"Simulator," Tommy corrected him. "I'm telling you, this is all fake! The deep space and the planet you saw out that huge window is just a projected image! *We are being played!*"

"I don't think so," Daisy begged to differ. "I felt the power of that orb rushing through my veins when it called this ship from the ground.
I felt invincible! *This is real.*"

"Wait, how does Bosco enter the pod?" Jack wondered.

Bosco whimpered, then sat and panted, his beady eyes looking up at Jack.

"Let's put him in first and see what happens," Victor suggested. "It's the only way we'll know if these things are safe."

"Good idea," Tommy agreed. "And he's already naked!"

"Nice. You want to make my dog a guinea pig," Jack griped. He glanced down at Bosco, who stared back up at him and wagged his tail.

Sighing, Jack stepped to the fifth pod and snapped his fingers over the square. Bosco trotted over to the area and sat. Jack knelt and rubbed the dog's ears. "You be a good boy, and I'll see you soon."

Bosco whined and licked Jack's face.

Jack kissed Bosco on his forehead and then lifted him and eased his back against the astrodome like Delanore had instructed. Then, when he felt a suctioning sensation pulling the dog through the pod's skin, he let go.

Bosco was absorbed into the transparent membrane, and the

pod's coating reformed to its normal state. Bosco appeared as a black spot wiggling inside for several seconds before he became motionless.

Daisy placed her hands over her mouth. "Did you see how he stopped moving!" she gasped. "Is he dead?"

"He should be sleeping," Jack presumed, stepping back from the pod.

"So . . . how do we do this?" Tommy asked. "I don't want anyone seeing me naked!"

"Cover your privates," Victor said bluntly.

"That's easy for you to say," Daisy said.

"What if we have to go to the bathroom?" Billy asked.

The room fell silent.

"I guess you go in the pod," Victor finally said. "I don't know where a bathroom is around here. Do you?"

"Gross." Daisy cringed.

"Just don't look at each other," Jack said. "I don't want to see any of you guys naked, either." Then he leaned toward Daisy and said softly out the side of his mouth while pointing his thumb at the guys, "I meant them!"

"I know," Daisy whispered.

"Well, what are we waiting for!" Tommy raised his voice. "Let's do this!"

Everyone stood in front of their assigned pods and undressed, keeping their blinders up and staring straight ahead. The guys stood like inmates entering prison, cupping their genitals as if they were about to get hosed with bug spray.

"Is it cold in here or what?" Victor joked.

"You're an idiot," Jack said.

"Do we all enter at once?" Tommy asked, keeping his eyes focused on the center of the room. He could see the flesh tones and body shapes of Billy and Victor on either side of him through his peripherals.

Jack came up with the idea to have Billy enter his pod first. "Count to three and lean back," he advised. Then to the group, he said, "After a few seconds when Billy has entered his pod, Tommy can check on him. If all looks okay, Tommy, you count to three and enter *your* pod. Repeat this down the line. Does that sound good?"

"What did I tell you about using your brain?" Victor said. "One of these days, you're gonna hurt yourself!"

"Don't listen to him." Daisy smiled.

"I usually don't," Jack replied.

"Okay, I'll take one for the team and go first," Billy volunteered. "See you guys on the other side! One . . . two . . . *three!*" He leaned back, and suctioning sounds filled the room as the pod swallowed him.

"Damn!" Victor hollered. "That kid wasted no time!"

Tommy counted to five in his head, thinking that was enough time before peeking at Billy's pod. Like when he saw Bosco distorted as a blotch through the pod's skin, he could see the same dark spot in the center of Billy's pod. He watched Billy squirming like a fetus in the womb. Then, a few seconds later, he was motionless.

Tommy stepped back to his square. "He's asleep . . . I guess."

"Okay," Jack said. "When you're ready, start the count."

Tommy took a deep breath and crossed his arms over his chest like he was about to take a ride on a waterslide. "One . . . two . . . *three!*" he said loud and clear, and leaned back.

"Check on him, Victor," Jack said.

Victor peered over at the pod. "He's good."

"Cool," Jack said. "You know the drill. Your turn!"

"Duh!" Victor blurted. "Shut up so I can concentrate."

"Concentrate on what? Counting to three?"

"On what's left of my life!" Victor said nervously.

Jack frowned, feeling pity for his brother. "Dude, you'll be fine. Just go."

"Wait! Before I go, I just want to let you know that you were always a good little brother to me," Victor said. "I hope you didn't take it personally when I always told you about using your brain. You're smart, bro."

"Is this a confession?" Jack asked.

Daisy giggled.

"Psych!" Victor smirked. "I'll see you on the other side! One . . . two . . . *three!*"

Jack waited a few seconds after his brother's count and turned to see him as a black dot floundering around inside the pod. "Ugh! He must've not eased into the pod as he was supposed to!"

"What's going on?" Daisy asked, keeping her eyes focused on the center of the room.

"He's fighting it."

After a few moments, Victor finally became still.

"Oh, now he's good," Jack said. He returned to his square, keeping his eyes forward.

"Your brother loves you, you know," Daisy said.

Jack nodded, his emotions getting to him. "I know. We rarely say nice things to each other in appropriate ways. We express our love through funny put-downs and physical altercations that are playful, if you know what I mean."

"Everyone expresses their love for one another differently," Daisy responded. "And I love you, Jack."

Jack felt a lump tighten in his throat. He never expected her to say those words to him. For years he wanted their friendship to go further, and he felt his wish was finally coming true!

"Jack?" Daisy said.

"Yeah?"

"If I go next, will you watch me?"

Jack swallowed. The lump seemed to have enlarged in his throat. "Are you sure?"

"Yes."

Jack could feel his heart racing in his chest. "Okay," he said with a scratchy voice.

Daisy smiled. "Jack?"

"Yeah?"

"Look."

Jack turned his head.

Daisy's curvaceous body was gorgeous, her skin pure and smooth. Her petite, perky breasts were perfect. It was all Jack had hoped for in her and more! She was a beautiful creation from God.

Daisy winked at him and giggled fervidly, biting the tip of the nail on her pinky finger. Then she began the count. "One . . . two . . . *three*!"

"Wait!" Jack gasped, stretching his arm out toward Daisy as she leaned back. But she was already enclosed in the pod. He closed his eyes, disappointed in himself for not telling her that he loved her, too. He breathed deeply and called out to her, hoping she could hear his voice from inside the pod. "I love you, Daisy Crawford!" Then he eased into the pod . . . and slept.

EPILOGUE

MONDAY, MARCH 20. 1:05 PM

The Jenkins brothers retreated to the sewer to evade the developing weather, Andy sitting at the outer rim of the pipe kicking his feet above the murky embankment.

"You might wanna scoot your little butt away from the edge," Stephen's voice rose from behind Andy. He was toying with the switchblade comb. "It looks like death out there." He folded the comb and concealed it in his pocket.

Kyle waved his flashlight through the tunnel and shone it in Andy's face. "Do as you're told, twerp!"

"But the sewer stinks!" Andy complained. "And it's hot. Can't we just go home?"

Grabbing Andy's shirt by the collar, Kyle dragged him further into the pipe. "We can't go home! Look at the sky, you idiot!"

"But Mom and Dad will think—"

"Don't worry about them!" Stephen interrupted sharply. "This is the safest place right now until the storm passes."

Andy spun around when Kyle let go of his shirt. The crotch of his jeans was soaked from being dragged through the water in the center of the pipe. He looked up at Stephen with tearful eyes. "I'm scared!"

"Grow up!" Kyle snapped.

Andy fell silent. His glassy eyes darted between Kyle's and Stephen's shoulders. Something was emerging from the shadows behind them!

Stephen threw his arms up. "Andy, get up!" he shouted like he was his father. "Look at you! You're ruining your pants!"

Andy scooched backward, shaking his head. The dark shape was still forming behind his brothers.

"Join us," a powerful voice suddenly cut through the darkness behind Kyle and Stewart.

The two older brothers jolted and spun around.

Devin Morton's face dipped from the shadows.

"Jeez!" Stephen screeched, then chuckled.

Kyle shined the flashlight at the sinister grin on Devin's discolored face. His broad shoulders and chiseled chest reflected in the light, his body covered in a black, gooey substance in a continuous drip like melted cheese. His hair was matted with the sticky tar-like stuff, and his clothes were shredded as if his bulging muscles had ripped through them. Devin looked like a sewer rat pumped with steroids, ugly and disproportioned.

"When did *you* start working out, Masquerade Morton?" Kyle teased. Then his face tightened at Devin's intimidating stare.

Devin tilted his head slightly, the veins in his face puffed underneath the dark goo and the blood vessels branching every which direction like spider veins.

Another figure silently stepped from the shadows behind Devin, and Kyle panned the flashlight to reveal a buff Denise Bevins, dripping with a dark substance like Devin!

"Join us!" Devin and Denise announced together, their voices lazy and hypnotic. Then, like snakes striking prey, they grabbed Kyle and Stephen by their throats and lifted them off their feet, their heads centimeters from scraping the ceiling of the pipe.

Kyle's flashlight slipped from his hand as his extremities fell limp.

Andy scooted back yet further, his legs pushing faster until he found himself at the rim of the sewer pipe. He clutched the outer edge and held his position, a warm flow of urine trickling down his pant leg.

Devin and Denise peered between Kyle and Stephen, glaring at Andy from afar with their bloodshot eyes before yanking his brothers into the darkness.

Andy's lower lip trembled. Staring into the dark sewer as the pungent smell of ammonia lingered between his legs. He didn't know what to do, and no one was around for him to get help. Then the waterworks began, and he cried until there were no more tears and his throat became dry and scratchy.

———

An explosion of contaminated water from the embankment mushroomed in the air, regurgitating a massive tar bubble from underneath.

Andy jerked his body around and watched as the sphere dripping with black muck lifted in the air and dipped back down, kissing the surface of the water. As it hovered, a mysterious rapid expansion of air produced bouncy waves in the water. At the same time, the massive gust of air forced Andy further into the sewer pipe, and he rolled like a tumbleweed, skinning his arms and legs until he found himself in a sitting position.

Outside the sewer, still hovering above the embankment, the black mass slowly rose again and then shot up into the sky, the force thrusting most of the water in the embankment into the sewer pipe.

Andy turned toward the mouth of the pipe and screamed as a tidal wave of contaminated water barreled through the pipe, engulfing him.

———

Water backwashed from the sewer, refilling the gutted embankment. And as it reduced to a drip at the mouth of the pipe, tiny hands, scraped and bloodied, clamped around the rim.

Andy struggled to pull himself up, then stood at the mouth of the sewer looking up at the sickening green sky. Then his eyes shifted below at the water sloshing around like bathwater.

Climbing out of the pipe, Andy followed the edge of the embankment to higher ground and staggard up the side to his bike that lay next to Kyle's and Stephen's underneath a wilted tree.

Everything around him was quiet. No singing birds, no traffic sounds, no construction noises, no people going about their daily lives. Instead, all Andy could hear was the water squishing in his shoes as he pedaled across Porter Park's grassy knoll and headed for home.

PHILLIP WOLF is the author of *Jeremiah the CHD Aware Bear and Friends*, a storybook for children touched by congenital heart defects. He is an [international] award-winning producer/director for his documentary feature film, *Silent Cries: Breaking Through CHD Awareness*. Wolf lives in Texas with his wife and two daughters.

PWBooks.NET

PWFilms.NET

Facebook.com/pwauthor

Instagram: @pwbooks

CPSIA information can be obtained
at www.ICGtesting.com
Printed in the USA
LVHW040337110522
718321LV00001B/3

9 780578 392714